P_{THE}OET

THE POET

LISA RENEE
NEW YORK TIMES BESTSELLING AUTHOR
JONES

Entangled Publishing, LLC
10940 S Parker Road
Suite 327
Parker, CO 80134
Visit our website at www.entangledpublishing.com.

Amara is an imprint of Entangled Publishing, LLC.

Edited by Liz Pelletier and Lydia Sharp
Cover design by Bree Archer
Cover art by miljko/GettyImages,
artisteer//GettyImages,
Renphoto/GettyImages
Interior design by Toni Kerr

Print ISBN 978-1-68281-517-5
ebook ISBN 978-1-68281-518-2

Manufactured in the United States of America

First Edition March 2021

AMARA

ALSO BY LISA RENEE JONES

A Perfect Lie

THE LILAH LOVE SERIES

Murder Notes
Murder Girl
Love Me Dead
Love Kills
Bloody Vows
Bloody Love

THE SECRET LIFE OF AMY BENSEN SERIES

Escaping Reality
Infinite Possibilities
Forsaken
Unbroken

PROLOGUE

Tap, tap, tap, tap…

I jerk my gaze from the pretty girl in the corner, who just joined our class today, to the front of the room where Sister Marion is beating her desk with a ruler, her sharp features pinched with anger. She's mad almost as often as my dad.

"Enough of this jabbering," she reprimands. "We're here to do our Lord justice by using our minds the way they were intended to be used. And how are our minds meant to be used, class?"

Me and the rest of the class quickly recite, "To their fullest potential, Sister Marion."

"That's right," she approves. "And we cannot do so if we are not listening carefully, which we are not doing when we're running our mouths at inappropriate times. We must speak with thoughtful discipline."

She moves behind her big wooden desk and sets the ruler down on top. Thank God. I hate that ruler.

"Today," she announces, "we start our poetry series." She flips open a book and begins reading a poem. It's boring. I hate it. I don't even understand the words coming out of her mouth.

My eyes are heavy, lids fluttering with the call of sleep. I fight it. I fight hard to stay awake, but somehow my chin wobbles forward and hits my chest. Oh God, no. Adrenaline surges, waking me with a sharp lift of my head. My heart races with the fear I might be caught. My eyes land on Sister

Marion, who is staring at a book, not at me, as she reads another boring poem. Relief washes over me, but I'm desperate to stay alert, so I do the only thing I know will keep me awake. I sneak another peek at the pretty girl again, her red curls waving around her freckled face. I frown. I think she's much older than the rest of us. Maybe twelve or thirteen when the rest of us are ten and eleven. I wonder why she's here. Did she fail a couple of grades? I wonder if her dad's mean, too, and that messed up her schoolwork like it has mine.

"Henry Oliver!"

My name is followed by the slamming of a ruler on my desk.

I jump, and my heart punches at my chest, the way it does when my dad yells real loud. Gasping, I look up to find the sister standing above me. "Sister Marion."

"Good to know you've at least learned my name this year, Henry," she replies.

The entire room erupts in laughter, and tears of embarrassment pinch my eyes, but I can't cry. My father says that crying is for babies. And babies get beat up.

"Enough!" Sister Marion snaps at the room. The students zip their lips, and all the sound in the room is sucked away, but everyone is looking at me, including Sister Marion. "We are not here to watch pretty little girls, Henry," she reprimands. "Yes, I saw you staring at the new girl."

Oh God, oh God. Please no. Please no. Don't do this to me. I fight the urge to stand up and run away.

"We are not here for that," Sister Marion adds. "We are here to honor God with our minds. Do you understand, young man?"

"Yes, Sister Marion," I agree quickly.

"Then make our Father proud," she says. "You

will be the first to read a poem today."

I quake inside. Oh no. "You're going to talk to my father, Sister Marion?"

"Our Father, the Lord Jesus. You will talk to him now. Get up and follow me." She turns on her heel and marches to the front of the room, waiting for me from behind her desk.

All eyes are on me and, afraid of losing my glasses, I shove them up my nose, my stupid hand trembling as I do. The kids saw. Of course, they saw. They're all watching me, waiting to laugh at me again. Forcing my legs to work, I stand because I have no choice, curling my fingers into my sweaty palms.

Two steps forward. Three. I'm doing good. Yes. Four. I stumble on my unlaced shoe, falling forward, landing with a hard smack of my bare knees on the concrete floor. The room erupts into laughter once more and I imagine quicksand, like I saw in some movie the other day, sucking me under. That would be good, really good, right now. I straighten and my ears are ringing, the room fading in and out. I can barely make out the ruler hitting Sister Marion's desk again. Every step I take shuffles heavily, like when I walk through the water in the river down by my house after Dad comes home, shouting and drinking his beer.

I'm almost to the front when Sister Marion loses patience with me like my dad does all the time. "Come now, son." She grabs my hand and yanks me forward, placing me in front of the class and shoving a book into my hand. "Read," she commands. "Give us the title and the author."

I can feel my cheeks reddening, blowing up like apples the way they do when I'm upset. Next, the smear of red will spread to my neck and then I'll look stupid. I need to get this over with now.

I clear my throat. "'Dreams' by Langston Hughes," I announce, and then I glance at Sister Marion to make sure I've said the name correctly. She gives a sharp nod of approval.

Someone snickers and a boy from the back of the class shouts out, "He's too fat for his uniform and he looks like he's going to poop his pants."

"I'm not too fat," I shout back. "It's too small because my mom and dad can't afford a new one."

"Enough, all of you!" Sister Marion snaps and waves her ruler across the room. "One more outburst from anyone and everyone in this room will write one hundred Hail Marys after the bell." She looks at me. "Continue."

I suck in air and force it out, promising myself I will not cry. I'm not fat. I'm not fat. I look at the book again, ready to do anything that lets me just sit back down. I start reading, and I can't dare say something stupid. I speak slowly, taking my time:

"Hold fast to dreams
For if dreams die
Life is a broken-winged bird
That cannot fly.
Hold fast to dreams
For when dreams go…"

I can't read a couple of the other words. They're too big for me, so I just stop there.

"Very good," Sister Marion says, clapping. I puff out a breath of relief. She didn't even notice I didn't read all of the poem. "Class, clap with me!"

Everyone claps but the redheaded girl and a boy in the back that I don't think I know. He's new, too.

The sister takes the book from me. "Return to your seat," she orders.

I want to run back to my seat, but I'm afraid of falling again. I walk. I walk really carefully, and when I slink back into my seat, I slide down low, snickers erupting behind me. My heart is pounding in my ears, my palms sweaty again. I'm going to get beat up after class, just like two weeks ago when that boy, Nicholas, took my lunch. Dad was mad, too. He said I was a pussy. I know that's bad, because Mom screamed at him and told him not to call me that.

Sister Marion begins reading another poem, and I plot my escape after class. One minute before the bell is to ring, my hand goes to my book bag, and when finally the bell blasts above, I launch into action. I dart for the door, determined to get out of here and just go home, hoping my dad won't be drinking beer tonight. I hate it when he drinks beer. I push through the other kids to the door, and I ignore the hall monitors screaming for me to "Walk, don't run."

I explode out of the school, running with all my might, looking over my shoulder, panting and wheezing by the time I reach the big tree past the playground. I drop my book bag and sit down. I made it. I'm not a pussy today.

"Hello, Henry."

I blink and Nicholas is standing above me, and five other kids all appear from behind the tree. I start to wheeze. I can't breathe. Nicholas shoves his foot on my chest and now I can't catch my breath at all. "Henry here almost pooped his pants today. Henry is a poo-poo pants."

The kids start singing that. "Henry is a poo-poo pants. Henry is a poo-poo pants."

"Read us some more poetry," Nicholas says, and he holds up a book. "I took Sister Marion's poetry book just for you." He opens it and shoves it into my lap. "Read."

Tears start streaming down my cheeks. Oh God, not the tears. "I—I—I can't," I sob.

"You can," Nicholas says, and he yanks me off the

tree, flattening me on my back. Then he's sitting on my chest, holding the book, reading it for me. "Now you," he says, shoving it against my face. I suck in air, but it won't come. I start to push against the book and Nicholas. But suddenly, he's gone. I scramble back and onto my hands to find the new boy punching Nicholas. Now Nicholas is on his back and the new boy is on top of him. I can't watch. I scramble to my feet and take off running.

. . .

"Thomas Whitaker! Kevin is here! It's time to leave for school."

At my mom's shout, I grab my book bag and run downstairs. I head for the door only to have her call out, "Stop right there, young man!"

"Oh, Mom," I moan, slumping forward and turning to look at her.

She wipes her hands on her apron and leans down, pointing at her cheek. I kiss her and she says, "Much better. Be safe and good."

"Yes, Mom," I murmur, and she motions me onward, offering me my freedom.

I don't wait for her to change her mind. I launch myself toward the door and exit to the porch, where I find Kevin at the bottom of the steps, stuffing his face with a chocolate-covered glazed doughnut. Intending to take half of that beauty for myself, I dash down the steps and vault to a finish in front of him. He laughs and shoves the last bite into his mouth.

Grimacing in disappointment, I watch him lick his fingers. "Dad made breakfast," he announces, "which means he brought home doughnuts. I love when Mom goes to work early."

"Jerk," I say.

He hands me a bag. "One for you."

"Not a jerk," I correct, hiking my bag on my shoulder and accepting my prize, while sirens scream in the distance. "Thank you."

We start walking and the sirens grow louder. "Wonder what that's all about," Kevin asks, looking over his shoulder and then back at me. "Maybe Old Man Michaels who owns that corner store is beating his wife again."

"Or the dog," I suggest. "I heard he beats his dog, too."

"No way," Kevin gasps. "The dog?"

I nod and assure him it's true. "That's what I heard."

"Man," he says. "That's bad."

I pull my doughnut from the bag. "That stuff after school yesterday was bad, too, right?"

"I know, right?" Kevin eyes me. "I wanted to help poor Henry, but I didn't want to get beat up, too."

"Me too." I test the chocolate with a lick of my tongue. "That new boy helped and he's big." I take a bite. It's really good. "I love this doughnut."

"Right?" Kevin says. "Those are the best. So is the new girl," he adds. "She's pretty."

I shrug and take another bite. "I guess."

"Hey! Hey! Heyyyy!"

We stop walking and turn to find our next best friend, Connor, running toward us, arms flying around wildly.

"What's his deal?" Kevin murmurs.

"Probably mad because we didn't ask him to walk to school with us," I suggest.

"I had only one extra doughnut," Kevin whispers. "What do I say to him?"

Connor screeches to a halt in front of us and leans forward, hands on his thighs, panting hard. "Class is cancelled."

I finish my doughnut. "Sister Marion sick or something?" Now I lick my fingers.

"No," Connor says, straightening, hands on his hips. "I heard my mom talking on the phone. One of the kids from class is dead. As in never coming to class again."

Kevin and I both drop our backpacks and together ask, "Who?"

"Don't know," Connor says. "But they found him down by the creek."

CHAPTER 1

PRESENT DAY

I sit in the back row of the theater-style Austin, Texas speakeasy, the air conditioner cranked on high, soothing the heat of a hot August night. A stage sits in the center of the room, and there is whiskey in my hand—an expensive pour of a high-end Macallan—my preferred drink. I'm loyal to what I believe to be quality in all things. There are other, more affordable whiskey choices, of course, but when I'm alone, without my family, I am no longer forced to play the frugal husband and father. A role that is cumbersome, but necessary to protect a higher purpose I must serve.

I glance at the attendees of tonight's poetry reading, counting twenty heads, the ages varied; one young woman can't be more than sixteen, while one man's shriveled skin ages to sixty-plus.

This is a cozy little spot indeed, and I sip my Macallan, oaky with a hot lick on the tongue, as Michael Summer steps to the microphone. He has thick dark hair, much like the look I've created for myself in this persona. He's tall, six-foot-two, I imagine, a good four inches above my five-foot-ten, with glasses and a bow tie accentuating his button-down. I appreciate the attention to detail, and considering his role as tonight's poetry guide, I've now raised my expectations. Perhaps he'll be good enough to continue in his role.

His gaze scans the crowd and finds me, "the professor," as he knows me from a prior event, one that led me to an invitation to this one.

He clears his throat and then says, "Good evening. I'm Michael Summer. Welcome to our poetry night, a night of literary delight. Now, to get started, I've placed a book of poems under your seat." I hear nothing else. Poetry is the bible of words, not meant to lie on the ground, not meant to be dirtied and disrespected. Poetry is history to be protected, lessons to be learned, a path to change our society or prevent its demise.

And I am the chosen master—not the original, of course, but the chosen one nevertheless.

I sit back, sipping the luxurious whiskey that I now know to be a mismatch to a night where I watch one person after another step to the microphone to butcher the great works: Frost, Shakespeare, Poe. The list goes on, but I don't blame the students. I blame the teacher, and the teacher must pay. He will not continue in his role, but he will serve a purpose.

I down my drink and slide my glass into my bag on the floor. The only part of me I ever leave behind is words, and my decision is made. Tonight is the night. Summer is *the one*. He's the one who will let her know it's time to fulfill her destiny. It's time for her to train, to prove her worth, to be tested. He's the one who will bring her to me, my perfect student, the future master.

CHAPTER 2

"Detective Samantha Jazz!"

At Captain Moore's bellow, my gaze jerks across my desk to Detective Ethan Langford, my sometimes partner and desk mate. "What did you do, Lang?"

He laughs, a big hearty laugh appropriate for a man of six-foot-three who believes in "go big or go home," and too often drags me along for the bumpy ride. The man doesn't understand the principles of research and preparation. He holds up his hands. "I did nothing. Just say that. It's perfect."

I scowl because he enjoys batting back and forth with the captain. I do not, and with good reason. Every encounter for me with Moore includes a ghost in the room: the former captain, my father, whom we buried only three months ago today, and not with the honor I would have liked. "Seriously, Lang?"

"I didn't do anything." He wiggles an eyebrow. "Not that he knows about."

I plop my hands on my hips and glare.

"Oh *come on*, brains," he chides, "you were the youngest detective in the precinct, at twenty-five, with the highest scores on record. You had some crazy-high IQ test. You can handle the captain."

"You're enjoying this," I accuse.

"I kind of am. Maybe he wants to know why you're thirty-two and won't take the sergeant's test."

"You're forty and you haven't taken the test," I counter.

"Because I'm a fuckup."

I love him, but he kind of is a fuckup, and it's always been interesting to me that my father partnered us so often. "Well then," I say. "I haven't taken the test because I don't want to manage people like you."

"Jazz!" the captain shouts. "Now!"

I shove strands of my long, light brown hair behind my ears, and do so for no good reason. To a detective like myself, it might seem like a nervous gesture. So would the way I stand up and run my hands over my blazer, the likes of which I often pair with a silk blouse and dress pants. The jacket hides my weapon and badge, and the silk says: "I'm female, hear me roar."

I'm not roaring now, though. My spine is stiff, and when I glance at the spot on my desk that once sported a photo of my father—tall and handsome, with green eyes that matched mine, and thick brown hair—I'm sick to my stomach. I'm also ready to get this over with.

Turning away from Lang, I tune out his, "Good luck!" that starts a symphony of the same from various detectives in the pit of desks. The captain isn't going to press me to take the sergeant's test. I'm the daughter of his dirty predecessor, only three months in the grave, for God's sake. And apparently, my desire to join Internal Affairs to be the better Jazz made me a worse traitor than my father.

Captain Moore doesn't trust me. The fact that my godfather is Chief of Police and my father's ex-best friend doesn't help matters.

I reach his doorway and without hesitation, I enter his office. That's the thing about being a homicide detective and my father's daughter. Even in the midst of uncomfortable situations, I haven't been bred to timidity. I know how to dive right in to the bloody moment. And every moment with the captain, at least for me, is a bloody moment.

He's behind his desk, a Black man in his forties

who is big in all ways; his presence is large and confident. His energy commanding. His office is cold, like the man, free of family photos. He's also a man who clearly enjoys the gym, and I know from my history with him that he does so far more than he ever enjoyed a day at the ice cream parlor. I, on the other hand, enjoy the gym *and* the ice cream parlor, but he's just not that divided on anything. He doesn't see the gray that I believe solves crimes. There is only black and white, which to me explains why, my father aside, I prickle every nerve Moore owns. We both know that I learned to see that gray from my father, who was inarguably a damn good detective in his day. He simply saw a little too much gray.

"Shut the door," Moore orders without looking up from his file.

Wonderful. A shut door is not good.

I do as I'm told and once I'm sealed in the rather small office with this extremely large man, he lifts his intelligent, brown, always-cranky stare to mine, judgment in its depths. Always the judgment, but that's not what comes out of his mouth. "I hear that you know something about poetry." He taps his computer screen. "That's what your employment record says. You ran a poetry club in college."

I frown. Maybe this *is* about the sergeant's test. "Why exactly are you looking up my college record?"

"I wasn't looking at *you*, Detective Jazz. I was looking for someone who knows poetry, even if it meant searching outside the department, but it turns out I got a hit with you." He slides a file across the desk and sets it in front of me. "This should explain."

My defenses lower, and the detective in me, the one who thrives on impossible puzzles, sits down, eager to work. Work is good. Work keeps me sane. It took me sixty days after my father died to convince the department shrink just how true that is. A month later, she's seen me solve cases and perform at my best. Now, she believes me. Now, I'm rid of her.

I open the file and I'm staring at a naked man tied to a chair by his ankles and waist, but interestingly enough, his hands dangle freely by his sides. His head is dropped forward, a mop of dark hair draping his face. Vomit forms an unevenly edged pool on the floor to his right. In my mind, I imagine the moment that sickness overcame him, imagine that he tried to escape that chair, and noting the burn marks by his ribcage, perhaps violently. When unable to untie himself, in desperation, it appears that he most likely leaned forward and heaved.

I scan the information sheet on the inside flap of the file.

Cause of death: Poison. Substance undetermined. Pending toxicology reports.

My memory conjures up an old case. A husband who'd forced his wife to ingest a cyanide pill under threat of her children's deaths. She'd never had a chance of survival. There's no turning back from a substantial intake of cyanide, no chance of being saved. You're dead in two to five brutal minutes. That mother was dead in two to five brutal minutes, never to see her children again.

That woman, that mother protecting her children, hadn't been tied to a chair like this man, but her monster of a husband later confessed to having given her a choice. He'd told her to take a cyanide pill he'd snapped up from the dark web or he'd kill the kids. He'd wanted her life insurance. She'd taken the pill to save her kids, but he'd given the kids pills as well and then tried to make it look like a murder-suicide that left him alone and devastated.

I shove aside that morbid memory to focus on this new case, already forming a hypothesis. Perhaps something similar to what happened to that mother happened to this man. That's why his hands are free. He was given a choice—freely submit to a poison-flavored death or an alternative that one can assume to have been worse.

For a moment, I believe that old case, and my history with a poison murder weapon, is why I'm looking at this file, but then I remember the captain's reference to my knowledge of poetry. I flip the page and find a photo of a typed poem, much like an oversized fortune in a fortune cookie. There's a note that indicates the poem had been shoved inside the victim's mouth, and yet it's free of the victim's vomit. That's interesting.

I set that thought aside for now and read the poem:

Who laugh in the teeth of disaster,
Yet hope through the darkness to find
A road past the stars to a Master

"We googled the poem," the captain says, obviously following my review of the file. "It's by—"

"Arthur Guiterman," I supply.

His brows furrow. "The poem's eight paragraphs. You have three lines. How did you know that?"

"Isn't that why you called me in here? Because I have a knowledge of poetry?"

"Indeed," he agrees. "I just didn't expect—"

"That I really did? Well, I do."

His eyes narrow. "What does the poem mean?"

"You could ask a handful of scholars that question and get a handful of disagreements."

His lips press together. He doesn't like my honesty, which is relevant to how impossible the question is to answer. "What does it mean to you?"

"My interpretation: it's about destiny."

Apparently, I passed the knowledge test, because he moves on. "The detective on this case made an abrupt decision to transfer to Houston, which leaves me reassigning the case."

My brows dip in confusion, my mind focused on the detective departing, not the case that's obviously going to land with me. We're a small department of twelve detectives who know one another at least reasonably well. No one has said a peep about transferring. "Who's leaving?"

"Roberts."

Now I'm really confused. I mean, Roberts and I aren't close, but I've known the man for years and he has roots here—a house, friends, an ex-wife he lives to fight with, a weekend football league. I shake my head with that confusion. "Why would he do that, Captain?"

"Personal decision." He offers no further explanation. "I'll let him know that he'll be briefing you on this case. You're taking it over. It's your decision to either pull in Detective Langford or fly solo. This case, as far as I'm concerned, is *your destiny*, Detective Jazz."

CHAPTER 3

I exit the captain's office with the file in my hand, and Roberts's rapid departure bugging the heck out of me for no real reason. Actually, that's not true. There's a reason. Roberts was close to my father, and knowing what I now know about my father, that's not a positive connection. Still, the man has a right to live his life and not tell a bunch of homicide detectives he works with in advance. I know this, of course, and yet when I arrive at my desk, with Lang waiting for me, I find myself ignoring him. Which isn't unusual. I'm as good at ignoring Lang as Lang is at ignoring me. Uneasy energy keeps me on my feet, leaning over my desk to my keyboard to look up Roberts's number before punching it into my cell phone.

Lang snaps his fingers in front of me. "What the hell is going on?"

Roberts's number plays a disconnected message in my ear that is both unexpected and downright odd. The captain said Roberts would be briefing me. Right now, it appears Roberts is already gone.

"Jazzy," Lang snaps. "Earth to—"

"You know Roberts pretty well, right?"

"Yeah. I worked a case with him last year. Good guy. Why?"

"I'm taking over one of his cases. He's making an abrupt move to Houston but was supposed to brief me on a case before he left. Apparently, that's no longer the plan. His phone's disconnected."

"Get the hell out of here. Roberts?" He scowls in my direction. "Are you sure?"

"Positive. I just tried to call him."

"This makes no sense. I had drinks with him last week and he said nothing about a damn move to Houston. You must have dialed wrong." He reaches for his phone to dial Roberts, but I know I didn't dial wrong. I cross the office again and poke my head into the captain's office.

He arches a brow. "Already solve the case, Detective Jazz?"

"Trying to," I say. "Anxious to talk to Roberts. Do you have a number for him?"

Irritation flicks across his face. "He's in the system."

"That number's disconnected."

His brows sink. "That's odd. He isn't leaving town until Friday. Did you dial wrong?"

I'd like to introduce him to Lang right now, the other guy wasting his time with that conclusion, but I refrain from that offer. Instead, I watch him punch a number into his phone, only to end the call almost immediately. "You're right. It's disconnected. Huh. Let me call Captain Newton down in his Houston precinct, or soon-to-be precinct. He should be able to reach him. I'll let you know when I talk to him."

In other words, get lost, but I don't follow that direction. Not yet. "Captain—"

"No. This has nothing to do with your father's scandal."

Scandal.

That word sours in the air and in my mind. So much so that I want to ask him if that's what we're calling my father getting caught on tape, commending a cop for his "good work" after he killed a suspect. But I don't. I bite my tongue and hard. It should be bleeding right about now.

The captain might not be my best friend, but I believe he absolutely hated my father for justified reasons. Moore's hard and difficult, but he's a good man and a good cop. My father was the reason I joined the force, and he was neither of those things, but that's a complicated piece of my psyche that most people, me included at times, wouldn't understand.

Feeling that double pinch in my chest that the counselor the department made me see after my father's death helped me identify as grief and anger, I fade back into the workspace and quickly return to my desk.

"You're right," Lang concludes. "His line's disconnected." He lowers his voice. "Is this—"

"No," I say before he can ask about Roberts's relationship with my father, because that's where this is going. I know him. He knows me. Five years of sharing a desk and a good hundred cases investigated together has that effect, and yet I didn't really know my father, whom I grew up with. Or maybe I did, and that's my real problem. I leave it at that one word and move on. "The captain's getting me a new number."

"Right." He doesn't look convinced or satisfied. "What's the case we're taking over?"

We're taking over.

I could shut him out, but I'm not going to do that. Not on this one. Not when he's already looking for a connection between the case and Roberts's departure. I am, too. I hand him the file and sit down, watching him scan the contents, waiting for his reaction.

"Obviously not connected," he says, glancing up from the file, "but it feels like old territory. That mother and her kids who were poisoned. Reads like a cyanide poisoning."

"Yes. I had the same thought."

He taps the file. "Did you notice that this guy threw up, but the poem that was in his mouth was clean?"

"I did. The killer must have washed out the mouth." I grab my phone. "I'm going to find out if the body is still with the medical examiner." A quick call and I have my answer. "The body is confirmed present," I say, disconnecting the line, and glancing at the time on my cell phone to confirm it's one thirty, safely after the sparsely operated lunch hour at the ME's office. "I'm headed in that direction. Want to join me?"

"If it includes a stop by Roberts's place first, I'm in." He flaps a piece of paper in the air. "I have the address."

Lang and I do not like the same movies or share the same politics, but when it comes to investigations, we collide and connect in all the right ways. We home in on the same things when it matters, and this is one of those moments. Something with Roberts isn't adding up. And when your life is all about death, you never ignore what doesn't add up. Or you end up dead, too.

CHAPTER 4

Lang and I decide to rally some computer forensics support on our way out of the precinct. My approach to such support is that while the way to a man's heart might not really be his belly, it seems to work on that team, all of whom tend to be overworked and underappreciated. Today, as is often the case, we find Chuck Waters, a man particularly fond of such attention, especially if it's chocolate, hard at work in his little cubicle and oblivious to his surroundings.

I reach in the bag now on my shoulder and pull out a Godiva bar. Lang gives me an approving wink and hangs back a bit, giving me room to work. I snag a chair from a nearby vacant cubicle and roll it in beside Chuck, joining him at his desk, where I set the bar in front of him. He grins at the sight of it and glances over at me, his fingers still working his keyboard. Muscle memory is a beautiful thing. My finger. My gun. His fingers. His magical keyboard that holds answers I need now and always. "You don't have to give me gifts."

"Almost every murder I've solved involved you and long hours. Which *I appreciate.* But I do actually need a couple of things again. Now."

He chuckles, and it's a low rough chuckle that is brawny and oversized for a man who stands level to me at five-foot-five and probably outweighs my one eighteen by about five pounds. "That means you need a lot of things." He shoves a yellow pad in front of me. "Make a list."

I don't reach for the pad. "Everything you can get me on the new Summer case. I'm headed to the ME's office, but I'm taking a leap of faith that the cause of death is poison by cyanide."

"And you need to know where the killer got the cyanide."

"Exactly. We worked a case a few years back, and that case file has a dark web contact we never caught up with."

"Case file: Roderick Kensington," Lang says, leaning on the edge of the cubicle wall on my side, his way of not overwhelming Chuck.

Chuck gives him a wave and writes it down. "Got it. On it. And I know the routine. I'll pull cameras for his home and work, search emails and phone records, and all the normal stuff."

"And pull the entire body of work for a poet named Arthur Guiterman," I add, "with emphasis on a poem titled 'Fate, The Jester.' Cross-reference it to the rest of his work."

"Arthur Guiterman," he says, scribbling additional notes. "'Fate, The Jester.' Summer case file. Got it all." He keys in the name and glances over at me. "Says here this is Roberts's case."

"About that," I say. "Roberts moved to Houston abruptly."

His brows dip. "This murder happened three days ago. He worked the scene and, according to these notes, one of my coworkers did quite a lot of work for him. You're sure he's gone?"

"That's right. He's gone. And we'll need your coworker's notes, or help, if you can recruit that person."

Chuck hasn't moved on from his present state of confusion. "That's more than abrupt."

"His phone is disconnected," Lang says. "We need to reach him. In fact, we're going to go by his house after we leave here."

Chuck's gaze latches onto Lang's, understanding in his stare. "Oh dear," he murmurs. "I'll ping his phone. You want me to dig deeper?"

"Not yet," I say, but I hesitate on a hunch. "Actually, look for any connection between Summer and Roberts. And cross-reference Summer to all of his cases in the past year. No, two years."

"Oh dear," Chuck murmurs again. "Yes. Of course. Right away. And just an FYI, Roberts's home security system was turned off with his power. Patrol is trying to find a neighbor who might have a camera angled toward his house."

"It seems no one has a working camera these days," I say dryly. "Thanks, Chuck."

Lang hulks his shoulders forward and growls. "Hulk Smash. The Chuck Smash."

Chuck looks at him as if he's crazy. He's not wrong.

A few minutes later, Lang and I are in his Ford Mustang, part of a pilot program that allows a few detectives to use their own vehicle, fully outfitted with police equipment. All part of an undercover job he did two years back that almost got him killed. He revs the engine and glances over at me. "My gut's roaring louder than my car, and I don't like what it's saying." He backs us out of the parking space with a squeal of tires.

Lang has never been small on dramatics, but in this case, it feels rather appropriate.

CHAPTER 5

Roberts lives, or lived, about ten hot August minutes from the precinct — well, ten minutes without traffic, which is something that happens in dreams, not reality. Hellish traffic is the way of the world in Austin these days, and I adjust my air vent, willing the coolness to follow. While I wait for that world wonder, I reach for the file in my bag, only to find an extra chocolate bar. In an effort to save it from melting, I open it and hand half to Lang.

He gives it a side-eye. "You and your chocolate," he murmurs, but he doesn't hesitate to grab his hunk of sugar.

"It was melting," I say. "We must save the chocolate. It saves the world, or at least my sanity. It might cause me to run about ten more miles a week than I would otherwise, but it's a small price to pay." I open the case file and start tabbing through the documents. "We have no camera footage at the crime scene, which is a three-story retail building with a bookstore at street level and a small theater on a basement level. There was a poetry reading in that theater the night of the murder."

"That explains the poem," Lang concludes.

"Maybe," I mutter. "I'm not sure it's that simple." I leave that thought dangling in the air, for now, ready to be plucked and examined later. "The victim's apartment, where he lived and died, was on the top level."

"Back to the topic of camera footage. This man lived and worked in a retail building and had *no* camera footage? In downtown Austin? He was smart enough to run a business. Surely he was smart enough to have had cameras."

I thumb through a few more documents, the air finally blowing blissfully cold. "Looks like he did have cameras installed, but they were conveniently offline the night he died."

"Compliments of the same person who gave him a permanent sleeping pill, I bet."

"Agreed," I say, continuing through the file, and when the car idles at a stoplight behind an eternally long row of cars, I angle in Lang's direction. "Roberts is a good detective. He covered a lot of material quickly. And he already pinpointed a person of interest."

"Well, hell. That works. Who?"

"He wrote 'the professor' with no other name referenced, but the interesting thing is that he interviewed everyone who attended that poetry reading with one exception."

"The professor," he assumes.

"Right. He really wanted to interview whoever this person is."

Lang shifts us into gear behind the now moving traffic. "Is there a description?"

"The lights were dim in the theater and directed toward the stage, so all we have is a vague description of a man who sat in the back row. Everyone said he 'seemed' to be tall, though no one saw him standing, so take that with a grain of salt."

"And?"

"Average weight with dark hair. That's all. No one seems to have seen him when the lights were up."

"Or standing," he grumbles. "Figures. So we have no DNA, a vague description that could be anyone, and a nickname of a man that no one really saw. *Jesus.* I thought you said Roberts did a good job."

"He *did* cover a lot of ground in a short few days. And we just got the file. There could be more here that I haven't uncovered." I tab through the evidence list. "We bagged mixed drink glasses used during the reading that are presently in line for DNA testing. I'm going to check the status." I dial the crime lab in a short, useless contact that has me disconnecting with a groan. "We're in line, but there's a backlog. Note to self: go to the forensics lab and do not leave until my testing gets priority."

Lang just grunts. That's his way. He saves the explosions for less opportune times, like crime scenes that require decorum that he forgets exists.

I scan the file and find a big gap in our investigation that needs to be fixed. I make a few more calls and arrange to have patrol collect the one thing that Roberts seems to have missed early on: a request for voluntary DNA from everyone at the poetry reading.

"Roberts didn't collect that DNA, huh?" Lang asks when I finally put my phone away. "Seems like a first step to me."

"Yes, it is," I confirm. "And no, he didn't. I'm not sure how he bypassed such an important step."

"Maybe he didn't do that great of a job, after all. Maybe something had him distracted, like dirty detective work."

He's back to connecting him to my father, and I'm not going to go there right now. "I don't know what's going on with Roberts, but it doesn't add up."

"Are you suggesting he's our killer? Because he's a damn cop, Jazz."

"Who you just suggested was dirty."

"Dirty is one thing. A monster is another. We're looking for a professor anyway. You said so yourself."

"Actually, Roberts said so."

"It's not Roberts," he snaps.

"We'll let the evidence lead us to our killer. Which means we need those samples to match them to the DNA on the glasses. And once we find this professor, which we will, we need to be able to prove he was at the event, which means isolating his DNA."

"Now, it's handled. And he's still missing." On that note, Lang pulls us into the driveway of a small, brown, brick house that I assume to be Roberts's home. I shove the file next to the seat. "Why am I nervous?" I ask without reaching for the door.

"Because you're a girl," he says, a joke he tells just because I hate it. Yes, partners are a bit like siblings, or so I hear. I've never had a sibling. Just a man I call Lang because he hates it. "And," he adds, "because Roberts is in trouble. It's in the air." He pops his door open and gets out of the car.

I follow him, my bag at my hip filled with investigative tools that I should have left in the car. This isn't a crime scene, but it's like my gut is telling me that I'll need it. We're almost to the door when my cell phone rings in my jacket pocket. I snag it, hoping it's the captain with an update on Roberts, only to find my mother's name on the caller ID. First time today, which is a miracle considering she's called me three times a day since I returned to work. With a stab of guilt, I decline the call, but already she's stirred a flashback to the night my father was murdered—him standing in front of me, while I confronted him over his many sins to the badge. Him telling me that I was a "judgmental know-it-all bitch." That was the last thing he'd said to me ever in this lifetime. A second later, a gunshot had cracked and he'd fallen on top of me.

Forcefully, I shake off the memory and shove my phone back into my purse. I know my mother's grieving and scared. I also know that if we'd caught the ex-con who killed my father, she'd be at least a little less clingy. But he had the chance to kill me. He didn't. He isn't coming back to do the job now, either. And if I let her make me afraid, I might make a stupid mistake and end up dead, too.

We step under an overhang in front of the house and Lang knocks on Roberts's door. I ring the bell. That's us, brawn and finesse. Neither method works. The door doesn't open. Lang tests the knob and it turns, then he gives me a sideways look. I shove back my jacket and rest my hand on my weapon, giving him a nod. He turns the knob, pulls his weapon, and uses his foot to shove the door open. Heat rushes out into the already-suffocating heat. A look groans between us that says it all. There's nothing worse than entering a Texas house with no air conditioning, except entering a Texas house with no air conditioning that has a dead body inside. The good news: so far, we're odor free.

Lang inclines his chin, and a second later, he's slicing through the heat. His big body bursts into the inferno that is the air-conditioning-free house, with me on his heels. We halt in a living area and Lang gives a curse at what we find. The room is empty, completely barren of furnishings, Roberts's departure quick and complete. Procedure, and our many years working together, kicks in and we automatically split up, searching the small house. We end our fruitless hunt for Roberts outside in the heat, where it's cooler than inside in the heat.

"No one leaves *this* fast," Lang says, shutting the front door behind us. "Not unless they're running scared."

"But he was mindful of his electric bill," I point out. "Turning off the air tells me that he cared about his future expenses." My cell phone rings again, and I glance at the caller ID. "The captain," I say, quickly answering the line. "Captain."

"Roberts asked for two weeks before he reported to Houston. At this point, they don't know how to contact him. You're on your own on the Summer case, at least until we can reach him."

I glance at Lang, and he nods, silently telling me that he can hear what's being said. "And this doesn't feel off to you, Captain?" I ask.

"This is a tough job, something you know better than most these days. Maybe he hit a wall. He needed air, but the good news is we have you. Go get our killer." He disconnects.

I slide my phone back into my pocket and fold my arms. Lang does the same.

"Do you think this is related to the Summer case?" I ask.

"I told you, I worked with Roberts. I can't imagine a monster scary enough to spook Roberts. He clearly made a decision to leave. He's got another job in the department."

"I agree that yes, it looks that way, but that could be by design. We need to speak to him."

He motions to the car, clicking the lock, and we start walking. "You keep working the case. I'll blow off my booty call for tonight and hunt down Roberts."

We both head to our sides of the car. "Booty call?" I ask incredulously, joining him inside. "Really, Lang?"

"That's her description, not mine." He starts the car and cranks the air. "She says that if I fall in love with her or some ridiculous shit like that, one of the killers I'm chasing might want to kill her to get back at me. And if she loves me and I end up dead, she'd be destroyed."

His booty call story has managed to hit a nerve, and I cut my gaze. "Our world does start and end in murder." A bitter taste gathers in the back of my throat, my mind going to my father. Ironically, he wasn't killed for his bad deeds, but his good ones. That ex-con just wanted to pay him back for locking him up a decade earlier.

"We might as well just accept fate and date each other," Lang jokes, baiting me and not by accident. No doubt, he read my reaction and knows what it's about. "We're together all the time anyway," he adds. "Two badges, one heart."

I shake my head at his silliness, and silliness *is* his intent. We spark together, but it's the kind of spark that sets the wrong kind of fire. The kind you run from, not to. "Funny thing," I say, "is that I tried dating someone in law enforcement and it didn't work. I don't need a repeat."

"I won't comment on what happened between you and FBI Agent Wade Miller. I'm going to focus on the here and now, you and me. You know you want my body."

I snort-laugh, something I've often wanted to do when someone is lying to me, but save just for Lang. I also point to the steering wheel. "Drive. We have a killer to catch and a detective to find safe and alive."

"You're right. You're right. Getting naked is proven to be the best way for two people to hate each other." There's bitterness to those words that tells me, yeah, he's joking around about his love life, but being labeled as a booty call bothers him. He's human. How can it not?

We're about halfway to the station, and I've long ago shifted back to the case when something Lang said earlier pops into my head: *I can't imagine a monster scary enough to spook Roberts.* And therein lies our problem. Just because we can't imagine that monster doesn't mean he doesn't exist.

CHAPTER 6

The drive from Roberts's house to the downtown medical examiner's office is not kind. Lang and I end up in a crush of rush hour traffic. When the six o'clock hour comes and goes, I still hang on to hope that the ME on the Summer case might still be at work, but it's clear that I need to call ahead. I scan the file for a name and groan. "Great. Trevor Richards is the ME."

"Sourpuss bastard," Lang mumbles, before adding, "He's likely gone for the day, and if he's not, he's not going to wait for you. Chocolate won't work on that man."

Considering Trevor *is* a sourpuss, he's right of course, but I'm not deterred. "I have to try. I have his cell number." I tab through my numbers and punch the autodial.

"Detective Jazz," he greets. "Whatever you want, this is a bad time."

I decide to make it a good time by continuing onward. "I'm calling about the Summer case. I'm taking over for Roberts."

"It's been a long week," he grumbles, but then, he always grumbles. He's forty-something, divorced, and forever mad at the world. Though I feel for him in some ways. Examining dead bodies all day and night can't help one's outlook on life, nor, and I can speak to this topic, one's love life. "I'm not staying tonight," he continues, "and I'm not here past noon tomorrow. I'm also too busy to see you before I leave."

"Yes, but—"

"I'm done with this one, anyway. The sister is just waiting for you folks to approve the release of the body to her home state."

"I'd like the chance to talk about the results with you and see the body before that happens. I can meet you at your office early."

"No." He offers no further explanation but states the obvious. "Summer is dead. He was poisoned. We're waiting on toxicology reports, but I can say conclusively that the toxin cyanide was the murder weapon. How I came about that conclusion with such speed, and before the toxicology reports, will be in my reports, which you will have tomorrow."

"Can I get them tonight?"

"No." His voice is snip and snipe. "Anything else?"

"The ropes—"

"Handed over to the crime lab, but they weren't ropes. They were ties from the victim's curtains."

Of course, I think. The Poet—that's what I decide right now to name him—wouldn't use anything that could be traced back to a purchase. The paper that the poem was typed on was most likely standard copy paper, found in every office in the country.

I make fast work of ending the call. "That went as expected," I announce, sliding my phone back into my jacket pocket before giving Lang the general rundown of the call.

"At least we confirmed the cyanide," he says. "What's the plan now? Back to the station? Or you want to ride along to hunt down Roberts?"

"We need to divide and conquer. I need to work this case."

With that plan in play, I decide to check out the crime scene and have Lang drop me off at my car in the station garage. On my own now, I climb inside my practical, five-year-old, silver Ford Focus. It's not sentimental to me like Lang's Mustang is to him, because it reminds him of a car his father used to own, but it gets me where I need to go. Lang was close to his father who, just like mine, died in the line of duty. I was *not* close to mine. I'm not sure why I thought working with him would change that, or, considering how he acted most of my life, why I even wanted to change it at all. But either way, it didn't work and it's over. He's gone.

Irritated that I'm even headed down that rabbit hole, I settle my things in my seat, lock up, and crank the engine and air. With a quick scan of the file, I confirm Summer's bookstore to be nearby, here in downtown.

A short drive later, I arrive at my destination to the sun flattening along the horizon. I pull my car into the sparsely lit parking lot of the property, which appears to square off the building in all directions. I park on the side where the front door sits, in the center of the empty lot, a location that allows me a bird's eye view of the location.

Thankfully, a rapidly rising bright full moon illuminates what turns out to be an adorable little bookstore painted teal with images of books floating along the stucco walls. And then I just sit here. That's what I do. I like to sit at a crime scene and just experience it, while I process the file and my thoughts. As crazy as some might call that, I've proven that just being at the scene of the crime delivers me to new and important revelations.

Killing my engine, I survey the darkness suffocating the sides of the building, shelter to anyone lurking about, a perfect veil to hide beneath and inside. There is no question that The Poet used that darkness to his benefit, a friend that helped him commit murder. No one would have seen him. Anyone could be there now, too, and I wouldn't know.

CHAPTER 7

My cell phone rings and I tear my gaze from the darkness to eye Chuck's number on caller ID. "What do you have for me?"

"I emailed you an encrypted file that has a lot of random data you should find helpful. As a point of interest though, I cross-referenced a connection between Roberts and the victim and found nothing."

Nothing means nothing with Chuck. He's that thorough.

"I went further than requested," he continues, driving home that thought. "I cross-referenced his family, his ex-wife, his cases, looking for anything that matched up to the Summer case. There's nothing there."

"There was a 'professor' noted in the file. Do you have anything on him?"

"Yes, I saw that and checked it out, but there's no one that I can connect to Summer or Roberts who fits that title. Not obviously at least. It could be a nickname."

A nickname's an interesting premise, I think, but we need to rule out the real deal at this point. "Look up professors with a literature and/or poetry connection. I'm sure you noticed, but we don't have much of a description."

"Right. I have the description in the file, which is pretty nondescript and includes no distinguishing marks. Got it. He should be easy to find."

I laugh. "Thank you, Chuck. And just in case I haven't told you lately, you are *brilliant*."

"Yeah, yeah. You gave me chocolate. You're spared excessive compliments until that high wears off." He hangs up.

I flip on my overhead light and grab my file, opening it to do exactly what I came here to do— read and think. For now, I focus on the people close to Summer. He had no girlfriend. His last known ex is now married with kids. Roberts interviewed her and her husband, as well as confirmed their alibis.

I read on and determine that Summer was alone in the world. His parents were killed in a car accident last year. His only sister lives in Ohio where Summer is from. She asked for the body to be transported when released. She did come to Austin right after the murder, and Roberts interviewed her and her husband. He also confirmed their alibi. Roberts was so fast and accurate that he already had bank records for everyone in question checked to look for signs of a paid hit. Nothing but "the professor" written down and circled a number of times.

God, I wish I could talk to Roberts.

I scan farther down the page and find notes that indicate the sister plans to sell the bookstore. Good luck with that. It's now the scene of a murder.

I scribble down a few notes: *Easy target. No close family. What about friends?* I flip to another page. Roberts covered that, too. He interviewed at least half a dozen friends and ruled them all out with alibis. I'm impressed.

I read the preliminary crime scene reports and not for the first time. I keep going back to the cleanliness of the crime scene. We found no foreign hair or DNA at the scene, but there were glove prints, indicating that the killer wore gloves. He knew what he was doing, and either his head and body are shaved, or he's covering up well, and that includes his head, perhaps using a skintight swim cap. To me, this skill level indicates experience. This was not a one and done. I make another note: *Killed before.*

We need to find his previous victims.

I've just shut the file and set it on my seat when my gaze catches on a shifting shadow near the bookstore. My body stiffens, stills, but that doesn't stop the surge of adrenaline jacking up my heart rate. I flip my overhead light off and stare into the inky blackness of the side of the store, into the very space I'd considered shelter for a killer, ironically looking for that killer now. Time ticks by in minutes, not seconds, while I wait for another shadow to appear, another shift of the darkness that doesn't come.

But I feel the energy charged around me. I'm not the only one here. He's here, our killer is here, and I can't—*I won't*—let him get away. My free hand settles on the butt of my weapon and I reach for the door.

CHAPTER 8

My father used to say, "Use your Spidey senses. If they tingle, beware." My Spidey senses aren't just tingling. They're conducting a rock concert on my nerves right now. And contrary to my mother's belief, I do not have a death wish.

I call for a silent approach backup. I also don't wait for backup to exit my vehicle for good reason. The Austin PD is close. Help will come quickly. If the killer is lurking about, watching me, thinking that I'm alone, he's more likely to keep watching. The minute he knows I'm not, he'll scramble away like a sewer rat, and the opportunity to catch him will be lost.

Once I'm outside my vehicle, I point a flashlight and my service weapon toward the black hole at the side of the bookstore. There are no hiding places besides the building: no trees, no dumpster. No other car. There is also only one streetlight, and it's not working, which feels a bit like the security system that was offline the night of the murder. I scan the scene for movement and find nothing. I could dismiss what I saw as wind or a squirrel, but that Spidey sense thing isn't going to let me be that foolish.

Keeping a wide distance, I pretend to go left, cutting fast in that direction, only to immediately go right. I'm about to turn the corner, to walk right into the shadow I'd seen from my car, but instinct halts me. Instinct yells for me to wait, not to go alone.

"Damn it," I murmur, dropping back toward my car.

But I know the killer's here. I *feel* him, evil crawling along my skin, trying to shove its way under and inside me. I'm suffocating in evil, in him. I feel his eyes on me, his stare, a burn that comes straight from hell. He can see me. I can't see him. That is not a matchup that ends well for me.

A car pulls into the street a few feet away, and I catch a glimpse of Lang in my peripheral vision. He's smart and sharp enough to approach silently, weapon drawn. He's halfway to me and I motion left, back toward the darkness and that shadow. He motions right. Another patrol car is pulling up behind his Mustang and just that quickly, I feel the shift in the air. I feel the evil coil and withdraw.

Damn it, again. We're losing him.

Fear gone now, I cut the corner around the building, flattening on the concrete wall, shining my light along the empty space. I don't wait here for him to escape from the rear. I run toward the back wall and pause, easing around the corner as Lang charges toward me.

We're clear. The killer is gone, but I have a crazy sensation of the familiar. Like this is not an evil I've felt only once.

CHAPTER 9

It doesn't take long after Lang and I give the go-ahead for the cavalry to light the bookstore up like Christmas. Or for us to decide we're going inside, just to be sure The Poet isn't seeking shelter there.

We converse with several officers, one of whom was a first responder on the initial crime scene. Officer Jackson is a tall redhead, a man in his thirties only two years out of the military and into the force, who is all muscle and stony-faced expressions. I know him from another case. He has a future. He's one of the good ones, and he's quick to contribute. "The front doors are glass and locked. No one got in or out from that location without breaking the glass that's intact."

"All right then," Lang agrees. "The rear entrance is our hot spot."

Decision made, and with a car illuminating the building and officers backing us up, Lang and I approach the back door, which is predictably secured. Lang breaks the lock and flips a light on. We're greeted with two sets of stairs, one going up and one going down. The archway to the left of both leads into the bookstore.

Officer Jackson joins us. "Hold the stairwells," Lang orders, and with Jackson's nod, Lang and I enter the store.

Side by side, we halt just inside the cozy little store, complete with wooden tables, a full bar, and rows of books. "Dude had a hell of a selection of IPA's," Lang murmurs, like a selection of beers is a dead man's legacy.

I scowl at him and then start walking. From there,

we divide and conquer, checking every row of books, and when we're all clear, I seek out a longer look at the poetry section, which is quite extensive. Considering the poem left in the victim's mouth, these books should have been bagged into evidence. They will be before we leave here tonight.

Lang and I reconvene with Jackson in the entry-way. "Get the poetry section into evidence," I instruct Jackson. "All of it. Every book." My attention turns to Lang. "Ready?"

He motions to the upper level. "Your case. You want the apartment? Where the murder happened."

"The murder began with planning. I'll take the theater. I want to be where the killer was, in the order that he was there."

"All right. Have it your way." He eyes Jackson. "Hold the fort, man." Jackson nods, and Lang heads up his set of stairs.

Weapon and flashlight in front of me, I start down my set of stairs, traveling well-lit territory into what appears to be a black hole below. Nerves quiver inside me, but they drive me forward. They make me want to strip away the unknown. I end my path at an open doorway. Aware that The Poet could be waiting inside, I shine my light in a quick scan of the space in front of me and reach to the inner wall, where I easily find a light switch. Once the room is glowing, I find exactly what I'd expected from a scan of the crime scene photos: a circular stage sits in the pit of the room, with theater-style seating chairs stacked around it. There are no hiding places, no room for a large man to conceal himself. The room is empty but for me, at least right now.

The killer was here before he killed Summer.

I already know what seat the witnesses claim was his and I go there now, standing in front of it and staring down at the stage. He was in a position of judge, higher than everyone else, and Summer was judged unworthy. I wonder if any of my thoughts mimic Roberts's thoughts. His detailed investigation doesn't support a disappearing act. Anyone who put this much work into a case would want to see it properly supported.

"Anything?" Lang asks from the doorway.

"All clear here," I say, twisting around to face him. "What about upstairs?"

"Clear. You want to walk the apartment?"

"I'll be right there," I say, but I don't move in his direction.

There's one last thing I need to do. I sit down in the same chair where our killer sat, and I see the room the way I need to see this murder: through the eyes of The Poet.

CHAPTER 10

The chair that Summer died in is no longer on the property, long gone and in our labs, but that area where it sat in his apartment is taped off and easily identified. I stand in front of that tape now, in the center of the tiny but immaculately clean apartment with simple furnishings and empty bookshelves. The books that were once neatly lined up on each shelf are now in our lab as well.

Lang steps to my side but doesn't speak, giving me time to process and share my thoughts. And that's exactly what I do. I force my mind into *his* mind, the mind of the man I know as The Poet.

"He waited until the building was empty, concrete walls sealing Summer's fate. He stood in perhaps this very spot, feeling powerful and larger than life. He looked upon a scared, naked man and welcomed his tears, even let him beg for freedom and escape. I don't think he enjoyed these things. They were simply inevitable. Summer, in his eyes, had to die. It was necessary. Judgment had already been handed down."

"I'll buy all of that," Lang says. "But how did he get him to take the pill? A threat against his sister?"

I reject that idea. "I don't think he'd bother with his sister. He wasn't worth that much of the killer's time. I'd gamble on a gun, which gave him the freedom to allow Summer's arms to be free. It would be a simple, clean threat because he knew he'd never have to fire it." I give the phantom chair my profile and face Lang. "I think he's actually a bit of a coward. He doesn't want to kill them himself. And I just won't buy into Summer as the first victim. The crime scene's just too clean."

"I damn sure don't think that Summer was his only victim. Which brings me to what I know that you don't know."

"What don't I know?"

"Roberts told no one before the captain that he was leaving. Roberts didn't even line up that job in Houston. The captain did it for him."

I could surmise about ten different things from those statements but choose to cut to the chase. "Where is this going, Lang?"

"Right back to you and this asshole being here tonight. Roberts's phone isn't just off, it's not even pinging." I open my mouth to speak, and he holds up a hand. "Just listen. He's missing. He's not the killer. He's in trouble. You know it. I know."

"That seems likely, yes."

"And this case was his last case," he continues. "Your case now. So here's my question and it's damn important, so listen up. If the killer was here tonight, did you stumble on him, or did he follow you?"

CHAPTER 11

I sit at the coffee shop across from Detective Jazz's apartment and watch her Ford Focus pull into the parking garage. She knew I was there tonight. Already she validates herself as a protégée, and by doing so, justifies everything I've done to bring us together.

The man she, and those around her, knew as Detective Roberts had to go. His departure was necessary. He, and his identity, were the sacrificial lamb for the greater cause. He stood between me and her, and that simply couldn't happen. Disposing of him properly demanded a rather complex execution, but it was necessary. I had to ensure that he simply vanished, gone and, eventually, as all basic humans are, forgotten. Of course, I arranged for his record to be dirtied up, the details of which will soon be discovered. Details that will make him look like he's sinned horribly, and done his badge a disservice, thus assumed to have run to avoid persecution.

A fade to black also ensured the FBI wouldn't nudge their way into the mix. And while I'd be quite entertained by their efforts to flex their weak muscles, they'd potentially remove Detective Jazz from the puzzle. And that isn't an option.

Detective Jazz must be prepared for the future. She must be taught how to step into her shoes as the future master, as I have my predecessor. She must learn to protect the poems that are the bible to our world. She must learn how to punish those who do not respect that bible. It's time, and I'm quite enjoying my mentoring.

My lips curve and I sip my coffee. I do believe I'll join her for her morning run.

CHAPTER 12

When murder is your job, you have to find a way to compartmentalize or you go insane. For me, that means flipping a switch off in my mind. That usually happens right now, as I enter my building and walk up the stairs toward my apartment. Tonight, it doesn't. I could blame it on Lang and his conspiracy theories about The Poet following me, but the truth is, I haven't managed that little trick since the night my father was murdered.

I reach my door, head inside, and lock up, but I stop there, leaning on the door's wooden surface. Standing there, I will myself to dispel the tension that I normally leave outside in the stairwell. This is my safe place, the apartment my grandfather persuaded me to buy seven years ago when I made detective. Brilliant man that he was before the dementia took over, he said the new downtown community would double in value. It quadrupled. Now I have something instead of nothing, but I'd much rather just have him back whole again.

I stand at the door another full minute and decide I'm still here for a reason and that reason is The Poet. I don't know if he followed me tonight, but he's under my skin and I can't shake the odd sensation of an evil that felt familiar. So much so that I cave and search my apartment, which doesn't take long. I have an open concept living room and kitchen, a master bedroom, an upstairs secret loft-style room, and a bathroom.

Once I know I'm alone, I prepare dinner. That means I sit down on my couch with my file, a glass of red wine, my favorite blend, and a bag of popcorn.

My faithful TV dinner is just not appealing. The gun I've set on the table next to me, however, is. I'm only on sip two of my wine, the edge of this evening still clear and present, when Lang calls.

"Are you home?"

"Yes, Papa Lang, I am indeed home. You do know I'm a detective and taking care of myself, right? And," I add, "I'm capable of kicking your ass."

"Should I come over and you can try?"

I kick off my shoes, heels that are somehow still on my feet. Another "girl power" statement. I can run in them and use them as a weapon quite effectively, should it become necessary; even I can admit that's a practiced skill. "Go service your booty call," I say, and I hang up.

I sip my wine and will myself to call my mother. I'm resisting her and I know it's not fair, but I'm self-analytical enough to know why. She pulls me into the deep, complicated puddle of grief, which muddies my mind and affects my performance.

For now, I settle on texting her: *Mom. I love you. I'm safe. I'm working a case. I'll call you tomorrow. I promise.*

"There you go," I murmur to myself. "I can take you out with my high heels and tell my mother I love you, all in the same night. I am empowered." Those last words trail off. *I am empowered.* I can't function in a place of fear, or I won't be able to do this job. And this job feels like my purpose. It has since I was a small child. I sip my wine and set down my glass. "Okay." I shrug out of my jacket, ready to dig in.

My mother returns my text: *I love you, too, honey. Thanks for letting me know you're okay. I worry.* Guilt stabs at me, but guilt is not empowering. I need to be a better daughter. I know this. I will fix this. I will call her in the morning as promised.

I pull my case file from my bag and lay it in front

of me. Next, I grab a pad and pen, scribbling down all my observations from the crime scene tonight. I circle: *He's killed before*. I tap my pen on the pad. I need to back that up with facts. I start by downloading the reports Chuck sent me, and my attention immediately goes to a list of professors, teachers, and instructors in the city and state who teach literature. He's gone so far as to turn the list itself into more lists and narrow down possible suspects based on random criteria: the description we have for the man at the poetry reading and any curriculum with poetry. Thankfully this narrows the list of thousands down to a short list, but I need to make it even shorter. Per Chuck's notes, there's also a poetry club on the UT campus, but he has no data on who runs it. More to come. And Lord help me, he's diving into off-campus poetry/book clubs tomorrow. The list is not going to end.

I move on and try to find clues with a narrower path to travel. I scan the phone records for Summer. Chuck has given me the details on each person Summer communicated with. This man is golden, I swear, and worth a million chocolate bars. Summer took all of his business calls on his cell phone, but none of the people who attended the reading that night are cross-referenced to his call log. I tab through the deluge of data, and as always at this stage, find it too excessive.

He killed before.

He will kill again.

I know it.

I feel it.

I feel the absolute need to cut time and take actions I wouldn't normally take, almost like a ticking clock on a bomb. And I know why. A husband killing his wife with cyanide is bad. A serial killer killing with cyanide is terrifying. His victims would have no chance of surviving.

Serial killer? Holy hell. He's killed *one person* who we've confirmed. One person does not make a serial killer, so why am I going there? Why am I certain that's exactly what we're dealing with?

My mind returns to the parking lot tonight, to that moment when I felt like evil was trying to crawl right into my soul. To that moment when that evil felt familiar. My mind goes to Roberts's swift departure and the possible connection he had to my father's bad deeds. It's time to consider this case somehow having a connection to me through my father.

CHAPTER 13

I text Chuck and have him cross-reference my father's cases with mine and Roberts, as well as anything connected to the Summer case. I text because I don't like to talk about my father. After I shoot off that message, I hesitate only a moment before I punch in an autodial number for Wade Miller, an FBI agent at the remote Austin office. His agent status is not only helpful right about now, it's how I met him and how he became my ex, the one who should have been perfect for me but never was going to work out.

"Sam," he greets, answering on the first ring. That's something about him I've always appreciated. He's reliable. "Is this personal or professional?"

I hesitate with my reply because this man was there for me, like *really there for me* in all ways, when my father died. I simply didn't have the emotional capacity to push forward with him at that point. I don't know if I ever will again, but we're not enemies. And we're not all business. We're *friends.* "Can't it be both?" I ask.

"You want a favor."

"I do, but now it sounds very dirty of me."

"I'm pretty okay with you being dirty, but we both know that's not where this is going." He doesn't give that comment time to be awkward. I don't think it would be anyway. It's hard to explain why that is when it would be from someone else. It just is. That's the thing with me and Wade; in fighting crime, horror movies, and occasional Chinese food outings, we are forever united. He proves this by saying, "I'll help. What do you got?"

"A case that feels bigger than the case itself."

"Any DNA?"

I like that he doesn't need an explanation of why it's bigger than itself. He gets it. He knows what I mean. "No," I say. "Not yet. This is three days fresh and I inherited it from a detective that suddenly went MIA, which is why I thought you could help me cut through the red tape to get what I need quickly."

"Is his disappearance connected?" Worry has now found its way into his tone. Law enforcement takes a threat to law enforcement seriously. "What are you into right now, Sam?"

"The detective who was handling this case before me supposedly asked for a transfer to Houston, but his phone is disconnected and it isn't pinging. In and of itself, that feels off, but he generally did a good job working the case. He did miss a DNA grab."

"You think that was intentional?"

"Based on how hard he worked the case from all other directions I tend to say no, but despite all that care he put into the case, he didn't even stay behind to brief me."

"It could be a personal problem. A cheating spouse. A sick family member. Any of those things apply?"

"I don't know yet. Lang's trying to track him down and figure things out. The captain doesn't seem concerned, though that was before we found out his phone isn't pinging. But the detective in question isn't due to report to Houston for two weeks, so a lot could happen in that time."

"What's your gut?" he asks. "What are you thinking?"

"I'm thinking I need to jump ahead of forensics and make sure I know as much about who I'm dealing with that I can possibly know. The good news is that Roberts, the missing detective in question, collected a ton of necessary data I'm already diving into."

"Does Roberts have family or close friends in Houston?"

"Unless it's a friend we don't know about, a new woman, or some long-lost cousin, no. His ex-wife is here. His parents are dead. We went by his house. It's cleaned out, which should make me feel better about the idea of a decisive action, but it doesn't."

He's silent a moment. "Sam—"

"No," I say, reading his mind easily. "I don't think he was involved in my father's dirty deeds, but they were friends. I can't rule it out." I leave out the part about this killer feeling like a familiar killer or my thoughts on that connecting him to my father. Anything to do with my father will have Wade at my doorstep.

The truth is that Wade and Lang suffocated me for two solid weeks after my father died until I couldn't take it anymore. I needed space in a bad way and before I forgot that I'm the badass with a weapon and brain I know how to use, and use well.

"I'll make some calls," he offers. "I'll find out if anything was about to come down on Roberts."

"Thank you." I sip my wine and then set my glass down. "Now," I say, moving on, "about the actual case. I think this guy has killed before and will kill again."

"Based on what?"

"The scene was clean, really clean. You asked about DNA. I don't think we're going to have some hidden source of DNA suddenly pop up."

"What *do* you have?"

"A glove print, which we both know is nothing, and a possible, extremely weak description, along with a poem he stuffed in the victim's mouth."

"A poem," he notes. "I see why this one landed on

your desk. What's the poem mean?"

"That's a subjective question, but it's about destiny."

"Sounds like they have a history, the killer and the victim."

"No," I say quickly. "I don't think so. I think this guy has a God complex. He judged his victim unworthy of living, a disruption to all those who remain. I'm just not sure why yet."

"Okay then." He doesn't ask how I came to this conclusion. "Cause of death?"

"Poison, and I've seen this before. I'm certain it's going to test out as cyanide."

I can hear his pencil scribbling on a pad. "I'll see if I get any hits on cyanide here and call a guy I know over at the ATF. And send me everything you can send me. I'll run a ViCAP report and see if we can find him hiding in those reports or across state lines."

"You read my mind. And one more thing."

"You want a profile."

I smile at how in sync we are. "Yes," I confirm. "Perfect."

"Have you done your own?" he says. "You spent months in an FBI training camp, where you were the badass everyone wanted to recruit. Again."

That's actually how Wade and I truly met the first time. The FBI used him to try to recruit me. They'd thought my flunking out of college had been a youthful mistake. There was a lot about why I followed my father that turned into a mistake I'm not going to visit right now, or perhaps ever again.

I move on to what I know. "The Poet, an organized killer, a planner. Highly intelligent. Well employed. These types like to appear stable and we're most likely looking at someone in a circle of family to shelter himself, even convince himself he's normal. None of this is on paper. And I don't feel like I have room for error on this one."

"The Poet?"

"That's what I'm calling him."

"Whatever you call him, do you really think he's a serial killer?"

"I *know* he's a serial killer. We just have to find his victims."

"I'll get you your profile for peace of mind."

"Thank you, Wade," I say, gratitude in my voice.

"Thank me by being careful. If this asshole came after Roberts, you could be next."

"If Roberts was his type, I am not."

"*Be careful*, Detective Jazz," he says, and this time he uses his best *Special Agent Wade Miller* voice, the detective title meant to make the "I'm serious" point.

"*I am.* I called you for a reason. I'm going to get him before he ever has the chance to get me."

We disconnect a few seconds later and I pull up the poem compilation Chuck put together for me on my MacBook. I gravitate toward the poem The Poet left called "Fate, The Jester." His message could be in those few lines or in another verse inside the full poem. I read it all slowly, all eight paragraphs, dissecting each one, but I return to the three lines he left in Summer's mouth:

Who laugh in the teeth of disaster,
Yet hope through the darkness to find
A road past the stars to a Master

A master, a statement that seems to reference superiority and drives home my earlier thoughts. The Poet judged Summer beneath him. Perhaps he judges us all beneath him. He believes he's above the law, and that's dangerous to those who come into contact with him.

That means I need to become dangerous to him, and quickly.

CHAPTER 14

After my call with Wade, I refill my wineglass, treat myself to another bag of popcorn, and tackle my next big problem. How to narrow my approach to the data dump I've been given. Deciding how to approach this takes me back to my teen years when I'd spent hours on end at a table with my father and godfather, now the chief of police, nosing into their case files. They'd tried to protect me from the horrors in those files but eventually gave in to my persistence. I'd become their protégée, and both lectured me not to get lost in the overload of data each case delivered, stressing how important it was to pick out the most productive angles of a case and focus. Most importantly, find "the system," my system, whatever that might be, and use it religiously.

For me, that means writing out lists the old-fashioned way, with pen and paper. It drives Lang crazy, probably because his system is all about pushing to the point of bullish demands of everyone who stands between him and solving the case. To each their own, but my lists have helped us catch more than a few killers.

And so, I do what I've been taught, what has worked for me over and over again. I spend hours sitting on my couch, working through the massive information dump Chuck has given me, trying to find the pieces inside the volume that matter. I have pages of notes, lists of things to do, and a plan of attack to unravel the mystery.

History and experience tell me that The Poet wants attention; otherwise, he'd simply disappear rather than leave law enforcement a message to decode. Sadly, I give him what he wants by retiring upstairs to my bedroom that overlooks the living area, with my Kindle and the book of poems Chuck put together for me. Propped against my headboard, snuggled under my down comforter, the air cranked a little too cold, I read while eating a healthy serving of chocolate. I've often wondered if serial killers eat chocolate, with the same conclusion. They do not, and perhaps that's their problem.

Somewhere in the middle of my studies, I jot down another page of notes filled with possible interpretations of the words before me. Poetry is often a bit of a mysterious, deep read, and my history interpreting it has often helped me decode a crime scene. But I don't feel like I have enough of The Poet's chosen words to tell me a real story.

When I finally turn out the lights, I stare into the darkness, my ice machine clunking loudly in the other room a few times while The Poet clunks just as loudly in my head. I know Roberts nicknamed him The Professor, while I call him The Poet. We could assume that means Roberts felt he was a professor, but perhaps he simply grabbed a nickname as I did, for his own mental processing. To believe he's an actual professor could be too small-minded. *Obvious* assumption is a good way to get outsmarted. And yet, ironically, I feel as if I'm missing something obvious.

I shut my eyes and drift into sleep with the poem The Poet left us in my head:

Who laugh in the teeth of disaster,
Yet hope through the darkness to find
A road past the stars to a Master

CHAPTER 15

I wake to a beam of sunshine, to that damn poem still playing in my head, to a freezing cold room, and to something about this case niggling at my mind. Frustrated that I can't just turn it into a coherent thought, and in need of a run to clear my head, I glance at my Apple watch. Confirming that it's only seven a.m., early enough to avoid the scorching sun, I suit up in workout tights, a tank top, and my sneakers.

Some cops drink their way out of hell, but one glass of wine—okay, two last night—is it for me and with reason. I'm a stupid drinker. Stupid is a good way to end up dead. That leaves running, karate, and the gym. I hate fat, out-of-shape cops. It's perhaps a mentality I inherited from my father, but one that I maintain. It's not about body shaming or judging at all. It's about staying alive for your family. It's about being fit enough to save an innocent life. Because any edge you have or don't have could cost someone their life. And sometimes having every humanly possible edge isn't enough, as proven by my father's murder.

Feeling that pinch of dueling emotions again, I slide a credit card into the pocket just inside my pants for a coffee run on the way home. I need that run. I really, really do.

Phone in hand, I hurry down the stairs, cross through my living room, and grab my keys from the table by the door. I exit my apartment into a foyer, which I thankfully share with no one, and then into the stairwell. Dashing down them now, I move quickly, hoping to avoid other human beings this morning, at least before my run. Not that I don't like people. I do. It's just that people are weird around law enforcement, all nervous and anxious, and this is one of those times when I don't need the distraction of making them remember that I'm another tenant. I need to stay in my headspace.

I exit to a humid August morning, the sun already pressing down on me, a weight sitting on my shoulders, a burden right along with murder. I begin my warm-up walk, tuning my music on my phone to my run playlist, but then pulling up Audible and looking for poetry. I find a few options, and one includes the poet that our killer quoted. I start the audio and begin my run.

I'm about a mile in when I stop dead in my tracks with the words: *A road past the stars to a Master* in my ear and now in my head. I pause the audio, and the obvious interpretation to that poem that I should have already realized is crystal clear now: *A road past the stars to a Master* means to God. This just confirms my earlier conclusions. He doesn't just think his victim was beneath him, he thinks he's God. Or a god. When you think you're a god, you think you're untouchable. He might actually be a professor, after all, an arrogant one who believes we might find him, but we can't catch him.

My mind goes to Roberts. Did Roberts prove him wrong? Did he get too close and move away too slowly?

CHAPTER 16

I finish my run with a sense of unease that I can't quite name and a decision to go to the university on my way to the station and find out who runs that poetry club. With my book still blasting in my ears, I step into the coffee shop and a line about five deep. I wave at Dave behind the counter, a mid-twenties medical student who I chat with rarely, but we're friendly. He grabs a cup and writes up my order on the side, showing me it's done and offering me a smile before helping his next customer.

I mouth a thank-you and continue to listen to my audiobook, but as we step forward, a tingling sensation slides up and down my spine, followed by a now-familiar evil. Which is crazy. The Poet is not here. That would mean he'd have had to follow me home last night.

A low breath trickles from my lips with that very real possibility. Discreetly, I glance to the jam-packed seating area of wooden tables, where a good twenty people of various sizes, ages, and attire are enjoying their coffees. What I don't see is a male with dark hair, but of course, the reality here is that The Poet may well have worn a wig to the poetry readings. I begin a closer inspection of each person when someone taps my shoulder. I jerk around to find the woman behind me pointing at the counter. I glance in that direction to discover that the line has cleared.

With a quick apology, I step to the counter. Dave is now talking to me, but my audiobook is still playing in my ear. I quickly fiddle with my phone and somehow manage to hit the wrong button. Poetry blasts from the microphone right at Dave, and I'm certain everyone waiting for their drinks at the end of the bar, and perhaps then some.

I punch the button again, ending the noise. "Sorry about that." I pull out my card and hand it to Dave.

"Poetry?" he inquires, ringing up my order.

"Words for the soul," I say automatically, something I used to say when I ran my poetry club, which became my thing only because I neglected a class in college. My professor made running the club my punishment, and extra credit, but it didn't turn out to be a punishment at all. The puzzles in the poems intrigued me and created a bonding experience with my grandfather, who spent countless hours helping me prepare for my club meetings.

"Words for the soul?" Dave asks with a snort. "More like a bunch of nonsense words thrown together to mean nothing, but to each their own."

"It's an acquired taste," I agree, as he hands me back my card. "Much like analyzing someone's bowel habits for a living. Which we both know is in your future."

He laughs. "Got me there. Have a good one, Sam."

"You too, Dave." And when I would move on down the counter, the barista steps to the counter and offers me my cup.

At this point, I would normally leave, but today I claim the one open seat in the place. Thankfully, it's well positioned in a corner, with a view of the shop. If The Poet's here, if he can see me now, I want to see him, too.

I sip my coffee, which is exceptionally good today, cataloging the people in the room: a Japanese couple smiling and laughing; a couple of guys in suits, battling over some document in front of them; a couple of teenagers; a man with curly light brown hair who sits in profile to me on the other side of the shop—something about him niggles me. There's also a bald man sitting with a beautiful blonde in a pretty pink dress. Bald would explain the lack of DNA at the crime scene. And he'd have my attention, but for one thing: the fact that the blonde has *his attention*, or rather that her breasts have his attention. He's definitely *not* here for me.

That's as far as I get before my cell phone rings with a call from my mother. I decline and use my camera to shoot a video of the room, and I'm not shy about it or quick. Yes, I'm bold like that when it comes to saving lives.

Once satisfied with my product, I shoot it over to Chuck, explain what it is, and once he confirms receipt, I stand up. Making my way to the trash can, I toss my cup and find that I'm still unable to get a good view of the curly-haired man. Looking for a better angle, I start a slow, even pace toward the door, past him, when he abruptly stands and gives me his back, effectively and perhaps intentionally, removing my vantage point. I rotate and watch him walk toward the trash can by the counter. He's tall. He's forty-ish, which qualifies as not too young or old. I'm not letting him walk out of the door without finding out who he is.

I pursue him and catch his arm. "Joe?" I ask, as if I think he's someone else.

He rotates, displaying a slash of a red scar on his face, which appears to be more birthmark than recent injury. "No. Sorry. Wrong guy."

And he is the wrong guy. At least he's not the man the witness saw at the poetry reading, considering none of them mentioned a scar. But makeup might hide the scar, and he was at the back of the theater, with dim lights.

"Maybe I forgot your name?" I press. "You're familiar."

"I'm not exactly easy to forget." His expression tightens and his eyes cut away before they find mine again, the slash of discomfort in his stare telling a story. He's talking about the scar. "Name's Jesse Row."

Jesse Row, who I now realize feels perfectly normal and not evil at all. It's a silly observation that has no factual merit, but in my gut, I know I'd know if he was the one. My hand, which hasn't left his arm, falls away. "Wrong person. Sorry to bother you. Have a good day."

I rotate away from him, exiting the coffee shop, but with no more peace of mind than when I sat down at the table. Either I've become paranoid in the wake of my father's murder and beyond what is reasonable, or my tingling Spidey senses are right and The Poet is here. *And*—I hate everything about the self-doubt I've projected in that thought. Never, ever have I doubted my instincts, but here I am. *Doubting.* And that simply isn't acceptable. I can't afford to doubt myself because The Poet damn sure isn't doubting himself.

CHAPTER 17

I text Chuck the name "Jesse Row" and a request for immediate information before I cross the street and sit on a bench, where I intend to do a little people watching. Chuck confirms receipt and the urgency. I'm about to text Lang when my mother calls again and this time, I answer. "Hi, Mom."

"Honey, so good to hear your voice."

The genuine joy in her voice stabs me in the heart. I'm such a bitch for avoiding her. "Sorry I haven't checked in. I've thrown myself into my work. How are you? How are things in general?"

"Hard, still really hard, but as for how I am? Busy at the hospital. It's good to be back to work."

Where she's a hospital administrator who faces death daily. I really need to be better about communicating. "Better right now, talking to you," she adds. "Your grandmother and grandfather would love to see you, too."

Except my grandfather doesn't remember my name, I think painfully.

"We'd love it if you'd come out to the house soon."

And I really can't make things right with her right now.

The last thing I'm going to do is to give The Poet a chance to turn his attention to my family. That leaves me two options: honesty or hurting her more than my silence already has. I opt for honesty. "Right now, Mom, I'm working a sensitive case, trying to catch someone who I believe will kill again and quickly."

"Oh my. You've dived right back in, I see."

"I have," I say, watching the bald man leave the coffee shop with the bosomy woman on his arm. "It's actually been good to be back, Mom," I say, still engaged in my call. "I needed this. I needed the same thing that I think you need, too—to stop feeling fear. These monsters don't get to make us cower."

"I don't know how you do it. You were *right there* with him."

But she wasn't, and I think that is part of the problem. Her mind keeps trying to imagine the horror and then denying that it's real. He died in my arms. For me, there's no denial.

"When this is done, we'll celebrate, because you brought me into this world, and I stopped him from killing again. Because you helped stop him."

"That's what it's all about, isn't it? Stopping the bad guys from hurting people."

"Yes. Yes, it is."

"Your dad did that his whole life."

There's a twist in my gut, a stirring of anger that I smash and smash quickly.

A man jogs past me, his shoes a neon green, his baseball hat one of those sweat grabbing types that prevents me from seeing his face. The two men who'd been arguing over a document in the coffee shop exit while an elderly woman sits down next to me and a siren shrieks past us.

"Oh my, that's loud. Where are you?"

"I'm out on my morning jog."

"Just be *very careful*. It's early and downtown is dangerous. Do you have your mace?"

"Mom, the part of this conversation where I'm a detective hunting bad guys. You were on that part of this call, right?"

"Yes, well, that's kind of the point, now isn't it? You live a death wish. *Do you have your mace*?"

I don't even try to understand why me carrying mace gives her some sense of comfort when someone could just shoot me, the way they did Dad.

I say the words she needs to hear right now. "I always have it on my key chain."

"Good. I *love* you."

"I love you, too."

"Call me. Don't make me call you."

"I will," I promise.

We disconnect and, unbidden, my mind flashes back to the long-gone past, to me as a teen, cowering in a closet:

I hug my knees to my chest and pray the shouting will stop, that my mother's tears will dry. The sound of something crashing jolts me, followed by the front door slamming. Silence follows but I'm afraid to hope that it's really over. Sometimes it starts all over again. Seconds tick by like hours and finally the closet door opens, and my mother kneels in front of me, and one of her eyes is swollen shut.

"Mom," I cry, throwing my arms around her and then pulling back. "He's a monster!"

"No." Her hands come down on my arms. "No. You've got that wrong. He's a hero who catches monsters. Sometimes the monsters mess with his head."

I shove away the anger fused in that memory as several people step inside while the man with the scar exits. I don't follow him. He's not The Poet. The woman next to me throws bread to a pigeon, which is basically a rat with wings, and three more birds scurry toward us.

I stand up. The neon shoe guy runs past us again, and my gaze follows him this time. This is a populated street where joggers pass by on the way elsewhere. They don't return. Hair prickles on my arms. He's approaching an intersection and I dash forward, running after him. I'm gaining on him quickly when a group of walkers crowds me and forces me to pause and sidestep.

By the time I'm free, he's disappeared. I sprint forward and stop at the intersection, scanning left and right, but he's nowhere to be found.

CHAPTER 18

I search the streets surrounding the area, jogging in several directions with no sign of "Neon Shoe Guy" anywhere. Drenched now from the extra workout and the rapidly heating temperature, my desire to find that jogger hasn't eased, but my opportunity has passed. Frustrated at my failure, I head back toward my building when Chuck calls me.

I answer, my gaze still flicking about, looking for the jogger who has managed to get under my skin, right along with The Poet. Perhaps because he was The Poet.

"What do you have for me?" I ask.

"Jesse Row's a financial analyst who just took a job a few blocks from the coffee shop. He relocated here from Tennessee two years ago. Nothing stands out. No warrants. No arrests. His hobby is cats. He owns a couple of cats that he shows professionally and is a judge for some sort of cat organization. Don't serial killers like to kill cats?"

"I certainly wouldn't have one pet sit for me," I say dryly, noting the woman on the bench is no longer on the bench, but the pigeons are still scurrying about. "He's not our guy." I'm already thinking about traffic camera footage that might give me a better picture of what set me off this morning, but if I say that to Chuck right now, Lang will get word, and he'll be on my doorstep when I don't want him there. I need to shower and think, without him hovering about in my apartment. "I'll be in soon, but call me if anything else stands out."

We disconnect, and I do one last visual scan of the area before I accept defeat and start the short walk home. I've just entered my building and made it halfway up the stairs leading to my apartment when I hear a familiar, gravelly voice yelling down at me. "Detective Jazz."

I halt and glance up to the next level, to find Old Lady Crawford leaning over the railing, her tropical shirt a blinding mix of orange and yellow, her shoulders perpetually hunched forward.

"Sam," I amend. "You know you can call me Sam."

"I like Detective Jazz."

My brow furrows with this reply. She never calls me Sam, but she's a bit eccentric and I just go with the flow. Or perhaps there's a problem and this is her way of telling me that she needs a detective? She does hold the self-assigned duty of "apartment mom."

"Is everything okay?"

"Who was that man hovering around your apartment last night? Made me nervous. You kick out a new boyfriend or something?"

The hair on my arms is standing on end again. "What man?"

"You know what man, honey. He was at *your* door."

"What did he look like?"

"I don't know. *You* should know."

"I *don't* know, Mrs. Crawford," I say, my voice calm but firm now. "*What* did he look like?"

"I couldn't see his face. He had on a baseball cap with a hoodie over the top of the hat. The brim stuck out wide over his face. The hoodie was pulled down low."

"How tall?"

She reaches way up over her head. "Tall."

Of course, anyone is tall to her. I doubt she reaches five feet. "Hair?"

"Under the hat."

"Clothes?"

"All black. Don't you know anything?" She sounds irritated now. "Who was he? You know now?"

A killer, I think, but I've learned sometimes a lie is the kindest words you can speak. Now is one of those times. "One of the detectives I work with," I tell her, at least for now. I don't want to scare her. "I'll get on him about scaring you. I didn't hear him knocking. I must have had my TV too loud." Adrenaline is coursing through me now, roughing up my nerves. "Better run and shower," I say, managing to sound breezy and easy. "Thanks, Mrs. Crawford."

I run up the stairs, unlock my door, and enter my apartment. I lock the door and then lean against the wooden surface.

I will not doubt myself again.

I felt his presence. I knew he was here.

And he was.

The Poet was here.

CHAPTER 19

I ran right past her this morning in my neon green sneakers. She was looking for me, and she knows me, she knows my face, but she just wasn't ready to *see* me. But she knew. She felt me there, as she should have. I'm her master, her mentor. She's ready to be pushed. She's ready to understand. On some level, she already knows her duty. She performed well this morning. She exposed an abuser who must be dealt with. And I will reward her by ending his sin.

For now, I park my family vehicle in our suburban-area garage and exit to have my wife open the door to the house and hold out a cup of coffee. She dotes on me. She dotes on the kids. We really are the perfect family, but then, that's by design. I join her and accept the coffee. "Thank you. Perfectly timed, too."

She smiles and tilts her chin, presenting me with her mouth, which I meet with my own. Happy wife, happy life. I head inside the house and stand at the end of the bar while the boys tell me all about the pancakes Mom just made. I play my role: father, husband, provider. A *necessary* role to ensure that I, too, follow my true destiny.

CHAPTER 20

I push off of the door, remove my backup weapon from the foyer table where I keep my keys, and make a trade; the keys go in the drawer. The gun goes on top of the table. Next, I dial Chuck. "I need any camera footage you can get me from my street."

"Ah wait, what?" He sounds confused. He won't be for long. "Your street?"

"Yes. Take down the address."

"I can look it up, but—"

I dictate the address anyway. "Have Louise, the new intern they gave me last week, ask the small businesses for security footage. Tell Louise I said she works for you now. I need you to have resources. And the Brew Coffee House is a top priority. Get me that footage and anything pointed toward it or my apartment first."

"Got it. Brew Coffee House and your building. Are you in danger?"

"I'm fine. I hunt monsters." I catch the edge in my voice that he doesn't deserve. "Sorry. I'm fine," I repeat, bringing my voice down a notch below my nerves. "Thank you for asking. I'm just being short because I'm working on a time-sensitive situation."

"Right, okay. I'm here. I'm on it."

"Thanks, Chuck. Chocolate for us both, lots of chocolate. Gotta go." I disconnect and dial the apartment office.

Tabitha, the long-term manager, answers in her famously nasal voice. "This is Tabitha. May I help you?"

"Tabitha, this is Samantha Jazz. *Detective* Samantha Jazz. I need you to pull the security footage for every angle of my building inside and out, for last night. Actually, for all of the buildings. I need that right now."

"Oh, I—I need to find out if that's allowed."

"The safety of your tenants is in question. Help me protect them."

"Oh. My. Yes." She sounds flustered. "I'm sure I can give it to you. I'll make a fast call. When do you need it?"

"Now," I repeat. "I'll be there within the hour to pick it up."

"That's fast. I don't—"

"Tell me when I get there." I hang up, and I have no choice but to search my apartment again. I can't not search my apartment after what I've just learned. And *I hate* that The Poet has that much control over me and my actions right now. That has to end. He wants to play. Let's play, but it has to be my game, my way. He is not in control.

I am.

CHAPTER 21

Even after I've confirmed that The Poet is not in my apartment, I can feel his evil pressing on the walls around me, systematically tearing them down.

I head to the bathroom, setting my weapon and badge on the sink. The weapon is to protect myself. The badge is to remind me that I'm not supposed to kill him if I can arrest him. I rotate to the shower and change my mind. I turn back and shove the badge into the drawer. If he comes into my house, I really am going to kill him.

Now, I feel better. I get in the shower, hurrying through it, eager to get to work. Soon, I'm standing in front of the mirror, dressed in my standard dress pants, which are black today, paired with a matching blazer, and a pink silk blouse. I chose the pink color for a reason. I reach for my hair to knot it at the back of my head, but on second thought, leave it long around my shoulders. I want to be underestimated because I'm female today. *Please.* Underestimate me. It will be a mistake.

I hook my badge and service weapon at my hip—a weapon that's never betrayed me, unlike my father.

Hurrying into the bedroom, eager to do what I need to do and get to the campus, I sit in the chair next to the bed and open my MacBook. With fresh eyes, I do a quick review of the material I'd prepared for Wade last night and then press send, hoping the report he's promised comes quickly.

I'm just settling my briefcase on my shoulder when there's a knock on my front door. Thinking it might be Tabitha coming to me before I make it to the office, I exit the bedroom and hurry down the stairs and across the living area.

And while I don't believe The Poet will knock and wait to be invited in, one can't be too careful. Spine stiff, shoulders knotted, I step to the door, hand on my weapon. "Who is it?"

"The big bad wolf."

At the sound of Lang's voice, the tension eases from my shoulders and I open the door. He's unshaven, his eyes bloodshot, and he seems to be wearing the same jeans and T-shirt he wore yesterday. Clearly, his booty call did end up happening and lasted all night. "You have something to tell me?" he demands.

"Chuck called you."

"Hell yeah, Chuck called me." He crowds his way in through my door and I back away, giving him space, and me, too.

I walk into my kitchen, which is a chef's kitchen with a beautiful navy blue and gray marbled island. Pots and pans hang from above that island on a pretty silver rack. I have never touched those pans since my mother put them there seven years ago, but I have had them cleaned, by someone who wasn't me. I walk to the fridge and grab a premade protein shake, tossing it to Lang as he steps to the end of the island.

"You need that, since we both know you aren't running on much sleep today."

He grunts, offering no denial.

I grab another for myself and step to the opposite side of the island, making sure I have a whole lot of marble between me and him. And a few pans to whack him with if needed. Maybe my mom was onto something. "Hope you didn't have to pry her legs from around your waist to come over here," I say, in an uncharacteristically crass comment, which I deliver all nice and cool before opening my drink and taking a swig.

The idea is to shock him and redirect the attention to where I want it: anywhere but on me. But this is Lang, and Lang is Lang. He knows me and what I'm doing. "I was right, wasn't I?" he demands. "He's hunting the detectives hunting him."

I abandon my drink and grip the edges of the island and speak what's been in the back of my mind for a good hour. "I don't think that we're going to get good news about Roberts."

He grimaces and looks skyward before leveling a fierce stare at me, anger bubbling beneath his surface. Anger I know is not at me. It's about fighting this fight and the wrong side winning. It's about losing a good man and a detective. "What happened?"

"I had one of those gut feelings that I get, right after my run this morning. It was when I entered the coffee shop. Like he was there. I *felt* him there, Ethan. I can't explain it. I felt him at the bookstore, too. Familiar. Like—" I stop myself before I make him more paranoid than he needs to be right now. "I stayed. I shot a video of everyone in the coffee shop. I even talked to one man who caught my attention. That's how strong the feeling was."

"And?"

"And he wasn't the guy. He has cats and judges cat shows, but that's not the real problem here. When I came home, Old Lady Crawford asked me who the man with the hat and hoodie was lurking around my door last night."

He curses and scrubs his jaw, planting his hands on the island. "He followed you from the building last night."

"One could assume. Yes." I stop there because the truth is that I'm not sure how I'm supposed to feel about this. I'm human. I'm a detective. I'm the daughter of a recently murdered father who was also a cop. All I know right now is that I want to focus and work the case. "I called the apartment office and had them pull the security footage."

"That's it?" he demands. "That's all you're going to say to me, Jazz?"

"What do you want me to say, Lang?" I snap, and now I'm angry. "What am I supposed to say?"

"That you get it. That you see what's happening here. If he kills the detectives who hunt him, you could be next."

"And so could you." I shove aside the anger. I need to work. I just need to work. "Which reminds me," I say, grabbing my phone, "I sent Wade the case file to have him get me a profile and a ViCAP report. I need to make sure he looks for cases where the detective working the case ended up dead." I text Wade, cautious not to set off any personal triggers: *Just to be safe, because of this situation with Roberts, check for cases where law enforcement disappeared.*

Message sent, I slide my phone back into my pocket and find Lang glaring at me.

"You're not going to talk about this, are you?"

"I'm just doing my job, Lang. What else can I do?"

"We need to talk to the captain."

"I don't want an overreaction that loses this guy," I say. "Let's just see what Wade says. In the meantime, Chuck is working on the camera action from the surrounding area and I'm headed to the apartment office to grab their security feed on my way to the UT campus. I want to follow up on the poetry club myself, in person."

"I'm in on this one. You don't get a say-so. I'm with you every step of the way. Let's go to the office. And I'll drive us to the campus."

I don't argue. Why would I? I have no goal here but to catch The Poet before he kills again.

CHAPTER 22

Tabitha, a pretty blonde who dresses like she's Saks Fifth Avenue, pops to her feet the minute we enter the office. Her eyes go wide at the sight of Lang, who is admittedly quite big and rather overwhelming in small spaces, such as this itty-bitty lobby. But she's not looking at him like she's intimidated. More like she wants to lick him all over, which is disgusting. He hasn't showered in two days. She bats long, mascara-laden lashes at him. "Hi."

"Hello there," he says in his best flirty voice that has me groaning and rolling my eyes.

"The security footage?" I say, and then, because I can't help myself, I say, "And do you make it a habit to flirt with tenants' boyfriends?"

Tabitha's cheeks flush. "Oh God. Oh sorry."

"Jesus, Jazz," Lang grumbles.

I don't set the record straight. I'm kind of enjoying this. "The security footage," I say tartly. "We're here for the security footage."

"The tech support team is working on it," Tabitha assures me. "And I'm sorry. I would never—"

Jeez, I think. "He's like a big brother. Take him. Have him. Remind him to shower for the rest of us to remain sane. We don't want to wait for the tech support team wherever they are. Can I access the feed from here in your office?"

Tabitha blinks and looks between us. "Ah. Yes. We do have a booth in the back room, but I don't know how to operate it."

"We do," Lang says, sounding a bit tart now, too. "Take us there."

"Of course," she agrees, hurrying away and

waving for us to follow.

And so we do. We follow like good little soldiers while Lang shoots me a look meant to freeze hell. Just another day in the neighborhood. I smile. He doesn't. We really are good friends. Everyone doesn't know that about us.

Once we're offered access to the booth, which is more of a closet, Lang sits down at the computer and keys the screen to life. I lean in close, hovering over his shoulder while Tabitha hovers by the door. "No feed for your apartment entryway," Lang says.

"Almost like he knew, isn't it?"

Lang gives a sharp nod. "Exactly what I was thinking. I'll check the building and the parking lot." He glances up at me. "What timeline are we thinking?"

"It had to have been nine when I got home, but I got the impression from Mrs. Crawford that he was at my door for an extended period."

He keys in a time stamp and then starts tabbing through timelines that seem to never end, to the point that I grab a chair and settle next to him. We hit the midnight hour and we have something: a man walking toward my building doorway in a hoodie. He opens the door and goes inside without ever looking up. I glance at Tabitha, who's still at the door. "Our building doors should have codes."

Her lips purse and she shifts her weight on top of her extremely high red stilettos. "I know. Mrs. Crawford expressed the same quite vocally this morning."

"I'm searching the parking lot now," Lang says, tabbing through the feed and then tabbing some more. "I can't find where he came from." He glances up at me. "It does seem like he had some inside knowledge of the security system here."

I dismiss that idea without questioning Tabitha.

"He wouldn't have known I existed until I took over for Roberts. And that just happened."

"Right," he says, but we stare at each other a long moment before he says, "Unless he did."

CHAPTER 23

Lang and I exit the apartment office and I immediately try to head off the blowup I know is coming. "I already asked Chuck to look for a connection between Roberts, my father, and this case."

"What do you know that I don't know? Spit it out. I'm not playing these bullshit games with you, Jazz."

"Games? I'm not playing games. There's nothing you don't know. Absolutely nothing."

"And yet you called Chuck, not me, this morning?"

"Because I knew you'd freak out and I needed to think, not fight."

"What don't I know, Jazz?" he repeats.

"Other than my theories?"

"Tell me," he orders.

"Roberts's abrupt departure made you ask about his friendship with my father. And Roberts is connected to this case. If The Poet knows me—"

"The Poet," he says thoughtfully. "I like it. Maybe we can turn him into The Dead Poet. Isn't that a book or something?"

"*Dead Poets Society* is a movie." I get back to what I was saying. "If The Poet knows me, it's logical that we look for a link to my father. I asked Chuck to search for a connection to all of us."

"In other words, this isn't a random serial killer. It's someone with a vendetta against your father."

"Who's dead." Those words punch and cut, but I press forward. "It doesn't quite add up, and I really don't think that's what's going on here, but it has to be considered."

"One way or another, he knows you and the security setup of your building."

"I know that."

His lips thin. "I have a few more questions for Tabitha." He turns around and walks back into the office. I don't follow. He'll get more out of her than I will.

I punch in Chuck's number before I end up punching Lang.

He answers on the first ring. "Jazz." He sounds so damn relieved. It's as if my mother has called the entire precinct and assured them that, my badge and gun be damned, I can't take care of myself. "Everything okay?"

"As okay as it ever is when I'm with Lang."

He laughs. "He is a rather *big* guy."

His diplomatic way of saying Lang overwhelms a room when he's present, and he does, but I for one know that isn't always a bad thing. "Any luck with the cameras?"

"We're making progress. We've pulled all public feed available and we're through a good chunk of the businesses in your area, including the coffee shop. I'm about to start a review. What am I looking for?"

"A man who might be shadowing me."

"Shit. He was shadowing *you*?"

"Yes." I don't want to say more, but he needs to know everything I can tell him if he's going to be effective reviewing any footage he gets his hands on. I give him the full rundown of my night and Mrs. Crawford's report.

"Everything I say right now will be wrong, but I'm going to speak anyway. I'm worried about you. I'm all in. I'll find him on that feed."

I can only hope he does. "Anything on the poetry club?"

"Yes, actually. It's defunct, but I found something

I think you're going to want to hear. There's a professor at UT Austin who works for the criminal justice department. He fits the description we're working with, and it gets better."

"I'm all about it getting better."

"Two years ago," he continues, "while he was working for UT San Antonio, and for only one semester, his curriculum included a class called Abstract Poetry and Criminology. Low enrollment sent it to the graveyard. I'm sending you his name, current schedule, a link to his faculty page, and the outline of the class in question, *right—now*."

"God, I love you, Chuck. If this is our guy, I swear I'll buy you a damn monthly delivery of chocolate for the rest of your life."

I disconnect and immediately key up the text he's sent me. The professor's name is Newman Smith and there's a photo. Tall, dark, average weight, but it's his green eyes that cut through me. Evil lives in those eyes.

Lang exits the office. "Tabitha is getting Chuck a list of everyone and anyone, including cable and electric crews, who might have had access to the building."

"We have a new person of interest," I say. "A professor at UT."

He rubs his hands together. "All right then. Why are we standing here?"

"Let's go."

We head toward the parking lot, and Lang says, "We're going to have to tell the captain what's going on. You know that, right?"

"I'm not arguing that point, but right now, time saves lives. I need to do my job, not defend my methods."

"I'll call the captain and let him know we need to talk to him tonight."

I stop walking and shake my phone at him. "*Don't* call the captain yet. He doesn't believe Roberts is missing. We have to have some kind of proof otherwise."

"And what do you propose that might be?"

"Finding The Poet on film while following me seems like a good start."

We glare at each other, but he silently concedes. We turn and start walking again.

Once we're inside his Mustang, the car rumbling with life, the air spraying us with heat instead of cold, Lang glances over at me with one of his intense looks. "I'm like a brother?"

"You irritated the hell out of me, so yeah. Brother."

"Hmm," he murmurs. "Best-looking big brother on planet Earth."

He's trying to blunt the tension and make me laugh. I want to, but I don't. I poke a finger in the air in his direction. "Whore around with whomever you want, but keep it away from my building."

"Damn. I wanted to whore around *right here*." This time his joke falls flat, the air thickening around it. He wouldn't be the only one whoring around here, considering The Poet's visit last night.

CHAPTER 24

On the ride to campus, I read through the material Chuck's given me on Newman. "Name is Newman Smith, no middle name."

"Oh hell, anyone without a middle name is a serial killer."

I don't even ask his logic on that one. I simply give him a "you're crazy" side-eye and then keep reading. "He's a criminal justice instructor with a master's in forensic science, which would explain the clean crime scene."

"I thought we were looking for a poet."

"Two years ago he taught a class called Abstract Poetry and Criminality. Among the topics discussed were 'Poetry: words that speak to the soul of a serial killer' and 'How poetry connects you to the mind of a killer.'" I hold up a finger. "And. It gets better. Also discussed was 'How poetry is death by words.'"

"From boredom," Lang grumbles. "Or brain scramble, just trying to figure out what the flip the poem means."

His comment has me thinking. The barista hates poetry. Lang hates poetry. Summer clearly loved poetry. He held readings in his theater. I love poetry. Maybe The Poet doesn't love poetry at all, as I've assumed. Maybe he uses it to mock those who do.

I glance over at Lang. "Did Roberts like poetry?"

He snorts. "I'd be shocked to find out Roberts liked poetry. He was a beer, bacon, and football guy."

"Is there someone we can ask?"

"His ex-wife."

"Call his ex-wife."

"I need to talk to her anyway about Roberts, but

I'd rather do that in person."

"Just call her now and ask if he liked poetry. We need to know."

"All right. I don't have the number, but I can get it." He idles at a stoplight and makes a few calls that finally catch up to Roberts's ex-wife. "Susie," he greets, and silently mouths, "ex-wife." "Got a bet I'm trying to win. Does Roberts like poetry?" He glances over at me, and says, "She laughed. The answer is not even a little."

"How long were they married?" I ask.

Lang relays the question and then says, "Twelve years."

A long time, I think. "Why'd they divorce?" I ask.

Lang scowls at me, and I scowl right back.

"Ask her."

He grimaces and says, "Why did you two divorce?"

He listens a moment and then looks at me. "He changed. He was gone all the time and when he was home he was moody and hard to handle."

Moody and hard to handle. At least, he doesn't fit the cool, calm calculation I'd expect from The Poet. And he doesn't like poetry. Or so the ex-wife believes. Assuming that to be true, because I have no other option, my mind races with this bit of new information; Roberts didn't like poetry. If The Poet did indeed kill both Summer and Roberts, then he killed a man who loved poetry and a man who hated poetry. What am I missing?

CHAPTER 25

We arrive at the campus while Newman is still teaching a class.

With twenty minutes left before dismissal, Lang and I enter a large auditorium on an upper level, where the lighting is dim and the students sit far below. We settle comfortably into the darkness, where we proceed to hold up a wall together. Teamwork. Occasionally Lang and I make it work.

Newman is, as expected, a tall, fit white man who, as per Chuck's notes, is forty-two, with an apparent love for bow ties. He's also standing center stage, discussing blood splatter.

"What if you aspired to outsmart law enforcement?" he asks his class. "Could you influence blood splatter to confuse the forensic science of a crime scene?"

The answer, I think, is yes, there are mechanisms a savvy killer might use to affect blood splatter intentionally, but there are cleaner ways to avoid detection. For instance, *cyanide*.

Students begin interjecting their thoughts while Lang leans over and whispers, "Better yet, why not just use cyanide?"

My lips quirk with that like-minded statement.

"Dude has a whole creepy thing going on," he adds.

Lang has a colorful way of saying things, but he's again proved our like minds with the same first impression. There is something off about Newman, something too perfectly pressed and put together, almost as if he's wearing a costume.

I scan the hundreds of students dotting the

stacked seating not so unlike that of the theater at Summer's bookstore. Students who could well be the future of law enforcement. Students being taught by a man who may well be a killer, but on the bright side, there's a lot to learn from a killer. There's a reason why I've studied killers quite extensively, met with them, even. You can't hunt and catch a killer you don't understand.

What I learned was that you can't fully know or trust anyone. Not your spouse. Not your best friend. Not your father. Everyone has secrets: secret fetishes, secret lovers, secret demons. Cheaters, liars, and killers lead the same double lives. I know too much to trust anyone completely.

And right now, listening to Newman lecture this class, I decide he, too, knows too much. At least, too much for our own good. Certainly, everything he needs to know to leave a murder scene squeaky clean and DNA-free. But is he the familiar evil I've felt from The Poet? We're about to find out.

CHAPTER 26

Class ends and students leave in a scramble for the auditorium doors and with such speed, you'd think there'd been a fire alarm. The crowd blows like the wind, and with its thinning, Lang and I step into action. Side by side, we head down the stairs, neither of us looking at each other or anyone but our person of interest: Newman Smith. Some might think I'd feel nervous with the anticipation of meeting my potential stalker.

I do not.

There is no hesitation in me, no fear of a man who may well have been stalking me, and for good reason. I simply find it easier to look into the eyes of a killer than have him look from the shadows upon me. The moment you unmask your adversary, you begin to understand and defeat him.

Newman's standing at his desk, shuffling papers, seemingly oblivious to our approach, but I do not believe this to be true. There are subtle hints to his awareness. His spine is still. His movements more robotic than natural. The fact that he retains this posture throughout our rather lengthy walk downward and toward him is also a telling factor. To me, this says he's guarding himself from our probing stares, denying us the opportunity to study his features, and inner turmoil, at length.

We're just stepping in front of his desk when he slides his bag over his shoulder and angles in the direction of the exit, as if he's going to leave.

"Newman Smith?" I ask, forcing him to halt.

He pauses, almost as if he's going to refuse to turn, but with obvious resistance, he concedes his position. He steps into a full-frontal pose behind the thick hunk of the wooden desk again. Lang and I are on the other side now, but it's me that Newman's sharp, green eyes fall upon, and they do so with a solid punch. In those seconds, I expect evil to wash over me. I reach for and welcome that familiar feeling, but it's not easily accessed. But there's something there, something unnatural, not like you and me.

"Who are you and what do you need?" he asks, a blunt edge to his tone.

If he knows me, there's no recognition in his eyes, but that could well be a prepared reaction, practiced even. I flash my badge. "Detective Samantha Jazz. And this"—I motion to Lang—"is Detective Langford. We'd like to ask you a few questions."

"If this is about that frat party some of my students were involved in, I've already told the police everything I know."

"Did they kill someone four nights ago in a bookstore?" Lang asks. "If so, yes, that's what this is about."

That's Lang's way. Shock and rock the bad cop routine while I observe and play the good cop when the time is strategically right.

Newman offers a convincing blanch. "What? I'm sorry." He sets his bag down. "Murder? I thought they just hung the kid up naked in the frat house."

"Just hung up naked, huh?" Lang comments.

"No. No." Newman is holding up his hands now. "I didn't intend to be dismissive, but the kid was alive. Murder is a whole other level of perversion."

Perversion.

This word bothers me for reasons I'll analyze later. "I understand you have an interest in poetry?" I interject.

He blanches all over again. "Forgive me if I'm

suffering whiplash right now, but these comments and questions are all over the place. *What* are we talking about?"

"We're working a case that might require a poetry expert," I say. "We pulled your name up as a possible option."

He narrows his eyes on me, blades of irritation spiking his stare. "I'm not falling for your bucket of tricks, Detective. What do you want? What do you *really* want?"

"You know what we want," I say and turn the question back on him. "What do we want?"

"Obviously to talk about a murder in a bookstore. So why don't we just do this?" He doesn't wait for a reply. He pulls his phone from his pocket. "Tell me the date and time of this murder. I'll give you my alibi. You confirm my alibi and then go do your jobs and find the real killer."

"August fourteenth," Lang supplies. "All day. All night. We need every detail."

He shoves his phone back in his pocket. "I don't even have to look at my calendar. August fourteenth was my son's birthday. I spent the day with my wife and family. All day. All night."

"She'll confirm this?" I ask.

"Of course, she'll confirm." His tone is arrogant and impatient. "What else?" He glances at his watch, a Rolex. I make a mental note to inquire about his paycheck. "I have a class to get to," he presses.

Lang snorts with disgust. "And we have a dead man who's going to his own funeral early. How old is your kid?"

Newman presses his lips together. "Twelve. What does that have to do with anything?"

"Where did you take him for his birthday party?" I ask.

"We stayed home. We're done here." He loads his

bag on his shoulder, turns, and walks away.

My takeaway: he didn't ask questions the way most people would ask questions. He didn't want to know who the victim was. He didn't want to know why we homed in on him. One might assume that he didn't have to. He already knew.

CHAPTER 27

Detective Jazz seeks the answers only I can give her, that only her master and teacher hold in my palm.

Why else would she be drawn to the campus, where learning is nothing if not monumental? She clearly understands the teacher/student dynamic in play but doesn't yet understand that these students, the ones who walk this campus, are not relevant to anyone or anything at all. *She* is the only student of any relevance at all, the student I once was, and to some degree will always be, to the great works.

She wasn't ready for the truth, though, she's *not* ready for the truth, and I'm growing impatient. In her haste to remove the veil of secrecy, she's ignoring important details—a mistake, and neither of us can afford her mistakes. I'll expect more of her in the immediate future. She must rise higher. She must study and learn the lessons that I'm teaching her, instead of scratching away at an itch she will never reach.

One thing is clear after today; she wants my attention. She needs my attention. She needs to know that I am not just watching, but watching closely, and that learning will be rewarded, while mistakes will be punished. It's time to ensure this lesson is learned. Tonight, she'll know that I'm right here. She'll know that I'm watching her, that I'm listening to her needs. She'll know that I'm guiding her work.

She'll know that failures have consequences.

CHAPTER 28

Lang and I leave our head-on collision with Newman with two agreed-upon points: we aren't done with him, and the man's an arrogant asshole. By the time we're in the scorching hot car, I've snagged the name and employment information on Newman's wife.

"Newman and Becky Smith have been married for ten years. They have a twelve-year-old and a seven-year-old. Becky is forty-one and an elementary school teacher."

"I bet he treats her like dirt under his shoe, too," Lang grumbles, starting the engine, and I burn my hand on the seat. God, you have to love Texas in August.

"Start driving toward Westlake. I want to catch her at work, away from Newman and her kids, if we can." I punch in the number for Becky's school, hoping to catch her before she leaves for the day.

Lang revs up the Mustang. "I'll drive to Westlake by way of a fast-food joint." He shifts to reverse.

My stomach growls its approval, but my call is a bust. "School doesn't start back until next week. She's off today." I dictate her home address from Chuck's text message. Lang detours to a drive-thru hamburger joint, and by the time we're handed our food, the AC is cranking out cold air, Chuck has sent me a full file on Newman, and we're on the highway.

In between stuffing my face with hot, salty fries, my splurge of the day, I scan a file and share important pieces with Lang. "His dad was a professor at UT Brownsville and get this—he taught literature."

"Was?" Lang asks while we idle in standstill traffic. "He's dead?"

"Yep." I sip my soda and scrunch up my face with the bitter taste. "I hate Diet Coke. Everyone in this city has nothing but Diet Coke. Can a girl just get a Diet Sprite please?"

"The real deal spares you that problem," he says, holding up his Coke.

"I hate real Coke, too."

"You're crazy."

"So are you. We're homicide detectives. It's a part of the job."

"Spoken like my booty call last night."

"All righty then," I say, and move back to the topic at hand: Newman's father. "He died of a heart attack when Newman was in junior high. His mother's dead as well. Fell and hit her head in her own home when Newman was twelve."

"So, did Newman or his father bash her head in? That's what I want to fucking know."

"There is the question," I say. "I'm betting on the father, who groomed his murderous son. Newman ended up in the foster system." I shoot some questions off to Chuck by way of text while multitasking and downing the remaining bite of my grilled chicken sandwich. Sipping my nasty Diet Coke again, I read onward until I'm poking at my screen and glancing over at Lang. "He was in the foster system, and one of the kids with him complained that he abused her dog and then molested her. She ran away and was never seen again."

"Ran away or she's dead?" Lang queries.

I point a finger at him. "Good question." I shoot off another text to Chuck.

"How did he end up a professor at UT himself?" Lang asks, working through this new bit of information. And why wouldn't he? It's not like the car is moving.

"A scholarship to UT, which I'm sure was aided

by his father's history there at the school. Not that he needed that aid. The man has a rocket-fueled brain. His IQ test and SATs were off the charts."

"Really? How do they compare to yours?"

My brows dip. "That matters why?"

"Brains against brains," he declares. "Like-minded gladiators fighting it out. It's an interesting matchup."

That like-minded comment hits a nerve that he should understand. It brings us full circle back to that "crazy" conversation. When you do this job long enough, you start questioning yourself, wondering how and why you're capable of seeing what you see and still remain human.

Lang gives me a wink. "Don't worry. You have the edge. You have me." He flexes his biceps. "This does count for more than a guy like that likes to admit."

I ignore his comment and glance at Newman's scores, which are right in line with mine. That doesn't say a lot to me. I've seen people with brains who should explode from their level of brilliance who simply couldn't apply common sense to life. Brains matter, but far more important is how that person accesses and applies that knowledge.

The Poet has already shown us he's the real deal, the full package: brains and execution. He's more than a worthy adversary, which is why he's a man willing to hide in plain sight. He will not be easy to take down, and he knows it.

CHAPTER 29

Lang pulls his Mustang into the driveway of Newman's sprawling mansion of a house in the elite Westlake area of Austin. Both of us lean forward, giving the two-story beauty painted a bluish-gray a better look. Lang gives a whistle. "That's a good two mil he's living in. He must rake in the bucks at UT."

"I'm sure he does," I agree, "but per his file, he inherited a five-million-dollar trust fund from his father."

"Bastard can't just be rich and happy," Lang mumbles. "If I had five million dollars, I'd be chasing women and buying a boat. What I wouldn't do is retire, because of pieces of shit like him. I mean, fuck me. This guy has it all, but he's still killing people."

"And he's not done yet," I say.

He turns sharply in my direction. "We both know that money and power is like a well-done steak. Hard to chew for the DA's office. They aren't going to allow us to arrest him without a clusterfuck of a whole lot of evidence."

"I'll get with the DA's office this afternoon and pin down what they're going to push for to make an arrest."

"Yeah. Do that, but they'll just change their minds when he gets a devil attorney who sets fire to the courthouse to keep him out of jail."

"Then I guess we'd better slam dunk this case." I reach for my door.

He grumbles something incoherent and does the same.

We exit the Mustang and trek down a sidewalk lined in decorative stones and yellow flowers. There's even a cute wooden chair in the center of the yard. On the outside, everything about this house screams of domestic bliss and perfection, but no family is perfect. Especially one with a serial killer using them as shelter.

We step onto the covered porch, where we are surrounded by ceramic pots filled with more yellow flowers. Lang jabs at the entry bell, and we don't have to wait long. The door opens and we're greeted by a woman dressed in jeans, a T-shirt, and the same white Chuck Taylor sneakers I favor on my days off.

"Can I help you?" she asks, her tone uncertain.

Her hair is brown, her eyes green, her skin pale. She can't weigh more than one-twenty.

She looks like me.

I'm not sure what to make of that observation popping into my head. I mean, technically, by way of coloring and height, you could say that about a lot of people. But a lot of people are not married to a man I believe to be a serial killer, and who joined me for my morning jog.

Lang flashes his badge. "Detective Langford, ma'am." He motions to me. "And this is Detective Jazz. Can we ask you a few questions?"

"Oh God." Her eyes go wide, panic in their depths, but she rockets into action. She steps onto the porch and pulls the door firmly shut behind her. "My kids are inside." Her voice is low, a hushed, urgent whisper. "Has something happened with my husband?"

I don't miss the word choice. She didn't ask if something happened "to" her husband but rather "*with*" her husband. "What do you think might have happened with your husband, Mrs. Smith?"

"Is he okay?" Her lips are parted, breath a pant. "Is he—okay?"

"He's fine," I say, surprised that Newman didn't

warn her that we were coming. Quite surprised, actually. "We saw him an hour ago at the campus."

She looks between us. "What is this?"

"We're investigating a homicide," Lang states. "We're in the process of eliminating suspects."

"Oh, I—" Her lips part on absent words before she tries again. "Is my husband a suspect?"

She knows.

That's what that question tells me.

On some level, she knows her husband is a killer. Lang catches that too, obviously, because he plays off of it. "What makes you think this is about your husband?"

"Am *I* a suspect?" Her voice lifts. "Why would I be a suspect?" Her hand balls in the center of her chest. "My God. Who died?"

"Michael Summer," I say. "Do you know him?"

She fast blinks. "No." Her brow dips. "That name isn't familiar at all. Am I a suspect? I don't know him."

"Fair enough," Lang replies, without confirming nor denying her status as a suspect. "Can you tell me where you were on the fourteenth?"

"That was our son's birthday," she says quickly. "We spent the day as a family. We were all together."

"Together doing what?" I ask.

"We were here." She motions to the house behind her. "We had a little family party, just us and the kids."

"From what time to what time?" Lang queries.

"All day and night," she says. "We barbecued in the afternoon by our pool, and then ordered pizzas that evening, which we ate while watching *Jumanji*."

"What time did you go to bed?" I ask.

"It was a Saturday, so the kids were up late, playing Monopoly. They love Monopoly. Newman and I both had papers to grade."

"All right then," Lang says. "What time did you go to bed?"

"I fell asleep at about ten o'clock. I think Newman was up a little longer. His papers are far more in-depth than mine."

"Would you have known if he left?" Lang asks.

She bristles. "Of course. He didn't leave."

And yet, so often that's exactly what happens in the family cover situations. The family sleeps. The killer simply slips away. "Do you have security cameras that can confirm no one left the house after ten that night?" Lang asks.

Her lips press together. "We don't have security cameras."

Lang arches a brow. "Nice house. You might want to protect it and your kids. We'll check with the neighbors. I'm sure they'll have cameras."

She folds her arms in front of her. "We probably should get cameras."

"One last thing," I say. "We'd like to glance at your husband's poetry collection."

"You want—you want to glance at—no." She holds her hands up. "No, I'm not inviting you inside to freak out my children. No." Her jaw sets hard. "If you need anything else, we'll find a lawyer."

"We'll leave," Lang says, reaching into his pocket and pulling out a card he then offers her. "Call if you think of anything we might need to know, anything at all."

She swipes the card from his hand. "I will."

I give an incline of my chin. "Have a nice evening, Mrs. Smith."

Lang and I head back to the car, and once we're settled inside the Mustang, with the engine running, Lang blurts out the last thing I expect. "She looks like you."

I ignore that comment and focus on our information gathering. "She admitted he has a poetry collection. And she believed we were here about her husband. She knows he's a monster. We can break her."

"Agreed," he says. "Now back to my prior point. She looks like you."

"So do millions of other women with brown hair and green eyes."

"Even her facial structure resembles yours. He was following you, Jazz. I don't like where this is headed."

CHAPTER 30

Lang pulls out of the driveway, and the lecturing has already started. "We're going to have a serious talk about your safety. We have a killer who's taken too much interest in you. When these monsters get personal, cops die."

Like my father, I think. He's talking about my father. And he keeps talking. And talking some more. I can feel heat rushing up my neck. I tune him out, turn him into white noise. He's pushing buttons that I don't want pushed.

Focus, I think. Follow the system and catch the killer.

I grab my phone and call patrol, arranging a hunt for the neighbors' security feeds, and when I'm done, Lang has stopped talking, thank you, Lord.

Still focused, still following the system, I glance at one of my lists I made last night and pinpoint what comes next. I pull out the case file and look for the District Attorney assignment for this case.

"The ADA is Evan Adams, whom you hate for reasons you won't share," I say as if Lang hasn't been lecturing and I haven't been ignoring him. "The good news is that he and I get along. We successfully charged and got a conviction together, recently."

"The bad news, outside of that bastard being involved?"

"Well, since you hate him and I suspect that's over a woman, you may know this, but he's good-looking and talented, which for him translates to arrogant and ambitious."

"I know all of that and then some. He won't charge if it's risky, but if bodies start dropping, he might well pressure us to charge too early."

"Exactly," I say. "He's a double-edged sword; one could almost call him an organized killer, much like The Poet. I'll call him. I'll go see him and try to get ahead of this problem."

"Back to you looking like Newman's wife."

I sigh and flip a page in the file.

"Sam," Lang presses.

We're on the highway now, idling in unmoving traffic again. There's no escaping this conversation. "I heard you, Lang."

"Did you? Because I don't think you did."

All my cool, calm focus slides right out of view. I whirl on him. "Ethan," I snap. "I hear you. I, of *all people*, am pretty damn clear on how dangerous this job is. I have never taken my safety or anyone's safety for granted, nor do I plan to start now."

"You need extra protection."

"What? Should I ask you to sleep over every night? Maybe get naked? Will that keep me safe? Don't divert attention from you to me."

"What are you doing right now, Sam?"

"What part of 'my father was shot dead in front of me' do you not understand? Blood splattered all over me. His blood, Ethan. Do you think I can ever wash that away? Do you think I will ever work a day on this job and forget that?"

A horn honks.

I turn away from Lang, and traffic is now moving. He sets us in motion, and silence is a sharp blade between us, ready to cut one or both of us. Lang turns up the radio, pumping out a country song, his way of telling me that he'll back off, at least for now. My foot is tapping on the floorboard, fingers playing a tune on my knee, neither of which has anything to do with the music. It's about the ten million nerves he's hit. It's a solid five minutes before the tension in the car eases to the point of being tolerable. My foot stops moving, my fingers still with it.

My cell phone buzzes with a text message. I welcome the entry back into a case that occupies my mind. It's Officer Jackson, letting me know that all voluntary DNA has been collected. He's achieved that goal in record time, but this doesn't surprise me. Jackson continues to impress. I forward the message to Lang. I just don't want to open a conversation with him again right now.

A few minutes later, he pulls us into the station parking area and into his assigned spot before killing the radio, but not the engine and air. "Jazz," he prods.

"I get it," I say. "You care. We're friends." I look over at him. "Maybe even best friends."

"I guess that's why having sex won't work, right?"

I laugh. "Do you ever stop?"

"Made you laugh, and you're the one who suggested I sleep over and we get naked."

"You know I wasn't suggesting that. We are never having sex, and I don't even think you want to have sex with me."

"What I want," he says, somber now when he is rarely somber, "is for you to stay alive and keep giving me hell. I thought you were dead that night, too. I knew you were with your father that night. When that call came in, I died inside. You know that, right?"

I recognize in that moment that I've been so burned by my own personal hell and desperate to escape that burn that I've blocked out everyone else's. Including my mother's. "I know you were affected, too. I do. But my father dying didn't make me a lesser detective. I need you to trust me again."

"I trust you more than anyone on the force. This case is not like other cases, and you know it. One of our own is missing."

"If The Poet is really following me, then me jumping off this case won't stop him from coming at me. And before you suggest I leave town or hide, I won't. If I don't have his attention, someone else will. My job is to protect that someone else. That's my oath."

"I know that."

"Then what do you want from me?"

"To stay alive."

"I plan to."

"Not everything goes as planned. Let's just go inside and find what we need to arrest this asshole." He opens his door and gets out.

CHAPTER 31

Lang and I enter the precinct prepared to divide and conquer, but before we even reach our desks, Chuck steps into our path. "We're still waiting on the apartment building footage," he says. "But—" He motions for us to follow. "I've got something to show you both."

We don't resist. Like good little detectives, we follow the information god toward a conference room. On the way there, he motions to three people sitting at a table outside of his cubicle—two men and a woman—pounding away on laptops.

"Our new interns," Chuck informs us, and when all three of the interns look up, he motions them back to their computers. "Keep working. We're trying to save lives. Time is critical." Chuck is already walking again, expecting us to follow, in charge and taking names.

"What is it with you short people?" Lang murmurs. "Are you all bossy and shouty?"

I laugh at the "shouty" word because he'd learned it from a little old lady just three days earlier when she'd told him to back off or she'd get shouty with him. It had not been in his official capacity. He'd stopped at a doughnut shop. They'd clashed over who got the last glazed doughnut. I'd sipped my coffee and watched him hand over the last glazed doughnut, losing that war. "What is it with you giants?" I counter. "Are you all incapable of listening unless we get shouty?"

He scowls. "No. Do not get shouty. It hurts my head."

I'm laughing as we step into one of several

conference rooms on this floor to discover a quite elaborate crime board is in fact already set up. Lang and I step to one side of a long conference table, facing the board. Chuck claims a spot on the other side of the table and beside the board, which is a mix of corkboard, whiteboard, and pictures and maps pinned directly on the wall.

Chuck waves a hand over a row of photos. "These are the people who were at the reading that we know of, including three staff members. I have their names, ages, and the models of the cars they drive. We're searching camera footage, looking for suspicious vehicles. I've also started information notebooks for us all, which include all evidence logged in to date, maps of the area near the crime scene, and much more."

"I'm impressed," I say. "You recruited help and it looks like you have a heck of a lot of detail already on that board." I give him the side-eye. "Why aren't you a detective?"

"I'm scared of guns, blood, and spiders. And you need me doing what I do."

"You look at photos of guns, and blood, and spiders in decayed earth all day long," I remind him.

"And even the photos give me nightmares."

I don't laugh, nor do I ask why he does this job. Neither does Lang, and with good reason. There aren't many of us in this line of work who don't have nightmares, but we still fight this fight. It's who we are. It's all we know. I settle my bag on the table and prepare to dig in. "Here's what I need right now. Reviewing the footage near my apartment is number one. And we should have a photo of Newman on the board. He's our focus right now. You did well finding him, Chuck. We need to get something, anything, substantial enough to support an arrest before he kills again."

Chuck's chin lowers, eyes keenly on my face. "He must have bombed the interview for you to be this convinced it's him."

"What we think doesn't matter. What we can prove does." I walk to the whiteboard at the end of the table and write "The Poet." I glance at Chuck. "That's his name until we have his real one." I don't wait for his reply. I start writing down the profile I've already done in my head:

An organized killer, a planner.

Highly intelligent.

Well employed.

In a circle of family to shelter himself, even convince himself he's normal.

Caucasian.

Age: Forties.

Important note: interest in poetry.

Possible knowledge of law enforcement procedures.

When I'm done, I turn to Chuck and Lang. "Newman Smith checks all of these boxes."

"Newman fits your profile," Lang says, "and he sets off my creep radar. We have our prime suspect. And the only good news you just gave me is telling me that we have a planner at work. A planner takes his time and 'plans' before he kills. In theory, we have a little breathing room. We should have time to catch him before he kills again."

My arms fold in front of me while objection screams through my body. "In theory," I agree, "we should have at least a little time, but we don't. Contrary to my profile, I don't believe he's going to wait to kill again."

CHAPTER 32

Lang stands up, hands settling on his hips. "This is one of your gut feelings, right?"

"Until he kills again and proves me right, yes. Yes, it is."

"Why is he different?"

"I don't know why." My voice rasps with frustration. "Because he can. Because he planned in advance. Because he wants us to know that he can do it right now, while we're all over him." My voice is louder now, and Chuck shuts the door, the very act of him doing so bringing me down a notch. "Because he knows exactly what to do. It's a science to him now. He's practiced. He's ready for anything." I repeat the portion of the poem he left behind. "'Who laugh in the teeth of disaster, Yet hope through the darkness to find, A road past the stars to a Master.' He's laughing at us. He sees himself as a master and we are not up to his level of greatness."

Lang smirks. "His arrogance is what will do him in. That's how this always plays out with these sick fucks."

Chuck is back on the other side of the table. "What can I do that I'm not already doing?"

"Let's circle back," Lang says. "Focus on him being a planner. No matter how fast he turns his victims, he's still that person, and a planner isn't going to kill someone at a place he's never visited before. At some point, he was at Summer's bookstore before the night he killed him."

"Maybe," I say. "Or maybe he's done this so many times that his system is perfect. Maybe part of that perfect system is that he never risks being seen twice."

"He was at the bookstore with you."

"Maybe I was worth the risk."

He grimaces. "I don't like how that sounds."

"Interjecting here," Chuck says. "Roberts's team checked for nearby cameras, Ubers, and parking lots related to Summer's murder. They found nothing to help us."

"Which reminds me," I say. "The cameras were off at Summer's place. He knew where the cameras were at my apartment."

"Your apartment management gave us a few names of service people for the building," Chuck says. "We're working on those. We'll cross-reference to anyone who shows up on Summer's history."

I move on, thinking out loud. "We didn't get a DNA sample from Newman today. We didn't get the chance. What about asking his wife for one?"

"Shake her up and force him to hand his over," Lang says, pointing at me. "I like it, but I do have to point out the obvious. We have no DNA to compare it to."

"If we can't place him at this scene, we need to find another scene, one where he wasn't yet as skilled as he is now. One where he might have left DNA."

Chuck waves a frustrated hand on that one and settles into a chair at the table. "I've gotten no hits on a homicide that involved cyanide or poetry. Zero. None. At least, not here in Texas."

"Expected, really," I say, sitting down across from him. "Which is why we have the Feds pulling a ViCAP report that will help us do a broader search. In the meantime, while we wait for that report, let's look for who he was before he was The Poet."

Lang sits down next to me, and I explain the hypothesis I'm forming in my head. "I believe our perp practiced at being this good at killing without leaving any evidence behind. And only now, now that he's at master status, does he leave his signature: a poem. Was this the first poem? I find that doubtful."

"With record keeping total shit half the time," Lang comments, "it's possible there were others."

"Or perhaps a different kind of signature each time?" Chuck offers.

"Maybe," I say. "Anything is possible. I'm hyper-focused on the poetry right now, because a reading like Summer held is specific taste, and the poem left was not something an unknowledgeable person would pull out of a hat. It spoke of real knowledge of the art of poetry. We have to work the current crime scene, but we need to think broader, to early crime scenes where he might have left DNA or another poem, or, as Chuck said, type of signature."

"But based on what you're thinking," Lang says, "the crimes before we had a signature would be the crimes with his lesser skill."

"Before he was the master and The Poet," Chuck concludes.

"Exactly," I agree. "We need to search for twists on our current crime scene. A different kind of poison or suspicious suicide, but the victims could still be near academics: students, teachers, literary experts. That's his realm. We'll find The Poet there, but the early version might not look quite like he looks now. We also need you to find out where he's been. What trips did he take in the past, say, five years?"

Lang rejects the five-year mark. "Let's go for ten years. These creeps start young." He glances between me and Chuck. "I'll get in touch with the detective who handled the missing girl from his foster home."

Chuck's cell phone buzzes. "One of our interns just arrived with a chunk of the security footage I'm waiting for."

"That's mine," I say. "I'll go through it."

"What else?" Chuck asks. "Because I have five interns right now, three newbies who I didn't expect to have. Let's use them."

"You got interns growing out of your ass like weeds, man," Lang says. "What's up with that and how soon are they going to vanish?"

"It's a special program over at the UT criminal justice department. First time they've ever loaded us down like this, and without notice."

An uneasy feeling slides through me, and I picture all those students stacked inside Newman's classroom. "Without notice? When did you get these interns?"

Chuck gathers a few papers and sticks them in a folder. "One of them is my long-term helper, Kent. And then Louise, your intern, but I had three extras show up just this afternoon. Great timing, so I didn't ask questions. I put them to work right before you got here."

Lang curses and his gaze rockets to mine. "Are you thinking what I'm thinking?"

"That he certainly works fast?" I ask. "Yes. I am."

"Lowlife bastard," Lang mumbles. "He's using them and their assignments to keep tabs on us."

"More like rattle us," I correct. "Or intimidate us."

Chuck's hands flatten on the desk. "Wait. What? He who?"

"Newman," I say. "They came from his department, and not long after we finished questioning him."

He blanches. "They work—they work for The Poet?"

"Seems a good assumption you've made there, Chuck," Lang confirms.

Chuck's jaw drops. "Oh God. They were pre-screened. That's why they were allowed in. I never—this can't—I didn't think—"

"You were right," Lang says, cutting him off and eyeing me. "He thinks he's already beat us."

"He doesn't just think he's already beat us. He's taunting us. Those interns don't know they're here at the direction of a killer. He was simply using them to send us a message. We can't get to him, but he can get to us, whenever, and however he wants to get to us, and do so in the blink of an eye."

"Which is why he stood outside your door last night."

"Yes," I agree, cotton in my throat, thickening my words. "That's exactly why he stood at my door last night."

CHAPTER 33

Chuck shoots to his feet. "I should get rid of the interns right now."

Lang points at him. "Sit. Wait."

Chuck's eyes widen and he settles into his seat.

"Good," Lang comments. "Now. We need to talk through our next moves."

Chuck's response is to spew words, lots of words. "They told me they were told to ask for Detective Sam Jazz. They were sent here by The Poet. They're his minions. They could be killers, too. They could—"

I intervene before he chokes on his own panic. "They are not killers, Chuck. We don't even have actual confirmation that Newman sent them. Can you get that confirmation?"

"Not this late in the day."

"Why don't you just ask them, Chuck?"

"Right. Ask them. That's okay?"

"Yes," I say. "Ask them."

He picks up the phone and punches a button. "Yes, hi, Lori," he says, when whoever is on the other line answers. "Who sent you over to work for Detective Jazz? Okay. Thank you." He hangs up. "Newman Smith. Now, do I send them home?"

"Not yet," I say. "Just pause a moment."

Chuck's cheeks redden. "They work for a killer."

"Newman's using them because that's what psychopaths do," I explain calmly. "They manipulate and use people."

Lang doesn't go down that rabbit hole with him, either. "I'm with Jazz on this. Those interns are game pieces being moved around by a man who sees himself as a master of some sort. Right now, we need to think about how to handle those interns and what message that sends to The Poet. Just wait." His attention turns to me. "If we send them away, we send one message. If we don't, we send another. This comes down to how he perceives either message and how he responds. He's a killer. Killers kill. So, I ask you, Jazz, based on your profile. Which move makes him kill again?"

Chuck gasps. "Sending them away could make him kill again?"

"Wait, Chuck," Lang snaps. "Just wait."

I'm not focused on Chuck. I'm focused on what Lang just presented, and he's right. This comes down to a quid pro quo—this for that. Newman wants a certain response, and that response determines what we're given in return. The weight of that question presses down on me. It's a burden Lang has now made mine to own.

I stand up and walk to the board where I've written my profile. I read the words I've written: planner, organized, highly intelligent. I will the answer to come to me, and when I turn to face them again, it's with a sense of helplessness. "I don't know how he's going to react to anything we do with the interns. What I do know is that any one of them could inadvertently update him on the case. Send them home. We'll talk to the captain about getting you additional help, Chuck. I'll talk to my contacts at the FBI and the DA and see what resources they can lend us as well."

The door bursts open and the captain charges into the room, bristling with agitation, his muscles bunched up, a bear about to claw us until we scream. Or die. He looks like he wants to kill us all. Lang and Chuck shoot to their feet, and now we're all just standing and staring at the captain, tension knotting between us. We're all waiting to take our bullets.

"I assume we're all here talking about Newman Smith?" he demands.

My brows furrow. "You know about Newman Smith?"

"Hell yes, I know about Newman Smith. He's lawyered up, ladies and gentlemen. How about warning me before you go after one of the mayor's biggest donors?"

Now *I* bristle, and not just a little. "With all due respect, Captain, I don't remember being handed a list of the mayor's donors and told to let them kill as they please. And I assure you that Newman Smith's invisible résumé, the profile I had to create in my head, didn't say 'professor,' 'donor,' and 'killer.' It just said 'professor' and 'killer' to me."

"Considering that attitude, Detective Jazz," the captain pretty much growls at me, "I now know why he referred to you by name. He doesn't like you."

"Is a killer supposed to like the detective trying to stop him from killing again?" I snap back.

His stare, now wholly reserved for me and me alone, turns a dark, hellish shade of anger. "Don't push me, Jazz." His voice is low, lethal. "You won't like the outcome. Do you have evidence against him?"

"Not yet, but—"

"Then stay the hell away from him!" He bellows that order.

Chuck clears his throat and raises a hand, a schoolkid afraid of the teacher, but clearly more afraid of a killer. "Captain."

The look the captain casts in his direction is impatience bordering on scathing. "What can I do for you, Chuck?"

"Newman sent over interns from his class and told them to ask for Detective Jazz." Chuck announced this as if it saves me and us, as if it changes anything the mayor wants from us or Newman.

The captain proves that as untrue as I mentally had predicted. "His attorney made me aware of that action. His way of reminding us of his many levels of support for our department. Treat him accordingly."

"An arrogant killer with the mayor wrapped around his finger," I state. "How absolutely lovely." I give him a sour smile.

"Enough, Detective Jazz," the captain snaps, and with that, he turns and walks out of the room.

Lang takes a step forward. "I'll talk to him."

"No," I say, pointing at him and passing him by on my way to the door. "I'm going to." I charge after the captain, well aware of how early I am off of mandatory leave and how quickly I could be sent home. But I don't care. I didn't take this job to be pushed around by the captain, let alone by a serial killer hiding behind an innocent family and his money.

CHAPTER 34

The hour is late, the administrative staff all but cleared from the building, which leaves the captain's path toward his office clear. Mine as well as I pursue him, my steps thundering on the floor right along with my temper. I'm right behind him when he enters his office, stepping into the small space before he can shut the door. Actually, he doesn't try. He knows I'm here.

He rounds his desk and I'm already there in front of it and him, in full confrontation mode. "I thought you weren't like my father, Captain."

He looks down his nose at me with the same arrogance I'd expect from Newman. My father didn't lead with arrogance, but I remind myself that he also didn't manage with honesty. I'm starting to wonder if Moore is just a different breed of bad. "What does that mean, Detective?" he demands.

"Since when do we let killers go free just because they make political donations?"

"You made a scene at the school."

I laugh and not with humor. "Really? Because I've made so many scenes in my career?"

"You just came off the loss of your father."

"That's how this is? You simply decide behavior that doesn't fit my own personal profile to be true, because my father died and I might be what? A new person now?"

He flinches, just barely—it's there and I see it—but it doesn't stop him from punching back. "You're making a scene right now."

"I'm defending myself when I shouldn't have to defend myself. I've earned more respect than this. I *did not* make even a small scene while interviewing Newman. If he told you that, he's lying. There's more going on here than you've taken the time to understand. I want to know why."

"I was there, too," Lang says, joining us and shutting the door. "He didn't mention me, did he?"

"No, Langford, he did not," the captain confirms. "Apparently, for once you kept your mouth shut."

Lang snorts out laughter. "In case you don't know me and her, I'm not the calm one. She is. That asshole is playing a game with Jazz. Her neighbor saw him lurking around last night. He showed up at her apartment and just stood outside her door for God knows how long."

The captain's gaze jerks to mine. "Is that true?"

"The security feed shows a man in a hoodie and a baseball hat," I say. "We believe it was him."

His expression tightens. "So you don't know it was him. We can't name him without proof. That's basic police work."

He's right. We have nothing on Newman aside from his personal interests and arrogance, neither of which is illegal. If not for Roberts's MIA status, I'd be ready to walk out the door and get to work proving he's The Poet, but Roberts *is* missing. This conversation can't end without tackling that topic.

"Look, Captain," Lang grinds out. "Jazz took this case—*we* took this case—when Roberts left town with too much abruptness to make sense."

Good. He's on track now, right where we need to direct this conversation. Then he opens his mouth again and goes sideways. "Then we had one confrontational interview and that was with Newman," he continues. "That same night, some guy hangs out by Jazz's door, and we think he followed her during her run this morning."

We're officially back to no proof and my gut

feeling, which will go over about as well as no proof and gut feelings ever do, which is never.

The captain's gaze swings back to me. "Talk."

I dodge the part where I never actually saw anyone following me. "We've collected the security footage available that tracks my running path. I'm about to go through it all now."

Lang swings us back to Roberts. "Bottom line, Captain, Jazz took over the case from Roberts. Now Roberts is missing and Jazz has this freaky shit going on."

The captain grimaces. "He's not missing. He's not due to be in Houston for two weeks."

"His phone isn't pinging," I say. "He left suddenly. It feels off, Captain. What did he say when he resigned?"

His expression tightens. "He called it in. He already had the job in Houston lined up." He looks between us, the hard lines of his face pierced by a hint of worry he isn't quite ready to admit. "Have you gone by his house?"

"Yes," I say. "And the good news is that he packed up and left. That supports the idea of him leaving of his own free will. I want to believe that's what happened."

Lang moves in closer, stepping to the end of the desk between us, the anger in the air between us all shifting to a calmer, conversational energy. "You need to hear what Jazz has to say about this Summer murder."

The captain gives me a stern, judgmental look that screams of distrust, but I don't hold back. I tell him everything. My theories about a killer I now call "The Poet" to include my profile, which fits Newman like that perfect winter glove that always manages to hide and never be found. Lang jumps in here and there and drives home the odd behavior of the wife. I finish my report with, "I called the FBI and asked for a profile to back mine up, and a ViCAP report."

"You're not all talk then," he observes. "You're taking this seriously."

That "all talk" comment reads like an insult, but I remind myself that I'm hypersensitive with this man who replaced my father. "As should the mayor," I say. "Better we catch this killer now before there's a trail of bodies in our city and the press accuses us of looking away because he's a political donor."

His jaw clenches so much I believe it might shatter, but then he surprises me by saying, "Agreed. I'll make that point. I'll put an alert out on Roberts." He lifts his chin at Lang. "What are you doing to find Roberts?"

"Finding him. Right now," Lang adds. "I'm going to go back to work and find the moving company or truck service he used."

"What about Newman?" I ask, wanting to hear the go-ahead to press him for answers.

The captain levels me in a hard stare. "I don't know if Newman's our guy, but I do *not* like the idea of Roberts being MIA and the 'freaky shit,' as Lang calls it, happening to you. Proceed cautiously and discreetly. And watch your damn back. I'm setting up patrols for your street and don't argue. You won't win." He eyes Lang. "Watch her back."

Lang gives him a nod and Captain Moore motions between us. "You're both off rotation until further notice. Shuffle your cases to Monroe and Gonzales."

I don't argue. In fact, I push for more. "We need resources. Manpower. I'd like to get Officer Jackson, one of the first responders at the Summer murder scene."

"I'll make it happen," he agrees and motions us to the door. "Go."

Lang and I don't stay around to find trouble. We head for the door when the captain calls out, "Detective Jazz." I half turn as he adds, "Find Newman on that film, and I'll personally call the DA and get you a warrant."

He's telling me that I was wrong about him. He's telling me that he can't be bought. To that I say, *we'll see.*

CHAPTER 35

Lang and I don't comment on that meeting with the captain. We settle for a shared look that says it all: *We won in there. Barely.* We leave it at that and head back to work, because work is the only way we'll get the job done.

Somehow, it's seven o'clock at night when we finally settle in at the conference table to dig in, him at the endcap and me with a wide side to myself. We're just discussing ordering food when Chuck joins us, claiming a seat across from me. "I sent the interns home, all of them, but those sent by Newman were told not to come back. Are we ordering dinner?"

"Go home, Chucky," Lang orders. "It's late. We got this."

His spine is stiff, chin hard with stubbornness. "I'm staying, and it's 'Chuck.'"

"Don't you have a family, man?" Lang asks.

"Had," Chuck says. "She and the kids left me. Like everyone else in the building. Did you know that statistically law enforcement officers have a divorce rate of fifty percent? In some high stress sectors, it's sixty to seventy percent."

"Don't let anyone tell you that you are not the King of Good Times," Lang says. "The pleasant shit you share is just motivational. And aren't you like twelve?"

"Lang," I scold.

He shrugs. "I'm the keeper of the real. You know it."

"Thirty-five," Chuck snips, looking at me. "And *I'm* the keeper of the real. I'm the facts guy. I'll stay. The job is all I have."

"We need you fresh," I say. "Go *home*. Rest. And the good news is that the captain is getting us help. The good kind that isn't wet behind the ears."

It takes some effort, but we finally persuade him to head on home.

Half an hour later, Lang and I are both working while inhaling sandwiches from one of our favorite takeout spots. Lang busies himself calling moving companies, the late hour throwing him roadblocks, while I read through the case file, looking for anything I missed. I'm presently putting off the security feed review, with good reason. I need to be focused, homing in on tiny details when I review it, and I'm not in a place that allows that hyper-focus right this minute. Food and Lang's loudmouth cursing at those roadblocks is not the way to achieve that goal.

I go through an inventory of everything collected at the crime scene, and the poetry books found in and under the seats are of particular interest. I can almost imagine The Poet picking one up and judging the material. I make a note. We need the forensics results on those books as a priority, and I'm not beyond pulling the missing cop card to get it done.

Roberts *is* missing, and with a twist of my gut, I know we won't find him alive. I frown with a thought and catch Lang between calls. "I just can't put two and two together on Roberts. He *did* resign."

"By phone." He scrubs his jaw and leans back in his chair. "Sounds fishy to me. Maybe he had a gun to his head."

"But he applied for a job in Houston. So he resigned and he applied for a job in Houston? Surely he talked to the Houston office himself at some point?"

"Seems like at some point he would, even if the captain made the initial call." He leans forward and grabs his phone. "I'll call Houston and do an information grab."

I sit there and wait, eager to find out what he learns. The answer is not much. He tries Roberts's new captain and the HR department. "Everyone's gone," he says. "We'll hear back tomorrow."

I nod, but this whole Roberts situation feels off. I don't doubt that he's dead or, if we're lucky, in hiding. There's no body. There's no poem. The Poet left that poem because he's proud of that murder; it feels justified to him. Roberts's situation just doesn't logically add up to The Poet.

CHAPTER 36

I sigh in resignation and refocus on my work, dialing the crime lab, only to land in voicemail yet again. Of course. It's late.

I decide I'll start my day tomorrow by swinging by there, at which time I'll shoot a little fire under a few backsides. I've just finished off the last of my sandwich when Lang curses and stands up. "This is getting me nowhere. I'm going to stop by Roberts's ex's house. They have a love/hate thing. She might know something helpful."

"Are you going to freak her out?"

"Yeah, maybe," he concedes. "But the truth is that at this point, if he's dead, there's no saving her that hell. Right now, there's still hope."

I heave a leaden sigh. "Right. Agreed." Though I know, we both know deep in our guts, that there is no hope. There is just justice, served by us, and if we have our way, served quickly. "Call me and let me know what happens."

"I'm coming back here to take you home. I'm sleeping on your couch." He winks. "Don't worry. I won't get naked."

"No. I don't need a babysitter, and please stop saying the word 'naked.'"

"You said it first in the car."

"Stop."

His mood shifts, sobers. "Roberts is proof we're all vulnerable to the bad guys."

"And I am prepared."

"You think he wasn't?" He doesn't give me time to reply. "There's no coming back from cyanide. If you're not here when I get back, I'm coming over.

Come on, Jazzy, I've slept on your couch before. All jokes aside, I'm a gentleman."

"I know you. I trust you, but I have a patrol backup."

"This guy's bold enough to send those interns and claim the deed. I'm coming over." He throws a bag over his shoulder. "End of story. If you go home, you text me. Otherwise, I'll see you back here to follow you home." He pauses at the door. "Anything on the security footage?"

"Just starting it now."

"Call me if you find the bastard," he orders, and with that, he exits the conference room.

I stare after him and decide this is exactly why we can never, ever date. We're friends and I don't ever want to lose that. Well, that and he's a damn slob. Turning my attention to my computer, I grab a chocolate bar from my bag and open it up. Armed with the good stuff, I pull up the data folder Chuck emailed me with the security footage.

The folder has fifteen total files. I force myself to start reviewing the recordings during the timeline that I jogged rather than jumping to the coffee shop. I want to experience every portion of my run and coffee visit in the order they occurred to ensure I spy anyone who recurs. And I know who was in the coffee shop. The question is, were any of them with me during my run?

I take my time, jotting notes about who I see where, but no one recurs, and no one looks familiar.

I'm just reaching the coffee shop portion of the recordings when my cell phone rings with Wade's number. Eyeing the clock, which reads eight thirty, I welcome the break. "Hey," I greet him. "Any news?"

"I'll have your report the day after tomorrow. The profile will take longer, but you know that."

"I do. Thanks for doing this."

Another call buzzes in. "That's Lang, I think. Give me just a minute." I click over to hear, "Jazz. It's Officer Jackson."

The captain worked fast. I open my mouth to tell him we're pulling him into the Summer case and I never get the chance. He jumps ahead of me and says, "We have another victim. Same story. Tied up. Paper sticking out of his mouth. I called it in to dispatch and told them to call you, but I thought you'd want to know directly."

My heart sinks. I was right. He didn't waste a second and we weren't fast enough to stop him. The Poet's killed again. "Yes," I say tightly. "Thank you. Text me the address. I'll be right there." Adrenaline surges through me and I hang up, reconnecting with Wade. "I've got another murder. Same guy. I have to go."

"Call me."

That's all he says, and that's because he gets this job and me. Questions are for later, and I do appreciate that part of Wade. "I will," I promise and disconnect right as dispatch is buzzing my phone. I accept the call, packing up my bag as I do. By the time I've confirmed I'm headed to the crime scene, both dispatch and Jackson have texted me the address.

I stare down at it and I go cold. It's three blocks from my apartment.

CHAPTER 37

I step into a hot, muggy August night, my feet lightning fast across the pavement, my skin instantly sticky. It's the kind of night that suffocates you in the death and violence of a crime scene. Right now, I'm suffocating in the idea that the location of this murder was to taunt me. I'm suffocating in the promise that The Poet murdered for me. I wonder if the Summer murder was for Roberts, the prelude to his murder, the promise he was next.

I'm edgy as I slide into my car, the feel of my weapon at my hip far more comforting than usual. Not that The Poet will come after me tonight. No. He'll want me to live out this night in hell while he basks in the glory of his most recent kill. That hell is what turns a short drive into eternity.

Once I'm within view of my destination, I discover the road is blocked off, lights flashing, people gathering. At this point, I'm literally three blocks from my apartment. I decide to just park at my building. I make a U-turn, and in a minute tops, I'm pulling into a spot street side to my building, rather than in the garage where I'd normally park. I'd like to say that's a convenience thing, but it's not. I'm smart enough to feel safer on the busy street than in a closed concrete box. "I'm a detective" is not supposed to be an excuse for being stupid.

Once I've killed my engine and climbed out of my car, I walk to my trunk and exchange my work bag for my field bag and toss on a pair of flats I keep for just such occasions. I lock up and start walking, the street humming with life, people bustling about here and there, the little Italian joint I love on the corner, overflowing with people who will not be disappointed as they wait for a table. It's always surreal to me, the way life goes on, without any realization of the life now gone.

I'm just passing a small apartment complex one block down from the crime scene, when the prickling sensation of being watched pulls my gaze left and right, with no source discovered. I'm just passing a small, yet-to-be-remodeled-and-developed complex when that sensation heightens and has me looking upwards toward a fire escape. The shadows shift and I swear someone fades into the darkness.

My hand settles on my weapon, but the street is busy and I resist my instinct to pull my weapon for fear of creating panic. Instead, I reach into my bag and remove my flashlight, scanning the fire escape to find no one present. I'm on edge, I tell myself. That's all this is. I'm so damn on edge. I'm letting him get to me, and that pisses me off. I need to be at the crime scene, not playing peek-a-boo with an empty fire escape.

I slide the flashlight back into my bag and charge forward, the curious crowd of about thirty or more gathering at the roadblock overflowing to the sidewalk not far ahead. Preparing for the crush, I palm my badge and lower one shoulder, bulleting forward and holding my credentials in the air. "APD coming through," I call out, repeating those words about half a dozen times before I'm at the first barricade, flashing my badge one last time at an officer, who motions me forward.

Free of the crowd, I walk toward one of the random stand-alone houses in this area, the place abuzz with law enforcement in various forms. I cross the lit-up and underwhelming front yard to the steps leading to the porch. Officer Jackson is there, easy to spot by way of his imposing stature and red hair, clearly waiting for me, while looking as stoic as usual.

"CSI and the coroner have yet to arrive," he announces. "We blocked off the scene and shot some preliminary photos. You've got the scene pretty fresh. The body's in the bedroom."

"Who found the body?"

"Anonymous tip. Same as with the Summer case, if I remember correctly."

"Interesting." I pull a pair of gloves from my bag as well as a pair of booties, offering them to him. "Join me."

He arches a brow. "You want me to join you?"

"You want to be a detective?"

"Hell yeah."

"Then put them on and follow me, but don't talk. That sounds cranky, but it's a thing for me. I need to process and so do you. And be at the precinct in the morning. You're joining our team on this case."

"I am?"

"You are. I had it approved today." I cover up and then arm myself with a crime scene camera I brought along as my extra set of eyes. "Do we know how the killer entered the house?"

"The back door was unlocked," he replies, "but we can only speculate. There's no sign of forced entry."

Nor was there forced entry at the prior murder, I think. "I wonder if the victims invited him inside," I consider out loud, but I don't expect an answer. I'm just processing and already turning away from him.

I open the front door to a rather loud squeak, which tells me this was not the entry point, not unless I'm correct and The Poet was invited inside. Or was he just here and waiting? That feels right. He's a planner. Planners want to be ahead of the game, set up, stage the scene and the murder to follow.

Jackson catches the door behind me and, even before I enter the house, the icy cold of an air conditioner turned to arctic conditions tortures my body. My mind goes to the Summer file and a reference I'd almost put out of mind. The apartment had been frigid. This could be The Poet's way of preserving the body for us to appreciate his work. Or perhaps his way to torture the victim before he kills them. Summer was found naked. I'm guessing this victim will be as well. I power through the cold, entering the house to a wall several feet in front of me. A framed picture of the human skeletal system is the centerpiece. Something stirs in me, something dark and uncomfortable that I cannot name.

I shoot a photo of that framed image and then glance to the hallway leading to the right, toward the bedroom. I'm not quite ready for the body. I don't know why. My mind pushes back against the idea when it should not. Instead, I glance left to the living room and open kitchen area. Basic discount-store furniture in shades of brown fills the space. This is a college student's rental. Summer was a well-established businessperson. On the surface, the two would have nothing in common and yet they did: *him*. They both captured his attention, to their end.

A bookshelf, the only piece of furniture in the place besides a couch and coffee table, catches my attention. I walk there now and study the one row of six books. Medical books, all medical books. That dark, uncomfortable feeling is back, a snake slithering through me with some realization I dread with almost nauseating certainty. I shove it aside, as well as the shiver sliding through my body, and focus on shooting photos of the bookshelf, ensuring

I capture every single title.

When I'm done, I make two obvious observations. I'm freezing my ass off, and Summer's personal bookshelves are filled with literary works, including some of the most well-known and respected poets. I'm back to the one thing these two victims have in common: him.

Rotating, I click photos of the room, resisting my urge to walk into the kitchen. I want a chance to view the bedroom and the body before CSI arrives, and I've already spent far too much time avoiding what I should be welcoming. I'm remotely aware of Jackson by my side, but I don't look at him. He's here to observe. I'm here to do the same, and he's not the subject of interest. I cross the room, and right as I'm about to head down the hallway, not one, but three members of the CSI team file in through the door, geared up in boots and cover-ups.

"Detective Jazz," I say. "This is my scene. Wait to enter the bedroom until Officer Jackson gives you the go-ahead." I glance at Jackson. "Hold the hall-way."

He nods and I head down the narrow, short hallway, and I'm now oblivious to the cold, a rush of adrenaline setting my heart racing. I halt at the one and only doorway. Grinding my teeth with a sense of dread—as if this scene is personal, which is crazy—I force myself to enter the bedroom. Pausing just past the doorway, I do a visual sweep of the simple room with a bed and nightstand, brown carpet throughout. And then there is, of course, the naked body of a man sitting in a chair in front of a bed.

I cross to get a better look at him, this man who is no longer a man at all. He's just a shell. His feet and waist are tied to the wooden chair. His head has dropped forward. The floor is clean. If he was poisoned, he didn't throw up.

Kneeling in front of him, I lean in to gain a better view of his face and suck in a breath with what I find. No, *who* I've found. It's Dave from the coffee shop, and suddenly the medical books make sense; the foreboding feeling makes sense. I knew this was Dave's house the minute I saw that framed image of the skeletal system on the wall.

I push to my feet and my mind replays my encounter with him yesterday, right after my poetry audio had blasted out of my cell phone speaker:

"Poetry?" he inquires, ringing up my order.

"Words for the soul," I say automatically, something I used to say when I ran my poetry club, which became my thing only because I neglected a class in college. My professor made running the club my punishment, and extra credit, but it didn't turn out to be a punishment at all. The puzzles in the poems intrigued me and created a bonding experience with my grandfather, who spent countless hours helping me prepare for my club meetings.

"Words for the soul?" Dave asks with a snort. "More like a bunch of nonsense words thrown together to mean nothing, but to each their own."

"It's an acquired taste," I agree, as he hands me back my card. "Much like analyzing someone's bowel habits for a living. Which we both know is in your future."

He was killed because of that encounter.

He was killed because of me.

There's a piece of paper in his mouth, and I grab a baggie from my field bag. I then pull the paper from Dave's mouth and as expected, I find a portion of a poem. Two verses that I know well. They're Shakespeare's "Sonnet 60":

My verse shall stand, Praising thy worth, despite his cruel hand.

I've analyzed this poem, as has many a scholar.

To most, it's about life and death, about the passing of time. To some, it's about immortality.

To me, it's about destiny again. It's The Poet's way of telling me this man had to die. It was necessary. It was for a greater cause: *his cause*.

CHAPTER 38

Dave is dead.

Because I walked into that coffee shop and spoke to him.

He made me a killer.

Those words rock me, slice me. I am bleeding inside. This is now personal. So very personal. Shock fades, and anger begins to burn inside me.

"Sam?"

At the voice of Hazel Lee, one of the most brilliant forensic medical examiners I've ever met, I jolt out of my head and back to duty and the investigation. Bagging the poem, I turn to find her in the doorway, geared up in a jumpsuit and gloves.

"Thank God you're not Trevor," I say, sticking the baggie in my field bag. "The last thing I need tonight is his level of difficult."

"He's on vacation. And yes. Thank God for us all."

Jackson pokes his head in. "She pushed past me." He glowers at her. "I told you to wait."

I'd laugh another time because Jackson has no idea who he's dealing with in Hazel, but then she's often underestimated, though I'm not sure why. Sure, she's youngish, in her thirties, and barely five feet, but she's also a savvy, educated, proud second-generation Chinese American who packs the kind of pushy charm that gets her everywhere.

"He's right," she says, glancing up at him. "Because I'm the ME, which means I get first dibs on all dead bodies. That means I get to walk past big, cranky police officers. Plus"—she wiggles a finger at me—"Sam likes me."

"She's right," I say. "She does and I do." I motion

her forward.

Hazel pats Jackson's arm. "It's okay. You're new. You'll get it."

He gives me a confused look, and I give him a simple thumbs-up. "Keep CSI out of here until she's done."

He nods and fades into the hallway. Hazel and I stand together in front of the body. "Holy crap," she murmurs, and when I expect some revelation about the body, that's not what I get. "Can we turn off the air?" She runs her gloved hands over her arms. "It's like the morgue in here." She grins. "Get it. Morgue?"

I don't even feel the cold anymore, though I'd welcome it over the guilt standing here in front of Dave is stabbing into my heart. "I'm not laughing at that joke. It's too bad. And no, we cannot turn up the temperature. Not yet. I need to read the scene exactly the way our killer intended me to read it. Did you take a look at the Summer body?"

"I assisted with the autopsy," she says. "And I read the file. The poem thing is freaky. Was there a poem left behind this time?"

"Yes. Already bagged."

"Interesting. Do you know what the poems mean?"

"Maybe." I don't offer more. The topic of poetry seems to get people killed.

Thankfully, she lets it go, focused on Dave again. "This one is fresh," she adds. "Rigor hasn't set in, but you know that. I'm sure it's one of the first things you noticed."

But I didn't. I didn't even think about the time of death. "I should have," I admit, "but I was a little distracted by the fact that I knew him."

"Oh crap," she murmurs, and I can feel her eyes on me. "You know him?"

"Just in passing. He worked at the coffee shop

across from my apartment, but I saw him earlier today. He's a med student. Or was. Was a med student."

"*Jesus.* Badass detective or not, that has to freak you out. I got called out for an ex-boyfriend once. That was a rough night. The last time I'd seen him, I'd called him a cunt." She holds up a hand. "Please don't judge. That's what God made my mother for. And I'd never used that word in my life until him, which only made the situation worse. Like I said, it was the last thing I said to him."

"What happened to him?"

"His new girlfriend killed him." She bends just enough to study Dave's face, shifting back to the scene, our small talk all just a part of coping with death. We all have our ways. Small talk, making the moment somehow normal, is often sanity. "He's discolored. He shows signs of oxygen deprivation." She pulls a sheet of plastic from a pocket and rolls it out on the floor before setting her medical case on top, squatting down in front of it. "Cyanide again is my bet," she says. "It deprives the body of oxygen."

I focus on what she's just revealed about the prior investigation. "About that. Trevor was supposed to send me his autopsy report on Summer, but I haven't seen it."

"He piled paperwork on me. You'll have it in the morning."

"How did he confirm the cyanide before the normal wait for a toxicology report?"

"There was a piece of the gel cap stuck in the victim's tooth with residue on it." She unzips her case and pushes to her feet. "My take was that the victim tried to hold the pill in his mouth and keep it from going down, but the gel dissolved. In fact, there shouldn't have been anything left of the casing, but those freak things happen. Two molars protected it. You'll get the report tomorrow. I'm taking over these cases. Unless you want Trevor?" She winks.

I snort. "I want Trevor like I want a hole in the head." It's not a good joke. Not tonight. Acid floods the back of my throat. "Do your thing," I croak, stepping back and watching her perform her tests, my mind thinking through the murder.

What do they have in common?

Poetry.

One loved it. One hated it.

He judges them by the poetry, and while I can assume why Dave's hate made him a target, what about Summer?

"Where's he getting the cyanide is my question," Hazel murmurs, bagging a swab of the victim's mouth. "Ex-military maybe? Could he have stockpiled it overseas? My father's ex-military. He's told me stories about how easily drugs, all drugs, were acquired in certain countries."

Ex-military. I consider that. It should feel right. He's clean. He's disciplined. He'd fit that profile, and yet it doesn't feel right. "I'll look into it," I promise.

Leaving her to work, I begin a walk-through of the room, but I already know that I won't find anything worth seeing. Neither will CSI. The Poet's outsmarting us, and that has to change. I step in front of the one window in the room, with a large frame that a large man could enter, but I rule that out as an entry point immediately. The Poet entered like he owned the place, and that would not be through a window.

I start to move away from the glass when a shadow passes on the other side. I stand stone still, staring out of that window, waiting for another movement.

Hazel's words come back to me. *This one's fresh.* I don't know if I saw something in the shadows or not, but he's still here. The Poet is still here.

CHAPTER 39

I turn away from the window, and without a word, I walk past Hazel, exiting the bedroom to find Officer Jackson missing. Ironically, after chasing down Hazel for ignoring instructions, he's ignored mine. I stalk down the hallway to the living room, where I count five CSI techs working in the house. Scooping the poem from inside my bag, I hand it to one of the techs. "Log this into evidence. Carefully." Once I have his agreement, I point at the room. "He's killed before," I call out to them all. "He thinks he's better than you. Make sure he's not."

Murmurs follow me as I exit to the porch, where another officer—not Jackson—is guarding the door. I don't ask about Jackson. I don't have time for his nonsense right now. I yank off my gloves and booties and bag them before handing them off to him. "Stick them in evidence." It's something I learned from my father, who once found trace evidence on a glove that solved a case.

He's barely taken them from me, and then I'm walking down the stairs, the shock of going from the cold house and into the hot night flushing my skin. Police lights rotate along the perimeter of the property, the sirens silent, but voices rumble in the distance. I cut right toward the side of the house, adrenaline surging through me, but I'm practiced at controlling how I respond to its sensation. Almost automatically at this stage of my career, I draw my weapon and flashlight, their weight in my hands easy and familiar, even comforting. Slowly, calculated like our Poet, I walk around the house, where CSI is hard at work.

"Detective Jazz," I call out to them. "I'm the detective in charge. Is anyone working the back of the house?"

"Not yet," one of the techs calls out. "We're working together, from one side to the other. Do you need a change in plan?"

"No. I just needed to know the plan." And who was behind the house, I think, since it doesn't appear to have been one of us. I mean it could be Jackson, but I don't think he'd go rogue and step out of his lane, plus CSI would have mentioned him passing by. I keep walking, bypassing a request for light that will risk driving The Poet away. At the edge of the house, I flatten on the wall, pausing there, and inching my way around to the rear, just enough to scan the darkness and search for movement. I find nothing, but I know what I saw in the window. I know what I felt when I saw it, too. He's here and he's waiting for me but he doesn't plan to kill me.

Taunt me, though?

That's another story.

With my flashlight on high, I boldly step around the house, shining the light into the darkness. The wind is absent, the night still but for the creep of death everywhere, an odd contrast to the sticky sweet honeysuckle of a nearby bush. Slowly, I move my flashlight over the yard, and when I land on the bushes that divide the house from an apartment complex, I suck in a slow breath, my heart thundering in my chest and swishing in my ears.

A man in a hoodie and a baseball cap stands there, waiting for me, his face shrouded in shadows.

CHAPTER 40

It's just me and him in the middle of the inky black night, with the man he killed a few feet away behind a window. I aim my weapon at him, my finger heavy on the trigger. I could shoot him right now and he'd never kill again. If, and when, he moves, I have two options: shoot or chase. I'd be obliged to chase. He's too smart not to know this. Perhaps he even knows the temptation that burns in my belly to end him so he will never kill again. He's gambled on my badge, on my honor. He clearly doesn't know how easily he's inspired a renewed love of being my father's daughter, able to justify anything for a good cause.

I step toward him, to get a closer view of his face, but his hoodie and hat combined shelter his features. He's tall. He's thin. I can't say if he's athletic. What he is for certain is fearless. I'm armed and he doesn't back away.

He's definitely taunting me, or maybe he really does want to kill me. "Police," I call out, though he knows who, and what, I am. We both know he knows. I'm simply proving I'm as predictable as he expects. At least one of us thinks he knows what I'll do next. I do not. "Put your hands up." I'm drawing nearer to him, one paced step at a time.

There's a flash across his face, a smile I think, and then he cuts into the bushes. *Damn it.* He's running and I already have his back. I can't shoot him. So I give him what he wants. I chase. I take off after him, but I can't just cut into those bushes without risking him grabbing me. I ease in and check my path, losing valuable seconds as I do. Once I'm through the jungle of leaves, I'm in the parking lot of the apartments, parked cars both my shelter and his.

I squat down, out of sight. There's a building in front of me and another to my right and left. The apartment buildings are smaller structures than most and close together. I stand there, weapon and flashlight still in my hand. I ease around the vehicles, eyeing my surroundings with no human in sight. I listen. I wait, and then there are footsteps. I round an old beat-up car to find my man running toward one of the buildings. I charge after him at full running speed, and well ahead of me, he cuts in between two of the complexes.

Flattening against one of them, I watch him dart toward the opposite building. I remain in the parking lot, but I'm running again, trying to catch up with him and cut him off, and I'm close, when a kid no more than ten darts into my path. I all but run him over before I manage to stop, and the moment he spies my gun, he screams bloody murder. "Mom! Mom!"

"Get in your house!" I order, setting him away from me and cutting around him, but that small delay probably just lost me The Poet.

I'm finally at the next building, and I plant myself on the wall again, when suddenly Jackson is standing in front of me. I jolt with his unexpected appearance, alarm bells ringing in my head. My weapon points at his chest. "How did you get here?"

He holds up his hands. "Whoa. Whoa. Easy. I saw you take off through the bushes. I thought you might need help."

"Where were you earlier?"

"Dave's mother showed up," he quickly explains. "She was freaking out. I'm good with freak-outs."

"I told you to stay in your position." My voice quakes with a mix of adrenaline and anger.

"I'm sorry." He eyes the gun. "Are you going to

shoot me for this?"

I don't like the way he disappeared and reappeared, and I don't know where that is leading me mentally right now, but it's no place good. "Not yet," I say. "Call for backup. Block off the apartment building. *Now*."

He does it, and he's just put away his radio when I hear, "Jazz!"

At Lang's voice, I call out, "Over here!" And it's only then that I lower my weapon from where it points at Officer Jackson.

CHAPTER 41

With my gun lowered, my gaze holds Jackson's. "Follow instructions. I could have mistaken you for the killer and killed you. Search for a man in a hoodie and baseball cap. Get an army searching." I rotate away from him, but only because Lang is in view. Something about Jackson at my back is no longer comfortable.

"What the hell is going on?" Lang demands, as I meet him in the middle of the parking lot.

"Aside from a murder? He was here. I stood all but face-to-face with him and then he ran. I *wanted* to shoot him, Ethan," I say, one of the rare moments when I use his real name. "I really *wanted* to kill him."

"You should have killed him. Why the hell didn't you call me when you got the dispatch?" he demands.

"It all happened lightning fast."

"And right here, blocks from your damn apartment. Why the *fuck* didn't you call me?"

I hate when he curses at me, but considering all that happened tonight, whatever. "The victim, Lang. Focus on the victim. He's the barista I talked to this morning after my run. My headphones came out and he heard the poetry I was listening to. He mocked it."

"Holy hell," he says, scrubbing his jaw. "And now he's dead."

"Yes. Now he's dead." A group of four officers exits the bushes, and Jackson is already there, greeting them. They aren't going to find The Poet, but we're going to go through the motions. Or they are. I focus on Lang and the bigger picture. "What happened with Roberts's ex?"

"She was freaked out. She didn't know he left. I had to take her to his house to prove it. She's certain he would have told her that he was leaving."

"And yet we have no body," I say. "The Poet likes the show he puts on for us. It makes no sense. It doesn't fit his profile."

"Don't start with this again. It's not him. And it can't be Newman if it's Roberts and we both know you have a hard-on for Newman being our guy."

"You're right. I do, but our killer likes to leave his victims for us to view. We have no body for Roberts."

"You're making this too complicated. Roberts got too close to The Poet and The Poet's smart enough to know that killing a cop brings heat he doesn't want. He wants to keep playing his game. He got rid of the body."

He wants to keep playing the game.

Lang's right. He does.

"Bottom line," I say. "We're having this conversation for one reason. I let The Poet get away tonight." I turn and start walking toward the crime scene that isn't going to connect the dots to Newman Smith or anyone else. The Poet is too skilled to let that happen. I'm going to have to connect the dots, and I will. He's not getting away alive again.

CHAPTER 42

I stand in the shadows right above the men in blue, on that same fire escape where Detective Jazz had spotted me earlier, watching the police officers scurry about like mice chasing cheese in all the wrong directions. But I'm not here for them. I'm here for her. I'm always here for her, so much closer than she realizes.

She knew I was here tonight, though, of course. Tonight she was expecting me.

I'd stood outside the bedroom window and watched her pull that poem from the sinner's mouth. Watched her read the words I'd written for her, and I'd seen the understanding slip onto her lovely face. She understands the great works and the implications those words have on our world, on our *very existence*. After tonight, she must understand that she is a part of the delicate balance of the universe that begins with those words. She must know that I did her work for her tonight. She revealed this sinner to me. I did what we both knew had to be done.

He spoke against the great works, the poems that are the word of man that guide us all. I righted the balance of good and evil.

Detective Jazz shows herself now, appearing through the line of bushes, dividing the apartment building from the sinner's house, pausing to talk to the officers with Detective Ethan Langford by her side. She and Detective Langford part ways with the officers and begin the walk down the sidewalk toward her apartment. I will allow him to remain in your life, for now, to hover and guard you for the same reason that I will go home and kiss my wife and kids tonight. These average humans we let in our lives allow us to look average. They shelter us to do our good work. As long as this Ethan Langford serves that purpose without getting in our way, he may stay on this Earth. Should that change, should he stray from his duty, then he too will be gone.

CHAPTER 43

Lang and I travel the short distance from the crime scene to my car in silence. We did our talking at the crime scene, while working the evidence. That's how we operate. That's how we make partnering up work. We both leave every crime scene without allowing ourselves to feel the emotion we could. We both need time to compartmentalize. It's survival, as necessary as breathing.

Lang eyes my car parked on the street. "What's with the street parking?"

"The road by the crime scene was a nightmare. This seemed a logical spot to park."

"Right," he says dryly. "You moving that into the garage?"

"I don't exactly like the idea of enclosed spaces right about now."

"Good decision." He motions to his car right across the street. "My head was in the same place."

I snag my keys and click the remote to unlock my trunk before walking to the back of the car, Lang sticking by my side. I trade out my field bag for my briefcase, but I leave the flats on and just shove my heels into my bag.

Lang shuts my trunk. "I'll walk you to your door."

I fold my arms and plant my feet. "You're not staying. I need to be alone."

He scowls, towering over me, a puffed-up, protective bear, and I can feel the tug-of-war inside him. I try to make it just a little easier on him. "I can't let him win. You staying with me tonight amounts to him winning. I know you know how that feels."

Understanding slides over his features. He gets it.

He gets me. Sometimes after the worst crime scenes, we need to battle our fear and beat it, or we can't go on. That has to be done alone. "We'll compromise," he offers. "I'll walk you to the door of your building."

I'm a little surprised at how easily he caves, but also relieved. I wasn't going to let him stay. I also wasn't looking forward to the battle that can erupt between the two of us when we bump heads. I nod and we start walking, again in silence. There is much we both will have to say about tonight's events, but those words will wait for tomorrow.

It's not long before we arrive at my building and prepare to say our final goodnight. Lang's way of doing so is an order. "I'm calling patrol to let them know you're walking up. And pull the damn trigger next time."

Regret fills me with those words. The Poet will kill again. I could have stopped him. "I will," I promise, reaching for the door and making quick work of entering my building. The walk is more tedious than normal, the stairwell tight but well enough lit, but I'm suffocating in the small space. I check my watch to find it's now nearing midnight and, as would be expected, not a peep can be heard but for me and my tired feet.

Relief fills me at the sight of my door, and I slide the key into the lock. I've barely cracked the door open when the glow of light tells me that someone is inside. Instinct kicks in and I drop my bag, pull my weapon, and kick the door open the rest of the way.

CHAPTER 44

I step inside the door and a man is suddenly in front of me, holding up his hands.

Wade.

It's Wade. Wade is here.

"Easy, baby," he murmurs, like calling me baby will somehow save his life. Men do that a lot. Call a woman "baby" and "sweetheart" to calm us down. Does that ever work? It damn sure doesn't for him. I'm suddenly pissed. Burning alive and hot under the collar.

I slam the door shut with my foot and walk toward him, shoving the gun into his chest. He's a good-looking man, and at thirty-eight, a younger Brad Pitt look-alike. His looks can't save him now. Not when his suit jacket is gone, flung over the table by the door, his blue tie that matches his blue eyes hanging low and loose. He's made himself comfortable, and while it would be a shame to mess up his pretty face, I think I could do it right about now.

"What are you doing in my apartment, Wade?"

"I still have a key. You know that."

"I don't remember you keeping my key."

"And you still have my key, which you haven't used in months, but we can talk about that later."

"You scared the shit out of me. I'll give it back. Talk complete. Why are you here?"

"Langford called. He told me about your visitor last night, the guy hanging out by your door. I grabbed a high-tech invisible camera and installed it by your door."

I grimace. I should have known. Lang gave up too easily downstairs. "He knows you're here?"

"Yes. He knows I'm here." He eyes the gun in my hand, now pressed to his chest. "Are you going to shoot me?"

"Did you bring wine and chocolate?"

"I did, in fact, bring wine and chocolate, Godiva and that Italian blend you love so much. And I have that late-night pizza joint on autodial, ready to call."

He wins. I lower my weapon.

Apparently, I'm not shooting anyone tonight, though I think I probably should have. I open the drawer to the entrance table and slide my gun inside. The minute the drawer is shut, he pulls me to him and wraps his arms around me. I'd forgotten how good it feels to have someone who doesn't think you're weak just because you're feeling beat-up in the moment. He pulls back and gives me a keen inspection. "Pizza?"

This man knows how well pizza replaces the acid burn of a bad night. I'm suddenly not as angry as I was moments before. "Please."

"Good. I'm starving. I'll order the pizza. The wine's on the counter."

A few minutes later, he's showing me my new state-of-the-art camera and security system, complete with a monitoring system that he installs on my phone.

"Thank you," I say, and a bit later, when we sit down at the coffee table with wine and pizza, I add, "You aren't staying the night."

His lips quirk and he says nothing. He just sips his wine.

"He killed a man tonight who just had a conversation with me this morning, Wade." And there it is. The words I've suppressed because speaking them somehow makes them far more real. It's out now, though. This isn't like any other case either of us has ever experienced. This killer is killing for me. "You can't stay." My voice is softer now, but it vibrates with emotion I can't afford to feel.

He ignores that declaration and takes a bite of his pizza. "You do know I've studied serial killers, right? Use me. I have a training class I'm teaching this week. Beyond tonight, my schedule is limited."

I take a bite of pizza and consider his offer. He really is well versed on this topic, which comes from his obsession with a long-uncaptured notorious serial killer before I even met him. Wade found him. He caught him. It made his career. Since then he's consulted on cases across the country. I'd be a fool not to go over this case with him.

"Off the record," he promises. "This is just me and you, discussing a case like the old days."

"Okay. Yes. Please. Let's talk it out."

"Let's do it." He refills our wineglasses.

I tell him everything about The Poet and my certainty that Newman Smith is our man. "He taught a class that connected serial killers with poetry, but that's circumstantial. Right now, I can't prove he's our man."

"He fits your profile," he says. "And I talked to Langford on my way over here. He told me that you think The Poet might have followed you this morning and that's how he picked Dave."

"I know he did." I share the story about my audiobook and Dave hearing the poetry on my phone. "The killer is more than just obsessed with poetry. He's protective of it as well."

"Well then, I'll praise Shakespeare and I'll be safe."

"Funny you say that. The poem he left tonight was from Shakespeare. 'Sonnet 60.'"

"Any idea what it means?"

"As I said to someone else, you could ask five scholars that question and get five different answers,

but as to what it means to The Poet, I need some
time to process. He was at that coffee shop. I took a
video of the entire place." I hand him my phone and
show him the video. "But none of those people were
close enough to hear my exchange with Dave." I grab
my computer and he moves the now-empty pizza
box to the floor.

"How do you know one of these people wasn't at
the end of the bar when you were talking to Dave?"

"I'm self-aware, and I don't remember him being
there." I pull up the footage from the coffee shop and
find the spot where I'm talking to Dave, frowning.

"This footage is limited," he points out. "You can't
see who's behind you and you can't see the entire
section of the pickup bar."

"You're right. The Poet could have been there
and never been caught on camera, but he'd have to
know where those cameras were."

"Maybe he did."

My brow furrows. "How?"

"That's the question," he says. "But my biggest
concern here is that this morning wasn't the first time
he followed you."

"The first murder that we know of was only days
ago, and Roberts was the detective handling the case.
The Poet didn't know I existed before I took over
this case."

"Unless he did," he counters. "I've already pointed this out before, but how many detectives have a
history in poetry?" He doesn't wait for an answer.
"One. You."

"That's ridiculous, Wade. A link to my father is
one thing, which I've considered, but there's no way
he would know my buried history."

"Unless he does. He killed for you tonight, Sam."

I immediately replay those words in my head: *He
killed for me tonight.*

It's an echo of the words I've already thought in my own head but somehow this assessment feels too simple. There's more to The Poet than an obsession with one person, which is where he's going with this. "Except this isn't about me, now, is it?" I challenge. "It's about him. He killed Dave because he dismissed poetry as irrelevant. I was simply the vehicle for Dave to offend The Poet." I stand up and walk to the opposite side of the table, my mind working hard and fast. "Dave offended The Poet. He dismissed poetry as unimportant. And maybe The Poet makes these kills about the poetry, but the truth is it's about him. When you dismiss poetry, you dismiss him."

Wade's lips curve and he fills our glasses with more wine before standing up and handing me my glass. "I do believe you understand The Poet better than The Poet understands himself. You're going to win this matchup. You're going to get him."

I drink my wine without the toast he offers me. I have nothing to celebrate. I spoke to Dave. And Dave is dead.

CHAPTER 45

The need to escape the hell of The Poet's games is real and present and answered by Wade. He stays the night and not on the couch. Morning arrives with our duties bleeding death and murder. Wade has an early commitment to teach a class on hunting serial killers to visiting recruits in the much-larger San Antonio office. A demand that has him rushing around to shower and dress—yes, he brought a change of clothes. I don't pick a fight with him over his presumptive behavior. He was good company for personal and professional reasons. He was here for me. I'm never going to bitch at him for being a good friend.

I'm still in the shorts and tank I pulled on earlier when he heads for the door, catching my hand and pulling me to him. He kisses me like I'm still his girlfriend and I don't complain. We did this same morning-after routine a few weeks before. We both know I'm not ready to keep doing this again. This is not that.

"Be careful," he orders, his voice rough with a mix of emotion and command that tells me he's really worried. "Do you understand me?"

"You too," I say, because despite how certain I am that the murders are rooted in poetry and not the people in my life, I'm still worried about him being here last night.

Wade and I stare at each other for a few beats, but we say nothing else. We both know there isn't anything *to say*. We risk our lives every day. There is only so much we can expect of each other, and maybe that's the problem with people like us. There is no one, especially those inside our world, who can ever feel comfortable and secure loving us. We are better off as loners.

I lock the door and grab my phone, pulling up the new application Wade installed. The one that allows me to see my front door. It works. I knew it worked, but I'm frustratingly *more* comfortable knowing it still works. The Poet is still under my skin.

I walk into the bedroom with the intent of throwing on my running clothes and taking my morning jog but halt by my closet. I can't go for a run. The Poet might be watching, and Lord only knows where that might lead. With a low growl, I head to my kitchen, drop the empty wine bottle in the trash, and fill my cup with coffee. Steaming brew in hand, I sit down with a copy of "Sonnet 60," and write out each line of the poem between sips, looking for a meaning beyond my initial reaction to identifying it last night. A quote on the SparkNotes website says, "This sonnet attempts to explain the nature of time as it passes and as it acts on human life."

While I don't completely agree with this assessment, human life ties back to a greater power, to a god. He thinks he's a god.

I do a quick read of both verses left with the bodies. First, the one left last night with Dave's body: *My verse shall stand, Praising thy worth, despite his cruel hand.*

Then the one left with Summer's body: *Who laugh in the teeth of disaster, Yet hope through the darkness to find, A road past the stars to a Master.*

My mind lands solidly back where it started. The Poet believes that he's a god.

He judged Summer and Dave unworthy of living, which brings me back to the contrast of the two men. Summer enjoyed poetry. Dave hated poetry. *But* they both had a connection to poetry, be it with love or hate. What about Roberts? Technically, he was connected to poetry by way of this case, but he's not dead and delivering a message by verse.

Frustrated, I head into the bathroom to shower, and by the time I'm dressed in my standard pantsuit, this time with an emerald green silk blouse, I have a thought. Perhaps they both offended The Poet. That's all that makes sense.

I wish desperately that my grandfather, who was once an expert on the topics of literature and poetry, was clear-minded enough to discuss this with me, but he's not. Those days are lost, and I decide I need a few scholars' input. I pull up my email and do some research before I shoot off a few messages.

I'm just packing up my briefcase to leave when Lang calls. "You're not here with a killer running loose. What the hell, woman?"

I glance at my watch and sure enough, it's nine o'clock, when I'd normally be to work by eight. "I got distracted by the case file, and what the hell was that with Wade last night?"

"I plead the fifth. Are you coming to work? We have an army of helpers right now."

"Have we found out where he got the cyanide?"

"One of our new tech guys is working on it," he replies. "Are you coming to work?" he repeats.

"I'll be there soon." I hang up.

He calls back. "Where the hell are you going?"

"I didn't get to run this morning. That's how I think. You know that. So I'm going to the firing range."

"I'll meet you there." He hangs up.

I call back. "Damn it, Lang."

"I'm meeting you."

"I'll come to the office."

"Come now or I'll come and get you. We have an

appointment to meet with Dave's landlord after lunch. We're trying to get some kind of camera feed around his house but coming up dry. His house sits off the road too far."

Of course it does, I think. "I'll be in the office."

I hang up again and head to the door, where I happily retrieve my weapon and place it on my person. A few minutes later, I'm in my car, and with Dave's house so near, it's impossible not to drive by the crime scene. I idle in front of his house, police tape drawn in all directions. One conversation changed his future. One conversation with me. They say the killer goes back to the scene of the crime. I feel like the killer. He made me feel like the killer.

Anger ripples through me and I pull around and start driving.

Lang calls yet again. "Where are you?"

"Jesus, Lang. I'm on my way. Work the case. Is Officer Jackson there?"

"He is. That shit that went down last night still bugging you?"

"I think we need to be careful. Hazel suggested that a good place to get cyanide would be overseas where drugs are easily accessed. She also suggested someone ex-military might have stockpiled cyanide. Jackson is ex-military."

"Wait. Now you think he's The Poet?"

"Not really, but I'm not prepared to ignore any possibility, are you?"

"No." His voice is tight. "I'm not."

"And can you make sure he turned in all the DNA samples from Summer's crime scene to forensics?"

"He did. I talked to them this morning."

"At least there's that. Any word on Roberts?"

"The captain called Houston. They haven't heard from him, but they're doing some digging for us.

Where are you?"

"I've been sitting in front of Dave's house, thinking." Which isn't a lie. I was. I'm just not now.

"Sitting there, inviting The Poet to show up?"

"If only it were that easy, Lang."

"Yeah. If only. Hurry up."

I hang up without saying goodbye, but I don't turn toward the station. I turn toward the college campus and the building where Newman Smith works.

CHAPTER 46

It's creeping up on ten a.m. when I park my car in the visitor parking of the faculty lot of the university, in a space that allows me a view of the faculty building door. For several seconds, I sit there, nervous energy thrumming through my fingers on the steering wheel. Newman was bold and arrogant enough to threaten the mayor once. He'll do it again, which means I have a tiny window before we're shut out completely.

I autodial Chuck, who answers on the first ring with a formal, "Chuck Waters. How can I help you?"

Clearly, he didn't look at his caller ID, which works out just fine right now. "Don't tell Lang I'm on the phone or I swear to you, you will *never* get another chocolate bar from me."

"I talk to him as little as possible," he says. "And I know my priorities. Chocolate wins. What do you need?"

"What's Newman's class schedule this morning?"

Keystrokes clack in my ear before he says, "He's out on break in half an hour. Then back at one."

"Thanks, Chuck. You're Superman." I disconnect, and wonder what a killer does with his break time the day after a murder. I plan to find out, but right now, I have a short half hour to get a look at his vehicle.

Decision made—albeit perhaps not a good one, but I'm committed to it either way—I open my door and climb out into what is now a low throb of hot sun beaming down upon me, and promising to burn hotter. I hate the heat, but at least I'm alive to bitch about it. Dave is not. After walking to my trunk, I once again exchange my briefcase for my field bag. I never leave my briefcase and notes out where they can be stolen. Men like Newman will do anything to save themselves.

Sliding the strap to my bag across my chest, I walk toward Newman's parking spot, scanning for anyone who might notice my attention to his vehicle. My audience is limited, and I step to the side of his minivan, a vehicle choice that is all about his sick façade of being the perfect family man. I think of Newman's kids, who are victims in their own way, of their father's monstrous actions. Kids who will be traumatized when his true self is exposed. I only hope they don't grow up to be just like their daddy.

Kneeling beside the rear tire, I shoot photos of the gravel caught between the hubcap and the rubber. I don't remember gravel at Dave's place, but there could be a nearby parking lot that does have gravel, and that offers us an opportunity to place his vehicle in the area. I push the limits I technically have with Newman at this point and grab a handful, scooping a tiny sample of the gravel and then slipping it into my bag. I then walk the full circle of the vehicle and stop at the driver's door, where I contemplate a swab for DNA. At this stage, it won't be admissible in court, but I'll get another later after I prove he's our guy.

"What do you think you're doing?"

At the sound of Newman's voice, cold and calm at my shoulder, and my back where I never want him, I whirl around to find him standing close, a few steps from contact, too damn close. He's wearing a yellowish-gold bow tie, the color of the flowers in his garden. I wonder if his wife picked it out, if that symbol of family and home helps her pretend that he's not a monster. Because she knows. I saw it in her eyes. I know she knows.

I hold my ground, and he holds his, intelligent green eyes locked on my face. Evil lives in the soul behind those eyes. "What are you doing?" he repeats.

"Waiting for you."

"More like lurking around my vehicle."

"Semantics. You people like semantics, right?"

"You people?"

Killers, I think, but I say, "Professors."

His lips quirk. I've amused him. "Is that how we're playing this game?"

"*We*," I say, "are not playing a game at all."

"Aren't we?" he challenges.

"Where were you last night?"

His brows sink into a scowl. "Last night? What does last night have to do with anything?"

"We had a second murder."

Understanding floods his expression, a hint of anger whitening the corners of his mouth. "That you believe I committed," he supplies.

I don't confirm or deny that statement. "Where were you last night?" I repeat.

He studies me for several cool moments, and despite that white around his mouth, the explosive response I'd have earned from most people is nowhere to be found. He simply says, "A university charity event with my wife. I had hundreds of witnesses. I went to bed with my wife. We cuddled."

Cuddled. Give me a break. My mind goes to Dave's lifeless face, and anger burns a hot spot in my chest. "Do you know a med student named Dave Gaines?"

"We don't have a medical school here, and I teach criminal justice."

"You've linked poetry and murder in at least one class you taught," I correct. "And UT's Dell Medical School is in Austin, and we both know you know this."

"The medical school is on Red River Street. Those students don't come to my location. They're beyond this level. We do not have a medical school here. I do not teach medical students."

"Did you know—"

"No. I did not know him. What else, Detective Jazz?" His lips quirk again, and he doesn't wait for a reply. "I wonder. Should I buy you a dozen doughnuts? Will that get you to go away? Cops do like doughnuts, correct?"

"Only to celebrate the killers we put behind bars. I'll have my doughnuts soon. As for me going away. You want me to go away?" I dare the question despite the fact that the man has lurked outside my door.

"Considering I don't even know the people you've accused me of killing, I do, in fact, want you to go away," he says. "It doesn't appear that I'm going to be that fortunate."

I reach into my bag and hold up a DNA swab. "Swab your cheek and give me a DNA sample."

His sharp gaze goes to the swab and then returns to my face, a wicked something in his eyes that I cannot name. "No. I don't believe I'll give up my DNA to a desperate detective who will do anything to close her case. I've heard about your father's dirty deeds. I'm beginning to think the apple doesn't fall far from the tree."

With that slap, he clicks the lock on his door and climbs into his minivan, successfully shutting himself out of my reach. I watch him drive away, and I've heard his message loud and clear. He just told me that he's made it a point to know far more about me than my name.

CHAPTER 47

My first instinct is to go to Newman's house and talk to his wife before he can corroborate his alibi, but that's an illogical move. Had I been thinking straight, I'd have gone to see her in the first place and asked her for a DNA sample. That was the plan Lang and I talked through. Using her to pressure him is my best next move. That's how the smarter me would have handled this morning. Instead, I've let emotion, not logic, dictate my actions, and this job has no room for emotional decisions, and therefore, I'm pissed. At myself. Which is always a sucky feeling.

At this point, I just head on to the station, a short drive that isn't tied up with traffic midmorning. Once there, I beeline to the conference room where I find a team of eight at work, Lang and Officer Jackson among that number. "When the captain throws support your way, he really throws support," I say, and instantly all eyes are on me.

Officer Jackson shoots to his feet at a spot near the opposite side of the table. "Can I talk to you, Detective Jazz?"

Lang, who is closer to the door and me, is now on his feet as well, waving off Jackson. "I'm first," he says, headed my way, and as usual, he's ignored a more formal dress code for detectives. He's wearing jeans yet again today, but on the plus side, he's managed a polo-style collared shirt. I guess he wants to impress all the little minion helpers and what better way than with a collared shirt paired with jeans?

He points toward the door and we end up in an empty cubicle in the sea of cubicles. "Jackson looks clean," he says, his voice low. "He was highly award-ed in the army. He could have been an officer but wanted to be near his family. He's got two sisters and he's close to them and his parents, who own a bakery. He's dating a baker who works at that bakery."

"The bad ones always look clean."

"I thought you were sure The Poet was Newman."

"We just had this conversation. I am. That doesn't mean I trust Jackson." I move on. "What about the cyanide?"

"One of our tech guys found a reference on the dark web to a cyanide sale that's two years old. He's trying to make a purchase himself. But assuming the buyer was The Poet, that means he's possessed that murder weapon for two years. We just don't have any proof he used it until now."

"He didn't start with cyanide. He tried other things." My lips press together and I steel myself for the explosion to come. "I went and saw Newman this morning."

"What the fuck?!" His voice is still low and yet he's managed a shout for my ears only. "I mean. *What. The. Fuck?* What the—"

"Lang," I warn.

"I know. You don't like to be cursed at. Well, *fuck* that. You shouldn't have gone there alone. You shouldn't have gone, period."

"We have a right to ask where he was last night, and I'd prefer to do that before the mayor shuts us down. I asked. He presented an alibi for us to check out. And I tried to get a DNA sample. He refused." I lower my voice a notch below its present level. "He accused me of being dirty like my father."

His eyes narrow. "How did he know about your father? That was an internal investigation kept under wraps and never completed."

"I don't know, but it was clearly his way of telling

me he is closer to me than I thought."

"I'm pretty sure he made that point on your doorstep."

"Detective Jazz."

At the captain's voice, I cringe. Lang and I rotate toward him, only to have him step into the cubicle. It's a move that forces the two of us against the wall, and how can it not? This is a cubicle for one that now has me and two giants inside it.

"What on God's green earth were you thinking?" he demands, his voice low, rough. Angry.

"Last night's victim—"

"You knew him," he supplies. "I know. Lang told me. But you know that Newman is in the mayor's good graces. *Talk* to me before you go after him. Do you understand?"

"Tell the mayor to force him to give us a DNA sample."

"And that does what?" the captain challenges. "Do you have DNA to compare it to?"

"No, but—"

"When you have DNA," he snaps, "ask again. Ask *me,* not him."

My lips press together. "I need to talk to his wife to corroborate his alibi last night."

"Call her," he states. "Do it by phone."

My objection is instant. "But—"

"Call her," he repeats. "Work your case, exclude everyone else, and then come back to Newman Smith. *The end.*"

"What about Roberts?" I demand. "What about finding him? He's the answer to finding Newman."

"I'm thinking of Roberts. You won't get to this guy if you give him the mayor's insulation."

"He has that," Lang says, finally speaking up. "And he shouldn't. Not with Roberts missing."

"I can't give the mayor a reason to believe this is

Newman," the captain snaps back. "We have no evidence. Work the case. You won't even have a small portion of the crime labs results back for a week from the first case, let alone this new one. Get me what I need to get you what you need."

"He killed Dave Gaines because I spoke to him, Captain. Because I *spoke* to him. This is no different than him sending in those interns. This was another taunt. One that took a life."

"Killing that young man is not the same as sending those interns," he argues. "We know who sent the interns. You can't prove who killed that young man. *Work* the case. Get the proof we need, and that isn't going to happen by you becoming a stalker." He turns and walks out of the cubicle.

"Stalker?" I take a step forward, and Lang catches my arm. I jerk around and square off with him. "Let go."

"No. The stalker comment sucks, Jazz, but he has a point. We need to work the case. We have witnesses and interviews coming in, starting in an hour."

I want to fight back, I do, but he's right. We have to work the case. My mistake is to allow the ticking clock to the next murder to be all I see, blinding me to the facts. The Poet is not a god, no matter what he believes. He's human. He makes mistakes. It's time to dig in and find those mistakes.

CHAPTER 48

Lang and I head back into the conference room, where I avoid eye contact with Officer Jackson, who thankfully doesn't push for my attention, which I'm not ready to spare yet. We'll talk. Just not now. I claim a seat next to Lang and across from Chuck to quickly review the interview list, which is fine, but too small and drawn out over a full week. We need to work the case but do it faster.

"Let's double up interviews," I suggest, eyeing Lang. "I'll take the Summer interviews. I'm the best person to get a read on a poetry event. I know what Dave did to set off our killer. I need to talk to the people who attended that reading to see if I can pinpoint what Summer did to end up dead."

"We don't even know if a trigger happened that night," he says, "but take the Summer interviews. The only thing I know about poetry is that it makes me dizzy and irritated."

It's not really funny, but everyone laughs as if they need to laugh, the rumbles strained and nervous with good reason: there's a young man now dead and he's dead for no reason other than his personal dislike of poetry. Dislike that could just as easily been another man's dislike of coffee, tea, or milk. We all hate and love, and that is our right as humans. But The Poet has now stripped that right away and made us all think about how easily life can change. And end.

Chuck clears his throat nervously and the mood shifts away from a morbid "death to us all" to a focused, investigative tone. I'm introduced to our new team, which now includes several tech guys and a couple of forensic investigators. The one person outside of Jackson and Chuck that stands out is Martin Rodriquez—a forty-something Latino, who has wavy dark hair with a hint of salt and pepper— and for more than one reason. For starters, he's the guy who hit the dark web for cyanide with excellent, rapid results.

He hands me his notes, which are impressive. I give him a curious look. "I'm in love with your skills. Where have you been all my life?"

"At the ATF. I worked a task force with Wade recently. He pulled some strings and inserted me into this."

And there's yet another reason that he stands out. The captain didn't arrange his help at all. It was Wade. "Is that right?"

"Yes," he confirms. "He says you owe him wine and chocolate. I say you owe *me* wine and chocolate. And a killer. I'm here to catch him. That's what I want out of this."

"I might like you," I surmise. "But I've met too many impressive killers to like anyone this quickly with any certainty. So, we'll see."

"That makes two of us," he agrees, and he gets right back to work. "I'm working on a meeting to purchase cyanide from the dealer, but it won't be here in Austin."

"Where?" Lang asks.

"Brownsville," Martin replies.

"Brownsville is where Newman grew up," I jump in.

"Circumstantial evidence," Lang says, "but something at least."

"Don't get too excited on my end," Martin says. "I have to warn you, our guy could have found someone else to buy the cyanide for him. I was born here, but my parents are from Mexico. If you know where to go, you don't even have to cross the border and you can find plenty of people who will do anything for cash money. We just have to hope he had his guard down at the border and showed his face to someone who talks. Or better yet, near a camera. I consider this a long shot, at best."

It is. A worthless one. The Poet didn't let his guard down. He doesn't leave behind DNA.

"If we can date the transaction, can we get his vehicle or plates at the Mexican border?" Lang asks.

It's a good angle. The Poet, I remind myself, is human. I flip open a folder to a picture of Dave tied to that chair and silently add, he's also a monster who I had a chance to shoot and didn't. Right now, I think that might just make me a monster.

CHAPTER 49

Dave's parents and girlfriend arrive early, not long after our talk with the captain, and well before any of my scheduled interviews. In my book, these particular interviews are certain to be emotional and useless. We know how The Poet found Dave, and that was me. Thus, I defer to Lang's expertise and stand down when I would otherwise sit in. He doesn't ask why. We both know why. Despite logic telling me and everyone I am not responsible for Dave's death, guilt crawls through me, and it has claws. Long, sharp, angry claws.

Once Lang is off to his interview, I spend some time listening to the team talk about cameras and vehicle identification among other investigative topics. It's a subject that reminds me of the bag of gravel in my bag that needs to make it to forensics in another building. I excuse myself from the group and find my way to that empty cubicle to call Wade. As expected, considering he's teaching a class, I leave a message. "I owe you in many, many ways, Agent Miller. Thank you, *Wade.*" I disconnect and turn to exit the cubicle to find Officer Jackson standing in my path.

"Do you have a second?"

"Of course." The words are welcoming, but my arms fold in front of me, that off feeling with him still clear and present.

"I disappointed you last night."

My arms fall to my sides, finger instantly jabbing in the air in his direction. "What you did was invite me to shoot you. You don't break from a command on an active murder scene. You don't pop up in front of a detective who's chasing a killer while she's chasing a killer."

"I thought I was protecting you." His voice lifts defensively. "I tried to have your back."

"And yet you weren't where I asked you to be to watch my back when I exited the bedroom."

His defense is instant. "In the army and on the street—"

"There are procedures for both. You have potential, but you know what you made me do? I had them investigate you this morning. You were in the same place as the killer."

"What?" He pales. "I—no. God. No. I was—"

"I could have killed you," I repeat. "Do you understand?"

"What if he would have killed you because I didn't show up to help you?"

My lips press together. He has a point, but he disappeared from where he was supposed to be and reappeared in a place where The Poet had led me. "If I tell you to hold a position, hold it."

"Understood. I'm sorry. I know it looks bad, but I *want* to learn. I want to do more."

In that moment, I believe him. Maybe I'm overreacting. My first instinct about him was a good one, but last night, my gut shifted. "I appreciate what you tried to do. I do. Just—"

"Believe me," he says, holding up his hands. "I won't invite you to shoot me again."

"Well," I say, my lips quirking, "that's definitely a good plan."

We laugh and exchange a few more words before he heads back to the conference room. I'm left wondering why I'm bothered by Jackson at all. Newman's The Poet.

CHAPTER 50

Before returning to the conference room, I try to call Newman's wife.

Of course, her voicemail picks up, and I don't leave a message. If by some unlikely chance Newman hasn't gotten to her yet, I'm not going to give her a chance to prepare. It's not long afterward that I begin my interviews. In a matter of two hours, I've met with five of the people who attended the poetry night, all of whom had been interviewed by Roberts. All of whom tell me some version of the same thing. It was a fabulous event. The theater is amazing. I can't believe the man running the event is dead. Some of the attendees knew Summer. They'd frequented past events. None of them knew him personally, and Roberts had already cleared them all. I'm again struck by how well and fast Roberts had worked this case. And once again, I can't help but wonder how close he got to The Poet.

Throughout the course of the interviews, I find several attendees who noticed the man in the back row who came in right after the lights went low and left before the event ended. Each consistently described him as tall, average build, with longish dark hair and a beard. A detail that's an illogical match for The Poet, who left behind no discernible evidence at the crime scene. There is natural shedding, and no one with as much hair as the witnesses describe avoids that shedding. In comparison to the man described, Newman is, in fact, tall with an average build. He does indeed have dark hair, but it's neatly trimmed, and could easily be shoved under a swim cap. He has no facial hair.

By the sixth interview, I have Officer Jackson visiting wig shops with photos of Newman Smith while another tech hits internet locations. Yet another investigator calls stores in the state. He wears a wig and fake facial hair. I'm certain of it. In between all of this, I attempt to contact Newman's wife again, with no success.

It's the seventh interview, and my last for the night, that stands out. That interview is with Debra Keyes, who is blonde, pretty, and far more youthful looking than her fifty-five years would suggest.

"Can you tell me about the event?" I ask as I have each interviewee.

"Of course." She sits up primly, her red dress a bold choice for a police interview, one that is almost too confident to suit me. "I hate that the man was murdered," she offers, sounding mortified. She reads like a woman above such things as death. "I want to help," she continues. "I'm afraid I don't have much to tell that I didn't tell Detective Roberts."

"It helps me to hear it firsthand," I assure her.

"Okay then. I was on a blind date that night. I didn't connect well with the guy."

"Who was your blind date?"

"Ted Bloom."

I don't check my notes. I've already interviewed Ted, who didn't mention her. "Are you still seeing him?"

"Oh gosh no. Ted is into poetry and mathematics and lives on zero carbs. The man was fit enough and all, but not enough to make me live like that. I don't like poetry. I hate math and I live for carbs. I declined another date."

I've read Roberts's notes. He not only checked out Ted, he seemed to feel he was too scared of his shadow to be a killer. I agree. Additionally, he placed Ted at his mother's place after dropping off Debra.

Debra, in turn, called her ex-boyfriend. Debra the player. Two men, one night.

"Go on," I urge, leaving her personal life alone. She's clear. It's not my business.

"Ted loved the event that night, but it was just odd to me. It was like we were in church."

Something about that word church resonates with me. "Explain what you mean, please."

"You know how they keep the bibles behind the seats in church and everyone reaches for a book and reads a verse? That's how it started. The poetry books were treated like bibles. Except the books were under the seats, on the floor. We all had to read random poems together, in between the solo readers. I hated it."

Bible.

Church.

Under the seat.

I start to piece together those thoughts. Any religious person knows that you never put a bible on the ground. It's disrespectful to God. The Poet believes he's a god. What if he believes placing a book of poetry on the floor was no different? It was disrespecting him? And as the person running the event, had he held Summer responsible for that disrespect? Of course, it's only a theory, but it feels like I might be onto something.

I finish the interview with Debra and meet Lang, who's just finished an interview of his own in the hallway. "I have one more," he says, "and nothing worth hearing to tell you so far. How about you?"

"I'm done with mine for tonight. I might have a few ideas the last interview sparked, but I'm not sure yet. I need to process and go by the forensics lab before they're gone. I want to see if I can clear one of the poetry books used for the guests at the Summer reading for my review."

"Definitely your kind of reading, not mine. You

want to meet up after?"

"I think I need to spend some time lost in poetry tonight."

"I'll come over."

"I don't need you to come over," I amend. "Wade set up a camera at my front door and I have my trusted friend right here, should I need her." I pat my weapon. She's a "her" and a badass, just like me. Except for last night. I failed the badass test last night for sure.

He looks like he wants to argue, but he settles on, "Call me when you're headed home."

"I don't need a phone check-in, Dad. I have a patrol by my place, remember? And yes, I know to call in and let patrol know when I head home."

"Just freaking call me," he snaps.

"Okay. *Okay.*"

He gives me one of his best glares and then stalks away to deal with his next interview. I take that as my cue to head for the door, and I do so relieved that I've gotten free of Lang for the moment. I have a few investigative steps left to take tonight, and at least one is best handled without him. For his own good, but probably not mine.

CHAPTER 51

I can almost hear, in my mind, a clock ticking off the minutes until someone else dies, but I can't allow that pressure to get to me the way it did this morning with Newman.

It's exactly why I don't dive into trouble that I know I will later when I leave Lang at the station. I start out by doing just what the captain ordered: I work the case in the expected, safe way. In fact, my first solo investigations of the evening are perfectly acceptable and without recourse.

Mostly.

After discovering that I've missed Hazel at the ME's office, I swing a few miles away from the precinct to the crime lab to drop off the sample I took from Newman's tire. While I'm there, I'll do a little begging and bartering to move us up to the front of the testing line.

Fortunately for me, once I'm in the building, I discover that Antonio Lopez, one of my preferred investigators, is present and working at this late six p.m. hour. He's my go-to guy when I can manage as much, for a reason: he's smart and dedicated. He lives to be a part of the solution.

Eager to rally his help, I hunt him down, and it's not long before I'm standing outside the glass of the evidence room, watching as he studies something under a microscope. I pound on the window, and he gives a little wave and hurries in my direction, yanking off his gloves as he does. He tosses them in a trash can and then exits the lab to join me in a small exterior office.

"Hola, Detective Jazz," he greets, his hands shoved into his lab coat. "What can I do ya for?"

I could chitchat, and I often do with Antonio, but

not this time. Not with that clock ticking in my mind. Tonight, I get right to the point. "I have a potential serial killer and a missing detective. I need answers."

His eyes go wide, as I'd expected. "What detective?"

"Detective Roberts."

"Roberts? He was just in here, riding my ass about a case."

"The Summer case?"

"Yes, Summer. He was all-in on that case. And now—*he's gone?*"

"Missing. We're concerned it's related to the investigation. I've taken over the Summer case, and we now have a second victim, Dave Gaines."

"Holy hell." He scrubs a lightly stubbled jaw, his hands settling on his hips. "What can I do?"

"I recognize that you're backed up and we're weeks out on most of our DNA results. But I need a few items pushed to the front of the line. If that can't happen, I need to see if the FBI lab can help."

"I'll make it happen." He points to the desk and grabs a pen and paper. "What do you need above all else? I'll get the right people to do the right things, fast."

I give him a list he jots down that includes the voluntary DNA samples we collected from guests at the Summer poetry event, forensics testing on the glasses collected from the Summer crime scene, the poetry books used at the event, and the actual notes left in the victims' mouths.

"Do you understand what the poems mean? Do any of us?"

"I'm a bit of a poetry expert, actually. That's why I need to see those poetry books rushed, to make sure there's not something there that might tell us where Roberts is or who the next victim might be. Something only a poetry scholar will understand."

"Scholar? You're a scholar?"

"I'm pretty darn close," I say, but I don't explain. I

don't talk about my past or my life in general. I focus on my present reality and my job. "Let's hope that knowledge helps us catch this monster."

"I need three days for the testing."

I push back. "It's been that long, longer even, since Summer was murdered."

"It's been three minutes since I promised you to rush this. We're buried in demand, but I'm going to move you to the front of the line. At least on these pieces of the puzzle. I'll get what you need done, but it's going to take three days."

I stop pushing, but I do step into that little bit of trouble I knew I'd entertain when I came here tonight. The trouble I wanted Lang to avoid. I reach in my bag and hand him the sample I'd technically, illegally, taken from Newman's tire. "I took that from the vehicle of the suspect in both cases this morning, which is relevant because the second murder was last night. No, I did not have a search warrant, but I did it anyway. This test will get thrown out in court, but if it places him at the scene of the crime, we'll get him. He's not easy to catch. He's that good at hiding."

It's these risk/reward decisions law enforcement has to make to save lives that I hope he understands. Yes, I'm standing firmly in the gray area where my father lived, where he justified bad to achieve good. But I'm visiting only out of desperation. I tell myself it's not the same. I tell myself this isn't how it started for my father.

Antonio studies me for a long, hard moment, perhaps weighing the impact of that gray for himself, but he ultimately gives a nod. "I'll make it a priority."

"Thank you," I say. "I *do* appreciate this. And I owe you."

"Just find Roberts and catch this killer."

"That's exactly what I'm trying to do."

Find Roberts and catch a killer. If only it were as simple as it sounds.

CHAPTER 52

I park my car outside the reach of a streetlight, a block down and in view of Newman's house, and I dial Chuck.

"Jazz," he answers, his voice a huff of exhaustion. "Hey."

"I was hoping you weren't still at work."

"You were hoping I was because you need me."

"I have your cell number. Why are you there?"

"I'm just trying to give you something to catch this guy with."

"And I love you for it," I say. "Where are we on Newman's alibi for last night?"

"The event he told you he attended was legit. I haven't gotten my hands on a guest list yet. There's no film of the actual event. I do have a campus guard now on autodial and feeding me what film exists."

"What's the bottom line?"

"Newman was at the campus and left at about nine o'clock."

"And his wife?"

"That's the interesting part of the story. I have her on camera at the campus, arriving at seven. She was dressed nicely, but she wasn't there long, for about an hour. She left in a rush and seemed to be upset. The guard says she was crying."

"I'd cry if that man were my husband, too," I murmur. "Just to confirm. She left at eight. He left at nine."

"Correct. The tip about Dave's murder came in at ten thirty. The campus is ten minutes from his house. He had plenty of time to kill Dave before that call."

Yes, he did, I think. "What about traffic camera

footage that puts his vehicle at Dave's house or nearby?"

"I've looked. His vehicle isn't on the footage, and we're trying to find a camera that shows us a spot where he might have pulled off and walked. We're also checking hired cars with pickup and drop-off locations somewhere nearby. So far—*nothing*."

"What about proof of when he went home?"

"We caught his vehicle on camera at one a.m., turning onto his street."

"He had to be on camera somewhere between nine and one."

"I'm trying, Jazz. I really am trying."

"I know. You did good. Now go home. Rest feeds the brain."

"Says the person I know who isn't home herself?"

"That's why they pay me the big bucks."

"They don't pay you the big bucks."

"Close enough. Go home. That's an order." I disconnect, certain that he'll go home. He's good at taking orders. I, however, am not, or I wouldn't be here.

It's right then that I watch the garage door open and Newman's minivan pull out to the street. Damn it. I need this time to talk to the wife, but what if he's on his way to kill someone else? My cell phone rings and it's Lang again. This time I answer. "Lang—"

"I'll follow him. You talk to the wife. And yes, I knew you'd be here. Bad Jazz. Bad."

God, I love this man. "That works," I say and disconnect, already reaching for my bag and the door.

My phone goes in my jacket pocket, my bag over my shoulder, and I step to the street, locking up behind me before pocketing my keys. The night is muggy, a heaviness to the air that suffocates. Appropriate considering The Poet's murder weapon is cyanide and that's how his victims spend the last few minutes of their lives: they suffocate while their organs die.

I step onto the sidewalk leading to the house, motion detectors flickering to life and guiding me past all the damn pretty little flowers. The world is full of pretty things that hide horrible, nasty secrets. This house, this place, and perhaps even this woman fit that description. I step onto the porch and ring the bell. I wait a few seconds and ring it again. And again.

Finally, the curtain moves, and then the door opens. Becky Smith stands there, wearing sweats and a tank top, her hair disheveled, her eyes puffy.

"Why are you here?" she demands.

"Are you okay?"

She folds her arms in front of her, a protective stance typical of someone hiding something. "I'm fine. What do you need?"

"There was another murder."

Her expression tightens, a flicker of panic in her eyes. "I'm sorry to hear that, but what does that have to do with me?"

"I just need to confirm what your husband told me about last night. Then I can make this go away for you and him. And for your kids."

She swallows hard. "We went to a party."

"At the campus. Yes. I know. He told me you had a fight, much like the one you had tonight, I assume. You left and were quite upset."

"I—yes."

"Can you confirm the nature of the fight?"

Her teeth scrape her bottom lip. "Why is that important?"

"What time did you get home?"

"Eight thirty, which I know because I let the babysitter go home."

"And what time did your husband get home?"

"Later."

"What time?"

"I don't remember."

"Maybe I can help. He left the event and hurried home after you. He was home half an hour after you, which would make his arrival here at nine."

Her lashes lower, her teeth digging into her bottom lip this time.

"Is that correct?" I press.

"Yes." Her gaze lifts to mine. "Yes. It's correct."

It's a lie that disappoints, that makes her complicit in ways I'm not yet ready to turn on her. Especially since I don't know if that lie comes from a place of fear, love, or guilt.

"Is that all?" she asks. "I'm tired. I need to get the kids to bed and me as well."

"Let me look at my notes." I grab my phone and pretend to scan for information. "Hmmm," I murmur, glancing up at her. "I got that wrong. He left the school at nine thirty."

"Oh. Yes. Well with the bustle of the sitter and kids, it just felt sooner."

"We don't show him arriving home until well after midnight."

Her eyes sharpen with anger. "Are you playing games?"

"I just want to know where he was until one in the morning."

"You need to leave."

"You're afraid of him."

"I'm not afraid of my husband."

"Two people are dead and the cop who worked this case before me is missing."

She quite obviously bristles, her spine stiffening. "Why are you blaming my husband?"

"You know why."

"He's—"

"Dangerous, and I don't want you or your kids to be next. You do know that by protecting him you're complicit in his crimes, correct?"

She swallows hard. "I don't know anything about any crimes."

I reach in my bag and pull out a swab, which I hold up. "Then you won't mind providing me a DNA sample."

A flicker of something flashes in her eyes—fear, I think. I've hit a nerve. "I need to talk to my attorney."

"Why? Did you kill someone?"

"I did not kill anyone. You need to leave." She tries to shut the door.

I catch it. "If you're afraid—"

"Let go of the door."

"Mrs. Smith—"

"Let go!" she shouts, and this time, I let the door go.

It slams in my face.

My cell phone rings with Lang's number. I answer it on my way down the sidewalk. "He's on his way back. Get out of there."

CHAPTER 53

Lang and I end up at a bar that's within walking distance from my apartment while an unmarked patrol car keeps tabs on Newman. Apparently, Lang had followed him on a grocery run for milk and toilet paper, to which Lang had joked, "We're so close, he's shitting himself." He's classy like that and I love him for it.

At present, we're sitting across from each other, tucked away in a back-corner booth. Garth Brooks is blasting through the speakers, with a neon Texas sign on the wall, while we contemplate our survival rate once Newman calls the mayor and the mayor calls the captain. I sip my cucumber jalapeño martini. "You weren't there. I was. No sense in us both going down."

"We're a team, Jazzy," Lang says, tipping back his Corona. "Live together, die together."

"I do love that you were there tonight."

"I hate that you didn't trust me enough to just tell me where you were going. What happened to live and die together?"

"You say that, I don't."

"Jazz—"

"My father happened, Lang. He pushed the limits of right and wrong and when wrong won, he took down some good people."

"Two detectives were fired after the Internal Affairs investigation finally concluded last month. And they wouldn't have gone down if they were good people."

"And five from patrol. Change the subject."

He studies me a long moment and then says, "I

talked to the captain up in Houston."

"And?"

"He knew Roberts from the police academy. Roberts called him and wanted a job. That's all it took."

"You think The Poet forced him to make the calls?"

"Or Roberts was trying to throw off whoever he might be running from."

I sigh. "We didn't change the subject at all. You still think this could be connected to my father?"

"I don't know. Your father never confessed his sins to anyone."

"He didn't have to." I down half my drink. "My godfather told me plenty."

"The chief gave you the dirty on your father?"

"That's right."

"When?"

"A few nights before my father died. The chief wanted to make sure I was clean before the shit hit the fan. I was embarrassed and angry. I respect him. He's family. My father was like a brother to him. I tried to keep it all to myself but failed. That's why I was fighting with my father the night he died. I confronted him."

"Fuck. I thought you overheard your father talking and figured out he was dirty."

"Technically, I did. The chief played a recording of my father celebrating the murder of a suspect."

"Holy hell. Why didn't you tell me?"

"Aside from the fact that I didn't want you to know anything you'd have to report to IA?" I finish off my drink. "I told you—it's embarrassing. I mean, Lord help me, in his own way, my father was much like The Poet. He had a God complex. If he couldn't take down a bad guy the right way, he found a way to hurt them. He got power hungry and started trading deals with the wrong people."

"What people?"

"Criminals," I say, stating what seems obvious. "And it doesn't matter at this point. He's dead. IA closed the case. As for Roberts, could he have done something while working for him that angered someone enough to put his life on the line? Yes. Of course he could have. Could it be a coincidence that it happened now, while this case was hot? Yes. Maybe. But how did Newman know about my father?"

"The mayor?" he suggests.

"Would IA allow that to slip to the mayor?"

"Captain Moore doesn't like the mayor, but if I remember correctly, your father was pretty darn chummy with him."

"Yeah. Yeah, he was, and believe it or not, I actually thought that was a good thing."

He snorts. "As good as bourbon and milk." He shows mercy on me and changes the topic from my father. "On a slightly different note," he says, "Chuck tried to find a connection between your father and these cases and came up dry."

My cell phone rings and I glance at the number; my spine instantly goes ramrod stiff. "My apartment office." I glance at the clock. "It's almost midnight." I punch the answer button. "Detective Samantha Jazz."

"It's Tabitha from the office."

"Hi, Tabitha," I say, eyeing Lang. "It's late. Did you wake up from a bad dream and have something new to share with us?"

"Well, no. Not really, but yes." She laughs nervously. "Sorry. That sounded absolutely stupid. Let me try again. We have a new foot patrolman who started tonight. One of the tenants came to him and told him an unknown man entered your building a few minutes ago."

"A strange man is in my building," I say, letting Lang know what's going on.

He curses and stands up, tossing money onto the table.

I'm already grabbing my bag and doing the same. "Do you have a description?" I ask Tabitha as Lang and I head for the door.

"I don't. This just happened and I confess, I was asleep when the call came in. I'm trying to get a grip on the full story. This really may be nothing. Thanks to Mrs. Crawford telling everyone to be on alert, the tenants seem to be a bit paranoid right now. But for safety's sake, we did call the police."

"Have your patrolman meet me at my building," I say, and we exit to the street. "I'll be right there."

CHAPTER 54

Lang calls for extra patrol support on the way to my apartment and instructs them to search for a man in a hoodie and baseball cap. Of course, we have no description of the man lurking about, but we both can assume who this person is. It seems that I went to Newman's place, stirred up trouble, and now he's making me as uncomfortable as possible. Next, Lang calls the patrol watching Newman, and I catch a few pieces of the conversation. "He slipped by you," Lang snaps. "Go confirm I'm right, because I am." He disconnects, an angry scowl on his face. "'Watch him' meant 'watch him,'" he complains. Apparently, that was too much to ask.

We arrive at my building to find a patrol unit already present and chatting with a security guard. The two cops are both bald, one tall and one short. I don't know this bald duo at all, and I don't have time to know them right now. Lang echoes that sentiment by getting right to the point. He flashes his badge. "Detective Langford." He motions to me. "Detective Sam Jazz."

The tall bald cop blinks. "I thought Sam was a man."

I wave off that comment that is old and overdone too many times in my life, dating back well before I joined law enforcement. I'm focused on my job right now. The end. I size up the guard, a stocky Hispanic man, who I estimate to be in his early thirties. His name tag reads "Daniel." The tattoo on his arm reads TS, which is the Texas Syndicate, a gang. I'll have questions about Daniel that I'll ask later.

"Who called in the concern?" Lang asks.

"A tenant is all I know," Daniel says. "The office manager called me."

"Did you"—I motion to the two officers as well—"or any of you get a look at this man?"

"No," Daniel replies for the group. "I got the call and came here. I searched the building but saw no one. The police were waiting when I exited the building."

I shove aside my jacket, hands settling on my waist. "Do we at least have a description?"

Daniel replies again. "I was told that he was in a hoodie and baseball cap."

Lang immediately motions to the two cops who haven't been much help. "Go search."

They back away and disappear, and I focus on Daniel. "Call the office and find out who reported this." I'm already turning away from him, assuming his compliance despite that tattoo, and motioning Lang toward my building. "I need a look at the film from the cameras Wade installed."

He opens the door and I file in first, starting the climb up the narrow steps. Lang follows, and once we're at my apartment door, we both reach for our weapons without pulling them out. I check the knob and the door is locked, which means nothing. An intruder could have locked it with himself inside.

I unlock it and pocket my keys. Lang doesn't even consider hanging back. He goes in and I follow. I let him search the place and I set my bag on the floor before kneeling beside the computer Wade left on the entry table, where I start tabbing through the feed. And there he is. The man in the hoodie. He was at my door, standing there with his back to me.

Lang finishes his search, holstering his weapon.

I hit the space bar and freeze the feed. "I found him on the footage, at my door again."

"It wasn't Newman," he says.

"Of course it was Newman," I argue.

"Nope. He's at home. Patrol knocked on the door and did a wellness check. He came to the door."

CHAPTER 55

I glance at the security footage, at the frozen image on the man in the hoodie, a chill running down my spine, before I refocus on Lang. "It was Newman," I insist. "That's Newman on my security feed. Him being home for the wellness check means nothing. He was here and rushed home, plain and simple."

"What time he was here on the film?"

"A full half hour. That's how bold and fearless he is. He left an hour ago."

"That's a tight ride to Westlake," Lang points out.

"It's a full hour and there's no traffic at this time of night," I argue.

"He'd have to make the drive, which isn't short, and enter his house." He holds up a finger, "Then," he adds, "he'd have to tuck himself into his bed *with* his wife, kiss her or bitch at her, whatever his thing is, and all before the police knocked. His wife would ask questions. She'd be suspicious that he races in the house, into the bed, and the police knock right afterwards."

"Maybe they sleep in separate beds. That's how the Golden State Killer managed to sneak out."

"Or this isn't him," Lang says. "The guy who killed your father is still missing. It could be him."

"He could have killed me that night. He didn't even try. And why would he want to taunt me? He didn't even taunt my father, who put him in jail. This *isn't* him. Why are you even going to him?"

Lang runs a hand through his hair. "This whole Roberts thing. That's what you have in common with Roberts. Your father. And we never got the asshole who killed your father."

"Roberts and I have the Summer case in common. You're letting Roberts be a distraction, and maybe that's exactly what The Poet wanted. What better way to distract law enforcement than making one of our own disappear?"

Daniel steps into the frame of the open door. "Anonymous caller," Daniel announces. "The report came from an anonymous caller. Male."

My gaze shoots to Lang's. "To my point. Just like the call last night. It's the same person."

Daniel motions to the security feed on my computer. "Did you catch him on camera?"

I bristle uncomfortably with what could be seen as a logical observation and question from a member of law enforcement. But he's not law enforcement and I don't know him. At all. It's time for Daniel to mosey on downstairs, and I'm about to say as much, but Lang isn't quite ready for him to go adios. "What I want to know, Daniel," he says, "is how you snagged a security job with that tattoo on your arm. How long you been in a gang?"

There's a barely perceivable stiffening of Daniel's spine.

"Most people aren't cops who know what it means. I got out a long time ago."

"When?" I ask. "Because that particular gang is known for its brutality."

"When I was eighteen, fifteen years ago now. Right after my pops got shot."

"He was in the gang, too," I assume.

"He pulled me in," he confirms, which isn't uncommon. These kids follow their fathers and siblings into a destructive future. "That was in San Antonio," he continues. "After that, I got sent here to Austin to live with my grandma. She whipped my ass into shape."

This all sounds reasonable, but I find myself

pushing for more. "Where's your mother?" I ask.

"She died when I was twelve of an overdose." His tone is flat, his expression unreadable, and I feel the cut of a young child losing his mother.

Lang shows no sympathy. "In other words, you have a sealed juvenile record."

"Look me up, man," Daniel challenges. "I have no record."

"And yet you're a robocop, not a real one?" Lang snaps back.

"My girlfriend's pregnant. This is my second job. I've been at this only a month."

"What's your day job?" I ask.

"Dell tech support." His fingers curl into his palms. "Why do I feel like I'm being questioned for a crime? I was in my uniform, doing my job."

Lang motions to his tattoo. "That gang you're representing on your body there is a slaughterhouse of killers, therefore that tattoo is always going to get you attention."

Daniel's expression tightens and when footsteps sound behind him, he's quick to seize an escape. "I better get back downstairs." He backs away, into the hallway, and Wade steps into my apartment, but I'm still focused on Daniel.

I'm bothered by our exchange with him. But isn't that The Poet's point in standing at my door and at Dave's bedroom window in a hoodie and baseball hat? For me to see monsters in every corner?

No. Not monsters. He wants me to see *him* everywhere.

CHAPTER 56

Three months earlier...

I sit at the end of the bar, in a hole-in-the-wall Mexican restaurant where Captain Jeremy Jazz chit-chats with a pretty blonde waitress half his age. He touches her arm and gives her cleavage a deep, lingering inspection, the kind of inspection a married man should save for his wife. His objectionable behavior doesn't come as a surprise. I've spent what is most of my life watching him sink deeper and deeper into a life of sin to such a degree that it's as if I'm watching my own father.

I sip my drink, a tequila and lime mixture that isn't my normal preference. I rarely deviate from my set structure—there is safety in what I know—but I want everything about this night to be memorable and unique. This is the night that will ensure she blossoms and becomes the magnificent poison rose of judgment that she is destined to become.

As if she heard me whispering her name, the poison rose walks into the restaurant, Detective Samantha Jazz, the future in ways her father can't begin to understand. Her spine is stiff, confrontation in the air, the sins of her father on her tongue.

She crosses the room toward his booth, a beauty: petite with long brown hair and piercing green eyes that have the liberty of disarming or charming. Skills she will find useful throughout her training. She settles into her father's booth, facing me, and I settle in to watch the show.

In *The Merchant of Venice*, Shakespeare wrote, "The sins of the father are to be laid upon the children."

A profound truth. We inherit our parents' sins, but

we decide in which way we allow them to influence our behavior. Samantha has proven her father will drown in the blood of his sins without her. We, she and I, live a destiny meant to protect the sinners that are all of humanity with the prophecies and truths of the great words, and while this is true, there are exceptions to that protection. Anyone who stands between destiny and a Master of the Word such as me, or his protégée, such as Samantha, must be eliminated.

A man slides onto the stool next to me, a beanie on his bald head. I rotate to face the bar and down my drink, sliding him an envelope of cash. My keen side-eye watches as he opens the fold and peers inside, scanning the funds, his thick lips curving. Tonight will be messy for necessary reasons, and I don't do messy. My visitor excels at such things. It's a kismet connection. We have a shared hatred of Jeremy Jazz. Captain Jeremy Jazz put this man in jail for a decade while he kept Samantha in a jail of his making for far too long. The man doesn't speak. He knows what is to be done. He knows what to do after it's over, where to go, how to shelter. He simply stands and exits the restaurant to prepare for what comes later this evening.

Jeremy Jazz has served one necessary purpose in Samantha's life. He's opened his daughter's eyes, which was abundantly necessary. To protect herself, she had to see sin clearly in all the places it hides and pretends to be something it isn't. Sin can pretend to be fragile, sweet, honest, pure, intelligent, and yes, even parental when it is none of those things and yet all of those things.

The bartender refills my glass and I sip my tequila again, savoring the bite of the liquor gliding down my throat and warming my chest. She'll feel the bite, too, tonight, but the burden that is that man will be lifted off her shoulders. She will rise stronger. We will rise stronger.

CHAPTER 57

Wade steps into the apartment and shuts the door. "I talked to patrol. I heard what happened. I don't like the attention this guy is giving you, Sam."

"No fear," Lang says sourly. "The apartment hired a gangbanger to keep an eye on things. And we don't even know if this guy was The Poet."

Irritation bristles and I whirl on Lang. "Oh come on. He stood at Dave's bedroom window last night. You think my father's killer followed me to the murder scene last night?"

Wade is now at the coffee table where he's set his briefcase, holding up his hands in a stop-sign fashion. "Back up. What am I missing?"

Lang's cell phone rings and he murmurs something under his breath before answering the call and walking into the kitchen.

Wade focuses on me. "What is going on?"

"Lang thinks—" My phone starts to buzz and my lips press together. "Of course. Now my cell phone is ringing." I pull it from my pocket to find Tabitha on caller ID. "The office manager. I have to take this." I accept the call. "Yes, Tabitha, what do you have for me?"

"I'm told that the police have cleared the property. I did ask the security company to send out an extra man starting tomorrow night. We're going to get a code on the door, too, but I'm told that won't happen until next week."

"That's all fine. Thank you."

"Okay. What else can I do? Because we want to get this under control. We thought security was the answer. We were wrong."

"Get me the security feed tomorrow morning first thing."

"I will. Absolutely."

We disconnect and I set my phone on the table, and at this point, Wade has removed his jacket to stay awhile. "The building was cleared by patrol," I shout out to Lang.

He leans out of the kitchen. "I know. I just talked to patrol. And what do I have to do to get you to keep beer in the fridge?"

"Bring your own," I mutter, claiming a spot on the couch.

Lang disappears again and I'm pretty ready for him to take himself home for a shower right about now. Wade sits down in the chair next to me. "Catch me up," he says. "Start with what the thorn in Lang's ass is right now, not that there isn't always a thorn in Lang's ass."

"We were having drinks at Dewy's. We got the call from the office manager that someone had reported a strange man at my building. An anonymous caller, which is how we found out about Dave's murder."

"And Lang's pissed he didn't get to finish his drink?"

"And at pretty much everything else," I murmur before I continue. "Patrol did a wellness check on Newman's home right after we found out about my visitor. Newman was there. Lang thinks that means it couldn't have been him at my door."

"He didn't have time to get home," Lang says, walking into the living room with a bottle of wine and three glasses in his hand.

"Was he standing at your door again?" Wade asks. "Because the security feed will time stamp when."

"He was," I confirm, "and I checked the feed. We have him on camera and time stamped. He had time to get home."

"He didn't have time to get home," Lang argues, filling the glasses.

"We've already had this discussion," I say, accepting a glass. "He had a full hour. That's plenty of time to get to Westlake. Lang thinks it's the same guy who killed my father, which makes no sense at all. He's letting Roberts's disappearance mess with his common sense. We have the hoodie guy placed at a Poet murder. That and his own stench. He whored himself out last night and has yet to shower."

Wade looks between us, sips his wine, and then sets his glass down. "Instead of getting in the middle of this fight, why don't I give you two something else to talk about?" He reaches inside his briefcase and produces a file. "I come bearing gifts. I had this done as part of my class today."

I set the wineglass down and scoot to the edge of the couch. "The report or the profile?"

"The report. I set you up to meet with a profiler in San Antonio tomorrow morning."

I purse my lips. "I know why you did that."

"Because you belong there and with us," he says. "Because you love it every time you're involved with the profile team. I also arranged for a couple of techs to meet with you and lend support, but this remains your case."

"Thank you." I accept the file. "Thank you for everything. Did you go through the report?"

"I had my whole class, some of the FBI's finest recruits, go through the file."

I perk up again and even Lang sits up straighter, setting his glass down. "And?" we both ask.

"And," Wade says, "there are hundreds of cases across the United States in the past ten years where a toxin is named as the cause of death, but the type of toxin is not properly documented. However, there

are only six that include bindings of the body to a
chair with some deviation from The Poet's current
methods. Additionally, there are two cases that include bindings of the body and hands with
suffocation with a plastic bag as the cause of death."

The hair on my arms prickles. I was right. He's
killed before. He trained. He practiced. He started
hunting and killing, and he got better at murder.
He got stronger, but his biggest regret will be the
day Roberts disappeared. Because that's the day I
appeared.

CHAPTER 58

My mind is racing a million miles an hour with questions, so many questions. I want to crawl into Wade's mind and into that file and know everything now, but I slow myself down. I remind myself not to get buried in the excess, to focus. I ask one simple, important question to start. "Were poems left?"

Wade gives a shake of his head. "But those types of details are easier discovered by calling the detectives on the targeted cases." He angles closer, his eyes alight with a secret he wants to share. "Ask the next question."

I'm not sure where he's going, but I'm eager to find out. "Were any of the cases in Texas?"

"Two."

Adrenaline surges through me, but I don't allow it to control me any more than I will allow the man in the hoodie and baseball cap to intimidate me. "When?"

"Both in the last six months," he says.

"Where?"

"Brownsville and Houston. Brownsville was the first of the two murders."

My gaze rockets to Lang's. "Brownsville. That's where Martin was trying to meet up with the person selling cyanide on the dark web."

"And Houston is where Roberts suddenly decided to transfer," Lang says, pulling his phone from his pocket. "I'll call Martin and the Brownsville and Houston PDs now. Maybe I'll get lucky and catch the right detectives working late." He's all action now and with good reason. We're getting close to him. We all feel it.

I turn my attention back to Wade. "What about the man with the hoodie? Were there sightings linked to any cases?"

"We're going to need to rerun the report to get that information."

"Right. Okay. Yes. I didn't give you that information when you were running the report." I shrug out of my jacket and kick off my heels. "There's suddenly a lot to do." I give Wade a pointed look. "And just so you know, I'm perfectly fine with you staying over and working all night."

He laughs, a deep, warm laugh, the kind of laugh that disarms humans and killers alike. I like that laugh, but even more so, the savvy skills hidden beneath it. "Good to know," he says, "especially since I'd already assumed as much. I'll order food."

"Perfect." I stand up, walk around the table, and head up the stairs to the attic, then flip the light on as I enter a compact room with an angled ceiling. The realtor pitched this space as a giant closet or small bedroom minus a window. I've since learned that this "closet" is the best place for photos of dead bodies and crime scene data if I plan to have guests. Not that I have many of those who aren't jaded members of law enforcement. I did at one point, back a few years ago when I tried a dating app. Traffic ticket advice and talking about episodes of *CSI* were far less appealing than solving crimes.

I've kept the space basic by necessity of size, with nothing but a built-in pale wooden desk against the far wall and a giant cushioned hammock couch framed by two simple side tables. That hammock was hell for Lang to get up here because he's so big and the room is so small.

My eyes catch on a record player on the desk. It triggers something in me, and I walk around the hammock to get a closer look. Next to the player is a collection of jazz albums I've traded back and forth with my grandfather for years. It's a special thing we've done, as granddaughter and grandfather and best friends. A pinch of guilt finds my chest. I haven't been to see him at the nursing home since Dad died, but he doesn't know; not that his son is gone or that I haven't visited. He doesn't remember much of anything, and that's hard to swallow. A different kind of pinch finds its way to my chest this time: pain and loss. I lost him before I lost my father.

I grab one of the albums, Chet Baker in Tokyo, one of his favorites. He loves jazz, and not because of our last name, which he's always thought was a fun gift passed down through the generations. A name I was blessed with because he adopted my father when he was ten. I fade back in time, sitting in Grandpa's den, otherwise known as his "jazz room."

"My dear Samantha," he'd say. "Jazz and poetry speak to the soul in the same deep and profound way as do many of the great literary works, of course." He'd held up a glass of whiskey and added, "But jazz, poetry, and good whiskey are magic together." Something stirs in my mind about the case with this memory, something I try to reach out and grab but can't quite manage.

Footsteps sound behind me, and I tuck that away in that place where I ping-pong things until they become more accessible. I set the album down and turn as Wade joins me and says, "I ordered from that late-night taco place you like."

"Perfect," I say, walking to the wall of whiteboards and corkboards, and use an eraser to wipe away notes I had left from a prior case Lang and I had worked a few weeks back. I glance at Wade over my shoulder. "Can you ask Lang to grab our case file from my briefcase on the way up?"

Lang pokes his head in the door. "I heard. I'll grab it." He points at Wade. "You got me ten tacos, right?"

"Yes, Lang," Wade replies heavily. "I got you ten tacos, though no normal human can eat ten tacos."

"Well, there you go." He flexes his muscle and taps it. "Superman." He drops his arm. "The tacos are small. I am big." He disappears.

I return to wiping the board, and then grab a pen and write three columns: *Austin, Houston, Brownsville.* Then I move on to another column: *Types of poison.* A thought occurs to me and I turn to Wade. "Did the two victims have a poetry or academic connection that the report found?"

Lang steps into the room with the file in his hand. "Just in time. I'm waiting for that answer as well."

"And a shower," I say, turning to eye his disheveled appearance. "Seriously, after we eat you have to go home and shower and change."

He sniffs his underarm and shrugs. "I keep clothes in the car. I'll use your shower." He motions to Wade. "Back to the question."

"The Brownsville victim was a female veterinarian, well established in her small city. The Houston victim was male and a science instructor at UT."

"I can see Summer and the instructor starting to form a victim profile," Lang says, sitting down on the floor against the wall, near the stairs. In other words, the closest spot to get to the food first. "He was an intellectual like Summer, but a vet? I guess technically that could be intellectual. Maybe they have a college connection?" He lifts a finger. "Dave was a medical student."

"Dave was a barista who took my order and made offensive remarks about poetry," I argue. "That's our victim profile. Each of these people somehow disrespected poetry in his presence." I wave my eraser between them. "Why do I believe this? I'll tell you. Aside from my obvious firsthand experience with Dave's disparaging remark about poetry, Summer had the poetry books for the reading stored under the seats. One of my interviewees told me the entire reading was like being in church. That made me think. The poetry book was like a bible to The Poet. Summer disrespected the bible."

"That seems like a stretch," Lang says.

"It doesn't," I argue. "It's not. He's had an encounter with each of these people. We have to locate the right camera feeds and we'll find him."

"Don't count on much in Brownsville outside of the border areas," Wade says. "There isn't much there but mom-and-pop shops. Face-to-face interviews will be critical."

"I already talked to Martin," Lang says. "He's all in to head to Houston and Brownsville tomorrow with me." I open my mouth to argue and Lang shuts me down. "You're going to San Antonio tomorrow. And Dave's murder is still fresh, the most critical for working a case. You work the present-day crimes. I'll come at this from behind."

I hesitate, fighting my deep-rooted control freak need to go along with him, but I finally concede with a short nod that he's right. I need to stay.

"On another note," Wade says. "There are three of the older cases that caught my eye, which I want you to look at. One man and one woman. They were all suffocated with a plastic bag and tied to a chair. Their hands, feet, and body were bound, but the cases are old enough and similar enough to warrant attention."

"Where were they and when?"

"2016 and 2017, almost exactly one year apart in

New York City, but the interesting part is this." He stands up and walks to the desk, flipping open the file he'd given me and removing something from inside. He then walks to the corkboard to pin two photos for our review. Both victims have a giant *U* carved into their chests.

CHAPTER 59

The three of us stand in front of the pictures pinned to the board, pictures of a naked man and a woman, each with a *U* carved in their chests. The woman appears Caucasian. The man Hispanic. The bags over their heads make little else obvious. The *U* on each is drawn in a perfect, thin line that oozed blood all over the bodies and dripped to the floor. It feels too dirty to be the same killer and yet maybe that's the point. It's too dirty. Trial and error. He learned from his mistakes.

"This doesn't feel like the same guy at all," Lang says.

"Unless it is," I reply.

"The Poet is clean, neat."

"So are the lines of that *U*. Impeccable, even. He wasn't always the killer he is now. That's my theory and I'm sticking with it." I glance at Wade. "Do we know what was used to carve the *U*s?"

"They never found a tool of any sort."

"Where did the bags come from?"

"They're manufactured in Canada and used to freeze dry foods. Without a suspect, that didn't get investigators far. And before you ask, they never had a solid lead."

"The timing sounds like a convention that comes to town the same time of year every year," Lang suggests.

I walk to the board and start a list:

•Did anyone in Newman's house buy those bags?

•Was Newman in New York on the dates of the murders?

•Was there a poetry or literary convention on

those dates?

•What conventions were in town, in general, those weeks?

•Do the suspects have any connection to our local suspects?

•What does the U mean?

Wade pins a list of words on the board. "The computer and my class made a list of potential meanings."

I step back and read the list:

Useless
User
Unanimous
Unknown
Undone
Unworthy
Ugly
Ulcer
Unacceptable

The list goes on and on. Lang steps closer and begins to read. "Holy hell," he mumbles. "I didn't know there were so many words that start with *U*."

I return to the word "unworthy" and think of a master and a god, the way I believe The Poet sees himself, and it feels right. I circle it. A poem by Roald Dahl called "The Three Little Pigs" comes to my mind and I begin quoting a small portion of what is a rather long work:

"The Wolf said, 'Okay, here we go!'

He then began to blow and blow. The little pig began to squeal.

He cried, 'Oh Wolf, you've had one meal! Why can't we talk and make a deal?'

The Wolf replied, 'Not on your nelly!' And soon the pig was in his belly."

I stop speaking and I can feel Wade and Lang looking at me, waiting for me to explain what feels obvious.

Seconds tick by in which I wait for them to understand, and finally Lang loses patience. "What the hell was that?"

Wade then breaks his silence. "What are you telling us?"

"Yeah," Lang snaps. "Cut through the poetry bullshit that means something only to you and maybe The Poet."

"That once he judges them, they can't win back his good graces. They can't feed him good words to make up for the bad. He's already decided they must die. They're unworthy."

CHAPTER 60

Lang, Wade, and I spend hours dissecting pieces of the case, calling everyone we can call despite the late hour, and pushing for answers and ways to catch The Poet. Lang and Martin set up flights that leave at noon. Somewhere in there, we eat tacos and listen to jazz while I try to capture whatever thought is fluttering around in my mind, and generally turn my wall into a collage of paper.

At some point, we divide and conquer. Wade claims the hammock, where he's looking through our two local cases, double-checking us, seeing if he can find things we've missed, which we welcome.

Lang is sitting on the floor, leaning on the desk with a pad of sticky notes, working through who he needs to see where tomorrow and what leads to follow up on. I claim the floor in front of the crime wall, looking through the FBI report and adding to my list of questions. For a good hour, I keep Chuck on the phone, going through all the conventions we can. After which, my MacBook is beside me, and I dictate what is certain to be a lengthy list of additional notes to be waiting for him when he arrives at work tomorrow. At some point, my back hurts, my eyes hurt, and my mind is frustrated. I lie back and stare up at the ceiling fan someone turned on. Maybe it was me. I'm too tired to remember. I shut my eyes for just a few seconds, the temptation of sleep overwhelming.

My eyes pop open, and I stare at the light fixture directly above me, a low glow of light slowly widening my irises. The smell of tacos torments my nostrils while the hard floor is no gentler on my back. There is also a low buzzing sound frustrating my ears.

I sit up and I'm staring at the crime scene wall. Groaning, I twist around to my hands and knees to find Wade asleep sitting up in the hammock, head drooping sideways to the cushion. Lang is passed out on the floor with papers all around him, still by the desk. And my phone, which stopped ringing and started again, is sitting on that desk. Don't ask me how it got there or how long we've all been asleep. I don't even have a window as a timeline guide.

Pushing to my feet, I run my hand through my hair and stumble forward, leaning over Lang to grab my phone. I fight a groan at the number and time, which is only six a.m. The drama I'd known would come this morning has arrived. "Morning, Captain."

Lang's eyes pop open with my voice and he sits up. "Shit," he mutters, and there's a sticky note stuck to his forehead that has some random address on it.

"My office," the captain snaps. "Eight a.m."

"I'm supposed to meet with an FBI profiler in San Antonio this morning."

"Now you're meeting me."

"We have a lead on four connected murders, Captain. There may be more. Lang is going to fly out to Houston and—"

"My office. Eight a.m." He hangs up.

At this point, Wade is standing up, his hair a tousled mess, his sleeves rolled to his elbows, hands on his hips. "What just happened?"

Lang pushes to his feet, his hair a disaster standing on end. Sometimes I do think he's my real soul mate. "She just got called into the firing squad," he says, running a hand over his two-day stubble and settling his hands on his hips as well. It must be the manly morning thing to do. "I'm going with you to see the captain," he offers. "I'm not letting you take the fall for confronting Newman's wife on your own."

"Get on a plane and go solve this crime," I say. "I

can slay the dragon that is Captain Moore." I glance at Wade. "My meetings in San Antonio—"

"I'll connect you with the profiler by phone and get the techs working on everything we put together last night." He glances at his watch as if he's not certain of that statement. "Right. Last night. You have an open invitation to come to San Antonio and meet the resources that are yours and Lang's to use. And I'll get them started researching the toxins on the cases that don't have them fully identified. If we can find another cyanide case for you, we will. We're close to what could be a much more notorious serial killer than we first thought. Captain Moore is going to hear what you have to say."

"It's what I don't have to say that worries me. I have no proof that Newman is our guy. None. Zero. Nothing. I need something to take to him and the DA's office that at least gets us a warrant."

"Tell him if he blows off Newman and he turns out to have victims across years and states, he'll lose his job."

"Right. I'll be sure to threaten my boss's job."

Lang snorts. "Yeah, good luck with that one." He motions to the door. "I'm headed out. I should probably go home and shower."

"You think?" I ask, and he winks before heading down the stairs.

Wade steps closer. "You could just come to work for the FBI, where the resources are plentiful and the assholes—"

"Are not?"

He grins. "Better looking."

I groan and turn for the stairs. Half an hour later, he's showered and headed for the door, with a promise to call me the minute he receives the travel report on Newman. I lock up, and walk to the pantry then open the door, my eyes falling on the box of

Frosted Flakes, my grandfather's favorite. My heart squeezes and I grab the box, fill a bowl with cereal and milk, and head back upstairs.

I ignore the excess of taco smells, sit down at the desk, and put that favorite album of my grandfather's on the record player. I start eating my cereal and searching my mind for what it wanted to tell me last night but did not. When my cereal is gone, I'm no closer to the answer. No wonder of course, considering the beating I'm about to take from the captain.

Maybe it's time to go see my grandfather. He has moments of clarity even if he doesn't remember them later. And he's far more a master of poetry than I am.

CHAPTER 61

I swing by my apartment office with the intent of grabbing the security feed of my night stalker before heading to the station, but they aren't open yet. Any other time, I'd run across the street for coffee and try again, but that's not going to happen now. It *will* happen, though. It absolutely will. He will not frighten me away from life or my own neighborhood. It still needs to happen, just at a time when I can deal with the emotional baggage that Dave being dead will inevitably stir.

With that in mind, I head to my car, and once I'm on the road, I swing by a Starbucks drive-thru. My order includes the green tea drink the captain drinks and two venti skinny white mochas for Chuck and me. While waiting for my turn at the window, I text Tabitha and Chuck to coordinate the security feed pickup.

Once I'm at the station, I stop by the conference room before heading to the firing squad, where I find Chuck and everyone on our team but Lang and Jackson. I tilt my head toward the door and Chuck stands, looking remarkably good considering he's probably slept about as well as I did on the floor of my giant attic. We pause in the hallway where I motion to the tray and his coffee.

"Thank you, Lord and Jazz," he says, grabbing his cup. "I need this badly."

I get rid of the tray and hold onto my cup and the captain's.

Chuck sips from his and crinkles his nose. "Is this skinny? Are we on a diet and I didn't know it?" He holds up a hand. "Not that I don't appreciate the caffeine immensely. I do."

"Extra fat next time. Promise. I save my calories for chocolate. I thought you might as well. You have more room for chocolate now." I switch gears. "I'm about to go in and get destroyed by the captain. Do you have anything to save me in there?"

"I'm trying, Jazz. I really am. I've bombed on any reason Newman's job or his wife's had them go to conventions in New York City. If we had any educational or criminal law events, I could go wide and look for additional suspects as well that might link to us here, but I got nothing."

"What about hobbies that might bring either to an annual convention?"

"I'm already looking into that angle. I'm also looking beyond the conventional angle to family or old friends with an annual get-together, things to that effect. That means going to the social media of anyone connected to them to try to piece it together. Because even if he didn't fly to New York, he could have driven. And we won't have warrants to look at his bank statements this early."

"Right." I sip my coffee. "Keep doing the great job you're doing. Where is Jackson, by the way?"

"Picking up the security feed from your office, and he's going to hit up anyone who had an angle on your place last night for camera feed."

"You really are Superman. I'd tell you I'd get you a raise, but I probably should make sure I keep my job first."

"That bad?" He eyes the extra cup in my hand. "Pretty bad."

"Yep. More soon." I point to my bag. "Can you take this?"

He grabs it eagerly and I move away from him, heading to the captain's office, arriving with only a few minutes to spare according to the clock in the hallway just outside his office.

I toss my cup in a nearby trash can and then step inside his open door to find him sitting behind his desk. He's not wearing a suit jacket, but his shirt is crisp and white. His tie a bright blue. His overall appearance is like a sword sharpened for war with me his target, but I've never let a battle send me running. I'm not going to start now.

Using my foot, I shut the door and cross to stand in front of his desk. "I brought you your favorite green tea." I set his cup in front of him. He stares at it and then lifts a steely, quite brutal stare at me before he picks up the tea.

"Tea won't save you." It *does* tempt the taste buds, though. He gulps a big drink. "At least you got this right," he mutters, setting his tea down while he stands, towering over me, which I'm sure is the whole idea. "What the hell were you thinking?" he demands, and I can almost imagine the wind blowing through my hair with the force of his bellow.

"I was—"

"Why didn't you warn me? I woke up to the mayor shouting in my ear."

"The man—"

"I know the man was back at your door. Chuck and Lang both told me. You should have told me. I should have gotten a call."

My defenses bristle. "Is that where we are now, Captain? I have to report every step of my investigations?"

"Since you can't follow a simple order, yes. I told you to call Newman Smith's wife. I told you—"

"We needed to shake her up enough to get her to turn on him. She was scared, Captain. She knows he's a problem."

"A detective showing up at your door is scary," he blasts back. "You think that wins her over?"

"He's going to kill again and quickly. I don't want that blood on my hands. Do you?"

"You're pushing your luck, Detective. I asked Lang this question and I'll ask you now. Can you connect Newman Smith to any of these cases?"

"I need a day or two."

"I told you, work the case around Newman."

Anger burns a hot spot in my chest and loosens my tongue. "Safe and slow for everyone but his next victim, right, Captain? Maybe the FBI needs to take over."

"Throwing around your FBI boyfriend, are you?"

"He's not my boyfriend."

"Right. He tried to recruit you. It seems you'd like to be there working for him now. Maybe you *need* to be working for him and not me."

I physically flinch and bite back the spew of words I'll regret, but they bubble in the back of my throat. I need air before they bubble to the tip of my tongue. I turn away and walk to the door, but the minute my hand is on the knob, he barks, "Do not open that door."

The spew begins. I whirl on him. "I tried to leave and get into IA, but you wouldn't let me."

"That was an emotional decision you would have regretted. You've let your father hold you back and dictate your damn life. Why?"

I'm back in front of his desk. I'm suddenly back in the department-mandated shrink's office after my father's murder, when she'd asked me that same question. In a weak moment, I'd blurted out a truth I didn't even know existed: *I needed to understand him. I needed to find the good in him.*

I found good in all the criminals he put away and people he saved, but I found just as much bad in the gray he allowed to blacken his soul. I never found that understanding. But none of this is the captain's business, and that he brings this up now is manipulation of the worst kind with motivation I'm not going to analyze. He's not my concern. The Poet's past and future victims are.

I straighten my spine, and he no longer looks as big as he did minutes ago, not with my proverbial fists drawn. "Roberts resigned by phone to you. He applied to the Houston captain by phone and email. What do you think happened to him?"

"Roberts disappearing doesn't fit your killer's playbook. He poses them, naked and tied to a chair, with a poem in their mouths."

"Roberts wasn't one of the intended targets. He was a nuisance he had to get out of the way."

"You don't know that."

"I know it. I feel it. I have the highest solve rate of the department and one of the highest solve rates in the country. It always starts here." I ball my fist over my gut. "Always."

"Feelings don't convict criminals."

"No, people do. I do. We have the ViCAP report in from the FBI, thanks to Wade, who isn't just some boy toy and you know it. That report, and his team, found four additional cases we're working to link to the ones here. But you have to know that. You talked to Lang. What if it's Newman? What if he killed one of our own? Give me a day or two to do what I need to get warrants. What happens when the press gets this, Captain? A serial killer headline won't be kind to our city. Wouldn't you and the mayor rather catch him before that happens, and tell the city he's in custody?"

His lips tighten. His entire expression tightens. "If you get your warrant and find nothing, both of us might be begging your boyfriend for a job when the mayor is done with us. If your Poet kills again, and we did nothing, we both might be begging your boyfriend for a job. In other words, get this bastard now. And get out of my office and do it now."

I don't need to be told twice. I get out of his office.

CHAPTER 62

I walk toward the conference room with my cell phone already in hand, tabbing through numbers to locate the one for the ADA on the Summer case, who's about to inherit a second case and me yet again.

He answers on the first ring. "Detective Jazz. I heard you're taking over the Summer case."

"It's not one case anymore. We have another murder with the same characteristics. Thanks to some FBI support, we believe we have connected cases in two different states over a number of years." I pause just outside the conference room. "I need to see you today."

"How many cases are we talking about?"

"Two in New York. One in Houston. One in Brownsville where Newman grew up. Two here where he lives now."

"Where he grew up and lives is circumstantial evidence."

"Six murders now if you count Roberts. He's missing."

"Holy hell. Roberts is missing?"

"Yes. Roberts is missing."

I can almost hear him thinking. "Okay. Okay. You have my attention. I don't even know when I can talk. I'm walking into court. I can't promise what time I'm going to be free. I'll have my assistant call you. It may be six or after."

"Name the time, I'll be there."

"See you soon, Detective Jazz." He disconnects.

I slide my phone back into my jacket and enter the conference room. "I meet with the ADA this evening. We have until then to get me something to support a warrant."

Seconds tick by in which the room is silent, eight sets of eyes staring at me. Chuck stands up and claps. "Let's go, people." The room erupts into action.

I step out of the room and dial Lang.

"What happened?" he asks.

"You couldn't warn me that you talked to him?"

"I guess it went like shit?"

"He basically said we're damned if we do and damned if we don't. I have a meeting with the ADA tonight. Get me something to use."

"We're on the ground by one thirty. A detective from the Brownsville PD is picking us up at the airport. Anything on the travel report?"

"Nothing, and no convention connection for Newman and the travel locations and dates of the murders."

An announcement sounds over his phone. "I gotta go. I'll call you when I'm on the ground." He disconnects.

I walk back toward the conference room to have Jackson meet me at the door. "I grabbed the coffee shop security feed again, too," he says. "They're more than a little eager to help. I figured this killer is arrogant enough to walk right back in to the place where he chose a victim. I thought maybe we'd catch him with a hat or hoodie."

He's not picking away at my Spidey senses today, which is always a good thing. And he's right. The Poet is arrogant enough to go right back to that coffee shop. "Good idea. Do me a favor and check out the security guard that was at my place last night, too, will you?"

"Of course. You want me to get started on the review of the security feed?"

"No. I'll handle it." My cell phone rings. "Just set

it on the table. I'll be right there." I grab my phone again and rotate away from him to find Wade calling.

Stepping into Chuck's cubicle, I answer. "Tell me something good."

"He did fly to New York City, but not on the dates of the murders."

"Close?"

"He was there within months of the first murder," he says. "No Houston or Brownsville travel, but he's close enough to drive to those. New York would be a long trip. Find a way to question the wife about the travel."

"This from the man who knew I was getting chewed out for questioning the wife today?"

"Obviously you survived," he says, "and I knew you would."

"Can you send me the report?"

"Already in your email. And I have our tech team looking for traffic camera proof he drove to any of the places in question. That's a big order, but we're trying."

"Thank you, Wade."

"Thank me by seriously considering the FBI again. You belong here, Sam, and before you push back, I've got my class to get back to anyway. I have to go, but the name and number of the profiler I recruited to help you out is in your email, too. You also have contact information for the lead tech I have helping out. Gotta run."

He disconnects, and I am ready to beat my head against the desk. I have murders. I have a killer. I have no proof. My mind goes back to my grandfather, and I'm not sure why it's pulling me to him. I need to go see him. I stand up and then immediately lean forward, hands on the desk, with the punch of an idea. But I can't go.

What if I lead The Poet to him and The Poet doesn't see him as worthy?

CHAPTER 63

The profiler is Judy Garland.

For real.

Her parents loved the movie star Judy Garland and named their daughter Judy. No wonder she chose to spend her days hunting killers. She needed to be bigger than the name. I know Judy well. I hide out at my desk for our talk, which is an easy one. She was one of my mentors in profiling, and it doesn't take long on the phone with her before we're batting things back and forth and creating a solid profile that ultimately matches mine with a bit more detail.

"You didn't need me," she says. "Why am I on the phone with you?"

"A wise man once told me you're never too good for a second opinion." That wise man was also a foolish man, but I leave that part out. He was my father.

Once I'm done with Judy, I head into the conference room and join the team, where I set up my computer and begin scanning the security footage. In the meantime, half the team is working on Newman and the other half opening the door to other suspects. Roberts, Summer, and Gaines shared the same cable company. They all had DIRECTV. The rabbit hole of information could drag me under, but I'm not tempted. I remain focused. The security feed at my building is useless.

I pull up the coffee bar footage for first thing this morning, and I'm about ten minutes in from the time they opened the doors when I freeze-frame on a shot of a tall man walking in, wearing a hoodie and a baseball hat. The same hoodie and baseball hat my stalker had been wearing in the film by my door. It's a bold move on his part, returning to the place where he'd chosen a victim. It's also a stupid mistake. The barista might remember him. The camera might catch his face. His mistake will be our gain.

My heart thunders in my chest as I push play again. He walks to the back of the room, where the condiments station sits, grabs something and then turns to leave, his chin low, his hat lower, his hoodie pulled over it. I can't see his face. "Damn it!"

Eyes turn on me with my unexpected outburst and I motion to Jackson. He stands and hurries over. I rewind and play the feed. "Holy shit," he murmurs, and Chuck is quick to join us.

I eye Officer Jackson. "Go and see if anyone remembers him, please."

"On my way."

He heads out of the room, and Chuck and I share a look. We know he isn't going to come back with what we want, but we have to try.

My cell phone rings and it's Lang. I answer. "Please tell me something good."

"The crime scene photos for the local victim, the female veterinarian, look identical. The use of a chair. Tying the victim up with bindings from her curtains. The way the ties are positioned. And once again, there was no DNA found."

"What about the drug that killed her?"

"The city had people dropping dead from a synthetic drug at the time. It read a lot like cyanide does postmortem. It looks to me that the testing wasn't properly conducted. We can't question the ME. He's dead."

"How did he die?"

"Car accident. And it gets worse."

I pinch the bridge of my nose. "I almost don't want to know."

"The lead we had on the cyanide dried up. Martin's

contact is deleted off the dark web and MIA."

"Jesus, Lang."

"I know. We're working the case. We're backing into it. We'll find something."

"You better. Right now, all I have to give the DA's office is Newman's early childhood in Brownsville."

We disconnect and Chuck is back on the opposite side of the table talking to someone on the landline. "Yes. She's right here."

"Me?" I whisper.

He nods and covers the receiver. "Newman Smith's wife."

My eyes go wide and I stand up, reaching over the table to grab the phone. "Mrs. Smith."

"I want to talk," she says.

"I'd like that. Can you come to the station?"

"No." Her voice is high, sharp. "No. I can't. No."

"When and where?"

"Lola Savannah coffee shop off Bee Caves Road. It's next to my yoga studio. Six o'clock."

"I'll be there."

"Okay." She hangs up.

CHAPTER 64

You can almost feel the sigh of relief from multiple directions after that call from Becky Smith. The captain, Lang, our entire team feel like we're about to get a break in this case. Evan is certainly pleased, and eager to be the ADA who closes a case involving a serial killer who happens to be a prominent member of society, so much so that he agrees to meet me for eight-thirty drinks. The mayor won't be happy to look dirty with him as a donor, but we can't please everyone.

I arrive at the coffee shop, a cute, artsy spot like so many places in Austin, fifteen minutes early. With time on my hands, I order my second skinny white mocha of the day. My mug with designer foam on top and I settle at a table, under a ceiling decorated with a giant canvas of coffee. My location is by a window, to view the parking lot.

Lang calls me about the time I've placed the first sweet sip of coffee and foam on my lips and tongue. Of course. Lang has perfect timing. I shorten the savoring moment, set my cup down, and answer the call. "Yes, oh great one?"

"I am pretty great, aren't I?"

"Did you call me to talk about yourself?" I ask. "Or do you have another, less vain purpose?"

"While I do believe I'm an excellent subject of conversation, I deliver the gift of information." His tone turns serious. "The vet's name was Carrie Ludwig. She went to A&M for her veterinary training but did part of her undergraduate and pre-vet program at UT Austin. Per her mother, that was because she hadn't decided to become a vet at that point, and she'd dreamed of going to school in Austin. She wanted out of the small-town mentality, which is where A&M took her again."

"Obviously she got over that and went to A&M and back to Brownsville."

"Obviously," he agrees. "And yes, I already have Chuck trying to find out if she was in any of Newman's classes."

"Sometimes, like right now, when you're two steps ahead of my questions, I think I love you, Lang."

He snorts. "For about thirty seconds before you want to kill me again, but whatever. Aren't you about to have your meeting with Becky?"

"I am." I glance at the time on my watch. "She's supposed to have already been here." My phone beeps and I glance at the number. "That's Chuck. Please tell me she didn't cancel. I'll call you back." I click over to Chuck. "What's up?" I ask.

"She cancelled with no explanation given. It was a short, fast hang-up."

"Text me her cell number."

"On its way."

When the text hits my messages, I punch the number and call Becky. She doesn't answer. I retry. I don't leave a message; Newman might hear. My face tilts skyward, frustration rippling through me. Why? Why? Why? I sip my coffee and try Becky again. Maybe Newman questioned her delay coming home.

A few minutes later, I've gotten my coffee poured into a to-go cup and I've stopped dialing Becky over and over. I'm worried about her safety. I head to my car to swing by her house. Once I'm on the road, I dial Chuck. "Where is Newman now? Find out." I hang up and continue my drive.

I've just turned onto Bee Caves Road, which is a short path to the Smiths' house when Chuck calls back.

"He's at home with his wife. She just pulled into the garage."

My cell phone rings again. "Please let that be her. I'll call you back." I eye my caller ID and sure enough, it's her. My heart punches at my chest and I punch the answer button. "Mrs. Smith?"

"I need you to leave us alone. That's what I wanted to tell you. Leave us alone. I don't want to talk to you."

"You called and said you did."

"That's what I'm telling you. This is hard enough on my kids. Leave us alone. He didn't kill anyone."

She hangs up.

He got to her.

And I'm back to having nothing but a scared wife and a loose Brownsville connection to give Evan during our meeting tonight.

CHAPTER 65

While Detective Jazz runs around chasing her tail, I move my late evening work away from the wife and kids, seeking the sanctuary of the library across from my office. At this hour, the recently remodeled massive glass complex is all but dead, the silence a welcome calm for my work. I settle into a small room on an upper level in one of several leather seats, surrounded by the great literary works. I pull out my MacBook and an egg salad sandwich from a nearby ThunderCloud Sub shop and take a big bite, savoring the flavors: red onion, tomato, and just the right amount of thinly shredded lettuce. ThunderCloud understands the gospel of doing things right. Too few do.

I open my bottle of water and tip it back, taking a long, thirsty drink, and then halfway into my meal, I key my computer to life. My messenger pops up in the corner with a note from the wifey: *Love you. Wish you didn't have to work late. Neal drew you a picture at school today and Tessa has a flower to show you.*

I type an automatic reply: *Love you, too. Kiss them goodnight for me. Tell them I'll make pancakes in the morning.*

That woman slows me down even when I want to speed up, a fact that I didn't appreciate at one point, but I do now. Speed is not always the smartest move, though I'm certainly skilled enough to operate at whatever pace I see fit at this point. But she and the kids are necessary.

Obligation complete, and with a rush of anticipation-driven adrenaline, I search the news for any hint of my recent kill, somewhat disappointed that it's not reported beyond a basic report on crimes for the week. There was a time when that would have been a relief, but that was during my training when I prepared to sit on the throne as master and judge. I'm seated now, and I plan to make a statement. It's time for respect to be given where deserved.

One of the rather elderly librarians passes by with a cart full of books for the daily restock, and I wait patiently for one of the works that is due back today. That work is why I'm here today. A slow-moving hour passes in which I toss my trash, finish off my water, and contemplate how two so obviously connected judgments have been kept quiet. But that won't last, because I'm not done. My duty will never be done.

Finally, the librarian moves along, and I walk to the shelf and pull the book I'm looking for: *The Annotated Waste Land with Eliot's Contemporary Prose: Second Edition.* Just holding it stirs a deep sense of value in me. And power. This book grants me power.

I walk back to my table and slide my MacBook aside, setting the book down in front of me and running an appreciative hand over the work of the late T.S. Eliot. The original poem was published in 1922, a masterpiece that dove deeply into the aftermath of World War I. To the few of us who truly speak the word, it also set a framework for preventing such a tragedy again. In five sections, it touches on war, trauma, disillusion, and death. In the final chapter, Eliot references three key components: Datta, Dayadhvam, and Damyata. These meanings translate to a demand to "Give, Sympathize, and Control." This summarization is as magical as the book. It's saying that these concepts navigate our world. Anyone beneath a master who is drawn to this book is drawn to it for a reason: to be judged and controlled before they destroy the balance of peace.

I draw in a deep breath, filling my chest fully, and flip open the book to the nostalgic, optional signature card the new library uses, not surprised when this reader has chosen to sign her name. I already know her name, of course. I've hacked the library's computer system. Ava Lloyd. Air trickles from my lips. I shut the book and stand up, walking back to the shelf, where I carefully replace it. I then return to my table and slide my MacBook inside my briefcase.

I don't have to look up Ava's address. I already know where she lives. I've already been watching her. I stand up to leave. Duty calls for both me and Detective Jazz.

CHAPTER 66

I'm afraid for Becky Smith, and for that reason I drive to her house, with no plan once I arrive, aside from confirming her safety. How I'll go about that, I don't know. Fortunately, the coffee shop is a short drive from her home, and it's not long before I'm idling in front of the park again with the house in view. I'm sitting there, trying to decide what comes next, when my cell phone rings. I grab it from my pocket to find Wade calling.

"How'd the meeting with Newman's wife go?" he says.

"It didn't. She chickened out."

"Well, that sucks, but you got her to call. You know how this works. You know sometimes you have to earn that real reveal."

"I just hope he didn't find out and she ends up dead because of me."

"He won't kill his cover story." He says this quickly and confidently, the voice of reason and experience saying what I know, but I'm afraid to believe. "He's proven to be smarter than that," he adds. "You know this. Don't let yourself lose focus."

Focus.

That's exactly right. I have to focus and rely on facts and training. I got this.

"Listen," he continues, "a case I had go cold on me a few months back just blew up. I'm going to have to stay here tonight. You want to stay at my place?"

"Do I want to hide from The Poet at your place? No, I don't, but thank you for offering anyway."

"If you were someone else, I'd have about ten

things to say right now, but you're not. So I won't. Be careful."

"Always."

We disconnect, and I'm relieved that Wade and Lang are out of town. That makes them out of the reach of The Poet. Newman's garage door opens, and he walks out to the driveway and then turns toward me, staring at my car. Crap. Crap. Crap. My cell phone rings and I grab it to find the captain calling. Crap all over again. I answer. "Captain."

"Leave his house now."

"Captain—"

"*Now*. His attorney has proof you called his wife eight times in a row tonight. He's filing a restraining order in the morning."

"I called because I was afraid for her, which is why—"

"Leave. I will not tell you again."

I grind my teeth and place my car in drive, but my foot remains on the brake. "I'm worried about her."

"Detective Jazz," he warns.

My lips press together. "I'm leaving."

"Good. You keep your distance, and that includes your team, unless you get that warrant from the DA. *Stay away*."

Anger burns a hot spot in my chest. "But he can stand at my door every night?"

"You can't prove it. And it's not me you have to convince at this point. It's the DA's office." He hangs up.

My gaze lifts across my dash to where Newman stands at the end of his driveway, daring me to get myself arrested. I won't take that bait. I hit the accelerator and drive past the monster and his house, but it's all I can do to keep driving.

CHAPTER 67

I call Lang on my way back downtown, where I'm going to meet with the ADA. "Did you hear?" he asks.

"I just hung up with the captain. Do you think she set you up?"

I don't even have to consider my answer. There's a reason I tried to confirm her safety. "No. She's scared. I heard it in her voice. I think she got busted and saved herself. Tell me you have something to take this bastard down."

"Nothing new. I tried to meet with Newman's foster parents, but they had no interest in talking to me. I mean, slammed the door in my face. Like they were scared. The foster kid who disappeared is a cold case. I'm bringing the file back with me. Other than that, I'm meeting with the ME on the local Brownsville cases in the morning and then flying out to Houston."

"In other words, we're depending on little old me, the one with the stalker, who is now labeled a stalker by her stalker, to win over the ADA. I don't think even Mr. Rogers would say it's a beautiful day in the neighborhood."

"You can do it," he says. "Go tiger."

"You are not a cheerleader, nor do I want to imagine you in a skirt."

"But I have cute knees."

"I'm hanging up."

I disconnect as thunder rumbles overhead, and "Zach the Flash," the local weatherman, predicts rain. The man spends too much time picking the funky ties he wears rather than offering advanced notice. The only positive about rain is that murder rates go down during downpours. Hopefully, it buys me a night without a visit from The Poet.

A few minutes later, I'm parked at a meter close to the door of the Cru wine bar, an elegant, quiet spot that plays soft piano music and allows conversation. I enter the bar, which is set up with clusters of wooden tables and an overabundance of dangling lights. The hostess greets me, but I've already spied Evan at a corner table by the window. He stands, and I motion in his direction, letting the hostess know I'm on my way there.

Evan remains on his feet, awaiting my approach, a man many call the proverbial tall, dark, and good-looking in an expensive gray suit and red tie. A suit over his pay grade, and I know for a fact that he doesn't come from money. Every decision he makes is about money, though, about his future and where the case can lead him. Therefore, every word I speak has to consider his motivation.

I arrive at the table and Evan offers me his hand. I'm not a big handshaker. I don't like germs. I blame my mother and her medical background. And it's really not that odd in my job. Gloves are a necessity in my line of work. That said, when you deal with the DA's office, you play the game. I shake his hand, and he motions to the bottle of wine already on the table. "I seem to remember you enjoy a good blend."

It's not every ADA who buys a detective wine, but this isn't a date. I've worked with Evan. We won a big case together. I know him. He likes wine. I'm just along for the good fortune of enjoying the bottle he wanted himself. "I do enjoy a good blend," I agree, and we both claim our seats.

Evan fills my glass. "I see you didn't bring your partner."

"He's in Brownsville, working the case." I sip the wine, a smooth, sweet blend with not a hint of a bite.

It's the only smooth thing about this day. "Good choice," I say before I shift back on topic. "And I wouldn't bring Ethan, anyway, since you two hate each other. That would be rather foolish of me."

"Indeed it would."

"Why don't you like each other?"

He arches a brow. "He hasn't told you?"

"Just wanted your version."

He laughs a low rumble of thunder in his chest. "Good try, *Detective*. Clearly, he didn't tell you. He did something right for once. I hear you got in some trouble with a suspect."

"You mean Newman Smith? The one showing up at my door every night, in a hoodie and hat to hide his face, while scaring my neighbors? I think he found out his wife was meeting me, and she saved herself by turning on me. I'm honestly worried about her. She's scared."

"Can you prove he's the one showing up at your door?"

"Not yet. We're getting there."

"And he's our guy on the Summer case? You said there was another murder."

"One more locally," I say, reaching in my bag to grab the file I put together for him earlier. I set it in front of him. "One in Houston and one in Browns-ville. There are two out of our jurisdiction in New York State as well. We believe there will be more when we pull the records all together."

"You can prove they're connected to our cases?"

"Not yet. We're close."

He doesn't even bother to open the file. "What *do* you have for me?"

"He ties them up. They're naked in a chair, legs and body bound, hands free. He uses whatever threat he uses, we don't know what, and offers them a cyanide pill. In several, painful minutes, their bodies shut down. He cleans their mouths and leaves a poem inside. The second murder was the barista at the coffee shop I frequent. He spoke to me about poetry, and not nicely. He was punished."

Evan reaches for his glass and leans back in his seat. "He punishes them for hating poetry?"

"He judges them unworthy. In fact, in his earlier murders, he carved the letter *U* into their chests."

He sips his wine. "What about Roberts?"

"Missing. We believe he got too close."

He taps the file. "What is in that file that helps me help you?"

"Newman was raised in Brownsville, where we've located another victim and where we believe he sourced the cyanide. His mother died mysteriously. He was then sent to foster care, where he abused animals, and a girl he lived with disappeared."

Evan sets his glass down and leans forward. "That's not enough for a warrant."

I set my glass down. "The right judge will look at this file and get me a warrant."

"You want me to go judge hunting," he assumes.

"Damn straight I want you to go judge hunting," I confirm. "Two people died here in our city in a week. I don't want to wait for three, do you?"

"Newman's a donor for the mayor's campaign," he says.

"Which emboldens him," I conclude.

"Which is why you can't expect me to go after him with nothing."

A muscle ticks in my jaw. "His wife came to me."

"His wife's filing a restraining order against you," the smart-ass reminds me.

"She's scared of him," I argue. "He forced her hand."

"Which you can't prove. You can't prove anything."

The air around us is downright crackling now. "If

he kills again, that blood is on your hands."

"No, sweetheart. You do your job. I do my job and I do it well. You haven't done your job. If he kills again, it's blood on *your* hands."

That's it. I'm done playing the game, at least his way. I glance at my watch. "Gotta go." I stand up and grab my bag. "I have a meeting with a reporter in half an hour. I figure it's better to let the world know about The Poet—that's what I'm calling this serial killer—in my own words. I'll be sure to let her know that we're not able to stop him from killing because he's one of the mayor's donors. I'll make sure she spells your name right. I know you want the credit." I start to turn.

"Wait," he bites out.

I angle toward him and arch a brow.

He taps the table. "Sit."

I don't move.

"Please," he adds.

I sit, but I don't settle my back on the seat. My bag stays on my arm. He fills my wineglass. "Stay." He grabs the file. "I'll read it. We'll talk about it."

I settle my bag on the seat and reach for my glass. "I'll watch."

He laughs. "You're tough."

"So is The Poet."

His smile fades and he nods, flipping open the file. A glass of wine later, he glances up at me. "He taught a class called Abstract Poetry and Criminology." He glances down and back up at it. "'Poetry: words that speak to the soul of a serial killer'? Seriously?"

"And how poetry connects you to the mind of a killer. Don't forget the part about poetry being death by words."

His lips press together and he closes the file again. "It's all circumstantial."

"The right judge—"

"I'll try." He scrubs his jaw. "I'm going to catch hell, but you have my word that I'll try."

I believe him. And that leaves me with nothing to say but, "Thank you. For the wine and the help."

A few minutes later, I step outside the bar, and the rain was nothing but a lie. It's gone, leaving the night a wide-open space for murder and mayhem.

"Watch your back," Evan calls from the sidewalk.

We all need to watch our backs, I think, climbing into my car, shutting the door, and flipping the locks.

CHAPTER 68

I head home in a moonless, starless night, and once again, I don't park in the parking garage.

A part of me is angry over this decision. I'm angry I have to make it. I'm angry The Poet forced me to make it. I'm just not stupid enough to rebel. Another thing my father taught me: pride is your prison. You know where it gets you? He'd asked me when I'd made a stupid rookie mistake. Dead, he said. It gets you dead. Now he's dead and I'm feeling the reality of just how easily the end can occur. I alert patrol that I'm home and then head to my building. Thunder rumbles promising a storm ahead, while the building security is, at present, as absent as the rain.

I text the office manager: *Tabitha, did you fire the security company already?*

Once I'm near my building's entrance, I feel the weight of this day heavy on my shoulders and I crave the moment that I'm inside my apartment. I'm just reaching for the door when Tabitha returns my call. I pause outside to avoid drawing attention to myself in the building, specifically from Mrs. Crawford.

"I'm sorry," she says, skipping a formal greeting. "I'm working to get a guard back in place. The company we're using appears to be having staffing problems."

"What happened to the guy who was here last night?"

"His wife had a miscarriage."

This niggles at me in all the wrong ways, but it's easy enough to confirm. And I will be confirming.

"They're supposed to have someone out in the

next couple of hours."

I glance at my watch that reads ten thirty, and I'm doubtful. "Text me when he's in place."

"Yes. Sure," she says. "Is there something I should know?"

"I'm the one with the gun. I just need to know who not to shoot."

"Oh. Right. Yes. Of course. I'm home if anyone needs me."

We disconnect and I enter my building. I'm halfway up the stairs when I hear, "Who is that man who keeps coming round here?"

I pause and tilt my chin upward to find Mrs. Crawford in an orange and lime-green blouse that makes my head hurt. Or it could be the fact that I haven't eaten since last night. "Did you see him again?"

"Last night. I know he's not a police officer. Is he coming back tonight?"

I don't lie to her at this point. She's proving right now that lies always get found out. "Let's hope not," I say. "Do you have my cell phone number?"

"No. No, I do not."

I hike up to her level and give her my number, letting her ask me questions I mostly dodge. "If you see him ever again, please call me right away."

"Okay. I will. Should I worry?"

I want to tell her just to say she loves poetry and she'll be fine. Instead, I say, "It's probably just a prank someone is playing."

"On only your apartment?"

"Better me than someone else. Goodnight, Mrs. Crawford."

I head on down the stairs and she calls out, "Be careful, Sam."

Not Detective Jazz, but Sam. I glance over my shoulder and up at her. "Always."

I hurry down the stairs, and I swear when I'm inside my apartment with the door locked, I still can't even rest. I search my own living space, and then finally set my gun by the door and head to the kitchen. I have just enough time to guzzle a protein shake and inhale a dozen grapes when Chuck calls. While we talk, I kneel in front of the computer with the security feed by my door and tab through the old footage.

"Do you think the DA's office will come through?" he asks.

"It's a fifty-fifty shot. I need something else to give him. Do you have anything?"

"I have pieces of a puzzle that takes time to put together. You know how this works."

"Unfortunately, I do, but tell me anyway." Thunder rumbles outside my room and rain begins to patter on my windows, and with it the tension eases in my shoulders. We're taking tonight off. Thank you, Lord.

Chuck and I dissect what he has, piece by piece, and thankfully my security feed is clear. We're about to hang up and I switch back to the live feed. That's when my breath lodges in my throat. The man in the hoodie is standing at my door. The Poet is at my door.

CHAPTER 69

Only a door separates me from The Poet, who stands with his back facing the camera. Chuck keeps talking, but there is this cold silence all around me. I don't move. The Poet doesn't move. He knows that I'm here. I sense this in every fiber of my being. Somehow, too, he knows that I'm watching him. His actions seem to taunt me and deliver a promise that he's untouchable. He's tempting me to act rashly, to prove I'm unworthy. I won't act rashly, and the only person unworthy is him.

With my earbuds in place, I pick up my phone and slide it into my jacket, thankful I never took it or my holster off. I reach for my weapon, the steel comforting in my hand, so much so that I ignore the holster. I hold the weapon.

And still, The Poet stands at my door.

Still, Chuck keeps talking. "One last thing before I get some rest," he says. "Let's talk about one thing several victims do have in common: yoga."

"Chuck," I say.

"Newman's wife does yoga as well and I—"

"You need to listen. Call the patrol watching my place and tell them I need wide support backup. The Poet is back at my door. I do not want them to scare him off. Do it now."

"I—oh God—I—"

The Poet moves suddenly, walking down the stairs, no, he starts to run. "Now!" I shout at Chuck, and dash for the door, unlock it, and fling it open. I don't take the time to shut it again. I leave it that way, running down the stairs, only to hear Mrs. Crawford yell, "He's here!"

"Go inside and lock your door!" I scream and damn it, The Poet is opening the building door, he's exiting. He's outside.

I'm not far behind him, but once I'm at the door, common sense forces me to pause. He could be outside waiting for me, right outside, hiding left or right. I crack open the door and rain smacks the ground in a hard, fast drumming that promises a blinding effect. I ease out of the opening I've created just enough to ensure no one is to my left and then I step into the downpour. Water hits me in an icy blast against the hot night, and with my weapon in front of me, I plant against the wall and scan right and then left, then left and right.

That's when I spy the movement, when I catch him in my view, running away with a big lead. I launch myself in that direction, and suddenly, as if the night inhales, the rain withdraws, the massive droplets turning to a gentle, barely present spray. The apartment lighting is now more effective, allowing me to track The Poet more clearly, and his path past two buildings. I gain on him, but I don't know that I should. He's a big, tall man, faster by genetics. Logically, I know he's drawing me in, but I can't let a killer escape who I might capture.

He cuts toward a fence that I know shelters a small dirt path the residents of my complex use to walk to a nearby store. If he turns that corner, my chances of catching him are slim to none, but if I call out, he'll know I'm here. I can't shoot a man running from me, so I make the decision that surprise is my friend. If he thinks this is his time to disappear, if he thinks the shadows of that walkway protect him and discourage me, he will be wrong, and I might catch him.

He turns the corner and disappears behind that fence.

I run faster and when I reach the fence myself, I flatten on the wooden surface, sucking in air and ignoring the vibration of my phone. I inch around the fence and scan the pitch-black night. Without my bag and flashlight, I grab my phone and hit the flashlight on it. I inch around the fence again and shine the light onto empty space.

I have about three seconds to contemplate how dangerous my next move will be, but a mental flash of Dave naked in a chair drives me forward. I can't let this man kill again. Decision made, gun in front of me, I step onto the muddy, dirt path, my light a tunnel in the darkness, guiding my steps, while I scan for The Poet, left and right. Suddenly, he darts out in front of me and starts running.

Adrenaline is the fire in my blood. "Police. Stop!" I shout. "Austin PD. Stop now or I'll—"

He turns and there's a flash of a weapon. The world seems to stand still in eternal seconds as instinct and training kick in and I fire my weapon. The Poet falls to the ground. Still running on instinct and adrenaline, my weapon remains ready as I move toward him. I'm aware that this man, of all men, could be just fine and waiting to take me down. I step closer, his feet at my feet, and I nudge his shoe. He doesn't move. I do this twice, with the same result. I move around him, outside the reach of his arms, and stand above his head, the hat and hoodie still hiding his face. I lean in just enough to check for a pulse that I don't find.

God.

I killed him.

It's a shocking, horrible feeling, despite his monster status. I suck in a breath and hit one on my phone, which autodials 911. "911, what's your emergency?"

"This is Detective Samantha Jazz, ID number

25K11. I've discharged my weapon and I have a suspect down and nonresponsive." I recite the address and hang up. Voices sound and then police officers are rushing toward me. I kneel and yank back The Poet's hood to administer CPR, and my world spins.

This isn't The Poet. It's a boy no older than twelve or thirteen, no more than five-foot-three, when I know I was chasing a man over six feet tall. And yet he's wearing the same clothes The Poet was wearing.

Desperation kicks in and I scream out, "Stop the bleeding!" while I administer CPR I know won't work. This boy is dead. And I killed him. Because that's what The Poet wanted. He wanted me to kill. He wanted me to be just like him.

CHAPTER 70

I stand in the shadows off the walkway and watch her drop to her knees beside the boy.

She killed him the way she was supposed to kill him.

I'd doubted her, I admit. I didn't think she had the stomach for such things, but I'm quite pleased to be wrong. She'll struggle this first time, question herself, more because of societal expectations than anything. She hasn't quite accepted her place above such things. And the messiness is beneath her, but that's how it starts. My first certainly wasn't clean and neat. How profound this is, though, truly profound.

I'd chosen this young sinner, a bully who'd knocked the poetry book I'd given another young homeless boy out of his hands and then mocked him. Our now-dead little bully had reminded me of another boy from a long time ago. I'd known this bully would be her first, as another bully had been my first. It had been so easy to set up. I'd convinced the bully we were playing a game, scaring the lady cop, and his reward would be a crisp one hundred dollar bill. All he had to do was jump in front of her and shine the flashlight on her.

As to how truly profound is this night, the boy who was bullying Detective Jazz, who just made her first judgment kill, was thirteen. The same age as the bully I'd killed when I, too, had been thirteen.

Sirens sound nearby, and I ease through a crack in the fence, disappearing into the stormy night, but I will not be forgotten. Of this, I am certain.

CHAPTER 71

In the moments that I try to save that boy, I have flashbacks to the night I'd leaned over my father, blood on my hands, life out of my reach.

And, just like that night, EMS arrives and I'm pushed back, out of the way. Patrol blocks off the scene and I ensure the entire complex is included. Lights are beamed into the walkway. EMS techs continue to work.

I stand there, helpless, utterly helpless and covered in blood from the wound seeping from the boy's chest. I didn't chase that boy or any boy. I chased a man, tall and broad. I know I didn't chase this little boy who has now left this world. I grab a patrol officer. "Do not let anyone go any farther down this path than they already have. Cover it now to protect it from the rain. Look for adult footprints. There was a man here. We need a shoe print. We need to prove he was here with the boy."

He nods and takes off, shouting out as he does to fellow officers.

The rain might lower the statistical rate of murder, but tonight it offered The Poet shelter in far too many ways.

One of the EMS techs steps to my side, giving me a grim shake of his head. The boy is beyond his ability. He's beyond saving.

"There was a gun," I breathe out, after the emergency crew cave to their failure and my weapon's success.

"I think it was a flashlight," one of the EMS techs replies.

"A flashlight." The words are acid on my tongue.

"I killed a little boy over a flashlight. That bastard tricked me into doing this. He's made me a killer all over again. Bag the flashlight!" I yell out to the patrol and motion another forward to bag my weapon.

The next hour goes by in a hurricane, rather than a rainstorm. There is a special investigative team from another agency that shows up, as per protocol when an officer shoots someone in the line of duty. I'm removed from the scene and my clothes become evidence. I'm now in uniform pants, a police T-shirt, and a jacket. The investigation team walks the scene. I then walk the scene. Detective Martinez, a twenty-year veteran of the police department, joins the scene as my liaison. He's a good guy who knows his job, compassionate, too, about the boy and what it's like to be in my shoes. He helps out rather than push my buttons. The press shows up. It's impossible to avoid, considering the apartment complex population.

The captain also makes a showing, here to do damage control. "What the hell happened?" he demands as if him punching words at me is what I need right now.

I can feel myself withdrawing. That's how I operate. I don't scream. I don't shout.

"The Poet was at my door. I have a video to prove it. It was him, not a boy. Somehow when I rounded the corner, the boy was wearing the same clothes. He flashed what I thought was a gun. It was a flashlight."

"How is that even possible?" he demands.

"The same way he leaves no DNA. He's smart. He turned me into a killer. That's what he wanted. I have them looking for footprints. I have the video. It's clearly a large man."

"What the fuck am I supposed to tell the press?"

"An evil monster used the kid as a shield. It's the truth."

"They know he's called The Poet." Accusation laces his tone. "You named him. Did you let this out to pressure the mayor over Newman?"

"That's what you think of me? He leaves poems in their mouths. A crime scene has a hundred other people on it. I'd like to think that my calling him The Poet was oh so inventive, but it's not. Now, if you'll excuse me, Captain. I'm covered in a little boy's blood. I need to go shower and get to the station to give my formal statement."

"While I stand here in the quicksand of your making."

"I used to think my father hated you because he was dirty and you weren't. I was wrong. He hated you because you're an asshole, Captain. Sir. I'm going to shower and pick up the security feed from my apartment. I'll text you a clip as well. Then I'm going to the morgue to try to figure out whose child I took." I don't wait for his approval or for him to tell me I'm on mandatory leave pending the investigation. I know. That's not stopping me from going to find this child's identity. I walk away, leaving him and Martinez in charge of the scene as if I have a choice.

I make my way through the many members of law enforcement now on the property and head into my building. I make it all the way to my door and halt when I find it open. Tension ripples down my spine. I know I left it open. What I don't know is if anyone, namely The Poet, might be inside waiting for me. And I'm unarmed.

"Detective Jazz."

At the sound of Officer Jackson's voice, an odd mix of unease and relief fills me. I rotate to place the door and him both in profile. "What are you doing here, Jackson?"

"Anything you need me to do. I'm on your team,

remember?" He eyes my door. "Is that supposed to be open?"

"I left it open. I'm unarmed. Can you search the apartment for me?"

"Right away." He draws his weapon and hurries into the apartment without any hesitation. It bothers me, but then, I'm back to the obvious. The Poet wants me so on edge that I see him everywhere. Even in a little boy.

CHAPTER 72

I don't stay in the hallway.

I follow Officer Jackson into my apartment, both of us streaking my hardwood floors with mud. Weapon drawn, Jackson scans the living room and kitchen and then walks toward my bedroom. I calmly enter the kitchen and open my special drawer. Anyplace I keep a gun right about now is special. I remove my personal Glock 43, a compact number that sits just right in my hand. I round the counter again and enter the living room as Officer Jackson is about to head upstairs to my war room.

"I'll take care of that room."

He eyes my weapon and then me. "You sure about that?"

"Positive. Thank you."

He hesitates. "I'll wait right here."

"No," I say, the idea of going up those stairs and being trapped in that room with anyone behind me not a good one. "I got it."

He hesitates again and then harnesses his weapon, rotating to fully face me. "You want me to leave."

I'm not big on denial. Reality is reality and I keep things real. "I need some time alone."

"Understood. If you need anything—"

To turn back time a few hours, I think, but I say, "Thank you. Just help me catch this guy."

"Understood." He walks to the door and I follow him and, despite one unsearched room, relief rolls off me as he steps into the hallway. I shut the door firmly behind him and flip the locks. I needed him out of here, but I waste no time standing there rejoicing his departure. That unsearched room calls me, and I pause at the bottom of the stairs. If The Poet is here waiting for me, I'm ready to play.

My cell phone rings. It's Lang with his impeccable timing. I decline his call for about the fifth time tonight. My Glock and I walk straight up the stairs to find the room empty and smelly, compliments of bags left behind after our taco takeout. Those bags and The Poet need to be taken to the trash, but neither is going anywhere right now. I walk downstairs and hurry into the bathroom, where I set my Glock on the counter. My cell phone rings and this time when I spy Lang on the caller ID, I answer.

"What the hell, Jazz? I've been worried."

"I had investigators and hell suffocating me. I needed to get past at least some of that."

"Right. I heard. What happened?"

I give him a quick recap, and just explaining it all is cutting, but necessary. I'll have to repeat everything at the station, probably ten times over. His response when I've spit it all out is, "Holy hell. You didn't kill that boy. You know that, right? He killed that boy."

The twist of my gut says differently. So do the facts. The Poet didn't kill that boy, I think. I did. I pulled the trigger. "I'm about to shower and head to the station to give my official statement."

"I'm coming back."

"No. You will not. You stay your big ass there and you find what we need to catch him. I have never wanted to catch him more than I do now."

"Sam—"

"I mean it, Lang. Stay. Work the case. Focus."

Silence fills the line. "What's your plan to cover your ass?"

"I have the security feed Wade installed. It'll show the grown man at my door. It's clear I was set up. I'll be fine."

"Right. Right. I know you will. You're tough as hell. Call me after the interviews."

"Yeah. I'll call." I hang up without another word. I just need a minute alone.

I set my phone on the counter next to my gun and strip, tossing everything I'm wearing into the trash. The hot shower that follows is a blessed relief and somehow, I force the night's events from my mind. I can't risk breaking down now, not until everything that has to be done is done, and I'm alone.

I've just stepped out of the shower and wrapped myself in a robe when Wade appears in the doorway, looking weary and, as is rarely the case for him, a bit haphazardly put together in jeans and a less-than-pressed T-shirt. "I came the minute I heard."

"What happened to your case?" I challenge, unreasonably angry. "Don't you have a killer to catch?"

"My case—"

"Do not come here and let a killer go. I can't be responsible for that right now, Wade." I turn toward the closet at the rear of the bathroom and he catches my arm, turning me to face him.

"I got him. And we'll get The Poet."

"More like he got me."

"We *will* get him."

I swallow hard, a flash of that boy in my mind I shove aside, clinging to sanity while I still can. "I killed a little boy, Wade."

"Don't do that," he chides. "Don't do that to yourself. The Poet—"

"Don't say he killed him. Lang said that, too, but making excuses for me is not okay. He didn't pull the damn trigger. I did. I pulled the trigger." My voice is raised, a dark bubble of something I can't name in my chest. I swallow again, a deep, hard swallow. "I need to get dressed. My liaison is waiting for me."

I start to turn away and he says, "About that."

I'm right back in front of him. "What do you mean *about that*?"

"I think you should name me as your liaison."

"Why would I do that?"

"Because your interview is supposed to happen tomorrow, and they want it to happen tonight."

My gut twists with the implications in that statement that I don't even fully understand. "I'm not very up to speed on this kind of thing," I admit. "I don't exactly shoot a lot of people."

"I am, which is another reason to name me your liaison. And yet another. I just talked to Martinez, he said 'the captain said' to me four times in five minutes. The mayor is trying to shelter himself from Newman, perhaps at the expense of you and the case, with the captain as his yes-man."

"Okay," I say, thankful for his help. "But you're FBI. Can you even be my liaison?"

"Say yes. I'll make it happen."

I'm no fool. He's right on all points. "Then yes. You're my liaison."

"Good. I'll ensure you have an attorney. You need one. And then I'll start by downloading the security feed we need to take with us while you get dressed."

I nod and watch him walk out of the bathroom, both relieved and concerned about his involvement. The Poet is obviously watching me and when he does, Wade keeps making sure he sees him. I'm not sure that's smart, but right now, I need to focus on getting through this interview.

Eager to do that, I hurry into the closet and throw on jeans and a T-shirt along with sneakers. I towel dry my hair and don't bother with makeup. A boy died tonight. All I care about right now is washing the blood away, and the shower didn't do the job. I'm not sure anything will.

I'm just reaching for the bag of clothes from the trash to throw out when my phone buzzes with a text from Chuck that reads: *Tried to call you over and over. Worried about you.* There's also a link to a news article titled: "The Poet Terrorizes the City."

It's official. The Poet gets what he wants. The entire city is waiting for his judgment.

CHAPTER 73

I slide my phone into my pocket and pick up my gun, walking into the living room to find Wade sitting on the couch, with the computer he installed with the security system in front of him. I suck in a breath meant to calm the sudden apprehension overwhelming me, but it does nothing to calm the drum now pounding inside my chest. My gaze goes to the front door. It was open. The Poet could have deleted that footage.

Desperate to find out if he did and yet terrified at the same time, I hurry forward and sit down next to Wade, setting my gun beside me where it comforts me just by existing.

"Show me," I order.

He gives me a sideways look, but he doesn't speak or offer commentary on what he's seen on the film. Wade's been doing this job long enough to know we each cope in our own ways. I need to see the film to cope. He understands. Without a word, he rewinds and pushes play. The Poet is standing at my door, all six feet plus of him. I don't know if I should feel relief or self-hatred. I should have known that boy wasn't The Poet. Whatever the case, the film is the proof that will set me free and show the investigators how I was tricked, but it won't bring that little boy back to life.

"What did you think you were going to find?" Wade asks when I finally breathe again.

"My door was open when I got here," I say.

"You were afraid he deleted the footage," he assumes.

"Yes, but that was a foolish fear. Of course, he

wouldn't delete the footage."

"Because he wants us to see the proof that he tricked you. He wants us to believe he's better than us."

"Yes," I agree, "but it's more than that." I quote the poem he'd left with Summer:

"*Who laugh in the teeth of disaster,*
Yet hope through the darkness to find
A road past the stars to a Master.

He wants us to see him as a master while showing us that we are not."

I say "we," but in my mind, I hear *me*. This was about me. He wanted me to see him as a master. This has become about me.

CHAPTER 74

There is nothing more suffocating than becoming the interrogated when you are normally the interrogator. Nothing like sitting in a cold box of a room with a two-way mirror and cameras, while who-knows-who watches you. I'm alone in that room, pacing to keep from picturing that poor boy's face, when my union-appointed attorney, a pretty woman with long dark hair, walks into the room.

"Nicole Richmond," she announces, shutting the door behind her. "I'm your attorney, here to shut down their bullshit." Even in her two a.m. outfit of jeans and a T-shirt, she owns a take-no-prisoners attitude, and I like it. "They shouldn't even be interviewing you tonight and they know it. They also know I think it's bullshit."

Oh yes, I think. I definitely like her.

"I've heard the general story," she says, and then getting right to business, adds, "Now I want to hear it from you."

I tell her everything, and when I'm done, she contradicts her tough side by hugging me. That's what people do in these situations. They hug you. After my father died, I wanted to carry a sign that said "no hugging." It's not that I don't appreciate the gesture, I do, but every hug starts to feel like pity, and it can be easy to wallow in pity, to weaken yourself. Hugs make you cry. I'd rather take action. I'd rather do something to make a difference.

Hug behind us, my new attorney lets everyone waiting to attack know that we are ready.

The first person to enter the room to question me is Evan. He's dressed in jeans and an AC/DC T-shirt that somehow humanizes him. There's stubble on his jaw, and he runs a frazzled hand through his hair when I'm not sure I've ever known him to show disorder in any way. Nothing about his actions are those of a man here to intimidate. "I walked the crime scene," he says, claiming the seat across from me.

Just hearing it called a crime scene rips out a piece of my heart.

"I also watched the security feed Wade brought us," he continues. "Just to get this out there. No one believes you did anything wrong."

"We're going to hold you to that," Nicole chimes in.

He flicks her an irritated look. "I'm sure you will. Save the claws for someone else." His attention returns to me. "I'm going to let the team here take your statements. I'm here for one reason. This asshole, The Poet, he did this, not you."

There it is, that cringe-worthy statement that stalks me the way The Poet himself stalks me.

"I've been calling judges," he continues, "trying to get a warrant, but everyone is afraid of this right now."

I lean forward. "There's a serial killer in our city. What more is there to be afraid of, Evan?"

"A lawsuit is coming at us after tonight," he says. "They don't want another from Newman."

"They? You mean the mayor, who's protecting his donor and his own ass?"

"Newman filed a restraining order against you and then you killed a young boy. It looks bad."

"You just said she didn't kill the boy," Nicole points out. "And why wouldn't a serial killer want a restraining order against the detective trying to stop him from killing?"

"She's right," I say, loving this woman. "I was

breathing down his throat, so he came at me to take the heat off him. And it worked. I'm on administrative leave, sitting here, instead of working on this case. I guess I should be glad, though. He killed the last cop hunting him. At least I'm alive."

"I'm not the enemy here," Evan says. "I'm just telling you where we are. There's going to be a press conference tomorrow. We'll downplay the threat because we have to avoid panic. And we'll let this cool down and go back at the warrant. That gives you time to gather more evidence."

"And him more time to kill."

"Get me something that isn't circumstantial, and I'll get past this wall now."

"That's what you were supposed to help with. We need electronic surveillance."

"I can't get that for you now."

The door opens and Raymond Winter, the chief and my godfather, joins us with a command. "We need the room."

The chief's an imposing man and not just because he's tall and muscular. His features are sharp, his eyes a piercing blue so penetrating they could cut through any level of bullshit right to your soul. He's a man who owns a room just by walking into it like he owns this one now.

Evan stands up. "Chief," he greets. "We're on her side."

"You better be," he says, his voice all gruff authority when he has none over Evan.

The two men shake hands and exchange a few muffled words I can't make out before the chief holds the door open for Evan, who quickly departs.

"Nicole," he says, and her name's clearly a warning.

"Chief, I can't—"

"This isn't official. She's my damn goddaughter.

We need the room."

"Oh." She looks at me in shock. "You didn't tell me he was your godfather."

"She doesn't throw me around like a weapon," the chief explains for me, pride in his voice.

Pride I don't deserve this night. Nicole eyes me and I nod. She gets up and walks to the door. "The cameras are off?"

"They're off," the chief assures her.

She leaves and when the door shuts, I stand up. The next thing I know the chief is in front of me, pulling me into a bear hug. "My baby girl."

My teeth clench. This is a test. His way of figuring out how ruined I am, how likely to be dead in the water, incapable of wearing my badge in the future. I will not fail. I'm not dead in the water. I want justice for that little boy. I want The Poet, and tears, at least not the public kind, will not make that happen.

"You do know I'm a badass detective, right?" It's an inside joke between us that we've been saying since I first joined the force and he brought me cupcakes to celebrate.

He usually laughs. This time, he doesn't. His hands settle on my shoulders and he leans back to inspect me. "And human. No one goes through what you did tonight without pain. You're going to come out of this just fine, though. You're tough as nails." He releases me and settles his hands on his hips. "But you'll have required counseling and a mandatory administrative leave for a month."

"A month?" I balk. "I thought the book said three days? I have a killer to catch."

"A month for you. It's only three months after your father died right in front of you. That shapes your recovery."

"Chief, damn it—"

"If you fall apart and something goes wrong, I

take that heat. Furthermore, the press will find you if you're underfoot. They will be stalking you right along with this killer. You're going to want to lay low. I *expect* you to lay low. Wade said he has a team supporting you in San Antonio. Head down that direction. Get out of sight. Enjoy a nice long walk on the damn Riverwalk."

"The Riverwalk stinks."

"It doesn't stink. It's beautiful."

"I don't *want* to go to San Antonio," I bite out.

"Newman's threatening to sue. This is the only way you stay active and the lead on this case."

"In other words, I'm on desk duty." I don't wait for him to reply. "This is what The Poet wants. Me out of the way."

His expression tightens. "He's obsessed with you. Seems to me he doesn't want you gone at all. He wants you as obsessed with him as he is with you. We can only hope that if you step back, he'll wait for you, and we'll catch him while he does." He leans in, kisses my cheek, and then walks to the door.

An image of me leaning over that little boy claws at me, and I stop him. "Chief?"

He glances over his shoulder. "Yes."

"Do we know who the boy is yet?"

"No." That's it. No. And with that he exits. I stare after him, stunned by his harshness. As of now, I decide, the scoreboard reads: The Poet wins. I lose.

CHAPTER 75

I wait until Wade and I are in his fancy black pickup truck, the Texas version of a Mercedes, before I ask the question that I've wanted to ask for an hour and a half. "Why would you suggest they send me to San Antonio?"

He starts the engine and cranks the air, then rotates to face me. "They were going to send you to Houston to wait on Roberts's return. I thought you'd prefer San Antonio, where you have more control over your investigation than you did here in Austin. And where you're close enough to come back nightly and meet with your team."

"They were going to send me to Houston?"

"Yeah. The mayor wants to get rid of you in a big way. And frankly, baby, so does your godfather. He might love you, but right now, he sees you as a liability."

Suddenly, his hug means even less than it did before. He was a close friend of my father's. They didn't share that bond without at least a few of the same views.

"And," Wade continues, "I'm starting to wonder if the mayor knows more about Newman than we know, and he's chosen to look the other way for financial reasons."

Based on what Wade just told me, he might be right. "Maybe the FBI needs to investigate him."

"I couldn't agree more, but we're going to keep that between you and me for the moment. Perhaps we need to discuss turning you into a covert operative."

"Now I see where this is going. You think a week

in San Antonio will finally recruit me to your side."

"I do, but right now, we need sleep. In light of the fact that your place is swarming with curious eyes and ears, I vote we go to my house and rest there. Once you're rested, you can decide what comes next."

"On that, you will get no argument."

We head toward his house on the west side of downtown, and I exchange a few text messages with Lang. The drive is short, and Wade's place is far bigger than mine, an actual house with a backyard, but still familiar and comfortable. He'd wanted me to move in with him at one point, and before my father died I'd considered that a possibility. Tonight, I take sanctuary in our relationship. I scream. I cry. I get angry—at The Poet, at the chief, at my father, at Lang for his betrayal but ultimately at myself because I let The Poet win at the cost of a little boy's life. He offers me an outlet in every way, but as I lie down in bed next to him, I know that where I go, The Poet will go, and one way or another, he'll make sure this showdown is between the two of us if I don't do it for him.

I won't stay here beyond tonight.

CHAPTER 76

The morning after Detective Jazz's first kill, I wake after only a few hours of sleep, feeling quite dapper, despite the limited hours of shut-eye. One might say I'm still riding the high of a night done well. So much so that the adrenaline rush rises high with the sun and I find myself having sex with my wife, quite intense, rather rough sex, the ropes I use on her legs and body tight, perhaps too tight, but she doesn't complain. She's seen this dark part of me that defies the reserved exterior I allow the world to view and drinks it up in ways one wouldn't expect from such a sweet woman. She allows me this outlet to sate an appetite for more, to hold me over until the right moment, for Ava Lloyd to become a lesson taught as a part of Detective Jazz's path to her destiny.

When it's over, she's breathless. "I love you, Shakes."

Shakes.

That's her nickname for me, short for Shakespeare. I do appreciate her understanding of my love of poetry. "I love you, too," I say. I don't actually love her; those types of trivial human emotions are beneath me, but she's an excellent outlet and a shelter in the storm of human interest I do not need nor do I invite.

When finally she's dressed in a pretty pink dress for work, and I'm in a blue suit with a blue silk tie she's chosen for me, I sit at the kitchen island, sipping coffee. The kids fight over cinnamon rolls, and the wife forces calm. Once she's found peace between the children, she sits down next to me, her coffee in hand. "Did you read about that serial killer?" she asks softly, careful not to let the kids overhear.

Inside, my heart flutters, a butterfly spreading its wings in joy. "Here?"

"Here," she says. "Crazy, right? Would you believe they're calling him The Poet?"

I feign surprise. The name suits me, but it's not as original as I'd hoped. "Really? Why?"

"He sticks poems in their mouths after he kills them, a message that law enforcement has to decode. I was thinking, maybe you should offer to consult. You're a poetry expert."

"No," I say shortly. "There are plenty of scholars available, and the last thing I want is to bring attention to my family."

"Right," she says. "Right. I should have thought of that."

I catch her hand and kiss it. "Relax. I'll take care of you and the kids. Always. You know that."

She nods. "Yes. Yes, I know you will."

CHAPTER 77

I wake from what is a surprisingly deep sleep to a call from Mrs. Crawford.

"Are you okay?" She doesn't give me time to answer. She's still talking. "What exactly happened? There are reporters everywhere and everyone is talking about what happened."

I sit up to find Wade walking into the bedroom, already dressed in a gray suit and freshly shaved, with two cups of coffee in hand. I mouth a thank you and accept the cup, wondering how I slept through him getting up.

"These reporters are crazy people, just crazy," Mrs. Crawford says. "Surely you can do something."

"The interest will fade in a few days. I promise."

She isn't so sure, because she launches into a story about a reporter who knocked on my door off and on for an hour and how she called the police. When she finally lets me off the phone, I sigh. "Good Lord. If this is how this day is going to start, I might need wine."

"That's not a bad idea. I talked to Martinez this morning. He wants me to tap our missing children's records. In the meantime, they're having a sketch artist do a sketch of the boy to put out in the press to try to identify him."

I inhale against the hot spot in my chest. "Okay," is all I manage and really, anything I might say would somehow be too much and not enough. "Are you headed to the office?"

"Not yet. Soon."

"I should shower." I stand up and take two steps before I turn back to him. "How can no one be missing a little boy?"

"We have jobs because it's a brutal world."

He's given me a profound answer that I don't expect and somehow, it's exactly what I need. I give a nod of thank you and walk into the bathroom. Wade doesn't follow. That's the benefit of being with someone in law enforcement. Again, he just gets it. I need time alone, but I don't shut the bathroom door. It's not necessary.

Soon I'm under a hot stream of water and in my own head, and I think of my life choices and vow to protect others. I failed in that last night, but I find Wade's words resonating, and beat back my self-doubt. I can wallow or I can fight. I'm going to fight. Focus. Work the case, I remind myself. And so I focus on what's important: justice for the victims, including that little boy, whoever he might be. As for me, survival is doing my job, working. I need to get back to work. I exit the shower, with last night as compartmentalized as anything this fresh can be, determined to get this asshole.

Thankfully, I still have a few clothes and toiletries remaining here at Wade's, and the truth is that I haven't rushed to amend that fact. Shoving aside any self-analysis of my personal life, I apply makeup. I dry my hair. I dress in jeans and a pink lacy blouse that doesn't scream "child killer." Not long after, with my empty coffee cup in hand, I find Wade in the kitchen, sitting at his large granite island on his phone. I grab the coffee pot, refill his cup and mine, pour creamer from the fridge in both, and then claim a spot next to him. He's still on the phone, talking about surveillance of some target when I unload my case file and computer to get to work.

He disconnects. "We're going to start poking around the mayor's business and see what we come up with. If I can get digital surveillance and he crosses any lines with Newman—"

"You could get surveillance approved on Newman as well."

His cell phone rings and he holds up a finger, letting me know he has to take it. Mine then rings, as well, with Chuck's number. I manage to finish half my coffee while he continues to talk about his yoga angle that isn't going anywhere.

He's nervously rambling, obviously afraid to stumble into the uncomfortable territory of last night when we're both saved by another call beeping in from the crime lab. I hang up with Chuck and answer the call. "Detective Jazz."

"Detective Jazz, it's Antonio."

I scoot to the edge of my seat. "What do you have for me?"

"I finished that urgent testing you requested. There's no unknown DNA on the glasses. They matched up with the voluntary DNA samples you submitted. As reusable items, the books are tricky. We got some random DNA from them, but nothing that matches our database."

"What about the gravel sample I submitted?"

"It didn't match the samples taken at either crime scene."

I sigh. "Damn."

"I know. Sorry it's not better news, but I do have the books being sent to the evidence room, clear for your review."

"Thanks, Antonio." We disconnect, and my phone buzzes with a call from Lang.

"Tell me something good," I say, answering the line. "I really need something good."

"You have me in your life. How is that?"

"That means you have nothing good to tell me."

"I'll pretend I'm not insulted," he says, but moves on. "Nothing from Roberts here in Houston, and I'm with the detectives on the suffocation case here. We're not getting anything from the physical evidence. We're about to start working the poetry angle and look for a way these victims connect the dots."

"I'm going to pick up the poetry books I got cleared from the lab a few minutes ago," I say. "The DNA samples on the glasses matched the voluntary samples. The books had random DNA, as would be expected of a reusable item, but nothing that matched our database."

"He's smart," he says. "He took anything he touched with him."

"That's what I think, too, but the bottom line here is that we have nothing which means I have to try something."

"What about our warrant?" he asks. "We need to get to his creepy secret hiding place. You know he has one. These assholes always do."

"Not going to happen. We need more, and I'm not exactly in a place to turn to his wife now."

"But I am. There's no restraining order against me. We'll see if I can get to her when I get back."

"I'm on desk duty."

"I'll take the lead."

"And how exactly are you going to get to her and not end up with a restraining order, too?"

"With my good looks and charm, baby."

"Okay well, in case your good looks and charm don't work on the married woman, I'm headed to San Antonio tomorrow to work with the FBI team Wade put together for us."

"Without a weapon, I assume?"

"Without a government-issued weapon."

"Good. I know what happened last night, but don't let that make you hesitate. Shoot that bastard if you get the chance." He hangs up.

Wade steps in front of me and presses his hands

on the island. "I need to go into the office. You know you can stay here. I have a kick-ass security system."

"I know."

"You're not going to stay here at my place, now are you?"

"No. I'm going to do what I just said to Lang and go to San Antonio and work with the FBI. Isn't that what you wanted?"

He studies me for several beats. "You know that's not what I meant, but I suppose it is." He pushes off the island. "When are you leaving?"

"I'll head up this afternoon."

"I'll have your credentials waiting for you. Where are you going to stay?"

"In a high-security hotel that I bill to the department."

He grunts and grabs his briefcase. "I'll be there tomorrow." He heads for the door, and moments after the door opens and closes, I hear the security system arm itself. I don't pretend that computerized alarm protects me or anyone else from killers like The Poet. I will, though, because as Wade said: we have jobs because it's a brutal world. And I'm going to do mine.

CHAPTER 78

I'm in San Antonio for five days.

The Poet doesn't kill anyone in those five days, which would sound positive if I didn't feel as if he were waiting for my return.

"The Incident," as Lang and Chuck call that horrid night at my apartment, also fades from the headlines after those five days. That's how important a life is to the media. It earns a mere five days of attention. The boy has yet to be identified. Maybe he'll never be identified, but it's not a part of this story that I can linger on while I'm hunting this monster. The problem is that I achieve very little in San Antonio besides shuffling through the excess unproductive data, and Lang achieves less in Houston.

On day six, Lang is set to return to Austin, and I'm scheduled to return as well for one of several obligatory therapy sessions to earn my reinstatement. The Poet won't wait for me forever anyway, and I'm not going to catch him hiding in the FBI offices, shuffling papers. I return to my home city just in time for my session, and shortly after, pick Lang up at the airport.

"Miss me?" he asks, tossing his bag into the back seat of my car and settling into the passenger seat.

I claim the driver's seat and buckle up. "You called me constantly," I remind him. "How could I miss you?"

"With all your heart?"

I snort. He laughs. "I need food," he says. "Take me to a drive-thru and I know just the spot."

He's up to something. "You're up to something."

"I'm craving a certain burger. What's wrong with that?" He motions me onward.

I drive, not sure what trouble he's getting us into because that's his plan: trouble, not a burger. Or trouble *and* a burger, knowing Lang. When we turn onto Bee Caves Road, the location of Becky Smith's yoga studio, I know what he's up to. "I can't be with you when you talk to Becky Smith."

"It's a yoga studio. I can't go alone."

"There's zero logic to that statement."

"I don't want to go alone."

"Lang—"

"Just drive. We're not going to the yoga place, anyway. Officer Jackson's following her. He's been following her for days. She goes to Lola Savannah's for coffee after every yoga session."

"Are you trying to get me kicked off the force?"

"I'm trying to catch this guy," he says. "Isn't that what you want?"

"Damn it, Lang," I grumble, but I don't stop driving. He's right. I do want to catch this guy.

I pull into the coffee shop and park. "What time is she supposed to be here?" I ask, glancing at my watch. It's five thirty.

"Five forty-five."

"I'm waiting in the car."

"We have time to set up inside. You can sit with your back to us. I'm on Bluetooth. We'll each take an earpiece and be on a call so you can coach me if I need coaching."

"Like you ever think you need coaching."

"Well, as charming and good-looking as I am, I want to get this guy, Jazzy. He's obsessed with you. You are not going to become one of his victims. You hear me?" He reaches into the back and pulls something from his bag, producing an envelope.

"What's that?"

"All she has to do is sign this and we get our surveillance."

"You thought this out."

"I talked to Evan. He got me what I needed."

"*You* talked to Evan? I thought you two hate each other."

"Not as much as we hate this asshole."

"If I go in, are you going to tell me why you two hate each other?"

"The night we arrest The Poet, and we will, I'll tell you," he promises. "Let's go." He pops open his door.

I inhale and despite my best judgment, I step out of my vehicle. Lang smirks with his achievement, walking toward the coffee shop door. I let him smirk. If this works, he deserves to smirk, gloat, and repeat.

A few minutes later, with coffees in front of us, Lang and I are sitting at a small wooden table right behind a display of coffee and near the pickup bar. The pickup bar is where Lang plans to approach Becky Smith. Lang can see the door. I have to inch back a bit, but I can as well. I just have to be careful not to be seen. We're both wearing a Bluetooth earpiece and he's called me to connect us. I'm on the line when Jackson calls him to tell him that Becky has just pulled up to the coffee shop. Lang ends that call and then calls me. We've already tested the range of the Bluetooth. He can walk all the way to the door without me losing him.

Lang waits until Becky finishes placing her order and then inclines his chin at me. "Mrs. Smith?" he says, just on the other side of the display. I inch forward and I can see her face between two bags of coffee.

"Yes?" she asks, and I don't miss the dark circles that frame tormented eyes. Her eyes go wide. "You."

"Yes. Me. My name's Ethan Langford."

"You mean *Detective* Ethan Langford."

"Yes. And I promise you I will not approach you again if you just give me two minutes."

"Why would I do that?"

"Because I think you're scared, and I want you to know that I can protect you."

"Like all the women who end up dead or deformed who trust the police to protect them?"

"That's an admission of fear and his guilt," I murmur to Lang.

"I don't know about anyone but you and me. And I'm not a man to fail someone I vow to protect. I'd lose my badge rather than lose you to him."

"You can't touch him. The mayor and his money and—"

"Sign a form that lets us do electronic surveillance. He'll never know. And if there isn't anything for us to find—"

"There is. There is. I just—I'm afraid—he knows I know. He keeps his computer locked up."

"What do you know?"

"Just—things." Her voice trembles. "Bad photos of naked people."

My heart starts to thunder in my chest. This is it. This is what we've been waiting for. Lang holds up the envelope. "Sign this for me. We'll get the photos. We'll get you out. Please."

"I don't think I can."

I stand up and walk around the coffee display. "Move, Lang."

He steps aside, with both of us in profile. "I'm sorry," I say. "I know I'm not supposed to be here, but I need to say this to you. He tricked me into killing a young boy, a thirteen-year-old boy. I don't want him to get the chance to hurt someone else."

Tears well in her eyes. "The boy I read about in the paper?"

"Yes," I whisper. "Him."

She breathes a hard breath, and her gaze shoots to Lang. "Give me the paper."

Lang hands her the paper and a pen. She leans over to the bar, signs it, and hands it back to him, but she's looking at me. "I didn't want to file the restraining order. He found out I called you. I had to save myself."

"I know," I say. "That's okay." And then I do what I never do. I hug her and whisper, "You're saving lives. You're the hero here."

"Just get him," she whispers before she grabs her drink and rushes toward the door.

Lang and I watch her leave. "We got him," Lang says, and I rotate to face him. "We got him."

I want him to be right, but for reasons I can't explain, something about this doesn't feel like the end. Something feels wrong.

CHAPTER 79

Hours after we have that paper signed, the surveillance is already being put into place, and everyone is riding a high, which is why I don't stomp all over them with any negative thoughts. We're on the right path. We're closer to catching The Poet. I let everyone celebrate. The only person who doesn't jump for joy is Wade, who is presently stuck in meetings in Dallas for three days.

"Let's hope Becky doesn't go home and tell Newman," he says during a short call we manage, despite me presently stuffing myself with takeout in the conference room at the station, with Chuck, Lang, and the whole team around me.

"Surely she won't."

"Happened to me once. I've learned to never count my chickens. Sometimes these spouses are so terrorized that the wrong look from the other spouse has them confessing things they didn't have to confess."

"What happened in your case?"

"The killer did what killers do. He killed his wife. Of course, we got him then, but it was not a happy ending."

We hang up with my bad feeling clawing my insides. Is that what I sensed at the coffee shop? A woman so on edge she'll give us up the way she did me? Since it's his investigative team that's handling the authorization and setup of the surveillance, I dial Evan's cell phone.

"Good news tonight," he says. "It's about time, right?"

"Just move quickly. I have a bad feeling about

leaving her in that house with him."

"We're moving fast. You have my word."

A long time later, Lang and I walk to the parking garage together. "You want me to stay at your place tonight?" he asks.

"I don't," I say. "I need to be home and I need to think, which I do best alone and at home."

"Call patrol."

"I am. I will."

"And text me—"

"I will."

He doesn't look pleased, but he's known me a long time and he knows when to let things go. I climb into my car and text the patrol detail on my building, whom I'd alerted earlier today of my return. A necessary stop by the store is fast, which includes a call from my mother, in which I promise I'll be home for the holidays. It's August. She's starting early this year. Once I'm at my apartment building, I decide to park in the garage. If The Poet doesn't know I'm back, I'm not prepared to announce it. And I'm armed with my little Glock 43. If he gives me a reason to shoot him, this would really be over.

Once I'm in my building, the very fact that I'm dodging Mrs. Crawford tells me it's time for me to face the facts: my job isn't conducive to community living. I need to call a realtor, sell my place, and move to a stand-alone like Wade smartly purchased. I lock up, search my apartment, and it's not long before I'm upstairs, my bowl of Frosted Flakes in front of me, jazz on the record player. I line up all the poems and grab my phone, dialing my grandfather. He doesn't answer. Of course, he doesn't answer. It's after ten.

I start writing the same words on the page: *Why me? Why me? Why me? Why is The Poet obsessed with me?*

I'd never met this man before Roberts disappeared. We believe that he started killing long ago, so why me? What is it about me that's drawn his attention? I stand up and start to pace. I'm missing something that feels important. *What* am I missing?

CHAPTER 80

I can almost feel the hum of her return to the city. Detective Samantha Jazz. The name has a ring to it. Samantha Jazz. For tonight, I allow her a quiet return home, but I have a proper greeting planned. It's my duty, in fact, as her master to ensure her homecoming is about progress forward. It's time for her to open her eyes and see all there is to see. It's time for me to step out of the shadows.

For now, this night, I sit in the library, with Ava Lloyd at a distant table, and watch her study a poetry book. She's a pretty girl, brunette, with big green eyes, and I favor her over others I've judged for the simple fact she favors Samantha Jazz. She'll be another profound ending, one that will remind Detective Jazz that those who resemble her are not like her, not at all.

Ava's twenty-three, single, and alone, which I find to be the case in most who have sinned. They're incapable of attracting love. In her case, her parents are no longer living; her one sibling, a brother, is too wrapped up in his Wall Street career to think of her. Ava herself is a student at the university, with big plans to be an English professor. That will never happen. I won't allow her to spread her sin to those who wish to study the great works.

Ava gathers her books together and packs them away inside a leather bag before heading in my direction. I expect her to walk by, but she surprises me by stopping at my table. "Hi."

Isn't this an interesting twist? "Hello."

"You're here often."

Her tone is flirty, interest in the depths of her

eyes. I do like to think I'm a respectfully attractive man, with a bit of a movie star look, I'm told, with sandy blond hair and blue eyes. "I am." I don't offer more. I never offer more than necessary.

"Would you like to join me for a cup of coffee?"

I indicate my wedding ring. "I'm a married man."

She offers a coy look. "I won't hold that against you."

The book she's signed and checked out here in this very library requires that I assess her and judge her. This process demands time and observation. She's certainly offering me an exceptional opportunity that I'm not foolish enough to take. "With regret," I say, "I must decline."

She pales, disappointment bleeding into her expression. "Right. Of course not. You're married. Sorry about that." She doesn't wait for my reply. She hurries away and I push to my feet, prepared to follow her.

CHAPTER 81

After hours of work, I sit in my bed with the air cranked to arctic, a cup of hot chocolate in my hand, and fighting the sleep I need desperately for one reason: it's a nightmare kind of night. That's a secret I keep. When I'm high strung before bed, as I am now, and since my father's murder, I suffer from intense nightmares. Somehow in those weeks after his death, with Wade by my side, I endured them without him finding out but they were part of the reason I needed a break in our relationship. I thought if I could just get some time to myself to heal, I'd conquer them.

I was wrong.

I stare at the clock: one a.m. Two. I force myself to turn out the lights and lie down. Now the room is dark and icy cold, the kind of cold that can freeze a person to death, not the kind of cold that allows a deep, restful sleep. Shivering, I pull the blanket to my chin, blinking into the inky black of my bedroom. The heaviness of nights spent tossing and turning weigh on me, but I dread the moment I drown in my own mind. I command myself to sleep. I command myself to stay awake, to fight the sleep where I have suffocated in nightmares for the past five nights, but I fail. The haze of a light slumber is a merciless quicksand dragging me under. And then I'm there, in my own personal hell, inside yet another nightmare, but it feels as if I'm awake, a spirit hanging over my own comatose body, watching a distorted reality of my past life events playing out in the present day.

This night, it starts with me on a playground, on a swing, the wind whipping viciously around me.

Leaves and dirt gust in the air, wickedly twisting and turning, tormented by the force of the storm. It's calm where I am, where I swing and sing a song that I can't make out. I'm always on this swing, and I try to figure out how old I am, but I can't.

Another second later, I'm in a pitch-black walkway behind the fence, shouting at the man running away from me, but he's still running. Pushing past the burn in my legs, I charge toward him, ready to make an arrest. I've almost caught him when he halts, turning to face me, a flash of steel following. His gun is pointed at me. My heart dances to the beat of a scared animal prepared to attack to survive, ready to claw its way to its next breath. That's where this chase has taken us. It's me or him, and he doesn't live and I die. I pull the trigger and time stands still, the swish of my own blood in my veins echoing in my ears. The man collapses on the ground, a limp rag doll. I fight the rest of the nightmare. I refuse to approach the body. I *can't* approach the body. I can't relive what happens next.

I can feel my body thrashing around, fighting my mind, but I can't escape its torment. As if punishing me for my resistance, I'm transported to another place, back at another familiar crime scene. I'm kneeling in front of Dave's dead body, where it's bound to a chair, just one of many victims, another victim of a killer who seems indiscriminate in his choices. It's true he kills the young, the old, the beautiful, the deformed, but they all have one thing in common: they've been judged unworthy.

I frown at the fresh knife wound on Dave's chest, the perfect *U* dripping with blood, but some part of my mind knows that's not what happened. The Poet didn't damage Dave's body as he did his earlier victims. He simply, so very simply, poisoned him. Clean and cautious in every way, he limited his risk of leaving DNA evidence.

Reaching my gloved hand into Dave's mouth, I pull out yet another poem and message left for us by The Poet. I unroll the piece of paper and read the words of a poem credited to bestselling poet, Mary Oliver:

And this scar I then remember
is a medallion of no emotion

Obviously, I now know why he cut him. He wanted him to have a scar to match the poem. No, my mind wanted him to have a scar to match the poem. This isn't real. This didn't happen.

Grimacing, I'm right back in the nightmare, and I start reading again, finding Oliver's words replaced now by The Poet's:

I know how those scars got there.
You know how those scars got there.
You cut her
You killed her, Detective Samantha Jazz

Bugs start crawling out of Dave's mouth and then they are all over me.

I gasp and sit up, hitting at myself, shoving away the bugs that don't exist, nor did they exist at that crime scene. My mind just seems to want to punish me in new ways. The hot Texas sunlight beams through the curtain, piercing my irises, while I might actually have icicles clinging to my eyelashes. Shivering, I all but sprint to the thermostat, turn it back up to a reasonable level, and then head to my closet.

Glancing at my Apple watch, and the seven a.m. hour, a perfect hour for a much-needed run, I decide I will not let The Poet strip me of my life or outlets. I throw on workout tights and a tank top before I settle on the bed and lace up my sneakers. A flashback to that nightmare and the bugs crawling all over me has me standing and running my hands over my arms.

Grabbing my phone and Bluetooth headphones,

I hurry down the stairs, crossing through my living room to grab my keys from the table by the door. With a sigh, I pull up the security footage and do a quick scan for activity alerts and find none.

Eager for my outlet, I all but explode into a small foyer, lock up, and head down the two flights of stairs, only to have Old Lady Crawford shout down at me, "When are you going to work again, Sam?"

At least it's Sam and not Detective Jazz, I think, wiping the grimace off my face that she doesn't deserve. I rotate to find her at the top of the stairs, standing in her perpetual hunched over position, her polyester pants a bright orange today. "I'm working, Mrs. Crawford." At a desk, without my service weapon, but close enough.

"Oh, pishposh," she says, her gravelly dismissal instant. "You get fired over that thing that happened?"

Now "the incident" is "that thing?" Someone dying is not "that thing."

"Gotta run, Mrs. Crawford, quite literally. Taking my morning jog before the heat suffocates me." And then, to soften my harsh dismissal of a seventy-something sweet old woman, and as for her question, I add, "I'll check on you later," and then hurry the rest of the way down the stairs.

Exiting to the sidewalk, the certainty that I have to sell my place slams into me right along with the Texas humidity. I don't let either thing hold me back. I start walking, tuning my music on my phone to my run playlist. That's the extent of my warm-up. I need to be moving. I start running, but the nightmare plays in my head. I'm back in the alleyway and this time, I approach the body. This time, I let myself live the moment that I roll the man over to discover he isn't a man at all.

I run harder, and I don't even notice the green light or the intersection I've entered. Horns blast and a car screeches to a halt. Someone shouts. "You idiot!"

Yes, I think, clearing the road to jog on the sidewalk, I *am* an idiot. I not only ran into a busy intersection, but I didn't do what it took to take down The Poet before that boy ended up dead. And how did I think that kid was The Poet? He was four inches shorter. I just don't know how he did the switch and how he convinced the boy to go along with him.

I round a corner and bring the university into view, halting on top of what is now my lookout hill, overseeing a parking lot to the liberal arts building. I didn't mean to come here. It just *happened*. I'm sure the captain would call me a stalker again. I don't know how a law enforcement officer trying to prevent another murder stalks a serial killer, but apparently, my captain believes I've mastered the craft.

Newman pulls his light blue minivan into his assigned faculty space, as I knew from reports he would right about now. A grassy mound and about ten parking spots divide me from him. I should step behind the ancient oak tree to my left before Newman reports me and his attorney threatens to sue the department again, but damn it, people are dead. I want him to see me. I want him to know I'm watching him, that I'll know if he tries to kill again.

Maybe I'm losing my mind. Maybe I am going off the deep end, but I'm not hiding. I wait for him. Maybe I'll have a little talk with him. Yes. I'm going to have a talk with him. Decision made, I start walking, and that's when the muted sounds of a discharging weapon inside a sealed vehicle is followed by blood splattering all over the inside of Newman Smith's minivan.

CHAPTER 82

The gunshot was muffled, lost to city sounds, but I know what I heard, and the blood on the windows tells the story.

A stunned moment overtakes me, but it's a breeze in the storm where I thrive. My training kicks in, my action automatic. I start running, clearing the grassy mound with a leap that has me landing in the parking lot, hyperaware of everything around me: Of the two middle-aged women chatting as they walk to their cars. Another man in a suit is rushing toward the building, a briefcase on his shoulder. Another woman, this one thirty-something, doing the same. At this point, my phone is in my hand, my finger automatically punching the autodial button that's been a part of my life for a decade now.

Dispatch answers in one ring.

"This is Detective Samantha Jazz, badge number 25K11, off duty and unarmed." I sound my normal cool and calm self, but the rock concert pounding against my ribcage argues otherwise. "Shooter alert," I add, still deceptively calm. "I'm requesting backup and an ambulance at an active scene. UT campus Calhoun building, faculty parking lot, now. Shooting, one known victim, possible suicide but undetermined."

A man runs toward me and I disconnect at the sight of him carrying a book bag. Bags of any type make great weapon cases.

"Austin PD!" I shout, approaching the van. "Stand back and get me security out here now!"

The man's eyes go wide, and he backs up. I squat at the rear of the vehicle, adrenaline coursing through my veins, driving away fear and leaving nothing but duty. Duty, however, rides a happier horse when it's holding a weapon. I don't have my service weapon or any weapon at all, for that matter, but that isn't going to change, and with a campus full of targets for a shooter, I can't wait for backup. I inch left to the door of the vehicle and find the driver's side sealed shut as expected. I do the same to the right and go cold inside. It's open. It wasn't open. And this isn't a suicide. Damn it, I *need* that weapon.

I unlink the mace I keep on my keychain attached to my pants, and inch to the side of the vehicle, still low, beneath the window, careful not to touch anything and screw up evidence, without gloves on. Oh, screw it. I rush to the door, the sweet, iron scent of blood blistering my nostrils even before I have a visual of the interior of the vehicle. That comes next with the gruesome view of Newman alone inside the van, sitting in the driver's seat, face down on the steering wheel, with the side and part of the back of his head missing. I don't bother to check for a pulse. No one has the Grand Canyon carved in their head and survives.

Blood and gore didn't bother my former captain, and father, but then, I'm just not the man he was, in all kinds of ways, and that's okay with me. A wave of nausea threatens to take hold, but I welcome the reminder that I'm alive, that I'm human, that I'm not immune to human suffering. That's what it takes for me to push past the gore, that's my light switch, my trigger. Or he is. Even from the grave, my father defines all I do not want to become. I begin to map the location of blood and tissue, but I home in on his right arm, hand palm up, and draped over the console toward the passenger seat. His fingers are relaxed, and the weapon is lying on the seat.

The weapon is a Smith and Wesson snub-nosed, single-action revolver, a common self-defense choice that packs a massive bullet, meant to get the job done. It also has a rough recoil that supports why his hand would be on the seat right now. The problem is that A) The Poet wouldn't kill himself. That's not his way. He's precise. Clean. He killed his victims with poison and then shoved a poem into their mouths. Even the *U* he carved in the chests of his earlier victims was delicate and precise. And B) Newman doesn't own a gun. Or he didn't. Not according to our files.

This was murder.

Someone killed this monster before I could claim that honor. That's my other secret, the one I'll never admit to anyone. The one I also faced quite vividly in that San Antonio hotel. I wanted him dead, gone forever so he could hurt no one else. Beneath my calculated, thoughtful investigations, with facts and knowledge as my preferred choice of weapons, my desire for this man's expiration was as complete as any desire any woman might possess. Perhaps the secret is the real root of my rapidly fading nausea. This one got to me. This killer was under my skin, and his death was what I wanted. Perhaps I'm more like my complicated father than I like to believe. I don't feel regret that The Poet is dead. I feel joy.

Perhaps that's how The Poet made me his victim. He turned me into my father.

CHAPTER 83

Voices sound all around me and I step back out of the vehicle where I lean around the door to find uniformed campus security, in a set of four, rushing toward me. "Lock down the campus," I call out to them.

"Who the hell are you?" a tall man wearing glasses demands.

"I know who she is," the chubby guy next to him snaps, his ruddy face set in a scowl directed at me. "She's that cop who's been harassing Newman."

"Focus," I order, sirens sounding nearby. "Newman is dead, and we need to rule out a shooter. Secure yourselves and the campus. Now!" This earns me shocked expressions and dropped jaws. It does not earn me action. "Now!" I shout again. This time all but one of them—a thin man with gaunt features—moves.

I grab Mr. Thin Man by the arm and look him in the eyes. "What's your name?"

"Mark."

"Will there be security feed for the parking lot?"

"Yes. Yes. There is. There will be." His voice vibrates, teeth all but chattering. The man does not belong in a uniform.

"Where's the camera room?" I ask.

"Just—it's—inside—inside the doorway."

"Go there now and watch the film. Find out who was in the car other than Newman. Call the police immediately with the description of anyone you identify. Then come back here."

He nods, head bobbing like a bobblehead, but he doesn't move.

"Go!" I shout.

His eyes fly wide and then he does the same, rotating and rushing away.

Behind me, a car screeches to a halt, and I turn to find Lang climbing out of his now parked Mustang. I scowl in anticipation of the hell he's about to give me and sure enough, hell begins.

"What the *hell* are you doing, Jazz?" he demands, because that's his word in situations like this: *hell*. Drama is also his thing, which is why, predictably, his door remains open, and all two hundred and ten pounds of angry, muscled man hunches into linebacker position and charges toward me. "Talk," he orders, once he's planted himself in front of me.

"Newman arrived to the campus in his minivan and then his brains exploded," I speak quickly, eager to get back into action. "I called it in, which you know, since you're here and—"

"Ya think? You're not even released back to full duty, so yeah. I came to save your stupid ass. Holy hell, woman, you're going to get us both fired."

"Focus, Lang," I snap, not bothering to point out the trouble he could have gotten me into with Newman's wife. "We have an active crime scene."

"Thank fuck it's a suicide or you might be a damn suspect."

I grit my teeth. "Except that he died in the driver's seat and the passenger side door is open."

"In other words," he says, his hard features bunching up, "it might not be a suicide."

"That's what I've been *trying* to tell you."

"And you were here? *Jesus,* Jazz." He curses and scrubs an overly square jaw that hasn't seen a shave in about three days too long. "Tell me you don't have your weapon with you."

"I'm going to kick you," I say. "And enjoy it. We don't have time for this." My hands fly to my sides.

"Where would I hide a weapon?" I show him the mace in my hand. "Aside from this, I'm not armed, but someone needs to be holding a weapon and searching for the shooter. You're the first active officer on the scene. If someone else gets shot, it's on you."

He draws the Glock from his shoulder holster. "I hate that you're attached to this shit, Jazz. Go home," he orders, only to curse again, which isn't unusual. In our five years of partnering, I know his dictionary, even if I don't subscribe to it myself. "No," he amends tightly. "Damn it, you can't go home. You called this in. Stay right here and do nothing or I swear to God, I'll lose my job for killing you. Or maybe I'll get a medal. I hope like hell there's security feed to prove you didn't do it."

"Did you really just say that to me?"

"Just preparing you for the verbal ass-whipping the captain's going to give you. *Don't* move. Do *not* make me hunt you down." He resumes his linebacker position and charges toward the van.

I'm about to join him when sirens shrill through the air, and I turn to find a fire truck and an ambulance filing into the faculty parking lot. I don't even consider staying put and doing nothing. This is my job. It's instinct. This job is the only thing I know. With quick steps, I plant myself in the path of the emergency vehicles and wave them to halt. I don't need a crew ready to save his life, but I didn't know he was gone already when I made that call. The problem is that Lang is right. Everyone might not believe that when they find out I was here when he died.

Perhaps everyone knows one of my secrets after all.

CHAPTER 84

I stand in the path of those emergency vehicles; my mind is processing what has happened.

The Poet is dead and that's my win today—it's my *only* win, considering I never proved he was The Poet, and the family is now likely to sue the police department. If Newman killed himself, I'll be blamed for pushing him over the edge. If Newman was murdered by a family member, I might well be blamed for pushing them over the edge. There is no win for me, so I have to go do what I do, what I've always done. When all else fails, work the crime scene. It's what my father and my godfather taught me, and it's where I land now.

The fire truck stops inches from where I stand, the grandstand of sirens silenced and replaced with my shout of, "Stop! Stay back!" I race toward the EMS team now coming up on the side of the fire truck. "Detective Samantha Jazz," I announce, turning my hands into a stop sign. "Stay back and call in CSI." It takes me about three minutes too long to rein them all in and save the evidence they might destroy. By the time they finally get a grip on what is happening, the hollow echoes of approaching sirens transform into screeching howls a moment before a good half dozen patrol cars explode past the entrance into the faculty parking lot.

That's my sign to get lost before I end up shut out of the scene. I need to examine the body and the vehicle, to read the story to be read there, but that's a good way to get noticed and shorten what little time I have left free to explore. I need to see that camera footage, and with that goal in mind, I head away from the approaching patrol cars and double step a fast walk toward the faculty entrance into the campus building. Lang is nowhere in sight, and I like it that way. Well, as long as he's not dead or injured, but that's highly unlikely. Whoever did this isn't looking to shoot up the school or the police force.

I approach the door with a clear path, the absence of students or faculty anywhere in view, telling me that campus police, for all their early pushback, are now doing their jobs. Pushing past double steel doors, I end up in a hallway just inside the building, and Officer Jackson is standing in front of me.

"What are you doing here?" I ask.

"Securing the building."

"You have a way of being everywhere I am."

"Isn't that what I'm supposed to be doing? I'm on your team."

He's right. The Poet is dead. I don't know why I'm pushing back with him. "Yes. You are. Are we clear?"

"We are."

"There's plenty more space to cover."

"Right. Going now." He exits the building and I shake off the encounter, focused on finding the security booth. My destination doesn't require a hunt. It's just off the entrance to my right. Entering the small office lined with cameras, I find no one here. Jesus. Someone should be here, watching the feed, looking for a shooter.

I sit down at the desk, a row of screens line the wall now directly in front of me, a setup that I've seen before. With nothing even locked down, I quickly and too easily key in camera views. What I find is not good. The camera feed for the parking lot where Newman was shot is nothing but fuzz. I try to bring it back up, but the camera's offline. Whoever killed him either killed the camera from the outside first or had access to the security booth I'm sitting in right now and knows technology better than me, which isn't saying much. Aside from that, there's little to see besides law enforcement scurrying about like rats on the campus, looking for blood, finding none. I tab through screens, looking for clues, one after another, and I find nothing.

The door jerks open. I launch to my feet and turn toward the door. Lang blasts into the small room, his big body awkwardly, well, big. He's big. It's not. He scans his surroundings and slams the door behind him. "What the hell are you doing, Jazz?" he demands. "I told you to stay where you were."

I wave that comment off and focus on what matters. "Whoever killed Newman probably killed the parking lot camera first, which, considering I can't get the camera back up, is likely. Which is weird considering Summer's security feed was offline and The Poet always knows how to maneuver around cameras."

"The Poet is dead," he snaps. "I don't know where you're going with this and I don't think I want to know."

I wave that off and focus on the here and now. "We need to know if that camera's knocked out, because if it's not, then the killer could have been here in this security booth where we stand right now."

"*You* have access to the security booth and you *alone,* which means that you could have cleared the footage. In other words, everyone whispers about me being the brawn and you being the brains. I'm officially the brawn and brains. The man had a restraining order against you, and you were here when he died."

"I'm more than aware of that fact," I snap.

"Alone, Jazz," he snaps right back.

My brows dip. "Alone?"

"You were here when you shouldn't have been here, gone rogue, and gone rogue *alone*. Only you're not alone this time, are you? I'm here."

I scowl. "I didn't call you."

"You should have and *before* you came. What happened to 'live together, die together,' remember?"

"That's what you say every time you drag me into a hellish situation I shouldn't be in, which is often. I don't do that to you."

"Right," he says, his tone taking on a mocking quality. "Ms. Morals. Better than me. We've never gone down for one of my hellish situations." He motions to the cameras. "What's on there that I need to know about?"

"Nothing. There's nothing worth seeing on that feed. What about when you were skulking around the building?"

"No one to shoot. Nothing to see. Because he killed himself. That's the whole point here. How about we make sure you don't go down for his choice to take his life?"

"The passenger door was open and the gun is in his hand in the passenger seat. He didn't make that choice."

"The door's shut, Jazz."

I blanch but recover quickly. "It was open."

"Read my lips," he says. "The door is shut. I saw it with my own eyes."

CHAPTER 85

Newman's door was shut when Lang got to him.

Those words replay in my mind and I flash back to me finding that very same door open.

My mind processes this information in a rapid formation of facts that all amount to validation.

"Did you hear me?" Lang presses. "The door was shut."

I snap back to the present and to Lang with a quick reply. "Further proof that he was murdered. I must have surprised the killer. He or she shut the door after I turned my back on the minivan to talk to you. Then that person escaped while the camera was off."

"Or Newman realized we were onto him and killed himself. That's the right answer, Jazz. He killed himself."

"The Poet wouldn't kill himself. That's not how he's made. That's not how he thinks. He believed the world was a better place because he was here. Someone killed him."

"They're going to say that someone was you. He killed himself. Accept that you didn't understand him as well as you thought you did and thank fuck for that. None of us need to understand him that well."

"You're not hearing me."

"I don't know what your problem is here. I might not have gone through all your profile training, but I know this. Killers kill themselves when they get trapped. It happens." He starts naming serial killers who killed themselves. "Joe Ball. Bitter Blood. Charlie Brandt. Dallen—"

"Stop. I get it. It happens. It didn't happen here."

"He was obsessed with you. Now you're *obsessed.*

It's over. Let it be over."

"I just—"

"Let it go. Who cares if some family member sought vengeance? Who cares? He's gone. Thank the good Lord, and let's get busy on the next one."

"Something is off." My jaw sets hard. "Maybe he wasn't working alone."

"That's not your profile," he profiles.

"Him controlling someone else, like Newman, that would fit. Him killing himself does not fit. The door was open. Someone shut it. And I know this because I can describe everything I saw inside that minivan. And you won't find my fingerprints because I didn't have to open the door. It was open. I leaned in."

"Or you killed him and that's how you know. That's what the investigators are going to say. Protect yourself. You saw the blood on the window. You called it in."

My heart begins to drum a rock concert in my chest all over again, almost as fiercely as it had when I ran toward that minivan. He's right. I'm going to be looked at, investigated, accused, and through all of it, I will remember my job over his death. It will drive a guilty response, it will be torture, but I will survive. And it's not like I'm going down the rabbit hole he's trying to drag me down anyway. "Even if I lied, and you know that's not who I am, I didn't let the emergency vehicle help him. I knew he was dead."

He draws in a sharp breath. "Fuck."

"Yes. That word, a bunch of times."

"It's okay if you say it. Your father damn sure would have."

He would have, and that's why I won't. "The door was open. That's the truth. It's the story I need to stick to. It's the story that proves someone else was there."

"Yes, you. The door was shut. And you were never in this room alone. I was here. We found the scrubbed feed together."

"No," I reject. "No. I'm telling the truth. You're telling the truth. Lies backfire." I think of the joy I'd felt earlier knowing The Poet was dead. I tell myself it's human. I tell myself it has nothing to do with me being my father's daughter, a man who did morning laps in a pool of lies. "Lies don't die. You will not lie for me."

He closes the space between us and shocks me by blasting into me and shoving me against the wall, knocking the breath out me. I'm trapped against a wall, a prisoner, at least momentarily, to a man twice my size, who has never, ever, gotten physical with me. "Time to wake up and smell the bloody fucking roses, Detective Jazz."

Adrenaline courses through me, anger spiked with confusion. He doesn't act like this. He doesn't do things like this. "What the hell are you doing, Lang?"

"I'm protecting you," he repeats. "Like I told your father I'd protect you, *at all costs.*"

I blanch and go cold inside. "What did you just say?"

"I always promised him I'd protect you. I didn't know how damn hard that would be."

I laugh incredulously. "You're the reason I've almost been killed too many times?"

"Are you dead?"

"No, but—"

"And you aren't going to jail for this, either."

Realization comes at me in that brutal way it always does when it hits close to home. "So let me get this straight. My dirty cop father wanted you to protect me and you drive a Mustang while the rest of us use government vehicles at work. Your story

about that car never made sense to me. We all do undercover work. We don't get Mustangs in exchange.
The captain was my father and the chief's my godfather, and I don't drive a Mustang."

"I can't even believe you just said that to me."

My mind tracks back in time, to the exact point
when Lang and I became partners. I'd started to read
my father, the real man, not my hero. I'd seen things.
I'd questioned things. And then came Lang, who may
or may not be protecting me as he claims, but it feels
more like he's protecting my father. I just don't know
why. What I do know is that he's not the man that I
thought he was. He's dirty. He's manhandling me.

And those two things are all I need to know.
Anger surges through me and mixes with a sense of
betrayal I can barely contain. I knee him in the groin.

He doubles over, grunts. "What the fuck? Why
would you even think I would take a car to protect
you? We're friends."

It's right then, with me standing over my six-foot-
three hulkish partner, who is presently howling like a
whale giving birth, that the door flies open again and
Captain Moore explodes into the room.

CHAPTER 86

Captain Moore slams the door to the security booth behind himself, shrinking the already tiny room to the size of a closet rather than a small bedroom. "What in high heaven are you doing here, Detective Jazz?" That question, spoken low and tight, still manages to crackle with anger.

"Captain," I greet, completely dodging his question, my mind picking through my best strategy. There isn't a best strategy. Lord help me, what *am* I doing here?

The captain arches a brow. "I'm still waiting for the words that are going to come out of your mouth to explain yourself, Detective Jazz."

Words that I will have to live with for the rest of my life. A life I don't want to be spent behind bars.

Lang grunts his way to his feet. "I can explain."

"She can explain," the captain amends, pointing at me. "Talk."

But I don't get a chance. Lang is already talking again. "She went jogging," he says. "I followed her here."

It's a lie that transforms into a possible truth in my mind. Did he? Is that how he got here so fast? "We were standing at the grassy mound just off the parking lot," he continues, "talking about why she shouldn't be here when Newman drove up."

It's a lie when I told him not to lie, and the only way I defy that lie is to throw him under a bus.

The captain's thick brows pull together, and his gaze swivels hard and lands on me with a perceivable thud. "I'm back to the obvious. Why the *fuck* were you even here, Detective Jazz?"

He doesn't use the F-word often, but when he does, you're screwed. I'm screwed right into an explanation that can lead nowhere else but being more screwed.

"I really was jogging," I confirm, "and believe it or not, I was reflecting on my right and wrong choices that led me here. In hindsight, I should have done my reflecting elsewhere."

He scowls and when the captain scowls, it's a tornado in a thunderstorm. "You think, Detective?" The snarky question is followed by another. "What else?"

"Newman pulled up in the minivan," I say quickly. "Blood splattered on the windows. I took off running and called in the emergency. I was unarmed."

"But I wasn't," Lang adds. "I approached the vehicle first."

Damn this man. That's a lie the campus police might dispute. "The door on the passenger side was open," he continues. "Once I determined Newman was dead, I had Jazz stop the emergency teams before they contaminated the scene. I know. I know I should have just sent her away, but the campus police were such a fuck-up. That's also why I shut the door. I didn't want someone screwing up the scene."

"You didn't shut the damn door," I snap, eyeing the captain, who is eerily silent. "Captain," I say, "someone else shut that door."

"I shut it," Lang insists, scowling at me. "You know I shut it. I'm willing to claim that sin."

My fingers curl into fists by my sides where they are least likely to land on Lang. "Captain—"

"Newman didn't know we were there," Lang interrupts again. "The pressure of hiding who and what he was got to him. We're all better off with him dead."

He's right. We're all better off with Newman dead,

but I'm not sure we're the only ones who believe that. Thanks to Lang, I can't say that, I can't suggest The Poet was two people, not one, without making us both look like liars.

The captain looks between us. "You two assholes better hope we can now prove he's The Poet, otherwise we're going to pay out the ass to the family."

I blanch when I never blanch. "Pay?" My tone is incredulous, bordering on angry. "Why would we pay a settlement?"

"Because you stalked the man."

"Surveillance is not stalking, and you were in on this, too, Captain. We all wanted to get him. And what would we have done if he killed again before he killed himself? Twiddle our thumbs?" I sound snippy and I am. I'm riled up now, my ability to analyze while containing my emotions apparently taking one of its random sabbaticals.

"You didn't have enough to charge him. You kept hounding him. And thanks to you, I've got word that he's officially suing the department; we now know that he's the one who went to the press and told the city there was a serial killer free."

"Serial killers crave attention," I argue. "That's why he went to the press."

"You drove him to kill himself," he states.

"And you know this because CSI did their job already?" I challenge, holding nothing back, on a rocky cliff about to jump off, and it has nothing to do with Newman and everything to do with that young boy I shot. No, that I killed. I *killed* him, but I can't win here. I'll end up pressing the department to name a killer and they could say it's me, or I just simply become responsible for a suicide.

The captain scowls at me. "Do I seem calm right now?"

This is a trap, but I take his bait because I have no

choice. Lips pulled tight, I say, "Reasonably calm."

"I'm not!" he shouts, and I cringe with the lion-ish roar. "I'm fucking not," he repeats again with that added "fuck" for effect as if I haven't quite gotten the point. "Go to the station. Stay there. Do not leave. Do not pass go. There is no reward to collect." He throws a few visual bullets at me and then levels a stare at Lang. "Do a better job of keeping her out of trouble than you've done so far."

I open my mouth to speak, and he slices a hand through the air in my direction. "Do not say whatever you plan to say. Spend all of your remaining effort leaving without the press seeing you here." He scrubs a hand over his face and drops it. "Let's hope we can magically have everyone here forget they saw you." He waves a hand in the air. "Just go. Both of you go before I start thinking of Detective Jazz calling in the incident and how damned that makes us all."

But I don't just go. I push his limits. "The camera's out in the parking lot. I can't say if that's because the camera was hacked or just busted. If it was busted—"

"Did you kill Newman, Detective?"

That question is yet another knife carving away every honorable moment of my career, cutting it away piece by piece. "I did not."

"Then I suggest you trust me to handle the scene and get out of my face before one of us gets charged with murder. And it might not be you or Lang." He grits his teeth, and still glaring at me, he speaks to Lang. "Get her out of here now."

I suck in a jagged breath and step around him, meeting Lang at the door, but I don't look at my paid partner. If I do, he'll take another knee. I reach for the doorknob and hear, "Stop."

At the captain's command, Lang and I turn to find the captain facing us, spine stiff, hands on his hips. He fixes his brown eyes—that shade almost black with his anger—on Lang. "Why did she knee you?"

Without even a second of hesitation, he replies with, "I shut the door," handling that dodgeball with a lie that he bats back with far too much ease.

The captain's stare finds me now. "Why did you knee him?"

I will not willingly tell a lie, so I stick to honesty. "If you had to put up with him every day for five years, you would, too, sir."

He just looks at me, his expression unchanged, unreadable. And keeps looking at me. Seconds tick by, heavy, tension-laden seconds before he simply orders, "Go." Now eager to comply, I begin to turn and he adds, "Not you, Detective Jazz."

I suck in another breath and turn to face the captain again. Lang might be a liar, but he's not a complete fool. He exits the room and shuts the door behind him. Now I'm alone with the hard brute of a man I call my boss. "I'm going to give you something to think about while you wait for me in my office," he says. "I believe that you hated your father."

My teeth grit. I'm not sure where he's going with this, but I'm certain it's no place good. "I loved my father," I correct, and it's true. I loved him. He was my idol. Until he wasn't, but the love didn't go away.

"And hated him," he corrects in turn. "Interesting thing to me," he continues, "is that just three months after he died, The Poet came into your life."

"You gave me the case."

"You became obsessed, and obsession became a monster that you couldn't control with this one. Almost," he pauses for effect, the blow he's about to deliver hanging in the air before he throws his punch and adds, "as if you needed someone to hate more than your father. And what do you have to show for that hate? A dead boy and a lawsuit."

I feel his words like a blade stabbing in my chest,

a bull's-eye in the center of my body that kills a piece of me that isn't coming back. I'm not coming back.

"You may leave now, Detective Jazz."

And I do. Without another word, I leave, in more ways than one.

CHAPTER 87

I could hate the captain for throwing that boy in my face, but I don't. It's not that simple. I don't think it will ever be that simple ever again. The truth is that when you work in homicide, there are moments when you fear that you are no longer human. Too cold. Too immune to blood and gore. Too much like the killers you hunt. Then there are those opposing moments when you pray to God that you can hold yourself together.

When I step out of that security booth, with the captain's words burning holes in my mind, I'm not having one of those familiar "please God" moments. Instead, there's a cold seeping inside me and a decision about my future brewing hot and quickly chilling. I do have a "thank God" moment when Lang gives me one look and says nothing. Regardless of why we partnered up, we have spent more time together than most spouses. He knows that I'm in what we have declared our ground zero, that place where we must gather ourselves, find ourselves, ground ourselves, or else we self-destruct.

Lang motions down the hallway toward an exit I don't know. I fall into step with him, still trusting him on some level when he doesn't deserve that trust. Or maybe he does. I need out of ground zero before I assess where I stand with Lang. For me, that means distance. I need distance from the recent events scratching holes in my soul.

We exit the building through a side door, and I don't ask how Lang's Mustang is conveniently waiting for us. I don't care. I climb inside the passenger side and settle into my seat. I'm starting to compartmentalize, a skill that is both underrated and necessary in this job. I'm no longer fighting my demons with labels like "my father" and "The Poet." They're boxed up. I've shut the lid. They're clawing at the lid, but their destructive effect is postponed until a later date. I don't have to analyze why they're in the same box. Despite the captain's desire to shock me with some stunning revelation I already know. I've known for a long time. But it's not what he thinks. It's not about displaced hate. It's about the only two monsters I've faced and failed to defeat.

Lang climbs into the vehicle and I don't look at him when I say, "Take me home. I'll drive myself to the station."

"Jazzy—"

"Take me home, Lang." I glance over at him. "I'll self-report and give my statement. As we're both aware, I'm far more by-the-book than you are. I'll do what I'm supposed to do."

"I protected you in there."

"I asked you not to lie, but apparently, you offer my dead father more respect than you do me. Don't say a word, either. If you know me at all—"

"If I know you at all? Really, Jazz? You know what? You're right. Why would I say a damn thing when you think I'd take a bribe from your damn father? He loved you, Jazz. He threatened me with my damn life if I didn't protect you, and I do mean that literally."

I don't say a word. That's the thing about being in a job like this one; too many people tell you lies. Honesty becomes everything.

Five minutes later, Lang pulls up beside my building and I get out without saying a word. In a measured pace, I walk to my building to find Daniel, our ex-gangster security guard from the other night, by the door. "Good morning, Detective Jazz."

I'm about to walk past him when my gaze lands on his hairless arm. I halt abruptly, a gut feeling churning inside me before my gaze jerks to his. His brows dip. "Something wrong?"

I wait to feel that familiar evil, but there's nothing there. "Why do you shave your arms?"

He laughs. "Kind of girly, right? I'm having the tattoos removed. I have to shave."

A breath I don't know I'm holding slides from my lips. What am I doing? Newman is dead. This is over. Or it will be soon. Supported by the fact that Lang was right when he said The Poet was obsessed with me. He was also too smart to ensure I got shut out of the case, which is exactly what happened tonight.

Unless he was part of the team and the other half of the team decided I was a problem.

"Detective Jazz?"

At Daniel's prod I snap back to the moment, a scold to the crazy places my head is going.

"Good decision on the tattoo removal," I say, and I hurry inside the building and to my door.

Once I'm inside, I fight the urge to search my apartment. He's gone, dead, there is no need. With that in mind and the fact that I won't be questioned for hours, I head into the bathroom and take a long, hot shower. Once I've dressed in my standard pantsuit with a pale blue blouse, I gather my work bag and stick my badge inside. My personal weapon is left behind this time, as I'm going to be questioned in a death investigation. I then do what I should have done days ago.

I face down the demons The Poet has left in his wake. I walk across the street and grab a coffee, but I'm not wearing my badge when I do. It stays in my bag. I just can't seem to make myself put it back on.

CHAPTER 88

I call Nicole, who is still acting as my union attorney, while waiting in line for my coffee, and she agrees to meet me at the station. Once we're there, the captain is already there too. My attorney heads to the interrogation room to meet with him, Evan, and Detective Martinez, who'll be taking my statement. I head to my desk to check my messages, when Chuck catches me in the hallway.

"Is it really over?" he says.

There is a clawing sensation in my chest that defies my full agreement which I cannot offer. Instead I say, "It appears that way." I do my best to give him a reassuring smile. I'm pretty sure I fail. "Great work, Chuck," I add, offering him a heartfelt compliment. "I mean, Superman. And you *really are* Superman."

I chitchat with him for a few minutes before heading to my desk, where I begin a review of anything that might have been overlooked while I worked on The Poet case. Wade calls, but I text him rather than answer: *Later. It's crazy here.*

I heard, he replies. *All of it. I know you have a rough few hours ahead of you. Call me when you can.*

I send a quick reply and set my phone aside as Lang sits down at his desk across from mine. We stare at each other, a crackle of tension between us that has never existed before now. We aren't good. I don't know if we will ever be good again.

"Detective Jazz."

It's the captain's voice, and I swivel around to find him towering over me, a scowl on his face. "We're ready for you."

I glance at Lang, and there's a warning in his stare. "Live and die together," he says, reminding me of the lie he told between us.

"What does that mean?" the captain demands.

Lang answers for us both. "We're going through this together, Captain. That's all."

The captain's expression is scathing. "Bullshit." He motions me forward.

I grab my bag and, without looking at Lang, head in the direction the captain indicates. A few minutes later, just like on the night that little boy died, Nicole and I sit side by side while Martinez asks me what feel like softball questions. Evan, in one of his expensive suits, enters the room, arrogance dripping off him. Today he exudes vibes of the future DA with an agenda, a power grab in the air. As if defying my mental assessment, he offers Nicole a nod. "No claws needed. I promise."

"We'll see," she says dryly, sensing what I sense.

He then claims the seat in front of me, his piercing blue eyes meeting mine. "He's gone. The world is a better place. I just need to be sure I have my ducks in a row if the family sues."

My lips press together with the evident plan in play. He was involved in taking down Newman, but he wants to distance himself and the DA's office. He and the department here need a fall guy. That's going to be me or Lang. "That's what I'm here for," I say, my tone measured and cool.

He sets a notebook on the table, opens it to a yellow pad and pen and scribbles the date down. "Why were you at the school?"

"I took a jog."

"But you knew Newman had a restraining order against you."

"I didn't cross that barrier until he was dead." It's technically true. I didn't step over the distance barrier of a restraining order until he was dead.

"How did you know he was dead?" Evan asks.

"Blood splattered all over his vehicle, and I ran to investigate."

"Was there a gunshot?"

"Muted. The car was sealed, but I've experienced a similar incident and knew what I was hearing."

"He just happened to kill himself when you were there." It's not a question, but rather an accusation.

It's a question that's niggled at my mind for hours. How is that even possible? "It happened. That's all there is."

"You hated him."

It would seem that Lang, the captain, and Evan have been talking. "The captain's words, not mine."

"Did you hate him?"

"I don't allow hate into my job."

"That's still not an answer," he says.

"Did you like him, Evan? I'd be interested to hear how you felt about a serial killer."

His lips purse. "I understand you didn't call for an ambulance."

"I looked inside the vehicle and he was dead."

"The door was open?"

I hesitate. "I don't know how it ended up open. I just know that I looked inside and it was clear he was dead."

He studies me for several long beats. "Who opened the door? Who shut the door?"

"I didn't open or shut the door."

"That's not an answer," he snaps back.

"That's my answer."

"I don't like your answer."

"What are you getting at?" Nicole demands.

He doesn't look at her. He looks at me. "Did he kill himself or was he murdered?"

My answer is simple and fast. "I wasn't allowed to

investigate the scene properly. You'll have to ask the investigators involved."

"Did you kill Newman Smith?"

The question isn't unexpected but it still smarts. "I did not."

"Who did?"

"Again," I say, "I didn't investigate the scene."

"Did he kill himself?"

No, I think, but I won't help him build a case that ends up against me. In other words, I say what I have to say. "It appears that way."

He leans in closer. "What aren't you saying?"

"Nothing I want to say to you. I need to speak to the captain."

He narrows his eyes on me. "Why not me?"

Now I lean in closer. "Because we both know you never really cared about this case. You care about only yourself and making yourself look good and covering your ass."

"She won't go down for you," Nicole interjects. "You come at her, we'll come at you. Hard."

He glances at her and then me. "This is not the way to earn my favor for the future."

The decision that has lurked in the back of my mind since the captain jabbed at me over that little boy sets hard and right in my belly. "I don't need or want your favor. Are we done?"

He closes his notebook. "We're done. For now." He stands up and walks toward the door.

The captain walks in immediately afterward and claims the seat Evan just left. "You'll be off a desk and on extended leave until we've finished our review."

I glance at Nicole, who knows my next move. She offers a nod of approval before I reply with, "Extended to a lifetime," and reach into my bag to palm my badge, which I set down in front of me. "I'm done," I say, and with that, I stand up and walk toward the door.

He doesn't stop me, which doesn't surprise me. I start walking and I don't stop. When I exit the station, I'm surprised at the load that lifts off my shoulders. I feel no regret.

"Jazzy."

At Lang's voice, I inhale a deep breath and turn as he jogs into a spot in front of me. "You turned in your badge."

"Yes. I'm done."

"Our story is good. I've got your back."

"That's just it, Lang. I don't want you to have my back if it means lying. And I've come to discover that this job is one big lie."

"I'll come over tonight and we'll talk."

"I won't be home." I turn and walk to my car. I get in and start the engine.

Once I'm idling at a stoplight, I do what I haven't done in far too long. I call my mother before she calls me. "Honey, how are you?" she says.

"How about that lunch, Mom?"

She laughs. "How about dinner? It is after five."

"Dinner it is." I hang up and I have no idea what my future holds besides dinner with my mother, but dinner's a good start. No one is my master but me now.

CHAPTER 89

The dinner with my mother is the best dinner I've had with my mother in years. I meet her at a little Mexican spot near the hospital where she works, and we chat for hours about my future. She tries to hide her relief at my departure from the police department, but she fails. And I'm okay with that. There are times when I'm angry with her over her rose-colored glasses where my father was concerned, but it's time I get beyond that. She loved him. And now he's gone, which has left her afraid that I will be, too.

After dinner, we sneak by the nursing home to find my grandfather sleeping. My mother steps out to speak to the nurse while I creep to his bedside and give him a kiss, disappointed when he doesn't stir. Mom and I are leaving when I spy the poetry book and box of Frosted Flakes by the window. There are two bowls sitting there as well, both floating with leftover milk. I'm sad that someone here has replaced me and vow to remember to visit. I pick up the poetry book and read the title.

There is a pad of paper with my grandfather's writing, and I sit down in front of it and read his still quite perfect script: *The Annotated Waste Land with Eliot's Contemporary Prose: Second Edition.* T. S. Eliot is not only a Nobel Prize winner and one of the most distinguished poets of his time and beyond, he has always been a poet my grandfather favored. "The Waste Land" is a deeply emotional, post-World War I piece broken into five parts.

1. "The Burial of the Dead"
2. "A Game of Chess"
3. "The Fire Sermon"

4. "Death by Water"

5. "What the Thunder Said"

The quote on the paper is from "What the Thunder Said." Ironically, considering The Poet's theme of judgment, this section concludes the work with an image of judgment.

In this decayed hole among the mountains
In the faint moonlight, the grass is singing
Over the tumbled graves

The words hit a nerve and a shiver runs down my spine, stirring something dark inside me that I quickly visualize. An image of Dave naked and bound to the chair has me launching myself to my feet. A foreboding feeling settles deep in my belly, and I know that while Newman Smith is dead, The Poet will live on in my nightmares.

CHAPTER 90

Wade calls right before I fall asleep that first night without a badge. "I'm not surprised you resigned."

"Even I'm surprised I resigned."

"It's been in the air since your father died and you wanted to go to Internal Affairs. You're ready for a change."

"Is this the FBI recruitment talk?"

"It's not. You took off your mother's rose-colored glasses and once you did, you changed."

He's referencing many a talk we've had over the months. "Is that bad?"

"It's necessary. It's a part of what we do and how we survive. It also makes us better at what we do. We become wider thinkers and more diverse."

"I don't know what that means for me."

"You'll figure it out. Rest. You're a free woman, and there's one less killer in the world."

We hang up and I replay the conversation, drifting into sleep without apprehension. In an unexpected and welcome twist, I wake up my first day without a badge also without memories of a nightmare.

Refreshed, I start my day with a run, frustrated that something about Newman and his suicide nags at me, but I resist a path to the school. I crank up a Garth Brooks song and force The Poet from my mind. I end my run at the coffee shop, suddenly aware that I haven't heard from Lang or the chief. Lang I understand, but the chief? Well, I thought a godfather would care that I resigned, but I guess I didn't go to him first, either.

Once I have my coffee cup in hand, I step out onto the street. The man with the neon shoes runs by me again, and I inhale with the memories he stirs of an evil that had felt too familiar and close. I'm sure he's just a neighbor. I see many of the same people all the time, but I call Chuck and ask him to do a scan for the "Neon Shoe Guy" on our various films. By afternoon, Chuck finds him, on feeds that go weeks back. He seems to be just a runner.

Shortly after Chuck's call, perhaps because of his call, I've smashed such thoughts and met with a realtor, placing my apartment on the market. With the profits from selling, I'll be able to buy another place and carry myself over until I decide what the next chapter of my life will become. That evening, I return to the karate studio I've neglected for one-on-one lessons with Hitman McCoy. He's a big, country cowboy of a man, who explains the nickname as he's good with his hands.

Day two, there are viewings of my apartment already, and I meet my mother at the hospital for lunch, leaving her delighted. I then drive out to the nursing home to find my grandfather awake and playing checkers with another man. He doesn't know who I am. It's one of those days, the ones that gut me. "You're such a pretty young woman," he says, his eyes a pale blue that are as striking as ever, and it's hard to explain, but the intelligence is still there, just not the clarity.

"And you, sir, are a handsome devil. I think I'll stay and watch you two play."

I leave with tears in my eyes and a promise from the nurse that he has moments when he's himself and he will remember me. "He talks about you often," she'd said.

I spend most of my afternoon at the firing range, thinking about all the years my career kept me away from family. Years in which I lost my grandfather, and yet I crave a purpose I no longer have. My evening is spent sipping wine, thinking about dinner I don't order, while watching the show everyone else has already watched: *The Witcher* with Henry Cavill. It's good, but a bit confusing, which suits me fine. I need a puzzle to unravel or I might just unravel myself.

By night three, I'm already losing my mind. I have to figure out what comes next for me. I'm so stir-crazy I have a double session with Hitman McCoy before heading home for the evening with a rumbling stomach and an urgent need for takeout. I open the door to the scent of delicious food and find Wade sitting on my couch. His jacket and tie are already gone.

"We have to talk about you and that key," I say.

"Before you yell about me letting myself in," he replies, "I celebrated returning home from Dallas by bringing you mac n cheese and wine."

"From Old Chicago Taphouse?" I ask hopefully.

"Yes," he promises, his lips curving. "From *Old Chicago*."

"Well then," I say, shutting the door and setting my things down. "We can talk about the key later."

Half an hour later, our stomachs are full and our glasses half empty. "Thank you," I say. "This was perfection."

"It was," he agrees. "I had one too many burgers in Dallas and not good ones, either. So," he adds, "are you ready to go back to work?"

"Is this where you make the FBI pitch?"

He sets his glass down and reaches in his briefcase before setting an envelope in front of me.

"What's this?"

"The pitch."

I glance at it and then him. "You want me to work for the FBI?"

"You act like that's a surprise."

"I have a case pending," I remind him. "And for all I know, they could come at me for Newman's death."

"They aren't," he says. "I talked to the chief and the DA's office."

Hope tempts me but I hold it in check. "You talked to the chief?"

His brows dip. "You haven't?"

"No. I guess the perks of him being my godfather lasted only as long as my father was alive." I don't give him time to offer me sympathy that I don't want over a man who obviously was just another kind of lie. "Did they prove Newman was The Poet?"

"Not yet," he says. "but they're doing a press conference to tell the public they have the suspect and no reason to believe the public is in danger. They're eventually going to name him."

"And the boy," I say, my gut twisting with the painful topic. "Did they ever identify him?"

"A homeless child several people knew from a nearby neighborhood. No lead on his parents." He doesn't let me linger on a bad subject, nor does he give me time to ask about Newman's wife and kids. He taps the envelope.

"I'm not ready."

"Lang told me you believed The Poet wouldn't commit suicide. If that's making you doubt your-self—"

"Lang's full of shit," I say. "He didn't kill himself, Wade. The passenger door was open when I got there. He didn't open the passenger door to kill himself. Lang covered it up. He said I'd be accused of the murder."

"Fair enough," he says. "I'm asking you to join the FBI. I clearly trust your judgment. Who do you think killed him?"

"Someone who wanted revenge, but my point is

that the truth didn't matter. Everyone involved did a little CYA. The truth should be the truth, but it's not. I'm not ready for the red tape bureaucracy of it all again."

"The truth should be the truth and it will be with me. You'll find that out. I believe that. That's why it's a consulting offer. A chance to get your feet wet. You can pick your cases. You'll have the freedom you never had before." He winks. "And me."

"You'd be my boss."

"You betcha, baby."

I snort. "Then it's a no."

He laughs because he knows we get along far too well for that to be my reason to say no. "Then let me give you a few reasons to say yes. The pay is excellent. The cases are interesting. And one day you might even walk into Captain Moore's office and claim jurisdiction over one of his cases."

"That's bad."

"And it would feel so good. You know it would." He hands me a folder.

I accept it with a curious look. "What's this?"

"Three open cases. Pick your flavor. All are hot and new."

"You're not going to give me time to find something else, are you?"

"Not a chance, and why would you with three puzzles in that file?"

The man does know me, it seems. Really curious now, I tab through potential serial killers, both originating in different states, and one Houston, Texas ransom kidnapping case. The kidnapping is an odd case for him to offer me. "I don't do kidnapping and ransoms," I remind him.

"Why not? It's a puzzle. And who better to help than a ten-year-old?"

I know what he's doing. He's offering me a way to

make peace with killing that little boy. Proving this point, he says. "Save the ones we can save."

I inhale a heavy breath and flip to the photo of a pretty blonde girl with blue eyes. Eyes that stare right into my soul. I shut the file. "I'll take the kidnapping case. Now what?"

He reaches in his bag yet again and hands me a badge. "You'll need this."

"I thought I was a contractor."

"You are. It's a pilot program I'm running with a handful of consultants. I can't promise it lasts forever, but for now, it's your start. There's paperwork to do in the morning, a weapon to issue. The basics." I stare at the shiny badge that reads "FBI." It's the future that might have been mine had I not followed my father, and I don't know why I continue to resist. That will take some self-analysis, but in the meantime, I'm not going to turn down the consulting job. I need a purpose. I need a puzzle.

I stand up and walk around the table.

"Where are you going?" Wade calls after me as I head toward my bedroom.

"To pack and get on a plane to Houston," I call over my shoulder. This is what I need, I think, as I grab my suitcase. This purpose helps someone in need and gets The Poet out of my head.

CHAPTER 91

Agent Jazz.

It takes me seven days to get used to people calling me this because of the badge, though I'm not technically Agent Jazz. Consultant Jazz, but I do admit that doesn't have quite the ring that Agent Jazz does. The idea of working for the FBI is growing on me.

It also takes me seven days in Houston to find the little girl, who wasn't kidnapped at all. Her parents were trying to get more from a rich grandparent. Returning home with a sense of accomplishment, and no contact with anyone at the Austin PD but Chuck, I'm also returning to the news that my apartment has been sold and the closing will be in three weeks. The time to hunt for a house is now. Therefore, my first day back in Austin is spent house hunting, which, not intentionally, leads me to a cute little white two-story stand-alone home not far from Wade's house.

It's near nine when I finally finish up at the grocery store and head home, where Wade will soon join me to discuss my future over takeout food. While I wait for his arrival, I open a bottle of red wine, fill a glass, and I'm not sure why, but I find myself drawn to the computer by the door connected to my security camera. I disconnect it and carry it with me to the couch to offer it a quick perusal, though I'm not sure why. Perhaps because this is the first time in a week that I'm back home and in the aftermath of all things The Poet.

I'm just pulling up last week's feed when there's a knock on my door, which wouldn't be possible if the apartment had installed coded entry panels as promised, but they have not. With the computer disconnected from the door, I check out my visitor the old-school way. "Who is it?"

"Evan."

Evan? What the heck. I open the door to find him dressed in jeans and a T-shirt, and on the surface, he appears relaxed and casual. But there is nothing relaxed about the hard lines of his face and jaw right now. "Why are you here and how do you even know where I live?"

"The chief gave me your address."

"The chief? What the heck is going on, Evan?"

"Can I come in?"

I remain planted in the doorway. "What's going on?"

"You need to let me inside. It's important."

I don't trust him. I don't like him. I want to get rid of him, which is why I back up to allow him the space he needs to enter, but not much more. He steps into my apartment and shuts the door. I plant my feet again and fold my arms in front of me.

"He's back," he says.

I go still and force a breath before I ask, "Who's back?"

"The Poet."

"I'm not a part of that investigation anymore, but the last time I checked, he was missing half his head. He's dead."

"Newman wasn't The Poet."

A ball of tension knots my belly. "And you know this how?"

"Because he's not just back, he's asking for you."

I blink at this craziness. "What are you talking about?"

He offers me his phone, and I stare down at a photo of a gloved hand holding a piece of paper. On that paper is a quote from the poet Robert Hayden:

Naked, he lies in the blinded room
Chain-smoking, cradled by drugs, by jazz
as never by any lover's cradling flesh.

The word "jazz" sets my heart racing.

"Clearly that message was left for you," Evan says.

My gaze jerks to his. "This was after Newman died?"

"Tonight. The crime scene is active right now. We want you to take a look. Now. Right now."

The Poet wasn't Newman. Or at least he wasn't working alone. God, I knew. On some level, I knew, but I was off my game, riding a wave of my father's sins that made me hate him even as I grieved him. "I'm not with the department anymore. I'm not a part of this."

"You don't have a choice but to be a part of this," he counters.

"I absolutely have a choice."

"The Poet asked for you. How many more is he going to kill before you answer?"

"That's a shitty thing to say and you know it."

"It's the truth."

My teeth grind on the real truth. "I thought he was Newman. Why would anyone trust me to help now?"

"You weren't wrong about Newman. He has sick-as-fuck child porn on his computer. He beat his wife. He would have eventually abused his children. You hyper-focused because you sensed his evil."

But not that familiar evil. I should have known Newman wasn't him. If I could turn back time—

"The chief wants you to come back, even as a consultant."

"The chief didn't even ask me to stay the day I left."

"Does it matter?" He flips through the photos on his phone and shows me a picture of a naked young woman tied to a chair. "She even looks like you. He's coming for you unless you get him first. I'll support you this time. We all will."

She looks like me.

I'm reminded of the day Lang said the same of Becky Smith, and that ended up meaning nothing, absolutely nothing. But The Poet is another bag of snakes. He is obsessed with me. He will come for me. And I can't be the lesser me of the last few months to survive and take him down.

The door opens and Wade walks in, still wearing his work suit for the day, delicious scents coming off the takeout bag in his hand. "Why are you here, Evan?" He glances at me. "What's going on?"

I lift my chin toward Evan's phone. Evan flips a screen on his device and then hands it to Wade. "Two back-to-back photos," he instructs.

Wade glances at the first photo, swipes with his thumb, and then eyes me. "The Poet wasn't Newman."

"But she wasn't wrong about Newman," Evan quickly says again. "We had plenty of reasons to lock him away, and I suspect he killed himself because he knew we were onto him."

I offer up a hard rejection. "He didn't kill himself. I tried to tell the captain that and he wouldn't listen."

Wade sets the takeout bag on the coffee table, and the three of us form a circle of conversation. "Did The Poet kill him?" he asks.

"The Poet isn't messy, and Newman died messily," I say. "That said, if he did it, he broke form. And I'm not saying he didn't. He's smart. If he broke form, he had a reason. As for why he might have killed Newman, if he did? Either he was taking attention The Poet wanted himself, or Newman was part of an agenda we don't understand."

"What we all understand is that he's obsessed with you," Evan says. "We want you back and you need to come back and finish what The Poet started."

"I'll make this easy for everyone," Wade interjects. "I'm claiming jurisdiction. And, since Sam is now on contract with the FBI, I'm placing Sam in charge of the case." He glances at me. "If you want the case."

My spine straightens and I give a nod. The Poet wants me. He's going to get me, the better me. The one that isn't muddied up with emotions. The one he can't beat.

CHAPTER 92

Wade sidesteps the captain and calls the chief on the way to the scene, informing him that the FBI is taking control of the crime scene and all related cases, and that I'll be taking the lead over his detectives. The call is short and terse, and when Wade disconnects, he offers no input. In other words, I won't like the chief's reply. Oh, how brutal the reality of how little the title "godfather" really means, at least to the chief. I don't ask Wade for details. The chief no longer deserves that emotional reaction from me. I'm focused on this case and the woman who lost her life tonight and deserves justice.

A few minutes later, Wade pulls his Texas Mercedes—AKA his pickup truck—to a meter a block outside the crime scene tape to avoid the congestion of people and law enforcement.

The crime scene is on a property set up as one of a half dozen row houses, each with their own little gated front and backyard. The area is a fun, quirky, campus-friendly area with little coffee shops, bars, restaurants, and even businesses set up in a little circular neighborhood with the school a mere three blocks down.

I let Wade do his thing, flashing his badge and declaring his authority and mine. Wade has a way about him, too. He assumes ownership and power, but he's not cocky and arrogant like Evan. In fact, over and over, he says to one person or another, "Keep doing what you do well. We're here to help make your jobs easier."

Of course, all FBI agents aren't like Wade, and my encounters with the arrogant assholes that act like gods are perhaps why I'd shied away from the job. Tonight, seeing him in action, I'm reminded that we choose how we walk and talk, and even how we chew our bubble gum. As a consultant, I can always walk away.

We cross the yard and walk up the stairs to a cute little porch where Officer Jackson stands guard. His presence is a little off-putting when the police force is a healthy size and the number of officers so plentiful. "I see you follow guard duty better when I'm not around," I comment.

"Detective Jazz," he greets. "We missed you."

"Agent Jazz now," Wade corrects. "She's with us now and is the agent in charge of this crime scene."

I'm an acting agent and consultant, and I'm pretty sure I'd like to keep it that way, but I don't push back. "How is it that you're always at The Poet's crime scenes?" I ask.

If the question rattles him, he doesn't show it. "Detective Langford called me. He's pulling our team back together."

It's a good answer. One I accept. For now.

"CSI is working now," he says. "And the medical examiner is already present."

"Hazel?"

"Hazel," he agrees. "Detective Langford asked for her."

Officer Jackson motions to someone, and Wade and I are offered jackets. "You're going to want these."

Because the house is turned to ice, I think. I don't know why The Poet freezes out his victims, aside from punishing them. He wants them to suffer and it's the only way he sees to get that result without getting messy.

"Let me guess," I say shrugging into my coat, as Wade does the same, "An anonymous caller reported the crime?"

"You guessed right," he confirms.

"What do we know about the victim?" Wade asks.

"Her name is Ava Lloyd. She's twenty-three. And interestingly enough, considering what we know of The Poet, she's an English major."

Who somehow insulted poetry in some way, I think. I give him a nod, and at this point, Wade and I both have on gloves. I reach for the door and step inside to a brutally cold room. Lang is front and center in the living area, standing with Hazel, both in APD jackets, both inspecting a naked woman tied to a chair.

Lang, of course, is yakking as usual and doesn't seem to know we're present, while he yaps on, telling a joke.

"A man was recently flying to New York. He decided to strike up a conversation with his seatmate. 'I've got a great FBI joke. Would you like to hear it?' The seatmate says, 'I should let you know first that I'm an FBI agent.' 'That's OK,' the man says. 'I'll tell it really slow!'"

Obviously, he *does* know we're here. I glance at Wade, who smirks. "He's always been an ass," he says. "That's not going to change." He clears his throat. "Detective Langford."

Lang turns and smirks himself now. "Agent Wade Miller." His gaze shifts to me. "And Agent Jazz. Didn't know you were here."

Hazel rotates away from the body to greet me. "Good to see you, Detective, I mean, *Agent* Jazz. Congratulations."

"Thanks, Hazel. What do we have?"

"It's what we don't have," she replies. "I'm not going to find a mistake this guy made."

"CSI is offering the same feedback," Lang says. "But there is one interesting difference to this murder." He motions with his head, and together, he and I step in front of the body of the once-beautiful brunette. That is until The Poet poisoned her and then used what looks like lipstick, most likely her lipstick, to draw a huge *U* on her face.

"Looks like he wanted us to connect him to the Houston and Brownsville murders," Lang comments. "And he found a way to avoid the mess you say he doesn't like."

"*U* is for 'unworthy.'"

"The question is," he says, glancing over at me, "if the poem was meant for you, is he telling us that she was unworthy? Or are you, Jazzy?"

CHAPTER 93

I stand at the coffee shop not far from the house where Ava Lloyd's body waits for Detective Jazz's inspection. Correction: FBI Agent Samantha Jazz. Agent. I like the ring of this new title. It suits her. It allows her more power, more freedom. I'd followed her and Agent Wade Miller to the neighborhood where Ava Lloyd's house still hosted her chilled body, watched her rush toward the crowd and the yellow tape. And now I stand here, just outside the coffee shop, sipping an espresso, enjoying the chaos that I know only she will understand as perfect order.

I wonder if she knows now the cold is part of the sinner's punishment. I wonder if she's figured out I force them to sit there, naked and freezing, when I make them choose life or death. When I make them choose to take the pill or let me shoot them in the head.

Of course, they all choose the pill. They believe it gives them a chance to survive.

It does not.

Sadly, my time here must be cut short. I walk to the trash can and toss my cup, focused on necessary progress. Progress that started with the expiration of Newman Smith, who'd served a purpose, a barrier between myself and Agent Jazz when she wasn't yet ready to see me in herself. A man easily disposed of when the time was right, a child molester who I knew Agent Jazz would judge unworthy, which she did. She simply wasn't ready to pass ultimate judgment, the eternal judgment, which was expected. Progress takes time.

She's obviously comfortable with judgment but still resists delivering proper punishment. That's coming for her the way she came to me tonight. Agent Jazz had chosen Dave. The book had chosen Ava. These were not random choices, and it's time she comes full circle. It's time she opens her eyes and sees me the way she used to see me.

I walk a few blocks to my BMW and climb inside, making the short drive to South Austin, where Richard Williams is presently staying in a rundown trailer park. I owe him payment for Newman's murder, and tonight, I've planned a little bonus for him that he's not expecting. Because he's a stupid embezzler. The trailers are broken down and spread apart and, as I have twice in the past, I drive to a wooded area just past his particular trailer, where I leave the money in our drop spot of a gutted tree. Tonight, his extra prize is an expensive bottle of whiskey.

Once I'm parked behind one of the neighboring trailers, one with a view of Richard's front door, and a for rent sign in the window, I step out of my car and head to my trunk, where the tools for my judgment await me. I tuck my hair under a skintight cap and apply a layer of wax over my eyebrows and lashes to prevent shedding. My shirt is removed, my chest and arms bare of any hair. My wife says she likes me like this. Why would I deny her what she likes? My gloves are rolled into place. I pull a scrub shirt over my head and scrub pants over my pants. Booties go on my feet. Next, I remove a throwaway phone from my trunk and dial his number.

"Who is this?" he demands, but he knows. Of course he knows. He's expecting me and the money I'll gladly sacrifice to terminate him and the problems he represents.

"The task is complete," I state. "I left you an extra

gift for a job well done."

"The gift will be the day you pay me to kill that other Jazz. The girl."

My lips thin with his sinful words, words that solidify why he must be ended. "You'll have to settle for what I left for you now." I hang up and remove the SIM card and pour bottled water over it before tossing it in a trash bag in my truck.

In all of sixty seconds, Richard bursts from his door and heads out on foot to retrieve his prize. Once he's out of sight, I quietly cross the terrain and enter his trailer through the back entry that he never locks. I move to the spare bedroom, where I wait, a crack in the door allowing me a full view of the tiny living room and kitchen. Richard returns quickly, and it's not long before he's sitting at his kitchen table with the cash and his gun on the table, downing the whiskey I've left him. He didn't even notice the bottle was open. The sedative I've included inside is fast-acting, and he's knocked out in minutes.

I exit the bedroom and remove the superglue from my pocket, squeezing the substance onto the gun as well as his hand before I press the steel into his palm. Once it's solidly attached to his skin, I rest both on the table. I set the bottle of glue next to the stack of money. I want this to look as if he did it himself, like the money just wasn't enough to make him happy. Once the setup is in place, I stick a couple of acid tablets, which I bought down at the border, under his tongue, pills laced with a little something extra. That something extra is well known on the streets and won't look suspicious. It's killed others, as it will kill Richard tonight. It also cost me a pretty penny, but money is of no consequence. I've been blessed with the financial freedom to allow my judgments. Finally, I set a handful of pills on the table, the same sedative that I put in the bottle. Pills that don't mix well with acid.

If I've done my job well, and I have, the police will think he was trying to get the courage to kill himself with the gun, then resorted to an overdose instead. They'll believe anything about a cop killer. They want him dead. Even more so if they find out he used this very gun to kill Detective Roberts. If they ever find Detective Roberts. That creek Richard left him in isn't exactly a family-friendly location.

My cell phone rings, and considering the late hour, my lips purse, but I grab it from my pocket. It's my wife. Of course, it's my wife. I answer quickly. "Hi, honey."

"How is the proposal coming?"

The proposal is a big project I've already locked down for my company, but she doesn't know this. She believes I'm slaving over a PowerPoint presentation at this very moment. Richard starts to convulse. Beautiful. He's dying. "Almost done," I say, "I'm about to head out. You think you might have time to read it in the morning?"

Irritatingly, Richard begins jerking about, making some guttural noises. I move out of the range of the gun. I wouldn't want to get shot by a moron in his last moments of life. "Of course," my wife says. "You know I will. I know how important this contract is to you." She hesitates. "What's that noise?"

"Janitor," I say quickly. "Fool is singing. Kool and the Gang, I think." I lower my voice conspiratorially. "I do believe he thinks he's good. He's not."

She laughs. "Obviously. Hurry home."

"Leaving here in about half an hour. Do you need anything?"

"It's midnight, baby. You just need to come home."

"Right. Holy hell. I didn't realize it was so late. Love you. I'm hurrying out of here." I hang up and slide my phone back into my pocket. Richard goes still. I check his pulse. There isn't one, but there's plenty of disgusting foam hanging out of his mouth. This was messier than I prefer but necessary to cover my tracks and clear a path for my real judgment and punishment.

About done here, I grab Richard's phone and dial 911.

"911, what's your emergency?"

With his phone far from my face, I whisper, "Help. Riverside — Trailer — Park." I don't give them the exact address and then drop the phone on the ground and leave.

I return to my car and drive away, but I park on a side street in a neighborhood just outside of the trailer park and wait for the EMS vehicles. It takes them ten minutes to arrive. My job here is done. The only thing left to do is find a spot to pull over where I won't be seen, bag my cover-up clothes for Goodwill, and get rid of my incidental trash.

Richard Williams is dead. The man who killed Agent Jazz's father is dead. Now, she can let that one go and focus on her future. My gifts to Agent Jazz are never-ending.

CHAPTER 94

Wade stays the night at my place, mostly because we're both exhausted. We literally eat cold gourmet pizza from the takeout bags at three in the morning before we fall into bed. The last thing on my mind before darkness consumes me is the poem left in Ava Lloyd's mouth, as if she were speaking to me.

Naked, he lies in the blinded room
Chain-smoking, cradled by drugs, by jazz
as never by any lover's cradling flesh.

I wake to the alarm only a few hours later, and those words are still in my head, and with good reason. He used my name. Evan was right. He was speaking to me. The jazz poetry connection plays in my mind, and I wonder if my name is the root of his obsession.

Wade heads to the shower, and I pull on a robe, following him to the bathroom but forgetting about the toothbrush I'd been intending to put to use. Instead, I lean on the bathroom counter, my mind chasing empty circles for so long that Wade finishes his shower. I blink him into view as he wraps a towel around his waist.

"Why is he obsessed with me?"

"I was thinking about that in the shower. Could it be your name?"

"Yes," I say, animated with the connected thought. "I had the same thought." I deflate quickly. "But that feels too simple."

"Simple to who? You and The Poet? Because I didn't know jazz and poetry had a connection until I met you and you talked about your grandfather."

My mind is still chasing those circles. "Jazz. Jazz.

Jazz," I murmur, and my eyes go wide. "Record stores and old jazz albums. What if he loves jazz and poetry like my grandfather? Maybe that's what he's telling me. God, I don't want to think that he knows me well enough to know that. I'm praying he just connected my name to poetry."

"Is that even possible?"

"It's a possibility. Jazz poetry is a subgenre, so yes. It's possible. I have to get the team checking with record stores." I push off the counter and disappear into the bedroom, grabbing my phone to dial Chuck.

He answers on the first ring. "You're really back."

"I am," I say, giving him directions and promising him chocolate, lots of it, soon.

The minute we hang up, I head to the shower myself. Not long later, I'm dressed in my standard uniform, guzzling coffee in the kitchen with Wade doing the same. "We should talk," he says. "About us."

"You're my boss now."

He arches a brow. "So I can sleep over, but we can't talk about us? I'm not going to die on you, Sam."

He hits ten nerves, all of them raw. "Neither of us can promise that, not in our jobs."

"So if we sleep together and eat together and enjoy each other, but pretend we aren't a couple, that somehow makes us immune to the pain if it happens?"

"This case has gotten personal, Wade. I shouldn't have you staying here at all. What if he comes after you?"

"Then I kill him and this is over."

Anger snaps inside me. "What if he kills you?"

He motions between us. "This exists. Pretending it doesn't won't make one of us dying easier. It makes living harder."

There's a knock on the door. Wade arches a brow. "Expecting someone?"

"No, but I never am. Wade, listen—"

"Save it." He downs another swallow of coffee. "I need to get out of here." He heads for the door.

I catch his arm and make my appeal. "Let's just get through this case. Then we'll figure it out. Please. Just be patient a little longer."

He leans in and kisses me, but he says nothing. I'm not sure what to think about that, and when he walks around the island and heads toward the living room, regret settles hard in my belly. I don't want to lose him, which is the entire point. The danger of him being close to me is real right now. Eager to reiterate that point, I quickly follow him, rounding the kitchen corner, but it's too late to catch him. I've forgotten the knock and visitor, while Wade is already opening the door.

He steps back enough to allow Lang to enter the apartment, his detective uniform for the day a dark pair of blue jeans and a matching blue polo shirt. He smirks in Wade's direction. "I guess I know who is back on overnight duty."

He's baiting Wade, but Wade isn't a man to be baited. Wade just gives him a far too tolerant look.

My look is not tolerant at all. "What are you doing here, Lang?" I ask, folding my arms.

"I come bearing news."

Wade lifts his hand in my direction. "Call me later."

"You're gonna want to hear this, too," Lang says, shutting the door before Wade can escape, and then drops his bombshell. "They found Richard Williams dead last night."

Richard Williams being the ex-con who killed my father. I swallow hard with a mental flash of my father's face the moment that bullet hit his chest.

"Where?" I ask.

"A trailer park off Riverside," Lang says. "He had a gun superglued to his hand and pills and money on the table. The first responders assume that the dumbass glued the gun to his hand to force himself to use it. He appears to have chickened out and taken pills instead. And then chickened out again. He called 911 to try to save himself, but it was too late. We'll never know for sure."

I inhale a hard-earned breath and let it slowly trickle from my lips. I expect to feel something life changing. I expect the ground to damn near quake under my feet, but it does not. It's one of those ground zero moments again, where I wonder if I'm becoming too cold, too removed, too much like the killers I hunt. "It's good news. Thanks for coming by."

Wade steps in front of me. "Are you okay?"

"I'm perfect," I say. "I'm motivated to do my job."

He studies me for a long, intense moment and proves once again why I've never walked away from Wade by saying, "I understand. I'll talk to you later." He nods and turns to leave.

I catch his arm. "You know—"

"Many things," he promises, his voice gentle with understanding that wasn't present in the kitchen. And with that, he leaves me more determined than ever to catch The Poet before someone else I love ends up dead.

CHAPTER 95

Wade leaves. Lang doesn't. And I know from his face that he's going to try to start a deep conversation.

Which is why when he says, "Jazz—" I cut him off.

"I just want to catch him, Lang. That's what I want to focus on. This is your investigation. That team at the Austin PD is your team. I'll just aid your efforts."

"You claimed jurisdiction."

"Because we're not going to be captive to the mayor and his foot soldiers." Which reminds me that I need to talk to Wade about his dive into the mayor's dirty deeds. "That means you aren't, either," I add. "Tell me what you need. I'll help you get it."

"Can we just take a minute and talk?"

"The day I heard about the man who killed my father is not the day for us to talk."

He cuts his stare and then nods. "Right. Fair enough. The autopsy's at three."

"I'll meet you there."

"Okay, Agent Jazz," he snaps. "But for the record, we're a good team. We want to catch this guy. Call me a cheat or a liar or whatever for now, I don't care. What I care about is letting this shit between us get in the way. You don't have to be my friend, but we started this together. Let's end it together, even if it's the end of us together. This is about catching The Poet, not about us."

He's right. His betrayal was personal, not professional. "You're right. What was your plan this morning?"

"We can't catch him with DNA, since he hasn't left any, but he comes and goes from the crime scene and he has to watch his victims. I already have patrol asking questions of neighbors and even the area merchants. I was going to go and help."

"I'm all in. Let's go." I grab my bag from the table by the door, right next to the computer I've reattached to my security system without reviewing the feed.

"I'll let you drive," he says.

"Don't be a baby," I say. "You hate driving my car and you hate my driving. We're taking the Mustang."

"That you think I obtained nefariously."

"Nefariously?" I laugh. "With you, that could mean a lot of things." I eye his unshaven jaw. "But you're probably too tired to do any of them. Come on." I open the door and exit, waiting for him in the foyer. He exits and pulls my door shut, while I lock up. It's a silly thing, but even in such a small act, I notice how automatic we are, how in tune. We are a good team. That's what matters right now.

"I do hate your driving," he teases, pulling his keys from his pocket.

"Then maybe I *should* drive," I joke, and as we head downstairs, somehow, we've slipped into our usual push and pull, and for now, that's enough. For now, this is about finally catching a killer.

CHAPTER 96

Fifteen minutes later, Lang parks the Mustang across the street from Ava's house. We talk with Officer Jackson, who is standing guard. The low burn of the heating sun contrasts with the chill of her home last night. It's mid-September now, but we're no closer to cooler weather, yet somehow closer to the holidays. I want this case over with by the holidays. I want that to be my gift to this city. And my family. The Poet is stalking me. That means he's stalking them.

"According to her best friend, Kelly, Ava frequented the Twilight Coffee Shop, the library, and the campus, all right here in the neighborhood," Jackson says, his freckled face stony, as usual, his red hair trimmed to the scalp. "She worked from home when she wasn't in school."

"What kind of work?" Lang asks.

"She was an English and math tutor," Jackson replies. He hesitates. "And—"

I jerk my head around. "And?"

His lips press together. "I don't want to assume improperly, but she had a lot of frequent male visitors."

"Oh Jesus," Lang grumbles. "If that means what I think it means, our suspect list just got enormous."

"It's unlikely he met her through an escort service," I say. "He's a meticulously clean, controlled man, but on the other hand, he *is* into bondage. He could have practiced such things with a hired escort. If she dared talk literature with him and spoke the wrong words, that would be her end." I look between Jackson and Lang. "I like that angle. He had to learn the bondage somewhere."

"I'll call Chuck and the FBI tech and get them on this," Lang says. "Well," he adds, "unless *you* prefer to call *your* FBI team."

I grimace. "Just call them. Don't be a jerk."

He smiles. "You snapping at me just like that — perfection. It works. Now it feels like old times."

I laugh in spite of myself.

"I'm trying to find out if she worked for a service," Jackson says, seemingly oblivious to our exchange.

"Talk to the best friend," Lang suggests. "She'll know, but if she's involved, she won't want to tell you."

I glance at Lang. "She'll tell you. All the pretty girls tell you."

"That is true," he says, wiggling his eyebrows and eyeing Jackson. "Where does she live?"

"By the Domain shopping center, but she works downtown for some senator at the capitol building."

"But she was best friends with a call girl," Lang says. "Interesting. What better place to get horny men with no morals than in politics?"

I snort. "Truth."

Lang doesn't linger on that truth. He's back to Jackson now. "Take another officer with you and start digging around the campus."

Jackson nods and takes off. "I'm going to hit the coffee shop and the library," I say. "I'll Uber it to the autopsy."

"You sure? I can come back and get you."

"I am. I think I want to spend some time in the neighborhood. I hadn't done that with the prior murders."

"All right," he says. "Call me if you change your mind."

I nod and head on out to the side street, where I pull up a collage of photos I made weeks ago of all of the victims, including the ones from other cities and states. I add one of Ava and then set out to ask if anyone knows any of the victims.

An hour later, I've visited ten businesses, and a few thought Ava was familiar, but none of the other photos rang a bell. I stop at the coffee shop, where I grab a coffee. The manager, a man in his mid-forties, knows Ava but no one else in the photos. "Did you see her talking to anyone here?"

"She was very social," he says. "She was always talking to someone."

"Anyone stand out or seem to be a frequent visitor with her?"

"Just another girl. Her friend. They came in together."

"Do you know her name?"

"Kelly, I think, but don't hold me to that."

A few minutes later, I stand just outside the door, sipping my skinny white mocha, and there's a clear view of Ava's house from here. The Poet's arrogant and bold. I wonder if he stood here and watched us last night. I shiver in the heat of a hot day, and for the first time in weeks, that evil slithers over me and seems to crawl deep under my skin.

He's here. The Poet is here.

What's terrifying to me is that I know. That I'm connected enough to this evil to feel his presence.

CHAPTER 97

I walk toward the library, that sense of evil following me, a sensation that has me dialing Lang.

He answers on the first ring. "Kelly confessed. She and Ava worked for a private madam. I'm on my way to see her now."

"I want to hear more, I do, but right now, I know this sounds crazy, but I can feel him here in the neighborhood. Get some plainclothes officers on the street."

"Where are you?"

"I just left the coffee shop and I'm walking toward the library."

"I'll handle it and come join the party," he says.

"No. If I'm right, and he's following me, he'll know you, too."

"Fuck. Right. I don't like leaving you out there with him and without me."

"I have a gun and I know how to shoot it."

"And a knee that you know how to use."

"Only when it's deserved."

"Or when you don't feel like letting another person explain themselves." He doesn't wait for a reply. "The autopsy is in an hour."

I let the exchange go as well, glancing at my watch to read two o'clock. "I didn't realize it was this late. No wonder I'm hungry. I'll skip the autopsy. It's going to be more of the same I can catch up on later. I need to stay here, where I feel like our killer is lurking about. Get me some officers on the street, please, and then call me back about Kelly."

"Right, but only since you said please." He hangs up without saying goodbye. I glance across the street and find ThunderCloud Sub. I love ThunderCloud Subs. I rush across the street and at the off-hour, I hurry inside where I show the photos to the staff with no success. I do, however, order a sandwich.

I'm waiting for it to be made when Lang calls again. I step to the end of the counter and answer. "Jackson and two other officers are headed to the area in street clothes," he says. "We're putting a rotation in the area. We also have traffic camera feed from last night and about a half dozen businesses so far. If we knew what the guy looked like beyond tall and fit and might be bald and wear a wig, we'd do a lot better with this."

"I know." A proverbial knife grinds through my belly. "It's my fault. I was hyper-focused on Newman."

"He was a bad dude and I thought it was him, too. Blaming ourselves does no good. We need to get The Poet. That's all."

"Right. We do. We will."

We disconnect, and I pay for my sandwich and a bottle of water, throw out my coffee, and step outside, with that evil at my back again. Aware that The Poet is shadowing me, I head toward the library. It's a short walk, and the minute I enter the library, it's as if a weight is removed from my shoulders. He's outside. I'm inside. I don't know if that is comforting or disappointing.

I hurry toward the information desk and show several staff members the photos. No one knows Ava or any of the others, but the staff rotates for the evening. I'll have to come back.

For now, I'll do some poetry research, and I ask directions to the poetry section.

The library is a beautiful, massive building with pathways jutting left and right above. I'm directed to an upstairs level.

I find what I'm looking for in a quaint little

corner on the third level, where I settle in at a small table with a cushy leather chair. It's the perfect spot to work and eat, which might not be allowed, but I'm doing it anyway. I walk to the poetry shelf, grab a stack of books, and return to the table. I pull out my water and sandwich and, feeling a bit light-headed, I open my egg salad sandwich and treat myself to a big bite. It's delicious and reminds me so much of the egg salad my grandmother used to make when I was growing up.

CHAPTER 98

I start shuffling through the books and looking for anything that stands out, though I don't know why. The basic library collection is present, and anyone taking a literature class would study any number of these books. Not to mention the fact that Ava was a private tutor who'd use these books for that purpose as well. This isn't helping.

I chat with Wade, who is flying out to Dallas for work tonight. Our personal drama will have to wait until his return. I'm relieved. I want The Poet to focus on me and no one else. We disconnect, and I still haven't asked him about his investigation of the mayor, but I don't think it matters right now. We don't need him to get to Newman. I don't need him to do my job now.

I replace the books I've been studying on the shelf and glance at my watch. The new shift just arrived. I stand up and hurry downstairs to the front desk again. My results with the evening staff are not much better than the day staff. No one remembers anyone in the photos I show them.

"What about regulars who visit the literature sections?"

I'm directed to a middle-aged woman named Maria, who's walking by with a return cart. She looks through the photos and decides Ava might be familiar. She's not sure. When asked about regular visitors, a man, in particular, she isn't of much more help. "We get a lot of people in and out. I don't often notice people."

I leave frustrated. I step into a cooler early evening and decide to walk back to the coffee shop where I first felt the evil of The Poet today. Once I have my coffee, this time I sit down and just watch those coming in and out. I'm a few sips into my coffee when my mother calls.

"You remember your grandfather's birthday party at the center is next weekend, right?"

"No. Did you tell me about this?"

"Twice."

I don't remember her telling me this. And I don't want to go to this party with The Poet on my heels, but how do I not go? My grandfather might not be here next year. He might not remember me missing this party, but I will. Forever.

"And you're not working anyway," she adds. "You have no excuse."

I haven't told her about the consultant gig. I need to tell her. I'll tell her next weekend. "I'll be there." We disconnect and for the next hour, I watch the people who come in and out, and I start to discover a theme. The mix is half college students and half from a big tech firm across the street.

I'm there a good hour when Lang calls. "The madam is a gorgeous bitch. We're not going to get her client list without a drawn-out investigation. I'm headed to the station to review the data Chuck's got together on Ava Lloyd's murder. Want to join me?"

"I'm still in her neighborhood. I want to stay on this course. I'll catch up on everything in the morning."

"I'll buy the pizza. I'll see you at your place at ten." He hangs up. I don't call him back. I'm thinking about the security system being out at Summer's place and the way The Poet navigates a path beyond cameras a bit too easily. The cameras were even out when Newman was murdered. Not for the first time, I wonder if The Poet killed him because Newman was getting my attention, not him.

I stand up and decide to pay a visit to the company across the street. I glance at my watch. It's almost eight. I can't imagine anyone will be present, but it's worth a try.

I hurry across the street to a four-story glass building with a sign on the door that reads Brooks Electronics, which is well-known in the city. I reach for the door, surprised when it opens, and step into a cozy lobby with rich navy high-back visitor chairs, a Thomas Kinkade painting, and a high-end wooden reception desk.

"Hello!" I call out. "Hello!"

A tall, good-looking man in a suit, with sandy blond hair enters the lobby. "May I help you?"

I'm stunned to realize this man is no stranger. I know him.

CHAPTER 99

"Nolan?"

"Samantha?"

"Oh my God," I say, shocked to be in the company of a boy I'd grown up with. "I can't believe it's you. How long has it been?"

"Forever," he says, laughing, rushing forward to shake my hand. "You look amazing."

"Thank you. So do you." I motion to his expensive suit. "You're Brooks Enterprises."

He offers a charming, humble smile. "I am. I graduated from MIT and had the trust fund my father left me. The rest is history. How are you here right now?"

I reach for my badge. "I'm with the FBI. I'm investigating a murder."

"The one here in the neighborhood?"

"Yes. Did you know Ava Lloyd?"

He pales. "Oh God," he murmurs. "It *was* her." His jaw clenches. "I'd hoped the whispers were wrong."

"Yes. You knew her then?"

"In passing. I go to the coffee shop on the corner often and so did she. I met her. We said hello, again though, only in passing." He shakes his head. "I can't believe she's dead. How can I help?"

"We're just doing some basic canvassing right now. May I get a list of your employees, or are you going to force me to get a warrant?"

"I'd be happy to give it to you, but let me check with legal and make sure I'm not opening myself up to a lawsuit. It shouldn't be an issue, though."

"Understood." I'm a little weird about knowing him, considering The Poet's interest in me, but I don't feel off with him. His surprise at seeing me reads genuine, but a little more digging won't hurt. "You want to grab some coffee?" I ask, despite the fact that I will never sleep again if I drink more coffee.

"I'm leaving for the weekend for Dallas with my wife and kids. We're headed to Six Flags. I'll be back Monday, though."

"How many kids?"

"Two."

"How old?"

"Grade school. I dread the high school dating thing." He gives me a knowing look. "I'm going to be one of those dads." He eyes me and prompts, "What about you? What's your story?"

"No kids. My job doesn't really allow it."

"That's too bad."

I offer him my new card, which Wade had made with remarkable speed. "Call me when you hear from legal."

"I'll get with you when I get back, Monday most likely. Maybe Tuesday."

"Thanks, Nolan."

"It's really nice to see you."

"You as well." I turn and exit, turning right toward the coffee shop again when another familiar face steps in front of me. It's Daniel, the security guard from my apartment, who I haven't seen for a while now, but then, I haven't exactly been home much either. "Detective Jazz."

"Agent Jazz now," I say. "What are you doing here?"

"I work here." He holds up a bag. "I grabbed dinner for a late night. I quit my security job and picked up some much-hoped-for overtime here at work. How's your problem there at the apartment building?"

"He seems to have moved elsewhere."

"Good," he says. "Stay safe. Gotta get back to work." He steps around me and enters Brooks Enterprises.

CHAPTER 100

Lang calls when I'm on my way home and cancels pizza. Roberts's ex-wife is freaking out and he's going to calm her down. Better him than me. She'd thought he was silent because he was sour about their breakup. Our questions told her there's more to this. I don't know how you calm her down without lying and telling her there's no real problem here. Clearly there is. Roberts has been gone too long, silent too completely. And I hate lies. They're unfair. They make the truth harder later.

Instead of pizza with Lang, I sit on my couch and eat popcorn while looking through my security feed that is now weeks neglected. Halfway through, I dial my mother. "Well, isn't this fresh and new," she greets me. "You calling me instead of me calling you. That makes twice. Miracles do happen."

"I will not reply to that uncalled-for comment."

She laughs. "I see how you are."

"Do you remember Nolan Brooks?"

"Nolan. Hmmm. I think I do." My memory jolts. "Oh right. His dad was that one who died in the boating accident, right?"

"He did. Does his mother still live around there?"

"Oh no. She died, too. Heart attack, I think, but I can't be sure. I think there was a bit of trouble for her after his father died, though that's expected."

"Trouble how?"

"Oh, I don't know. It's a vague memory. Why?"

"I ran into him today. He's the owner of Brooks Enterprises. *The* Brooks Enterprises. The one that is now running a streaming service and cable network."

"That's impressive."

We chat for a few more minutes, and I finish reviewing the security feed. There's nothing there. It's almost like when Newman Smith died, so did my stalker. I supposed he could have been Newman. Newman hated me. Then again, he could have simply been the living, breathing puppet for The Poet, now deceased and therefore off duty.

Later, when I finally go to bed, I crank down the air, aware of the dark clawing in my mind. I try to blank my mind, but it doesn't work. I tumble into my personal hell, but this time, I'm back reliving the night my father died. We're fighting, shouting at each other, and then Richard Williams is right there, behind him. I'd looked into his angry eyes, screamed my father's name, but it was too late.

In slow motion, it seems I'm calling 911 and trying to stop the bleeding. I'm shouting for help. I'm shouting at a man standing in the distance, just out of view, wearing a hoodie and baseball cap. "Help! Help us please!" But he just turns and walks away.

CHAPTER 101

I think of that nightmare often over the next few days. Of course, The Poet was not present when my father died. I found out Richard Williams was dead yesterday. I'd twisted two monsters into one in my sleep. But still, the nightmare haunts me.

The next few days go by in a whirlwind of frustration for me that barely leaves time for such nonsense.

I make my return to the station and have an awkward encounter with the captain. The chief just stays away. Our team begins a suspect list, and it's not long. I have Nolan Brooks and my security guard checked out, though we'd already looked into Daniel. Both fit the age and family profiles, but not much else. I vow not to remain hyper-focused on any one person, but the Nolan encounter bothers me. His offices have been in that plaza for a decade. So he didn't just pop up suddenly. I simply found him.

Wade is now on a manhunt across several states for a cop killer who's struck three times, so my nights are spent alone—well, once I kick Lang out. I decide Lang and I might have made a great married couple. We've become excessively good at avoiding what's wrong between us. So much so that I start to wonder why it matters. I can't change the deal he made with my father, and I'm no longer with the APD.

Ultimately, we're at the stage of every case that becomes frustrating. We've gotten some results on random cases back from the lab, but nothing that adds up. We're working ten different angles from the madam to careful eyes on the employees at Brooks Enterprises. We know that the last two victims of The Poet were close together, which ups the pressure.

These investigative matters all take time, and we all feel the ticking of the clock.

I'm in the conference room, working with Lang and Chuck, when Nolan Brooks calls me on Tuesday afternoon. "Good news. We have a disclaimer in our policies that cites our compliance with law enforcement. I'll have the list ready for you by tomorrow evening."

"That sounds good," I say. "We appreciate that."

"How about that coffee? I can give you the list then."

"That works. What time?"

"How about seven at the coffee shop by me? Sorry, it can't be earlier. We're working crazy hours here."

"That works."

We disconnect.

"Brooks is getting me that employee list tomorrow night. We're meeting for coffee."

"You still feel weird about him?" Lang asks.

"I do. I don't like the connection to my past, but you know, I ran into another friend I knew a few months back, too. I've had several find me on Facebook. It happens."

"But they didn't bother you," Lang points out.

"No, but I also wasn't being stalked by a serial killer. I'll see how I feel after the coffee meeting."

"Want me to come with?" Lang asks.

"I think I'd better make this friendly. I'll go alone."

He pushes back, but we have our hands full, and our time is better spent divided. It's a few hours later when I exit the station and run smack into the chief. "There she is," he says, his tone doting as usual and yet somehow cold. "Agent Jazz herself. How are we coming on the case?"

I bristle with the question that assumes his

authority but smash my reaction. "Too slowly."

"We calmed the public with that early press conference we had about a single suspect, but I've had a reporter snooping around again. We won't silence this for long."

"If necessary, the FBI can hold a joint press conference with your team."

His eyes flare with anger, but his expression is unchanged. "If necessary. Just catch him already." He steps around me.

I turn and call out to him before he enters the building. "That's all? You have nothing else to say to me?"

He pauses and turns back. "You left without talking to me. I let you. End of story." He heads into the building.

I'm left with the slap of his words, uncertain what just happened. Then again, I don't think anything just happened. I'm just figuring it out now. Actually, I don't understand at all, but I don't have the time and energy to waste trying to find out. I have a killer to catch. The cranky chief and ex-godfather can wait.

CHAPTER 102

I arrive at the coffee shop right on time for my meeting with Nolan. I already have my much-needed white mocha with an extra shot when he arrives a few minutes later. He waves on his way to the counter and orders for himself as well, and I watch him joke with the barista in his expensive blue suit that he's paired with an emerald green tie. He's good with people, charismatic, successful. A man who has it all and no reason to kill anyone.

He joins me while we wait for his own brew to be made, sitting down across from me with a charming smile. "Good to see you again. I believe this is what you need." He offers me the large envelope he's been holding since he walked in.

"Thank you. We do appreciate the help."

They call out his order and he stands up and grabs it, but not before I notice that he isn't wearing a wedding ring. But then, not all men do. He returns and sits down. "Follow in your dad's footsteps, did you?"

"I did," I say.

"How is he?"

"Dead."

His eyes go wide. "Oh. Well. I'm—"

"Don't say sorry. I've heard that too much. I can't remember. What does your father do for a living?"

"He was a programmer. I, too, followed in my father's footsteps."

"And how's your mother?"

"Dead."

I don't blanch with his similar reply to mine. This job prepares you for about anything. "I see," I say simply. "How?"

"Heart attack when I was in college. I met my wife shortly after. She helped me get through it. Oh, how are your grandparents?"

"Good. Well," I reluctantly add, "my grandfather has dementia. But otherwise good."

"Ouch. That's rough. He was a brilliant mind, if I remember correctly. Why does it always happen to them?"

"I don't know."

We're solemn for a moment and then he brings up one of our old teachers. That leads us to talk about a few of the other students, and I'm surprised by how hard I end up laughing. "Those were good times," I say, relaxed now.

"Except for that one incident. The boy who died."

Unease I can't explain slides down my spine. I know the incident. Of course I do. We lived in a small town and, while I was home sick the day of our poetry studies, one of my girlfriends told me about another student, poor awkward Henry, being mocked during his reading, and then beat up after class. Later, his bully ended up dead. Why even bring this up? "The murder," I say, looking for a reaction.

"That's what they said way back when. All I know is we were all different after whatever it was happened." His cell phone rings and he grabs it. "Wifey." He holds up a finger. "Hey, honey. Yes. Yes, I can bring home milk. Yes, I can help with homework. I'm on my way. Love you, too." He disconnects. "Well, this has been fun. I'd better run." He motions to the folder. "Let me know if you need anything else."

"I will."

I watch him leave, and I'm bothered by the talk of

the boy who died, but I set that aside. I didn't feel
that familiar evil with Nolan. I didn't feel it with
Newman, either. Newman was a different kind of
evil. I'm not going to ignore my feeling this time and
hyper-focus on the wrong person.

CHAPTER 103

Friday, I sign the papers on my new house and then it's back to work. I head to my home office, otherwise known as the room with the coffee pot, and follow up with the lead tech at the FBI office in San Antonio, who I'd tasked with researching the list of Nolan's hundreds of employees. I drink my late morning coffee while chatting about our possible suspects, but the bottom line ends with a less than encouraging result. We don't have a good suspect, and I'm left feeling like I need to depend on me.

Determined to figure out what we're missing, I spend most of the rest of my day in my apartment, staring at the poetry now plastered on my upstairs wall. I read through random expert opinions about deeper meanings of each work to no real end. The answer to who The Poet is, and how to find him, has to be in the poems. I just can't figure out the puzzle they represent.

Hours later, I settle into bed, still working the puzzle, scribbling notes on a pad of paper. When I finally lie down and drift into sleep it's with that pad on my chest. It's not a restful sleep, either. The nightmare haunts me again, the one about my father dying and the man in the hoodie watching us, ignoring my plea for help.

I wake with a vise around my chest and a call from Wade. "We got him, baby. My manhunt is over. The bastard killed five people, but he didn't get another after I got involved."

"I had no doubt you would get him. I just hate that so many people died." We talk a bit about the manhunt and all that went into it as I try to shake off a bad night of no real rest.

"I'm coming home tonight," Wade says. "How about a late dinner out?"

I counteroffer. "How about a working dinner? I'm going to my grandfather's birthday party this afternoon and I'm still no further ahead on this case."

"That works. I'll be there. I'll call you when I land."

We disconnect, and I head out for my morning run. I end with my normal coffee stop, and this time when I exit to have the neon shoe guy run by, I feel an odd tingle of discomfort. I hand my coffee to a stranger and take off after him, but by the time I reach the corner, he's gone. I call Chuck and ask him to check the traffic cameras, but our luck is no better this time. The runner's hat covers his face, and he disappears off camera not far from my apartment.

This incident bothers me all morning, tangling with my nightmare for top billing. With excess energy and a few hours to kill, I head to Ava's neighborhood. Once there, I grab another egg salad sandwich and head to the library. Fortunately, my little table I'd enjoyed on my prior visit is available. I load up on poetry books, sit down, and start to scan the stack for any clues to my unsolved puzzle that is The Poet and the messages he's left with his victims.

I'm halfway through my sandwich when my hand stills on a book titled *The Annotated Waste Land with Eliot's Contemporary Prose* by T. S. Eliot. It's a version of the same book that my grandfather had been reading when I'd visited him. The coincidence is chilling, almost as if the universe is trying to tell me something.

I open the book and manage to land on the optional signature card. Ice slides down my spine with the scripted signature of a name I know well: Ava Lloyd.

Inhaling sharply, I do not like the idea that my grandfather had a version of this book out in his room, only a few days ago. I calm myself with a reminder that this is a famous work, used regularly in many classrooms. This isn't about my grandfather. It's about a madman I call The Poet. The clue here could very well be leading me full circle, back to the classroom and Roberts's first nickname for The Poet: *The Professor*.

I dial Chuck. "Are we looking at Ava's professors yet?"

"None of them fit the profile."

"Look deeper, at their families and friends. We need to look for any class that includes an analysis of *The Annotated Waste Land with Eliot's Contemporary Prose* by T. S. Eliot. And find out if any of the other victims, in any city or state, took a class that included that book in their curriculum." My brows dip with a thought. "Ava offered private tutoring. Maybe she used it herself in her curriculum. Find out if CSI has anything that might indicate poetry in her curriculums, especially this work."

I certainly used it, I think. I highlighted it in my poetry club for its unique structure and content, but I did so because I was inspired by my grandfather's love of the work. Someone might have inspired her to love it as well.

"Got it," he says. "Got it all. I'm on it."

"And look for any families she's connected to who might know and love poetry." I hesitate. "Or jazz."

"About that. We've exhausted the jazz shops as leads across the state. No one noticed anyone who stands out as someone we're looking for."

"Of course not," I murmur. "Thanks, Chuck. I know it's Saturday and I just keep on keeping on with you."

"Because The Poet keeps on keeping on."

We disconnect, and I'm aware that I'm perhaps barking up the wrong tree with this work of poetry, but it feels right. Then again, so did Newman. I shove aside that negative thought. Lang is right. That gets me nowhere. Newman was a pedophile. I wasn't wrong about him being a monster. I'm not going to start doubting myself or I won't be able to do this job.

Fortunately, to do that now, I don't have to analyze *The Waste Land*. I've spent hours on end with my grandfather studying this particular work and poet. My gut says that I'm onto something here until I start looking through the rest of the poetry books. Ava signed out most of them, not just *The Waste Land*.

I want to scream.

Instead, I stand up and head down to the information desk and flash my badge. "I need a list of anyone who checked out a poetry book in the past two years."

A deer-in-the-headlights look greets me, and a woman who identifies herself as the manager finally says, "We need a warrant."

Frustrated, I head back to my seat and make the call to Evan to get the warrant. "One of the victims checked out the poetry book," I say. "Don't tell me it's not enough. Get me the warrant."

"It's going to be Monday."

"We both know you could rattle cages now."

"This isn't big enough to do that," he says.

"So much for you helping this time."

"You have the FBI behind you now."

I grind my teeth. "Let's hope he doesn't kill again before Monday."

I hang up and shoot a picture of all of the signatures in the books, pausing when I return to *The Waste*

Land and scan the second signature card, where I find the name of the veterinarian in Brownsville. I wasn't wrong. We're onto something here. Adrenaline surges through me and I dial Evan again. "Two of the victims."

"Two?"

"That's right. Two. Get me my warrant."

"I'll rattle cages."

I hang up. Or maybe he does. It doesn't matter. I just want my warrant and I want it now.

Standing, I return the books to the shelf and gather my things, hurrying to my car. Once I'm behind the wheel with the air cranking, I dial Lang. "You're invited to my grandfather's birthday party. We need to talk."

"Will there be cake?"

I grimace and hang up.

CHAPTER 104

I've barely hung up with Lang when a thought hits me and I call him back. "I'll bring you cake. I have to go to this party, Lang. It's important to my grandfather, but I have a time-sensitive situation."

"What does that mean and what do you need?"

"The library is going to close for the day before I'm done with my grandfather's birthday party that I don't want to rush away from. We need their security footage. Look for anyone who might be on our radar or anyone who frequents the poetry section. Both Ava and our Brownsville victim, who went to school here, signed the signature card in a poetry book that has a judgment theme."

"I'm headed there now. I'll call you once I get the footage."

We disconnect, and my mind races. Our perp could be someone we haven't even considered. It's likely someone we don't even have on our radar. I dial Chuck and update him, making sure he knows how important the research he's doing right now has become.

Fifteen minutes later, I pull up to the Georgetown nursing home a few miles from where I grew up, and park, only to have my cell phone ring with Lang's number. "Anything?" I answer.

"The staff here has called their security person. He's on his way to help me."

"Our killer could be—"

"The security person. I know. I'm on it."

We disconnect and, since my mother doesn't know I'm back in law enforcement, I remove my weapon and badge. I then head inside the nursing home, where I'm directed to the recreation room. I find a party underway, with balloons and streamers, cake and laughter. There is also dancing, and the residents and guests boogie on down, including my grandma and grandpa. A smile breaks on my face and my mother appears in front of me, giving me a hug. For the next hour, I'm drawn into family and fun. We eat cake and I sit with my grandfather, singing along to old sixties music and he remembers the words. But he forgets my name.

In the middle of it all, Lang sends me a text, letting me know that he's got six months of footage to review. He's headed back to the station to get some help. Just knowing he's handling this relaxes me back into the party. It's a good two hours later that I'm sitting in my grandfather's room with him resting while I chat with my mom and Grandma Carol.

They're laughing, and I'm struck by how close my mother is to Grandma Carol, when the truth is, they aren't blood. Since my grandfather adopted my father, and my grandma Carol was his wife of fifty years, she's not my mother's blood relative, either. But both my grandparents moved in with us when I was a teen, and my mom was the one who cared for them. She was closer to them than my father ever was. Perhaps because she lost her parents as a child. Or maybe it's because my father's mood swings were reined in once they moved in with us.

"I'm glad you came, honey," my mom says, squeezing my hand.

"I know you think he doesn't know you're here," my grandma adds, "but I believe he does."

I smile and squeeze her hand. She's a kind woman who still colors her gray hair brown and loves to fuss in the kitchen. My grandfather loves her baking. I can't imagine how hard it is for her, for him to remember nothing of their life together.

"I miss the days when he and I listened to jazz and talked about poetry."

"That reminds me, honey," she says. "Your mom has all of his old poetry and jazz albums in the attic at her place. If you want them, they're yours."

I sit up straighter. "Really?"

"Really," my grandma says. "Take them. Enjoy them. That would please him."

The idea that there might be something in those memories that could be a trigger I can use to solve this case has me pushing to my feet. "I'm going there now."

My mother catches my hand. "Oh God. You're working that case I heard about, The Poet, aren't you?"

"Mom—"

"I thought you quit." Her tone is sharp, accusing even.

"I'm consulting for the FBI. We *need* to catch this guy."

"I thought the press conference said they had the killer isolated and there was no mass population danger." The sharpness is gone. The worry is back.

My lips press together. "They lied. He's hurt a lot of people. A lot more than the public knows."

Her lashes lower and then lift. "Just don't get killed."

"I won't." I don't promise. We both know I can't promise.

My grandmother stands up and hugs me, her head coming to my chest. She's the kind of person who lights up lives and deserves to be protected. The kind of person I do this job for. She gazes up at me and pats my cheek. "I hope something in that attic helps catch him."

"Me, too, Grandma." I kiss her and my mother

before gently placing a kiss on my sleeping grand-father's forehead. My heart squeezes. God, how I wish I could talk about this case with him. Instead, I'll have to settle for his memories as inspiration to catch The Poet.

I'm heading for the door when my mom calls out. "Oh, honey."

I turn. "Yes, Mom?"

"I put your stuff from that poetry club you taught in a box with the stuff from Grandpa's poetry club."

I blanch. "Grandpa taught a poetry club?"

"You don't remember?" my mom asks. "He had the kids over all the time. Random students he men-tored."

My heart is racing now, adrenaline shooting through me. "I don't remember this. I mean he helped me set mine up, but I didn't know he ran one, too."

My mom waves a hand. "It was after school while he still taught. Maybe it wasn't a club. Like I said. Mentoring."

"Yes," Grandma agrees. "And tutoring. He didn't have a club. Your mother's confused. You'd think she was as old as me." She laughs. "Your grandfather loved mentoring and tutoring more one-on-one. There's lots of fun stuff in the boxes. Enjoy, honey."

I nod and turn away, certain now that The Poet's obsession with me is really an obsession with me *and* my grandfather.

CHAPTER 105

The first thing I do when I get back to my car is to return my gun and badge to my person where they belong. The drive to my family home is a short one, down a country road. The house is sprawling and white, a real mansion in its day—that I should have questioned. My father was a detective. Detectives don't buy mansions unless they're doing something other than being a detective.

I hurry into the house and lock up behind me, the scent of cinnamon clinging to the air today. There's always some delicious scent in this house with my grandmother living here. I hurry through the cozy living room of overstuffed brown furnishings and shelves of books and trinkets, to the hallway where I pull down the attic stairs. Hurrying up them, it's a bit like the scene from *Christmas Vacation* where Chevy Chase is under a slanted ceiling, enjoying boxes of memories. I find the record player, plug it in, and play a Louis Armstrong album.

After some searching, I find the boxes my grand-mother referenced, filled with my grandfather's books on poetry and jazz. I start reading, smiling often, and I go through a journal that's in his own writing, but this isn't what I need, not right now. I dig through the boxes and find my poetry club materials. Underneath them, I find my grandfather's tutoring files. I do vaguely remember random students coming to the house. There are years of tutoring and mentoring notes. The students even had what he called, oh God, "master patches."

My heart is about to explode in my chest right now. There are notes about my grandfather's most impressive students. I flip the page and start reading a bit about each. I've read the notes on the first four, vaguely remembering them, when I flip to number five and go cold. The name is *Nolan Brooks*.

Cotton thickens my throat and I grab my phone, dialing Lang. "It's Nolan. Pick him up now."

"You're sure?"

"Positive. Lang, I went to school with him. I knew him. My grandfather knew him."

"Holy shit. I'm going after him now."

"I'm getting protection here for my family and then coming in." I hang up and dial Captain Moore.

"Agent Jazz, what can I—"

"I know who The Poet is. This is personal. It's about me and my family. I need them protected now. Call the Georgetown PD and get me help here now. Actually, I need them to meet me at the Sun City Retirement Center. Ethan Langford knows the rest of the story. I have to get to them."

"I'm calling now. I'll call you back once they're on the way."

"Thank you." I hang up and rush down the stairs, dialing my mother as I do. She doesn't pick up. I redial, running for my car. Again, my mother doesn't answer.

I climb inside my vehicle and start the engine. My mother calls me back.

"Listen to me, Mom. The Poet, the killer I'm hunting, is Nolan Brooks, someone Grandpa tutored. He's dangerous. He's obsessed with me and Grandpa."

"I remember Nolan. He was a nice young man."

"He's not a nice anything. I'm coming to you with police support. Where are you now?"

"Oh my. Oh my."

"Mom—"

"We're still with your grandpa."

"Stay where you are."

"Yes, I— Yes, we will. I'll get security."

We disconnect, and I can't drive fast enough. My heart won't calm. My cell rings and I answer without checking caller ID to hear the captain's voice. "Georgetown PD has two cars on the way now."

"Thank you, Captain."

"Langford told me what's going on. Be careful."

"Yes." That's all I say. I hang up. If Nolan knew I was onto him, what would he do? Who would he hurt? I bring the retirement center into view and whip into the parking lot. Relief washes over me as the police cruisers pull in behind me.

A few minutes later, I've hugged my family one by one and left them with two competent officers. Now, it's time to go get Nolan and end this.

CHAPTER 106

I'm halfway back to Austin when Lang calls. "He's not home. He's not at work. We have an APB out on him."

"He knows. He must have seen me at the library. What I don't understand is why I didn't sense this was him."

"Oh come on, Jazzy. You're human, not Spider-Man. That Spidey-Sense stuff is bullshit."

"But I could feel him when he was watching me. Why didn't I feel it when he was in front of me?"

"I don't know. Maybe he's got a split personality. You feel only one of his sick personalities. Where are you now?"

"Almost back to the station."

"He's going to be looking for you. Call him. Try to get him to meet you."

"Good idea. Where?"

"You tell me."

"My apartment," I say.

"He'll feel trapped there."

"I'll just see where he wants to meet. I think he called me from his cell phone. I'll call you back." I hang up and tab through my call log for his number, punching the autodial. It goes to his voicemail. "Nolan, hi. This is Samantha. I just visited with my grandfather, and we were talking about you. I didn't realize you'd spent so much time with him. I'd love to catch up. It's hard now, with his mind so gone. I was shocked at how much he remembered about you. Call me." I hang up and call Lang back. "I left a message. Damn it, this is going to turn into a manhunt. I'll meet you at the station. I'm calling

Wade to get reinforcements."

"Be careful."

"Always." I hang up and dial Wade.

"Hey," he says. "I'm about to get on a plane."

"I need help now."

"What's up?"

"I know who he is, but he figured out that I know. He's missing."

"I'm getting off the plane," he says, cool and calm, but there's an urgency hidden just beneath the surface. "I'll take a later flight. Text me his information so I can call this in now."

I pull into a gas station and idle by the curb. "Doing it now. Thanks, Wade. I know him. I grew up with him."

"Holy hell. This *is* about you."

"And my grandfather."

"Where are you?"

"On my way to the station."

"Good. I know you'll be safe there. Be careful."

"Always," I assure him.

"Don't give me that standard answer you give. I mean it, Sam. *Be careful*."

"I know. I am. You too."

"I'll call you when I get things moving."

"Okay. Thanks."

"Sam—I'm—we—"

"I know. Me, too. I just—just come home."

"Soon."

He disconnects and I call Lang again. "Anything?"

"Not a damn thing. We're checking traffic cameras near his home and work, but he's a tech genius. We now know how he avoids detection on our security feeds. From what I'm reading, this guy can out-tech any tech we have on staff. Hurry the fuck up and get to the station."

We disconnect, and for once, I don't mind being cursed at. He's worried. So am I. Killers like Nolan do one or two things when trapped. They go on a killing rampage or they disappear and sometimes are never found. Nolan has money and resources. He may have had a plan to disappear, but the FBI will send out travel alerts immediately. Nolan is smart enough to know that will happen.

I think back to that boy in my class who was killed so many years ago. We'd all thought he'd been killed for bullying Henry, by Henry. Nolan was in my class, too. I now think it was Nolan that killed the bully. I'm not sure why, perhaps because the bully mocked Henry for reading a poem. We'd been thirteen. My stomach churns with realization. The same age as the boy I'd shot and killed.

Oh my God.

Oh my God.

Feeling downright sick now, certain we're dealing with a man with a long history of murder, a history that may well run far longer and deeper than we ever imagined, I pull back onto the highway, thinking about what Lang said. What if Nolan had more than one personality? Could one of them be evil and the others not, and therefore, I didn't feel his evil when I was with him? The idea that this kind of evil can hide so easily is a terrifying thought. We have to catch him before that evil hides somewhere we can't find him. Because that evil might hide, but it's not going away.

CHAPTER 107

Wade doesn't come to the station when he lands in Austin. He heads to his local FBI office and coordinates resources that he's pulled in across the state. Everyone on our team is present at the precinct, including the captain, but at near two in the morning, we agree to take shifts. It takes a lot of effort to get Chuck to go home. Lang stubbornly insists on staying with the night detectives despite being dead tired.

"We need you and Chuck with working brains," he insists. "He's a genius we need pitted against Nolan. And you understand Nolan's poetry bullshit. I'll take a nap in the captain's office." He gives the captain a challenging look.

"It's all yours."

"The only reason I'm agreeing is that I want to go through all my research at home and try to figure out where he might go. Maybe there's a clue in the poetry I'm missing. And Wade is meeting me at my place."

Lang motions to Officer Jackson, who's been hard at work with us. "Make sure she gets home safely and that patrol is at her damn door. Then you get some rest, too."

Jackson scrubs his jaw. "Let's get you home, Agent Jazz."

We move toward the door and the captain stops me. "Agent Jazz."

"Yes, Captain?"

"Be careful."

The same words I keep hearing from everyone, but from him, there's an apology beneath those

words that I accept with a small nod. Then I get back
to business. "Someone needs to check on his wife
and kids."

"We have patrol there now."

I give another small nod, and the exchange ends
there.

Officer Jackson follows me home and, as I have
been doing lately, I park on the street beside my
apartment. Jackson is right there at my door when I
exit, and another officer joins him. None of us speak.
We're all on edge, watching our surroundings. Once
we're at my building door, the second officer remains
outside at the entrance, while Jackson and I head
upstairs. At my door, Jackson holds up a hand. "I'll
clear the apartment."

"I can clear the apartment, but thank you."

"No. I'm doing this," he insists. "I've been tasked
with protecting you."

I'm too tired to argue. I offer him my key and step
back. He disappears inside and I wait. And wait. I
wait too long. My adrenaline begins a slow rise. I
pace back and forth. Something feels off. I dial
patrol. My phone won't work. I try again. It still won't
work. Someone is using a portable cell phone
jammer. And there is only one person I know of who
has that kind of skill.

I draw my weapon and cautiously enter the
apartment. Silence greets me and I can't get eyes on
Jackson. I begin a search, clearing the kitchen and
then the bedroom, heading cautiously into the
bathroom and closet. Finding nothing, I head back
downstairs and go to the one place that is left. The
stairs that lead to the attic.

Slowly, I take one step at a time, my heart thundering in my ears. I inhale as I step into the room, a
vise closing around my throat at what I find. Jackson
is knocked out at my feet, a syringe beside him.

Wade is tied to a chair and unconscious, but he's not naked, which tells me he refused to undress. I'm not sure how Nolan knocked him out or how he got him in the chair.

Nolan is standing beside Wade with a pill pressed to Wade's lips, and in the depths of Nolan's eyes is an evil I hadn't seen during our prior encounters. I feel that evil now, too. Lang was right. Nolan is not one man, but two, at the very least. This is the killer's side of Nolan's personality, the one I haven't met in person until today. Stubble covers his normally clean-shaven jaw, and his white button-down shirt is wrinkled. He looks frazzled, drugged even, running on no sleep. A man of control losing control, which, in my experience, is a bomb about to blow.

"They aren't dead," he says. "Yet. They'll end up like Roberts and be dead if you don't do as I say."

The confirmation that Roberts is dead is a brutal one that does what he hopes. It tells me he really will kill Wade and Jackson, and probably me, too. "What do you want, Nolan?"

"Drop your gun or I'll shove this in your boyfriend's mouth and kill him right now."

I decide right then that I will never complain about someone calling Wade my boyfriend ever again. I'm fairly certain Jackson injected himself to save Wade.

I kneel and set my gun down, but there's a second one in my desk drawer. I'm paranoid that way. "Okay. Now what?"

He motions to another chair that used to be in my kitchen against the wall, beside the desk. "Sit."

I don't argue. That desk is closer to him and Wade. It also has my backup weapon inside it. I need to be in that chair. I do as he says, crossing the room and claiming the chair. Now he's got Wade positioned in profile to me and Jackson. He's behind Wade, but he's on this side of him, which is a problem. He could grab for me if I reach for the drawer.

"How did you get Wade to sit down?" I ask, trying to keep him talking. "He's a big guy."

"Big isn't a weapon against drugs. He didn't even know I was here."

He got him from behind, I think. "And Jackson? Did he inject himself to protect Wade?"

"He did. I wasn't sure he was that brave, but he proved otherwise."

And I doubted him. I couldn't feel shittier right now. "What did you inject them with?"

"Heroin. A heavy dose." He reaches into his pocket. "They'll need these." He holds up two syringes. "An epinephrine boost. It could cause a heart attack, but that's their only hope."

My own heart about stops with those words. "Give them the shots and I'll do anything you want."

He's still holding the pill, and he also has the syringes. The pill is no longer at Wade's mouth, but I'm not sure I can get to him before he changes that.

As if he senses my thought process, he throws the syringes across the room, out of reach and then, to my surprise, grabs a gun from the back of his pants and shoves it at Wade's head. "You understand this a little better, don't you? Now maybe you won't consider coming at me. You were, weren't you?"

"I wasn't," I lie, and while I'm aware that he could shoot us all, I don't believe he will. He doesn't like to get dirty, but I don't know where the cyanide pill went, either, and his hand is shaking now. He's losing it. He's on edge. He doesn't have the control he values. He's going to act out if I don't act first.

"I did all of this for you and the greater good," he says. "You need to commit to the greater good. The world depends on it. I killed your father. I killed Roberts. They were distracting you. They were keeping us apart."

"You didn't kill my father," I say. "Richard Williams killed my father."

"I paid him to kill your father. Your father didn't deserve the Jazz name and what it *means* to this world. The Jazz name is everything. The Jazz name is royalty. It must be protected. Your father had to be removed from the lineage. And Roberts got in the way. You had to be close to me. You have to be trained. They were all in the way. I paid him to get rid of all of them: your father, Roberts, and Newman."

I suck in a breath, trying to calm the shock rolling through me right now. He had my father killed? He thinks we're really blood relatives to my grandfather and if I tell him differently, he might kill us all right now. I try to focus, I try to just focus and keep calm, keep him talking. My father is too close to me, an emotional topic for me when I can't afford emotion. I go elsewhere. "Why kill Newman? Why involve him? What was that all about?"

"I set him up, I gave him to you. I wanted you to judge him, to feel pleasure when he was dead. To know that was the right thing, the right judgment."

And I had. I'd felt pleasure at his death, and that terrifies me. "Richard Williams killed himself."

"I killed him because he wanted to kill you, too." He kneels in front of me. "I will always protect you. I love you. I love your grandfather. You just need to prove you understand your destiny. You have a duty. You have a duty!" He shouts the last declaration right in my face.

Somehow, I don't react. My voice is low, controlled. "Inject Wade and Jackson and we'll leave. We'll get out of here and you can teach me. I want to do what I need to do."

"You don't understand. You're just saying that. You don't—"

"I do," I say quickly. I really have no idea what he's talking about, but I wing it. "I saw my grandfather today. It all started to come together."

"Did it now?"

"It did."

"Tell me."

I use what I have pieced together. "Poetry is the bible of life. It's the gospel." His hand is still shaking. He doesn't like the gun. He had to hire someone else to shoot my father. I could tackle him. I *have* to tackle him.

"That's right," he says, stepping in front of me. "That's right. Those who sin against the great words must be eliminated before they damage the balance of the universe. Your grandfather, he was Jazz, for a reason. You are Jazz for a reason. Jazz and poetry are born in the soul of the universe. He kept that balance. I helped him keep the balance, the way you are destined to keep that balance."

I blink, momentarily confused and stunned. Is he saying my grandfather was a killer? God, no. Please tell me that isn't what he's saying.

CHAPTER 108

My grandfather can't be a killer. No. I don't believe that for a minute. "My grandfather?" I ask, pressing Nolan for real answers.

"Yes. Your grandfather, of course. He taught me the importance of the great works, of how they have affected the world. He kept a balance, but when he got put in that home, he lost his mind. He lost the ability to keep peace, and the world went crazy. I felt it coming. I stepped in even before he went to that horrid place that's so beneath him. I had to. I had to manage the great works and kill the sinners for him."

"My grandfather killed the sinners?" I ask, holding my breath as I await his reply.

"No." He says the word as if appalled. "No. He had me. *He had me.* I did these things for him. We read the book together. I knew what he wanted."

My mind goes to the cereal and the book at the nursing home. "You visit him."

"Often."

"We should go together."

"Yes." His eyes light, but the craziness is there, so very there. "Yes, we should."

I lean forward. "Tell me what you need me to do."

"Your duty."

The gun is between us. He could shoot me, but he's close. So very close. I am running on instinct, and I reach out and press my hand to his face. "Thank you. Thank you for being there for my grandfather."

He leans in to the touch, and this is my moment, the only one I might get. I grab the tape dispenser on the desk and crash it into his head. He jolts and drops the gun. I go for it, but he shoves me back into the chair and against the wall. He's against me, screaming, "Bitch! Bitch! You sinner!"

I reach for anything, anything at all, and my hand finds the record on the player. I smash it against his face. It breaks and he jolts backward again, but before I can reach for his gun near my foot, he throws me to my back, air catching in my chest as he comes down on top of me. My hands grab again for something to hit him with, but all I find is a piece of the jazz record.

Nolan's fingers are on my neck, choking me. I squirm, but he's big and holding me down. I can't breathe, and the pill is coming at me. I turn my head and desperately shove the album at his face as hard as I can. The edge makes contact and he rolls off me, screaming. I roll to my knees, and the edge of the album is lodged in his eye. I grab the gun and somehow, he's launching himself at me, screaming some demon cry.

I don't even hesitate.

I shoot him in the chest and he falls backward. I shoot him again for good measure. I can't save Wade and Jackson if he's coming back to life.

"Jazz! Sam!"

At Lang's voice, I shout, "Up here!"

I scramble for the adrenalin syringes and grab them. Lang appears in the doorway and I throw him one of the syringes, praying it is what Nolan said it was, because we don't have time to wait.

"What's this?" Lang asks.

"Adrenalin, I hope," I tell him. "Inject Jackson in the heart."

I scramble to Wade's side, unbutton his shirt and feel for the right spot. I don't hesitate. I can't hesitate. I shove the needle into his heart. He gasps immediately and comes to life. Beside me, Jackson does the same with Lang's help. "Oh, thank God," I murmur, sagging over him in relief.

Lang is on the phone to 911. Tears burn my eyes and I cup Wade's face. "Damn you, you do not get to die. Do you hear me?"

"I'm not going anywhere, baby," he promises, and the name "baby" has never sounded so good.

"You should probably cut him loose," Lang says. "Bondage games are fine and all, but you might want to keep them private."

I laugh through my tears and cut him free. The EMS team overtakes the room a few seconds later, and I'm right there in the ambulance with Wade. I hold his hand and he kisses mine. "I'm fine. It's over. That's what matters."

It's over. Nolan is dead, but his impact will linger in many lives forever, including ours.

CHAPTER 109

A search of Nolan's home and company offices do little to close the open murder cases we believe he committed. His technical skills and resources leave us with a maze of possible hiding places we may never fully uncover. The most painful part of it all is that we still haven't found Roberts. Some part of me thinks we will one day, but that may be wishful thinking.

Not long after Nolan's death, I meet with his wife, who is little help. She claims to have had no idea her husband was a killer. Ultimately, I decide that I believe her, but I'm not sure how I feel about her ignorance. I meet her children, too, who are adorable kids. I don't want to believe they're just like their father, in all the wrong ways, but I privately vow to keep them on my radar.

Not long after that meeting, I visit the river where the bully named Mark Meadows was murdered. With a chill down my spine, I discover a tree trunk there carved with the letter *U*.

When finally the case is officially closed, life begins to return to its routines, and I do my best to define my new normal. I move into my new house, not far from Wade's place, and install a security system. I still struggle with commitment, but Wade and I are working through that. Perhaps that's why I cling to my role as a consultant to the FBI rather than accepting a full-time job.

Lang and I never talk about my father, but we're working through things as well. He still shows up when I don't expect him and he's still a pain in my ass, but one I'd miss if he were gone.

And I'm being a better daughter and grand-daughter, especially today, on Thanksgiving. My grandfather is home today, and still agile in body despite his lagging mind. I manage to get him to the attic, where we now sit together, reading poetry and listening to jazz. And the moment he looks at me and says, "My Samantha," wipes away all the bad in my life, and leaves me with the good. The kind I need after finding the evil that was Nolan Brooks. The kind of good that makes me ready to go fight evil all over again.

ACKNOWLEDGMENTS

Thank you Detective Ramiro De Jesus aka Chepin for allowing me to text and call you like crazy to ask a ridiculous number of questions. I am blessed by your knowledge and generosity. I'm proud to call you "cousin." You were an invaluable resource when writing so many scenes in this book. Truly, you gave me the knowledge to color scenes with so much more depth than I might have otherwise.

And thank you, Detective Trey White, for the tips to writing an officer-involved investigation. Congrats on the ACP 40 under 40 award! What a incredible international achievement.

Thanks to Dr. Anne Bode for sharing your knowledge of the autopsy process and invaluable advice on cyanide.

To my husband, Diego, thank you for sharing your love for fiction and suspense with me. Your vast love for reading, watching, and talking about murder is contagious. Only you would tell a waiter we aren't ready to order yet, because we're still plotting murder.

Much love to Emily for years of friendship and support. From romance to murder. We do it all together!

Thank you to Louise Fury, my agent, for years of support and guidance.

Liz Pelletier, my editor and publisher, for the support that made this possible. You are an inspiration in so many ways. Thank you as well to Lydia and Jessica. I appreciate all that you both do.

—Lisa